The

"J. D. Barker is a one-of-a-kind writer and that's a rare and special thing. Stephen King comes to mind and Lee Child, John Sandford. All one-of-a-kinds. Don't miss anything J.D. writes." —**James Patterson**

"The craftsmanship here is outstanding. The story is intricate without being annoyingly so; the characters are sharply defined; the dialogue is fluid; and the ending—well, let's just say that when the book ends, it's like a speeding train slamming into the side of a mountain: unexpected, abrupt, painful. The story is scheduled to conclude in the next book, which better get here soon." —***Booklist***

"Competent . . . The cliffhanger ending points to more mayhem in a third volume." —***Publishers Weekly***

"Well-written, haunting, and insanely addictive . . . Bottom line, this is what a crime thriller is supposed to look like. Think Stephen King meets Michael Connelly—J. D. Barker was born to write crime thrillers, and *The Fifth to Die* is his latest masterpiece." —***Real Book Spy***

"I described J. D. Barker's first story about Chicago detective Sam Porter and his hunt for serial killer Anson Bishop, entitled *The Fourth Monkey,* as bearing comparison with Thomas Harris's creation of Hannibal Lecter. This sequel confirms my view: It is a superbly paced, beautifully constructed evocation of evil. Genuinely frightening, and with a terrific villain, it underlines just how good Barker is." —***Daily Mail***

"A talented writer with a delightfully devious mind!" —**Jeffery Deaver**, *New York Times* best-selling author

"I don't say this lightly: J. D. Barker is a force to be reckoned with." —**Tosca Lee**, *New York Times* best-selling author

"Barker knows how to evoke chilling imagery and will have readers anxiously looking over their shoulders with each terrifying 'clickity, click, click.'"
— *Library Journal*

"Barker is a master wordsmith." — **AudioBookReviewer.com**

"Masterful storytelling." — **Bookish**

"It is clear Barker is a name to watch." — *Horror Bookshelf*

"Barker's sleight of literary hand is absolute genius. He builds tension and then rips the rug right out from under you, just to do it all over again." — *Quitterstrip*

"Mr. Barker may have begun by following in the footsteps of such literary royalty as Stephen King, Thomas Harris, and Dean Koontz, but he has blazed a unique path all his own." — **Fresh Fiction**

"J. D. Barker is quite frankly one of the best crime-thriller writers out there who should be on everyone's radar!" — *Novel Delights*

"Barker is an award-winning writer who is the second coming of Thomas Harris." — **BookReporter.com**

"Barker is such a skilled and exciting writer, delivering a chilling, slow-build thriller, a final, jaw-dropping twist, and a cliffhanger ending that leaves readers dangling precariously by their fingertips." — *Lancashire Evening Post*

The
Fifth to Die

BOOKS BY J. D. BARKER

4MK Thrillers

The Fourth Monkey

The Fifth to Die

The Sixth Wicked Child

Dracul (with Dacre Stoker)

Shadow Cove Saga

Forsaken

The
Fifth to Die

J. D. Barker

HARPER

An Imprint of HarperCollins*Publishers*

Boston   New York

First Mariner Books edition 2019
Copyright © 2018 by J. D. Barker
Teaser chapter © 2019 by J. D. Barker

www.harpercollins.com

Library of Congress Cataloging-in-Publication Data
Names: Barker, J. D. (Jonathan Dylan), 1971– author.
Title: The fifth to die / J.D. Barker.
Description: Boston ; New York : HarperCollins Publishers, 2018. |
Series: A 4MK thriller ; 2
Identifiers: LCCN 2017058446 (print) | LCCN 2018001184 (ebook) |
ISBN 9780544980662 (ebook) | ISBN 9780544973978 (hardback) |
ISBN 9781328589811 (pbk.)
Subjects: LCSH: Detectives—Illinois—Chicago—Fiction. | Serial
murderers—Fiction. | BISAC: FICTION / Suspense. | FICTION / Mystery &
Detective / Police Procedural. | FICTION / Thrillers. | GSAFD: Mystery
fiction. | Suspense fiction.
Classification: LCC PS3602.A775525 (ebook) |
LCC PS3602.A775525 F58 2018 (print) |
DDC 813/.6—dc23
LC record available at https://lccn.loc.gov/2017058446

Book design by Chrissy Kurpeski

Printed in the United States of America
24 25 26 27 28 LBC 10 9 8 7 6

For Father

1

Porter

Day 1 • 8:23 p.m.

Darkness.

It swirled around him deep and thick, eating the light and leaving nothing behind but an inky void. A fog choked his thoughts—the words tried to come together, tried to form a cohesive sentence, to find meaning, but the moment they seemed close, they were swallowed up and gone, replaced by a growing sense of dread, a feeling of heaviness—his body sinking into the murky depths of a long-forgotten body of water.

Moist scent.

Mildew.

Damp.

Sam Porter wanted to open his eyes.

Had to open his eyes.

They fought him though, held tight.

His head ached, throbbed.

A pulsing pain behind his right ear—at his temple too.

"Try not to move, Sam. Wouldn't want you to get sick."

The voice was distant, muffled, familiar.

Porter was lying down.

Cold steel beneath the tips of his fingers.

He remembered the shot then. A needle at the base of his neck, a quick stab, cold liquid rushing under his skin into the muscle, then—

Porter forced his eyes to open, the heavy lids fighting him. Dry, burning.

He tried to rub them, his right hand reaching out only to be pulled back when the chain at his wrist went taut.

His breath caught, and he forced himself to a sitting position, his head spinning as the blood rushed out. He almost fell back.

"Whoa, easy, Sam. The etorphine will work out of your system quickly now that you're awake. Just give it a minute."

A light blinked on, a bright halogen aimed squarely at his face. Porter squinted but refused to look away, his eyes fixed on the man beside the light, the dull, shadowed shape.

"Bishop?" Porter barely recognized his own voice, the dry gravel of it.

"How you been, Sam?" The shadow took a step to his right, turned over an empty five-gallon paint bucket, and sat.

"Get that damn light out of my eyes."

Porter yanked at the chain on his wrist—the other end of the handcuffs rattled around a thick pipe—water, maybe gas. "What the fuck is this?"

Anson Bishop reached over to the light and turned it slightly to the left. A shop light, mounted on some kind of stand. The light struck a cinder-block wall with a water heater in the far corner, an old washer and dryer along the far side.

"Better?"

Porter tugged at the chain again.

Bishop gave him a half smile and shrugged.

The last time Porter saw him, his hair was dark brown and close cropped. It was longer now, and lighter, unruly. Three or four days of scruff marred his face. His business casual attire was gone, replaced by jeans and a dark gray hoodie.

"You're looking a little ratty," Porter said.

"Desperate times."

He couldn't change his eyes, the coldness behind them.

His eyes never changed.

Bishop pulled a small spoon out of his back pocket, a grapefruit spoon, and twirled it absent-mindedly between his fingers, the serrated edge catching the light.

Porter didn't acknowledge the utensil. Instead, he looked down, tapping the metal beneath him with his index finger. "Is this the same kind of gurney you chained Emory to?"

"More or less."

"Couldn't find a cot?"

"Cots break."

A dark red stain pooled out from under the gurney, a deep blemish on the filthy concrete floor. Porter didn't ask about that. His fingers came away sticky after touching the underside of the metal. He didn't ask about that, either. A few shelves lined the wall to his left, stacked full with random painting supplies—cans, brushes, tarps. The ceiling above was constructed of wood, two-by-six boards spaced about sixteen inches apart. Exposed electrical wiring, water pipes, and air ducts filled the space between. "This is a residential basement. Not a big house. Older, though. That pipe above your head is shielded in asbestos, so I wouldn't recommend chewing on it. I'm guessing the place is abandoned, because your light there is plugged in to an extension cord running upstairs to . . . what, some kind of battery pack? Not a generator. We'd hear that. You didn't bother with any of these plugs along the wall, so that tells me the power isn't on in this place. It's also cold as balls. I can see my breath, so the heat isn't on. Again, that points to an abandoned house. Nobody wants to risk frozen pipes."

Bishop appeared pleased with this, a thin smile edging his lips.

Porter continued. "Wall to wall, this house is fairly narrow. That suggests a shotgun home. Considering you wouldn't want to be in one of the trendier neighborhoods where residents have Starbucks, the Internet, and tend to report known felons to the police on sight, I'd say you're more likely to stick to the West Side. Maybe someplace like Wood Street. A lot of empty houses on Wood."

With his free hand, Porter reached for his gun under his thick coat but found only the empty holster. His cell phone was gone too.

"Always the cop."

Wood Street was a good fifteen-minute drive without traffic from his apartment on Wabash, and Porter had been a block from his house when he felt the stab at his neck. Of course, this was all a complete guess, but Porter wanted to keep Bishop talking. The more he talked, the less he thought about that spoon.

The throbbing in Porter's head settled behind his right eye.

"Aren't you going to try and convince me to turn myself in? How you can spare me from the death penalty if I cooperate?"

"Nope."

This time Bishop did smile. "Hey, you want to see something?"

Porter would have said no, but he knew whatever he said didn't really matter. This man had a plan in mind, a purpose. Snatching a Chicago Metro detective off the street was not a risk one would take without a good reason.

He could feel his key ring in his right front pocket. Bishop had left it when he took his gun and phone. He had a handcuff key on his key ring, and most handcuffs took the same key. While he was a rookie, he was told this was because the person who cuffed a perp most likely wouldn't be the same person who would later uncuff the perp. A suspect could easily be transferred two or three times during booking. That in mind, they were taught to take away keys when patting someone down, *all keys*. Any criminal worth their salt owned their own handcuff key on the off chance some rookie forgot to check. Porter would have to remove the key ring from his right pocket, somehow maneuver it to his left hand, unlock the handcuffs, and take down Bishop before the man could cross the five feet that separated them.

The man didn't appear to have a weapon, only a spoon.

"Eyes front, Sam," Bishop said.

Porter turned back to him.

Bishop stood up and crossed the basement to a small table next to the washing machine. He returned to his seat, carrying a small wooden box with Porter's Glock sitting on top. He set the gun down on the floor beside him and thumbed the latch on the box, opening the lid.

Six eyeballs stared up at Porter from the red velvet lining inside.

Bishop's past victims.

Porter looked down at the gun.

"Eyes front," Bishop repeated with a soft chuckle.

This wasn't right. Bishop always followed the same pattern. He would remove his victims' ear, then the eyes, followed by the tongue, and mail each to the victim's family along with a note in a white box tied off with a black string. Always. He never deviated from this. He didn't keep trophies. He believed he was punishing the family for some wrong they committed. Twisted vigilante justice. He didn't keep the eyes. He never kept the—

"We'd better get started. "Bishop ran his hand over the top of the box, a loving caress, then set it down on the floor beside the gun and held the spoon up to the light.

Porter rolled off the gurney, crying out when the metal of the handcuff tore into the flesh of his wrist, the pipe pulled back. He tried to ignore the pain and awkwardly shoved his left hand down into his right pocket to retrieve the keys while also kicking the gurney in Bishop's direction. His fingers slipped over the keys as Bishop dodged the gurney and thrust his leg out, impacting Porter's left shin. Porter's leg fell out from beneath him, and he crashed down to the ground, the handcuff on his right arm catching on the pipe and yanking him hard enough to dislocate his shoulder.

Before he could react, he felt the sting of another needle, this one at his thigh. He tried to look down, but Bishop pulled at his hair, snapping his head back.

Consciousness began to drift away. Porter fought it, fought with all he had. He fought long enough to see the grapefruit spoon approach his left eye, long enough to feel the serrated edge cut into the tarsal plate beneath his eyeball as Bishop forced the spoon into his eye socket, long enough for—

"Was she hot?"

Porter jerked in his seat, a seat belt holding him back. He took in a deep breath, his head thrashing side to side, his eyes landing on Nash in the driver's seat. "What? Who?"

Nash smirked. "The girl from your dream. You were moaning."

Six eyeballs.

Porter, still disoriented, realized he was in the passenger seat of Nash's Chevy, an old '72 Nova he'd picked up two months back when his prized Ford Fiesta sputtered and died on the 290 at three in the morning, forcing him to call headquarters for a ride when he couldn't reach Porter.

Porter looked out the window. It was coated in a thin film of road grime and ice. "Where are we?"

"We're on Hayes, coming up on the park," he replied, flipping on his blinker. "Maybe you should sit this one out."

Porter shook his head. "I'm all right."

Nash made the left into Jackson Park and followed the recently plowed access road, the red and blue flashing lights bouncing off the dark trees around them. "It's been four months, Sam. If you're still having trouble sleeping, you should talk to someone. Doesn't have to be me or Clair, just . . . someone."

"I'm all right," Porter repeated.

They passed a baseball field on the right, forgotten for the winter, and continued deeper into the bare trees. Up ahead there were more lights—a half dozen cars, maybe more. Four uniform patrol vehicles, an ambulance, a fire department van. Large floodlights lined the edge of the lagoon, and propane heaters littered an area roped in by yellow crime scene tape.

Nash pulled to a stop behind the van, dropped the car into Park, and killed the engine. It sputtered twice and sounded like it was gearing up for a stellar backfire before finally going silent. Porter noted several officers staring in their direction as they climbed out of the car into the icy winter air.

"We could have driven my car," Porter told Nash, his boots crunching in the newly fallen snow.

Porter owned a 2011 Dodge Charger.

Most of their coworkers referred to the vehicle as Porter's "midlife crisis car"—it had replaced a Toyota Camry two years back on his fiftieth birthday. Porter's late wife, Heather, bought the sports car for him as a surprise after their Toyota was vandalized and left for dead in one of the less "police-friendly" parts of town on the South Side. Porter was first to admit sitting behind the wheel shaved a few years off his subconscious age, but mostly the car just made him smile.

Heather had baked the key into his birthday cake, and he almost chipped a tooth when he found it.

She led him down the steps and out in front of their apartment blindfolded, then sang "Happy Birthday" to him in a voice that had little chance of getting her on *American Idol*.

Porter thought of her every time he climbed in, but it seemed fewer and fewer things reminded him of her these days, her face gradually becoming a little more fuzzy in his mind.

"Your car is part of the problem. We always drive your car, and Connie over there spends her days rotting in my driveway. If I drive her, I'm reminded of the fact that I want to restore her. If I'm reminded of the fact that I want to restore her, I might actually get out to the garage and work on it."

"Connie?"

"Cars should have a name."

"No, they shouldn't. Cars shouldn't have names, and you have no idea how to restore her . . . it . . . whatever. I think you got that beater home, and the first time you picked up a wrench you realized you wouldn't be done in forty-three minutes like those guys on *Overhaulin'*," Porter said.

"That show is bullshit. They should tell you how long it really takes."

"Could be worse. At least you didn't get hooked on HGTV and convince yourself you can flip a house in your spare time."

"This is true. Although, they knock those out in twenty-two minutes for a much bigger return on investment," Nash replied. "If I did a house or two, I could pay someone to restore the car. Hey, there's Clair—"

They crossed under the yellow crime scene tape and made their way toward the shore of the lagoon. Clair was standing next to one of the heaters, her cell phone pressed to her ear. When she saw them, she nodded toward the shoreline, covered the microphone, and said, "We think that's Ella Reynolds," before returning to her call.

Porter's heart sank.

Ella Reynolds was a fifteen-year-old girl who had gone missing after school near Logan Square three weeks earlier. She was last seen getting off her bus about two blocks from her home. Her parents wasted no time reporting her missing, and the Amber Alerts were running within an hour of her disappearance. Little good they did. The police hadn't received a single worthwhile tip.

Nash started toward the water's edge, and Porter followed.

The lagoon was frozen.

Four orange cones lined the ice offshore, yellow tape running between them, creating a rectangle. The snow had been swept away.

Porter tentatively stepped out onto the ice, listening for the telltale crackle beneath his feet. No matter how many boot tracks waffled the lagoon's frozen surface, it always made him nervous when they were his boots.

As Porter edged closer, the girl came into view. The ice was clear as glass.

She stared up through it with blank eyes.

Her skin was horribly pale, with a blue tint except around those eyes. There, her skin was a dark purple. Her lips were parted as if she were about to say something, words that would never come.

Porter knelt to get a better look.

She wore a red coat, black jeans, a white knit cap with matching gloves, and what looked like pink tennis shoes. Her arms were loose at her sides, and her legs curved beneath her, disappearing into the dark water. Water normally bloated bodies, but at these temperatures the cold tended to preserve them. Porter preferred bloated. When they appeared less human, he found it easier to process what he was looking at—he was less emotional.

This girl looked like somebody's baby, helpless and alone, sleeping under a blanket of glass.

Nash stood behind him, his eyes scanning the trees across the water. "They held the World's Fair out here in 1893. There used to be a Japanese garden across the lagoon, that whole wooded area over there. My father used to bring me up here when I was a kid. He said it went to shit during World War II. I think I read somewhere they got the funding to restore it in the spring. See all the marked trees? They're coming down."

Porter followed his partner's gaze. The lagoon split into two branches—east and west—enclosing a small island. Many of the trees on Wooded Island had pink ribbons tied around them. A couple of benches littered the opposite shore, covered in a thin layer of white. "When do you suppose this freezes?"

Nash thought about this for a second. "Maybe late December, early January. Why?"

"If this is Ella Reynolds, how'd she get under the ice? She disappeared three weeks ago. It would have been frozen solid at that point."

Nash loaded a recent photo of Ella Reynolds on his phone and showed it to Porter. "Looks like her, but maybe it's just a coincidence—some other girl who fell through back when it was still soft."

"Looks just like her, though."

Clair came up beside them. She blew into her hands and rubbed them together. "That was Sophie Rodriguez with Missing Children—I sent her a picture, and she swears this is Ella Reynolds, but the clothes aren't a match. She says Ella was wearing a black coat when she disappeared. Three corroborating witnesses put her in a black coat on the bus, not red. She called the girl's mother—she said her daughter doesn't own a red coat, white hat, or white gloves."

"So either this is an entirely different girl, or somebody changed her clothes," Porter said. "We're a good fifteen miles from where Ella disappeared."

Clair bit at her lower lip. "The ME will have to get a positive ID."

"Who found her?"

Clair pointed to a patrol car at the far perimeter. "A little boy and his father—the kid's twelve." She glanced at the notes on her phone. "Scott Watts. He came out here with his father to see if the lagoons had frozen over enough for some skating lessons. Father's name is Brian. Said his son brushed away the snow and saw part of her arm. The father told his son to stand back and cleared away a little more on his own—enough to confirm it was a person—then he called 911. That was about an hour ago. The call came in at seven twenty-nine. I stowed them in a patrol car, in case you wanted to speak to them."

Porter scraped at the ice with his pointer finger, then glanced along the shoreline. Two CSI officers stood off to their left, eyeing the three of them warily. "Which one of you cleared this?" he asked.

The younger of the two, a woman who looked to be about thirty, with short blond hair, glasses, and a thick pink coat, raised her hand. "I did, sir."

Her partner shuffled his feet. He looked to be about five years her senior. "I supervised. Why?"

"Nash? Hand me that?" He pointed toward a brush with long, white bristles sitting on top of one of the CSI officers' kits.

Porter motioned for the two officers to come over. "It's okay, I don't usually bite."

Back in November, Porter returned early from a leave of absence forced on him when his wife was killed during the robbery of a local convenience store. He had wanted to keep working, mainly because the work distracted him, kept his mind off what happened.

The days following her death, when he locked himself in their apartment, those were by far the worst. Reminders were everywhere.

Her face watched him from pictures on nearly every shelf. Her scent was in the air—for the first week, he couldn't sleep unless he spread some of her clothes on the bed. He sat in that apartment and thought of nothing but what he would do to the guy who killed her, thoughts he didn't want in his head.

Ultimately, the Four Monkey Killer had gotten him out of that apartment.

It was also 4MK who exacted revenge on the man who killed Porter's wife. 4MK was the reason people like these two CSI officers acted odd around him. Not exactly intimidation, more like awe.

He was the cop who had let 4MK into the investigation under the guise of CSI. He was the cop 4MK stabbed in his own home. He was the cop who caught the serial killer and let him go.

Four months later, and they all talked about it, just not to him.

The two officers walked over.

The woman crouched down beside him.

Porter used the brush to clear away the snow nearest the shoreline and along the outer edges they'd previously cleared. When he expanded the circle by another two feet, he set the brush down and ran his palm over the ice, starting at the center and slowly moving out toward the edge. He stopped about four inches from the snow. "There. Feel that."

The younger investigator removed her glove and hesitantly followed his lead, her fingertips brushing the ice.

She stopped about an inch from his palm.

"Do you feel that?"

She nodded. "There's a small dip. Not much, but it's there."

"Follow it around. Mark it with this." He handed her a Sharpie.

A minute later she had drawn a neat square over the body, with two smaller squares approximately four inches wide jutting out on each side.

"Guess that answers that," Porter said.

Nash frowned. "What are we looking at?"

Porter stood, helping the woman to her feet. "What's your name?"

"CSI Lindsy Rolfes, sir."

"CSI Rolfes, can you explain what this means?"

She thought about it for a second, her eyes darting from Porter to the ice, then back again. Then she understood. "The lagoon was frozen, and someone cut the ice, probably with a cordless chainsaw, then put her in the water. If she'd fallen in, there'd be a jagged break, not a square like this. But this doesn't make sense . . ."

"What?"

She frowned, reached into her kit, took out a cordless drill, attached a one-inch bit, and made two holes, one outside her line, the other near the body. With a ruler, she then measured the depth of both from the top to the water. "I don't get it—she's beneath the freeze line."

"I don't follow," Clair said.

"He replaced the water," Porter said.

Rolfes nodded. "Yeah, but why? He could have cut a hole and pushed her body under the existing ice, then let the hole freeze up naturally. That would have been much faster and easier. She would have disappeared, maybe for good."

Clair sighed. "Can you explain for those of us who didn't take Icehole 101?"

Porter motioned for the ruler, and Rolfes handed it to him. "The ice here is at least four inches thick. You can see the water line here." He pointed at the mark on the ruler. "If you cut out a square of this ice and removed it, there would be a four-inch ledge from the top of the ice to the water. Then let's say you put the girl's body in the hole, she sinks, and you want to make the hole disappear. There's only one way to do that. You'd have to wait for the water to freeze around her, at least a thin layer, then fill the hole with more water to the top of the ice, level it off."

"It would take at least two hours to freeze," Rolfes said. "Maybe a little less, with the temperatures we've had lately."

Porter was nodding. "He kept adding water until this fresh ice was at the same height as the surrounding ice. Our unsub is patient. This was very time consuming." He turned to the CSI supervisor. "We'll need this ice. Everything on top of her, and at least a few inches surrounding this square. There's a good chance some trace got in with the water while it froze. Our unsub hovered here for a long time."

The supervisor looked like he was about to argue, then nodded reluctantly. He knew Porter was right.

Porter's gaze went back to the overgrown mess of trees across the water. "What I don't understand is why whoever did this didn't dump her over there. Dragging a body out here in the open, taking the time to cut the ice, fill it, wait for it to freeze . . . that's a lot of risk. The unsub could have carried her across the bridge and left her anywhere over there, and she'd go undiscovered until spring when they started work. Instead, he spends hours to stage her in the water near a high-traffic area. Risks getting caught. Why? To create the illusion that she was here much longer than she really had been? He had to know we'd figure that out."

"Dead bodies don't float," Nash pointed out. "At least, not for a few days. Look at her. She's perfectly preserved. I'm still not sure why she's floating."

Porter ran his finger along the edge of the square, stopping at one of the two smaller squares on the side. He lowered his face to the ice, looking down at her from the side. "I'll be damned."

"What?" Rolfes leaned in.

Porter ran his hand over the ice, above the girl's shoulders. When he found what he was looking for, he placed Rolfes's hand over it. She looked at him, her eyes growing as her fingers dug slightly into the ice. She reached for the same spot on the other side. "He kept her from sinking by placing something over this hole, probably a length of two-by-four based on these marks, then ran a string or thin rope around her body at the shoulders, and secured it to the board while the replacement water froze. When he was done, he cut the string. You can still feel the nubs here in the ice. There's enough left to keep her near the surface. You can see a thin rope if you look through the ice at the right angle."

"He wanted her to be found?" Clair said.

"He wanted to make an impact *if* she was found," Porter replied. "He went through a lot of trouble to stage this so it appeared like she froze beneath the lake's surface months ago, even though she's only been here for a few days at best, possibly less. We need to figure out why."

"This guy is playing with us," CSI Rolfes said. "Twisting the crime scene to fit some kind of narrative."

Self-preservation and fear are two of the strongest instincts of the human condition. Porter wasn't sure he wanted to meet the man who possessed neither. "Get her out of there," he finally said.

2

Porter

Day 1 • 11:24 p.m.

"You want me to come up?"

They were parked in front of Porter's building on Wabash. Nash tapped at the gas to keep Connie from stalling. The night had grown bitterly cold.

Porter shook his head. "Go home and get some rest. We'll hit the ground running in the morning."

Using chainsaws, CSI had cut the ice around the girl as one large square, then carefully broke the ice away in manageable pieces, which were loaded into buckets and transported back to the crime lab for analysis. The girl's body went to the morgue for identification. Porter put a call in to Tom Eisley, and the man agreed to go in early and contact him as soon as they made a positive identification. Uniformed patrol officers were still searching the park when Porter and Nash left, but at that point they had not found anything. Clair agreed to stay and review footage taken by the lone security camera placed at the park's entrance. She wasn't quite sure what she was looking for, and Porter couldn't give her any direction other than to watch for something unusual over the previous three weeks, particularly after hours. The park itself closed at dusk, and after that, aside from a few lights in the most common areas, the grounds were dark. There were no permanent lights at the lagoon. Anyone coming or going after dark would stand out.

"About earlier, on the way to the lagoon—" Porter began.

Nash cut him off. "You don't have to explain. It's okay."

Porter waved a hand in the air. "I haven't been getting a lot of sleep. Not since Heather died. Every time I step into our apartment, the place feels so empty. I expect her to come walking in from one of the other rooms or through the front door with an armload of groceries, and she never does. I don't want to glance over and see her side of the bed empty. I don't want to see her toothbrush in the bathroom, but I can't bring myself to throw it out. Same with her clothes. About a week ago I nearly boxed everything up for Goodwill. I got the first blouse into a box but had to stop. Shuffling her clothes around had filled the air with her scent, and it was almost like she was back again, if only for a little while. I know I have to move forward, but I'm not sure I can. Not yet, anyway."

Nash reached over and squeezed his friend's shoulder. "You will. When the time is right, you will. Nobody is rushing you. You just need to know we're all here for you. If you need anything at all." Nash fumbled with the steering wheel, tugging at a flap in the faux leather. "Maybe it would help to move. Find a new place, start over."

Porter shook his head. "I can't do that. We found this place together. It's home."

"Maybe a vacation, then?" Nash suggested. "You've got plenty of time off saved up."

"Maybe, yeah." Porter stared up at the face of his building.

He wouldn't move. Not anytime soon.

The door of the Chevy squeaked as Porter tugged the handle and stepped out. "Holy balls, it's cold."

"Time to break out the long johns and whiskey."

Porter knocked on the roof of the car twice. "If you put some time into this thing, it could be one sweet ride."

Nash offered a smile. "Meet in the war room at seven?"

"Yeah, seven's good."

Then he was gone.

Porter watched the car disappear down the road before making his way into the small foyer of his building, carefully avoiding the piles of frozen dog poop on the steps. He passed the mailboxes and took the stairs. He didn't do elevators anymore, not if given a choice.

Stepping into his apartment, he was assaulted by the mixed odors of a dozen take-out meals. The worst of the perpetrators, a pile of pizza boxes on the kitchen table, filled the air with stale cheese and old pepperoni.

Porter hung his coat over the back of a chair and stepped into the bedroom, flipping on the light.

The bed had been pushed to the far corner of the room, along with the two nightstands.

Hundreds of pictures and notes, Post-its, and newspaper articles filled the wall where the bed used to be. Some were connected by string. When he ran out of string, he drew lines with a black marker.

This was everything he had on 4MK, or Anson Bishop, or Paul Watson—all of them one and the same. He had details on Bishop's past crimes, but mostly he focused on just where Bishop might have gone after his escape.

In the corner of the room, a laptop sat on the floor, the screen glowing bright. Porter lifted it up and studied the display. He used Google alerts (surprisingly simple for someone lacking the most basic computer skills) to flag every mention, every story, every sighting of Bishop, Watson, or 4MK on the Internet and drop the results into his personal e-mail account. Sometimes it would take hours, but he would sort through each message and plot out the locations mentioned on the large world map tacked to the wall at the center of all his other data. Maps too. Dozens of detailed maps, all the major cities.

Four months of data.

Thumbtacks filled the maps—red represented a sighting, blue for the location of the reporter writing the story, and yellow for the home of anyone who had gone missing or had been murdered in a way similar to 4MK's MO. The copycats were everywhere. While many of the thumbtacks centered on Chicago, they went as far as Brazil and Moscow.

Porter picked up a yellow thumbtack and located the lagoon at Jackson Park on the Chicago map. "Ella Reynolds, missing since January 22, 2015, possibly found February 12, 2015," he mumbled to himself. He had no reason to believe 4MK was responsible, but that tack would stay there until he was sure he was not.

His eyes were heavy with lack of sleep.

He had a brutal headache.

He sat in the middle of the floor and began sifting through all the Google alerts for today, all 159 of them.

When his phone rang two hours later, he considered ignoring the call, then thought better of it. Nobody called at one thirty in the morning without reason.

"Porter," he said.

Why did his voice always sound louder in the middle of the night?

At first there was silence. Then: "Detective? This is Sophie Rodriguez with Missing Children. I got your number from Clair Norton."

"What can I do for you, Ms. Rodriguez?"

More silence. "We have another missing girl. You and your partner need to get down here."

3

Porter

Day 2 • 2:21 a.m.

Here turned out to be a graystone in Bronzeville on King Drive.

Rodriguez didn't provide any details when she called, only said this case tied to the body of the girl found in the park earlier, and he'd want to be there.

Porter parked his Charger on the street behind Nash's Chevy and trudged through the snowbank at the side of the road and up into the home at the corner. There was no need to knock. A uniformed officer at the door recognized him and ushered him inside. He found Nash and a woman he didn't recognize sitting in a parlor to the left of the entrance. A man in his late forties, salt-and-pepper hair, fit, wearing a tweed sport coat and jeans, stood beside Nash. Another woman, no doubt his wife, sat on the couch with a crushed tissue in her hand.

The woman sitting beside her rose as Porter entered the room. "Detective Porter? I'm Sophie Rodriguez from Missing Children. Thank you for coming. I know it's late."

Porter shook her hand and studied the room.

Most of these graystones had been built around the turn of the twentieth century. This particular one had been painstakingly restored with original trim and fixtures. The rugs looked authentic too but had to be knockoffs, careful reproductions of the originals. Antique furniture filled the space.

The man who had been speaking to Nash offered his hand. "I'm Dr. Randal Davies, and this is my wife, Grace. Thank you so much for coming out at this hour."

The man gestured to a chair next to the couch.

Porter declined. "It's been a rather long night. I think I'd better stand."

"Coffee, then?"

"Please. Black is fine."

Dr. Davies excused himself and disappeared down the hall.

Porter glanced at Rodriguez, who had returned to her seat on the couch.

"My office received a call from Mrs. Davies shortly after midnight, when her daughter didn't come home," Rodriguez said.

Mrs. Davies looked up, her eyes red and swollen. "Lili works downtown at an art gallery. On Thursdays she goes straight there after school and takes an Uber home when they close at eleven. She is always home by eleven thirty. If for some reason she's running late, she texts me—she knows her father and I worry, so she *always* texts me. She is a responsible young lady, and this is her first job and she knows we worry . . ." She dabbed at her eyes with the tissue. "I hadn't heard from her by eleven forty-five, so I called her, and it went straight to voice mail. Then I called the gallery and spoke to her supervisor, Ms. Edwins. She said Lili didn't show up for her shift. She had tried to reach her several times and got the same thing: voice mail. No rings, just voice mail. I know that means her phone is off, which is very unlike her. She never turns her phone off. She knows I worry. I called her best friend, Gabby, then—"

"What is Gabby's last name?" Porter asked.

"Deegan. Gabrielle Deegan. I gave her contact information to your partner." When she said this, she glanced at Rodriguez. Porter didn't correct her.

Mrs. Davies continued. "Gabby said she hadn't seen her all day. She wasn't at school, and she wasn't replying to text messages. This isn't like Lili, you understand. She's a straight-A student. She hasn't missed a day of school since the fourth grade, when she had chicken pox." Mrs. Davies paused, studying Porter's face. "You're the detective who chased . . . oh God, do you think 4MK took our daughter? Is that why you're here?" Her eyes went wide and flooded with tears.

"This isn't 4MK," Porter assured her, although he wasn't certain of that himself. "At this point there is no reason to assume anyone has taken your daughter."

"She wouldn't disappear like this."

Porter tried to change the subject. "Where does she go to school?"

"Wilcox Academy."

Dr. Davies returned and handed Porter a steaming cup of coffee, then stood beside his wife on the couch. "I know what you're thinking, and like we told your partners here, Lili doesn't have a boyfriend. She wouldn't skip school. She most definitely wouldn't skip work— she loves that gallery. Something is wrong. The Find My iPhone feature is activated on her phone, but it's not coming up on our account. I called Apple, and they said her phone is offline. Our daughter would not turn off her phone."

Nash cleared his throat. "Mrs. Davies, can you tell Detective Porter what Lili was wearing today when she was last seen?"

Mrs. Davies nodded. "Her favorite coat, a red Perro parka, a white hat, matching gloves, and dark jeans. On cold days, Lili preferred to change into her uniform once she arrived on campus. She stopped in the kitchen and said goodbye to me before she left for school this morning. That's her favorite coat. She bought it at Barneys with her first paycheck. She was so proud of that coat."

Rodriguez pursed her lips.

Porter said nothing.

4

Porter

"How is that even possible?"

"We can show them a photo of the jacket to try and confirm," Nash suggested.

Porter shook his head. "We can't show them a picture of a dead girl."

The three of them stood outside the Davieses' graystone, their breath creating an icy fog between them.

"There is no way someone had time to kidnap Lili Davies, put her clothes on Ella Reynolds, and bury her under the ice at the park. There is no way. There just isn't enough time." Porter shuffled his feet. The temperature must be in single digits. "That means he would have been out at the lake during daylight hours, while it was open. Somebody would have seen him."

Nash thought about this for a second. "In this weather, the park is nearly deserted. The only real risk would be when the unsub carried the body from his vehicle to the water. Unless someone got close, nothing else would really jump out as a red flag. He would just look like some guy out by the lagoon, maybe ice-fishing or something. If he set up with a fishing pole, I bet he could spend the day without anyone giving him a second glance."

"Logistics aside," Rodriguez said, "what's the point?"

Porter and Nash exchanged a glance. They both knew serial killers rarely had a point, at least not one that made sense to anyone but them. And although they only had one victim, if she tied to this second missing girl, they might be looking at a serial.

"Do Ella Reynolds and Lili Davies know each other?" Porter asked Rodriguez.

Rodriguez shook her head. "Her parents only knew the name from television."

"We should check with Lili's friend Gabby," Porter suggested. "What time did she leave for school?"

Rodriguez glanced at her notes. "Quarter after seven."

Nash closed his eyes and crunched the numbers. "That only allows about twelve hours from the time Lili disappeared to the time Ella was found frozen in the lake."

"Look at you doing math." Porter said, and snickered.

"If this is one guy, he's fast. Efficient," Nash said.

Porter turned back to Rodriguez. "Sophie, right?"

She nodded.

"Go back in and search the girl's room. Look for anything out of the ordinary. Get her computer—check her e-mails, saved documents. Look for a diary, photos . . . You find anything at all, you call me. Find out her route to school. Does she walk or get a ride? With friends or alone? Got it?"

Rodriguez chewed on her bottom lip. "What does this mean for Lili?"

Porter wasn't ready to go there. He turned back to Nash. "Let's go wake up Eisley."

5

Porter

Day 2 • 4:18 a.m.

The Cook County Medical Examiner's Office and morgue was off West Harrison in downtown Chicago. At this hour, Porter and Nash ran into little traffic, and they found the parking spaces out front to be relatively deserted. The guard at the front desk looked up at them with groggy eyes and nodded a hello. "Sign in, please."

Porter scribbled *Burt Reynolds* on the clipboard and handed it to Nash, who wrote *Dolly Parton* before returning it to the desk and following him to the bank of elevators at the back of the lobby. Porter wasn't a fan of elevators but he was even less a fan of several flights of stairs.

The second elevator from the left arrived first, and he followed Nash inside before he could change his mind.

Porter hit the button marked 3. "Dolly was hot back in the day."

"Still is," Nash replied. "A true GILF."

"GILF?"

"I'll explain when you're a little older, Sam."

The doors opened on an empty hallway.

Nash eyed the vending machine, then gave it a pass, heading for the double doors at the end of the hallway.

They found Tom Eisley at his desk. He glanced up at them as they came in before returning to whatever he was reading.

Porter expected him to say something about the time. Instead, he asked, "Have either of you ever seen the ocean?"

Porter and Nash exchanged a look.

Eisley closed the book on his desk and stood. "Never mind. Not sure I'm ready to talk about this yet."

"I take it you're working on our girl?" Porter asked.

Eisley sighed. "I'm trying. We've been warming up her body since they brought her in here. She wasn't quite frozen, you understand, just way below normal temperature. It's going to make time of death difficult to determine."

"Do you know the cause?"

Eisley opened his mouth, prepared to say something, then thought better of it. "Not yet. I'm going to need a few more hours. You're welcome to wait, if you'd like."

Before they could respond, he disappeared through the door leading to the autopsy room.

Nash nodded at Porter. "Sounds like this might be a while."

Porter fell into a yellow vinyl chair near Eisley's door, his eyes heavy with lack of sleep.

6

Porter

"Gentlemen?"

Porter's eyes fluttered open, and it took him a moment to realize he was in Eisley's office at the morgue. He had slid down in the yellow vinyl chair, his neck cricked from being at an odd angle. Nash was slumped over at Eisley's desk, his head resting on a stack of papers.

Eisley picked up a medical text, lifted the book about three feet above the desk, then released. The book crashed down, loud and hard, and Nash snapped back in the chair, drool rolling down his chin. "What the—"

"Chicago's finest, hard at work," Eisley chided. "Follow me."

Porter glanced up at the clock on the far wall—about half past seven. A little over three hours had passed since they arrived here. "Shit, didn't mean to fall asleep," he mumbled. He pulled his cell phone from his pocket—three missed calls from Clair, no voice mail.

Eisley led them past his desk and through the double doors at the back of his office into the large examination room. Both Porter and Nash grabbed gloves from the box hanging on the wall near the door.

Noises echoed in here.

This was always the first thought that popped into Porter's head when he entered. Everything sounded different due to the beige tile on the floor and walls. The second thing that always hit him was the temperature—he didn't know what the actual temperature was in the room, but it felt like it dropped nearly twenty degrees. Goose bumps prickled the back of his neck, and a shiver ran over him. The third thing, the one he'd never get used to, was the smell. It didn't smell bad, not today anyway, but the room smelled *strong*. The heavy scent of industrial cleaners attempted to mask the underlying odor of something else, something Porter preferred not to think about.

Fluorescent lights burned bright above, glimmering on stainless steel cabinets. A large, round surgical light arched over the examination table at the center of the room where the body they pulled out of the lake rested.

Eisley had closed the girl's eyes.

Sleeping beauty.

An electric blanket and four large lamps sat off to the side.

Eisley caught Porter looking at them. "We got lucky. She wasn't in the lake very long, and her body was below the freeze line. If she froze through and through, we'd need to wait a few days before we could autopsy. In her case it only took a few hours to raise her body temp enough to proceed."

"You haven't cut her open yet," Nash pointed out. "It doesn't look like you've started at all."

"You'd be surprised what a body can tell you if you know where to look," Eisley replied. "I won't be able to open her up until tomorrow; she's still quite cold. If I warm her up too fast, we run the risk of crystallization and cellular damage. That doesn't mean she can't offer up some answers while we wait. Unlike you two, I've been busy." He ran his hand through her hair. "She's been talking, and I've been listening."

"Okay, now you're creeping me out," Porter said.

Eisley offered a smile and took a step back from the table. "Would you like to know what I found?"

"That would be lovely."

He walked over to the side of the table and lifted her hand. "The cold water was extremely preserving. With most bodies found in the water, they can be difficult to print. The skin tends to expand, and we have to reverse the effect before we can print. Like an extreme version of the pruning you probably experience in the bath."

"I'm more of a shower guy," Porter told him.

Eisley ignored the comment. "The near-freezing water kept her fingerprints completely intact, probably would through spring thaw." He lowered her hand back to the table, placing it gently at her side. "The results came back about two hours ago. I confirmed this is Ella Reynolds, the girl who disappeared three weeks ago."

Porter sighed. He expected as much, but there was something deflating about hearing the words spoken aloud. "What about a time of death or the cause?"

"As I said earlier, time of death can be a bit tricky because of the icy water. At this point, I would have to say no more than forty-eight hours ago but at least twenty-four. I'm hoping to narrow that down once I can get a look at her liver and other organs," he explained. "Help me turn her over?"

Porter and Nash exchanged a look. Nash took a slight step back. For a homicide detective, he had an odd aversion to dead bodies.

Porter took the girl's legs, and Eisley held her shoulders. Together, they turned her over.

Eisley ran a finger along a long, dark mark running across her back. "This is from the rope he used to hold her up in the water. The coloration tells me she was suspended post mortem. Soon after, though, otherwise it wouldn't be so prominent, particularly through that thick coat she was wearing." He nodded at her clothing, neatly piled on the stainless steel counter.

Nash walked, picked up the red coat, and began going through the pockets. "Did you see any identifying information on the clothing?"

"The clothing isn't hers, is it." Eisley said this more as fact than a question.

Porter turned to him. "Did you come to that conclusion?"

"I suspected as much, but I'm not sure I'd be willing to call it a conclusion. Everything seemed like a tight fit on her. Under normal circumstances, I would chalk that up to bloating from the water, but since there was so little, it seemed strange. Her undergarments and jeans in particular were at least a size or two too small. She squeezed into them, but they're tight, uncomfortable even. Take a look at the hat," he said, gesturing at the counter. "There are letters written on the tag, most likely initials."

Nash set down the coat and picked up the white hat, turned it inside out. "L.D. It's a bit faded, but that's definitely what it says."

"Lili Davies," Porter said.

"Yeah, probably."

"Who's that?" Eisley asked.

"Another girl, went missing sometime yesterday," Porter told him.

"So whoever killed this girl dressed her in the other girl's clothing?"

"Looks that way."

"Huh."

Porter asked, "What about cause of death? I don't really see anything on the body. No wounds, no strangulation marks."

At this, Eisley lit up. "Ah, yes. And you're going to find this strange."

"How did she die?"

"She drowned."

Nash frowned. "That doesn't sound so strange. We found her under the ice in a lake."

Porter raised a hand. "You said the mark on her back was post mortem. Are you saying she was alive when he put her in the water?"

"Oh no, she was dead at that point. I'm saying she drowned, and then he put her in the lake." He went over to a microscope on a raised table to his left. "Take a look at this," he said, pointing at the device.

Porter walked over and looked down into the eyepiece. "What am I looking at?"

"When they first brought her in, I was able to snake a tube down into her lungs, and I extracted water, that water."

Porter frowned. "What are these specks floating in it?"

The edge of Eisley's mouth curled up, "That, my friend, is salt."

"She drowned in salt water?"

"Precisely."

Nash's face went from lost to confused, then back again. "We're in Chicago . . . the nearest ocean is what, a thousand miles from here?"

"The Atlantic would be the closest," Eisley told him. "Baltimore, Maryland. About seven hundred miles."

Porter's cell phone rang. He glanced at the display, then answered. "Hey, Clair."

"Back from vacation? I called you about a dozen times."

"You called me three times."

"So your phone *is* working," she replied. "You should never ignore a woman, Sam. It won't end well."

Porter rolled his eyes and walked slowly across the room. "We're at the morgue with Eisley. He confirmed the girl in the lake is Ella Reynolds. It also looks like she was wearing Lili Davies's clothes."

"Who's Lili Davies?"

He thought he'd told her about the second missing girl, then realized he never had. They hadn't talked since the park. He needed sleep; his head was a foggy mess. "Can you meet Nash and me in the war room in thirty minutes? We all need to get up to speed."

"Sure thing," she said. "Aren't you going to ask me why I've been calling you?"

Porter closed his eyes and ran his hand through his hair. "Why have you been calling me, Clair?"

"I found something on the park video."

"Thirty minutes in the war room. We'll talk then. Grab Kloz."

7

Lili

Day 2 • 7:26 a.m.

"Would you like a glass of milk?"

Lili Davies heard his voice before she saw him, truly saw him.

He spoke slowly, softly, only a breath, each word enunciated with the utmost care as if he put great thought into what he wanted to say before releasing the words. He spoke with a slight lisp, the *s* in *glass* troubling him.

He'd come down the stairs nearly five minutes earlier, the boards creaking under his weight. But when he reached the bottom, when he stood at the foot of the steps, he remained still. Shadows engulfed him, and Lili could make nothing out but the outline of a man.

And this was a man, not a boy.

Something about the way he stood, his broad shoulders, the deepness of his breaths, these things told her he was a man, not one of the boys from school. Not someone she knew playing some kind of sick joke, but a man, a man who had taken her.

Lili *did* want milk.

Her throat was as dry as sand.

She was hungry too.

Her stomach kept making little gurgling noises to remind her of just how hungry.

She said nothing, though; she didn't utter a sound. Instead, she huddled deeper into the corner, her back pressing into the damp wall. She pulled the smelly green quilt tighter around her body. Something about the material made her feel safe, like being wrapped in her mother's arms.

He'd been gone for at least an hour, maybe more. Lili used that time to try to figure out where she was. She hadn't allowed herself to be afraid, she wouldn't allow herself to be afraid. This was a problem, and she was good at solving problems.

She was in the basement of an older home.

She knew this because her house was older, and she remembered what the basement looked like before her parents brought in the contractors and construction crews to renovate it. The ceilings were low and the floor was uneven. Everything smelled like mildew, and spiders thrived. Every corner and cranny had either an old web or a new web, and the spiders crawled everywhere. When her parents brought in the contractors at her home, they gutted the basement, leveled the floor, sealed the walls, and coated everything in fresh drywall and paint. That drove the spiders out, at least for a little while.

Her friend Gabby lived in a brand-new house, built only two years ago, and her basement was completely different. High ceilings and level floors, bright and airy. They carpeted, brought in furniture, and turned the space into a fun family room. Basements in old homes could never be fun family rooms, no matter how much work was done. You could cover up the moisture, even level the floors, drywall, and paint, but the spiders always came back. The spiders wouldn't give up their space.

This basement had spiders.

Although she couldn't see them from where she sat, she knew they were right above her, creeping in and out of the exposed floor joists. They watched her with a thousand eyes as they spun their webs.

He gave her clothes, but they were not *her* clothes.

When she woke on the floor, wrapped in the green quilt, she quickly realized she had been stripped nude and left here, in this cage, a stranger's clothes folded neatly and left near her head. They didn't fit. They were at least a few sizes too big, but she put them on because she had nothing else, because they were better than the green quilt. Then she wrapped herself in the green quilt anyway.

She was in a dimly lit, damp basement. More precisely, she was in a chainlink enclosure set up in a dimly lit, damp basement.

The enclosure went from floor to ceiling, and the pieces were welded together. It was meant to be a dog kennel. She knew this because Gabby's family owned a dog, a husky named Dakota, and they had a very similar, if not the same, kennel in their backyard. They bought it at Home Depot, and she and Gabby had watched her father put it together over the summer. It didn't take him long, maybe an hour, but he hadn't welded it.

When Lili stood up, wrapped in her green quilt, and ran her fingers over the various pipes and thick metal wire that made up her cage, she sought out joints, remembering how Gabby's father assembled his, then her heart sank as she found the bumpy welds. The gate at the front was locked tight with not one padlock but two—one near the top and the other near the bottom. She rattled the gate, but it barely moved. The entire structure had been bolted down into the concrete floor. It was secure, and she was trapped inside.

"You should drink something, you need to be strong for what is to come," the man said, his voice catching for a second on the *s* in *something*.

Lili said nothing. She wouldn't say anything. To talk to him would give him power, and she wasn't ready to do that. He didn't deserve anything from her.

The only light came from what was probably an open door at the top of the stairs. He stood perfectly still at the base.

Lili's eyes fought with the darkness, slowly adjusting.

He remained out of focus though, a darker shadow among other shadows, an outline against the wall.

"Turn around. Face the back wall, and don't turn back again until I say it's okay," he instructed.

Lili didn't move, her posture firming.

"Please turn around." Softer, pleading.

She gripped the quilt and pulled it tighter around her small frame.

"Turn the fuck around!" he shouted, his voice booming through the basement, echoing off the walls.

Lili gasped and took a step backward, nearly tripping.

Then all went quiet again.

"Please don't make me shout. I prefer not to shout."

Lili felt her heart pounding in her chest, a heavy *thump, thump, thump.*

She took a step back, then another, and another after that. When she reached the wall, the back of her cage, she willed her feet to turn around and faced the corner.

Lili heard him as he walked closer, the living shadow. Something about his gait was off. Rather than steady steps, she heard one foot land, then the other slid for a second on the concrete floor before it too fell into place, repeating again with the next step. A shuffle or limp, a slight drag of the foot, she couldn't be sure.

Lili forced her eyes to close. She didn't want to close them, but she did anyway. She forced her eyes to close so she could concentrate on the sounds, *picture* the sounds behind her.

She heard the jingle of keys before the telltale *click* of a padlock—it sounded like the top lock—then the other a moment later. She heard him slip both locks from the gate, then lift the handle and open the door.

Lili cringed in anticipation of what would come next.

She expected his hand on her, a touch somewhere or a grab from behind. That touch never came. Instead, she heard him close the gate and replace the locks, both clicking securely back into place.

His uneven shuffle away from her cage.

"You can turn back around now."

Lili did as he asked.

He returned to the stairs, lost to the dark again.

A glass of milk sat on the floor just inside the cage, a thin bead of water dripping down the side.

"It's not drugged," he said. "I need you awake."

8

Porter
Day 2 • 7:56 a.m.

"I'll see you in there. I need to hit the head," Nash said as they stepped off the elevator at the basement level of Chicago Metro headquarters on Michigan Avenue. Nash took a right down the hallway and disappeared behind the bathroom door. Porter went left.

After Bishop escaped, the feds had stepped in and taken over the 4MK manhunt. Porter had been on medical leave at that point, but from what Nash told him, they initially tried to take over the war room. Nash used his incredible charm, and threats of violence, on the interlopers and banished them to the room across the hall known primarily for the odd odor that permeated it, which seemed to come from the far left corner. Since that point, they coexisted with the civility of North and South Korea.

The lights in the FBI room were off.

Porter waited for the sound of Nash locking the restroom door, then tried the door to the feds' room.

Open.

With a quick glance back down the hall, Porter slipped inside. He left the lights off.

Six eyeballs.

Seven victims. Eight, if he counted Emory.

His subconscious was trying to tell him something.

He crossed the room to the two whiteboards at the front and studied the victims' photographs. The familiar faces looked back, their unknowing smiles captured forever in a moment of happiness. In those final moments on the eleventh floor of 314 West Belmont, Bishop pled his case, he laid his cards bare, so proud in the twisted logic of his plan. "These people deserved to be punished," he told Porter. And it was true. Each of his victims did something horribly wrong, something worthy of punishment. But he didn't go after them. Instead, he took their children. He made the children suffer in death so their parents would suffer forevermore in life. Each of these girls died not because of something she did but because of something a member of her family did. Each of these beautiful young faces snuffed out to pay for another's crimes.

Porter stepped closer to the first board and ran his fingers over the photo of Calli Tremell, Bishop's first victim. Twenty years of age, taken March 15, 2009. Bishop's first victim as 4MK—Klozowski was always quick to point this out. So thorough and sure in his methods, the pattern strongly suggested he'd killed before, developed a technique after honing a practice over years. He was too sophisticated to be a first-timer, and the thought of someone like him existing out there, taking lives, leading up to this . . . If this was his beginning as 4MK, Porter couldn't imagine where he came from. The diary gave him some insight, but not enough, only a glimpse—a quick look through an open curtain before Bishop dropped the fabric back into place.

Calli Tremell's parents reported her missing that Tuesday. They received her ear in the mail on Thursday. Her eyes followed on Saturday, and her tongue arrived the next Tuesday. All were packaged in small white boxes tied with black strings, handwritten shipping labels, and zero prints. He never left prints.

Three days after the last box arrived, a jogger found her body in Almond Park, propped up on a bench with a cardboard sign glued to her hands that read DO NO EVIL. Porter and his team had picked up on his MO by that point, and the sign confirmed their theory.

Do no evil turned out to be the key to Bishop's focus, something they realized with 4MK's second victim, Elle Borton. She disappeared on April 2, 2010, more than a year after his first victim. Porter's team caught the case from Missing Children when her parents reported receiving an ear in the mail. When her body was found a little over a week later, she held a tax return in her grandmother's name covering tax year 2008. After some digging, they found out the grandmother had died in 2005. Matt Hosman in Financial Crimes discovered that Elle's father filed tax returns on more than a dozen residents of the nursing home he managed, all deceased. Bishop killed Elle Borton, only twenty-three years old, because of crimes committed by her father.

When 4MK's motive became clear, they went back and looked at Calli Tremell's family and discovered her mother had been laundering money from the bank where she worked, upward of three million dollars over the previous ten years.

Porter stepped to his right and looked at the third photograph. Missy Lumax, June 24, 2011. Her father sold kiddie porn. Susan Devoro's father swapped fake diamonds for real ones at his jewelry store. She was victim number four—May 3, 2012. Number five— Barbara McInley, seventeen years old. She disappeared on April 18, 2013. Her sister had hit and killed a pedestrian six years before, and Bishop killed Barbara as punishment. Allison Crammer's brother ran a sweatshop full of illegals down in Florida. She was number six, disappearing on November 9, 2013, at only nineteen years of age. Jodi Blumington followed only a few months later. On May 13, 2014, she went missing at age twenty-two. 4MK killed her because her father imported coke for a cartel.

The very last photo on the board was of a girl Porter knew well, the only one he actually met, the only one not to die. Emory Connors, fifteen years old, taken in November of last year. Although she lost an ear and spent days in captivity, Bishop didn't kill her. Most likely he would have, if Porter hadn't found him first. At least, that was how the papers printed it. Porter knew damn well Bishop let her live. He also knew that Bishop had let Porter find him. He wanted the chance to explain himself, explain his purpose, his manifesto, before killing Arthur Talbot and disappearing.

Talbot, who turned out to be Emory's father, was the worst criminal of the lot. And although Bishop had kidnapped Emory, he ultimately punished Talbot by mutilating the man before pushing him down an elevator shaft—he killed him and spared Emory.

Emory went on to inherit her father's billions, his untimely death triggering a clause in his will, a condition left by her mother years prior.

Emory lived, and Bishop eluded capture.

Six eyeballs.

Porter stared up at the photos of 4MK's victims.

Seven deaths, one girl freed.

Anson Bishop had managed to integrate himself into Porter's task force when he posed as a CSI photographer back in November. During his first briefing with the team, they reviewed each of 4MK's past victims, tried to bring him up to speed while searching for Emory. He listened to them with attentive ears, soaking in what they knew, pretending all this was new to him. Porter often looked back on that moment, searching for anything that should have given away his true identity, but there was none. Bishop no doubt stared up at this board with a feeling of great accomplishment while portraying just the right amount of horror on the outside, just the right amount of interest. He asked the right questions and refrained from embellishing on the information provided. Porter imagined this was extremely difficult for him. During that last confrontation at Belmont, Bishop bubbled over with the need to share what he knew, to explain himself. That urge must have been overwhelming as he stood looking at these boards, as he heard what they knew about each victim.

Bishop made several points, though, latched on to a few details.

Porter closed his eyes and thought back on that day, on his words.

He recalled Bishop pointing out information access—find out who had access to information on all these crimes, and work back from there. That had been a moot point, though, because ultimately they discovered that it was Talbot himself who knew of all these crimes, and Bishop had pilfered the information from him. He mentioned the dates, pointed out 4MK was escalating. This was true, but if a reason existed, they never determined what it was. They believed 4MK was dead at that point. Only finding Emory mattered.

Then there was the hair color.

Porter recalled how Bishop fixated on the photo of Barbara McIn-ley, the only blonde. An anomaly, he called her. The only blonde among a group of attractive brunettes. He went on to ask if any of the girls had been sexually assaulted—they had not. He also asked if 4MK had any male victims. Specifically, he asked if any of the girls had brothers, then said something like, "If we assume half these fami-lies had at least one son and he grabbed their children at random, one or two male victims should have presented. That didn't happen. There was a reason he took the daughters over the sons—we just don't know it." Porter believed 4MK took female victims simply because they were easier to control, less likely to fight back.

Six eyeballs.

Seven dead girls.

Porter returned to the photo of Barbara McInley. Punished be-cause her sister killed someone in a hit-and-run. McInley was the only girl to really hold Bishop's interest during their briefing, the only one he had honed in on. Porter could still picture him, tapping on her photo, the wheels of his mind racing.

Porter glanced over at the door, listening for anyone in the hall-way, but heard no one.

A table stood against the wall on his left, stacked high with file boxes—everything they'd collected on 4MK. The third box from the left had the word *Victims* written on the front with red marker, Por-ter's own handwriting. He crossed the room, removed the lid, and shuffled through the contents until he located Barbara McInley's file, the name also written in his handwriting.

These were his files. His team's files. They did not belong to the FBI.

"Fuck it."

Porter wrapped the file in his coat, then replaced the lid on the file box and crossed the room to the door. When he was certain the hall-way was still deserted, he slipped out of the room and pulled the door quietly shut behind him.

He ducked into the war room at the end of the hall and flicked on the overhead fluorescents.

"I was beginning to think you took the morning off," Special Agent Stewart Diener said. He was sitting at Nash's desk, his feet up, poking away at the tiny screen of his phone.

Porter hoped an indoor breeze would catch the man's delicate comb-over. No such luck.

9

Porter

Day 2 • 7:59 a.m.

Porter stared at Diener. "We caught a body and a second missing girl. I've been up all night. What do you want?"

Has he been in here the entire time?

"Yeah, great job keeping a lid on that." Diener tossed a folded copy of the *Chicago Tribune* over to Porter's desk.

Porter glanced down at the headline:

4MK BACK AND TAKING OUR DAUGHTERS?

This was followed by a photo of Emory Connors walking on the sidewalk, head down. Both the story and photo were above the fold—main headline. Below the fold were two other shots—a telephoto lens capturing the scene at the Jackson Park Lagoon and another of the Davieses' house.

Diener stood and walked around to the side of Porter's desk, pointed at the paper. "They name both Ella Reynolds and Lili Davies in here."

"How is that possible? We haven't released anything. I just met with Lili Davies's parents a few hours ago."

Diener shrugged. "One of your crack team of investigators has loose lips."

"That's ridiculous," Porter muttered, skimming the text.

The story mentioned the body found at Jackson Park Lagoon and speculated that she was most likely missing teen Ella Reynolds. The reporter also revealed that quick on the heels of this discovery, another girl vanished. Lili Davies was last seen leaving for school yesterday, but she never got to class. The remainder of the story detailed 4MK's past victims and implied that Anson Bishop was forced to change his MO after his botched arrest.

"What's that nut sack doing in here?" Nash said from the doorway.

Porter held up the paper. "Delivering the news."

Nash walked over and dropped his coat onto the chair Diener had vacated. He brushed a piece of lint from the man's shoulder. "Nice to see you exploring your career options. If you behave, maybe after school today we can go down to Walmart and pick you out a nice bike so you can expand your route."

Porter dropped the paper onto Nash's desk and pointed at the photos of the lagoon and the Davieses' home. "This isn't Bishop. It's completely irresponsible for them to go out on a limb and say that it is. They're just trying to sell more papers."

Diener said, "How can you be so sure? Maybe Bishop decided to change things up, just like they say."

"Serial killers don't change their MO, you know that. Their signature is fixed."

Diener shrugged. "Bishop is no ordinary serial killer. Each of his murders was part of an elaborate revenge plot. A plot he wrapped up when he killed Talbot. Maybe he planned to retire after that and quickly realized he still had a taste for young girls. When he couldn't keep it under control, he grabbed Ella Reynolds. He finished up with her and snagged Lili Davies." Diener started for the door. "You take a step back and look from a little distance, and it makes sense."

Porter dropped his coat onto his desk, Barbara McInley's file still wrapped inside. His heart pounding.

"That guy's a tool," Nash said.

"Heard that!" Diener shouted from the hallway. "If you're wrong and they are 4MK's vics, then you need to kick them over to us!"

"The other guy's a little better," Porter said. "His partner—Stool, Drool, Mule . . . ?"

"Poole. Frank Poole. Also a tool, the whole room full of 'em. Hey, see what I did there?" Nash reached for the door, ready to slam it, when Clair pushed past holding an iPad. Kloz was right behind her, with three white boxes perched precariously on top of his laptop. "Little help here," he said.

Nash plucked the top box off and carried it back to his desk.

"Don't go too far with those," Kloz implored. "They need to last me for the week."

"What is it?" Porter asked.

"Three dozen from that new place down the block, Peace, Love, and Little Donuts," Clair told them. "The little bugger was going to hoard them back at his desk, until I explained the virtues of sharing with his coworkers."

Kloz snickered. "You said if I didn't bring them down here, you'd send a mass e-mail to the department telling everyone I had these in my desk. I couldn't leave them upstairs undefended with all those vultures. They'd be gone in a minute. And there's only eighteen—six in each box, not twelve."

Nash opened the box he pilfered, and his eyes grew wide. "My baby Jesus, these are beautiful."

Porter grabbed the second box from the pile and settled at his desk. Clair grabbed the third.

"Hey!" Kloz cried out. "Those are mine!"

"Why are they so small?" Porter asked, his mouth full of cream filling.

Clair plucked a donut from her box and held it up. It was covered in Oreo crumbles. "They're *gourmet*. I'd do air quotes, but my fingers are busy. They make them small and sell them as artsy-fartsy fancy food for twice the price of regular donuts. If they didn't taste so damn good, they'd never get away with it, but these little guys are heaven. I can feel my ass getting bigger with each bite, and I don't care."

Kloz settled into his usual desk next to the conference table. He placed both palms on the metal top and took a long, soothing breath, his face turning red. "Okay, you can each have one, only one."

"I may have eaten four," Nash said, wiping the culinary evidence from his lips. His eyes fell on the decimated box before him. "And I'm keeping the rest."

Ten minutes later all three boxes were empty with the exception of one strawberry-frosted donut. Porter felt the sugar kick in. He stood up, walked over to their single remaining whiteboard, and wrote ELLEN REYNOLDS at the top.

"It's *Ella* Reynolds," Nash told him.

Porter grunted, wiped away the first name with the back of his hand, replaced it with ELLA. "Okay, what do we know?"

Clair said, "Ella Reynolds was reported missing on January twenty-second and found yesterday, February twelfth. Her body was discovered frozen under the ice at Jackson Park Lagoon."

"She wasn't frozen," Nash broke in. "Not entirely, anyway. That's what Eisley said. But the lagoon was."

"Yeah, sorry," Clair said. "According to the park, the lagoon was completely frozen over by January 2, twenty days before she went missing. Also, I have something on video we'll want to watch after we update the board."

Porter nodded. "When found, she wasn't wearing her own clothes but clothes believed to belong to our second missing girl, Lili Davies." He wrote her name on the board, then went back to Ella's column. "Ella was last seen getting off her bus about two blocks from her house in a black coat, near Logan Square, approximately fifteen miles from where she was found. I think we can safely say the unsub staged the scene at the lagoon to appear as if Ella's body had been there for weeks, which would be impossible if her clothes turn out to be Lili's."

Nash got up from his desk and went to the conference table in front of the whiteboard, taking a seat. "What's the point of that? He went through a lot of trouble to put Ella under the ice, but then he dresses her in Lili's clothes, giving us a firm date on the timeline. It doesn't make sense."

"It makes sense to him," Porter pointed out. "All of this does. Including this—"

Porter wrote DROWNED IN SALT WATER beneath Ella's name.

"Are you serious?" Kloz said.

"Eisley said he found salt water in her lungs and stomach. He's fairly certain cause of death was drowning," Porter told him.

"Drowning," Clair repeated. "In salt water."

Nash added, "The nearest ocean is about seven hundred miles away."

"We'll need to check out local aquariums and aquarium supply houses," Porter said. "I think we can rule out a trip to the coast. This timeline is too tight."

Clair was shaking her head. "I haven't slept enough to deal with this."

"I think we're all running on fumes," Porter agreed. "What do we know about the second girl, Lili Davies?"

Nash opened his small notebook. "Parents are Dr. Randal Davies and Grace Davies. Her best friend is Gabrielle Deegan. She goes to Wilcox Academy. She was last seen wearing a red coat, according to her mother—a Perro red nylon diamond-quilted hooded parka. She also had on a white hat, white gloves, dark jeans, and pink tennis shoes. She never made it to school yesterday, which means she was most likely taken on the morning of February twelfth. Her mother said she saw her leaving for school. That was about a quarter after seven in the morning. Classes start at ten to eight, and she's walking distance to the school."

"Does she walk with anyone to school?" Porter asked.

Nash shook his head. "Her mother said the school is only four blocks, so she goes alone."

Kloz gave the donut boxes a sad glance, then went to the conference table. "Four blocks isn't very far. That doesn't leave a lot of time for someone to grab her."

Clair took a seat next to Nash. "Assuming she went straight to school, which we can't assume. She might've run into a friend on the way and gotten into their car. I know it's only a few blocks, but I used to do that all the time when I walked to school. When you're that close to campus, the drivers and walkers tend to converge in the parking lot, and many of the students hang out there waiting on that first bell."

"May I come in?"

The three of them looked up. Sophie Rodriguez stood at the door. Porter noted she was wearing the same tan sweater she had on at the Davieses' house. Most likely she hadn't gone home yet, either. "Please," he said. "Take a seat, we're running through everything."

"Uh, Sam?" Kloz said, his eyes giving her a once-over. "Remember what happened the last time you invited a stray into the clubhouse?"

Clair smacked his shoulder. "I've known Sophie for almost four years. She's been vetted." She motioned to the chair to her left.

Sophie set her bag down by the door, removed her coat, and took a seat studying the board. "I know you're all working this from Homicide and Lili is just missing at this point, but we have an obvious connection. Probably best for us to work together, at least for now. Until we have a handle on what's going on."

"Welcome to the team, Sophie," Porter said.

Nash gave him a weary look but said nothing.

Sophie studied the faces in the room. "Ella was one of my girls, too. You always hope for the best, but when they don't turn up for more than forty-eight hours, it usually means they're a runaway or something worse. Both of these girls have solid home lives, so I think my heart was telling me it was 'something worse.' When you told me about the clothes, I guess you confirmed it for me. I'm just hoping we find Lili in time."

"Did you show the clothing photos to Lili's parents?" Porter asked. He had e-mailed them to her from the morgue.

Sophie nodded. "Her mother confirmed they belonged to Lili. She said she wrote the initials in the hat herself."

Porter wrote FOUND IN LILI DAVIES'S CLOTHES under ELLA REYNOLDS on the board. Then he turned back to her. "What else can you tell us about Ella?"

Sophie studied the board for a moment. "I walked the scene a few weeks back, right after she disappeared. The bus lets her off about two blocks from her house, near Logan Square, but her parents told me she would sometimes go to Starbucks on Kedzie to do her homework. I took both routes. It took me four minutes to walk from the bus stop to her house, seven minutes to walk from the bus stop to Starbucks, and nine minutes for me to walk the route from Starbucks to her house. The entire area is very public, people everywhere. I don't see how someone could have grabbed her without being seen."

Nash asked, "Did you talk to the manager at the Starbucks?"

Sophie nodded. "He recognized Ella from the photo I showed him, but he couldn't tell me if she was in on that particular day. She typically pays with cash, so I couldn't reference debit or credit card receipts."

"Any security cameras?"

"There is one, but it recycles daily. They don't store the footage. By the time we got there, it was gone."

Kloz cleared his throat. "Maybe I should take a look? I've never known a security system that really erased the previous day's footage. If the system is hard-drive-based, fragments may still exist, even if the manager thinks the footage is gone."

Porter nodded and wrote STARBUCKS FOOTAGE (1 DAY CYCLE?) — KLOZ on the board. "What else?"

"We searched her computer and e-mail but didn't find anything out of the ordinary," Sophie replied. "Her phone disappeared with her. It last connected to the tower near Logan Square and dropped off four minutes after the bus's scheduled stop."

"Kloz?"

Kloz was already nodding, making a note on his laptop. "I'll take a look at that too."

Porter turned back to Sophie. "Did you find anything in Lili's room?"

"Nothing out of the ordinary. Lots of clothes strewn about. Nothing hidden in any of the drawers or under the mattress, the typical places. There was a photo taped to the mirror of her and another girl. Her mother said it was her friend Gabby. Her father said she had both a cell phone and a laptop, but neither were in her room. Her mom told me she would have taken them to school, said she was carrying her backpack when she left." She paused for a second, reading a text message on her phone. "My office pinged her cell, but it was off. The results just came back. The last tower it hit was near her house.

It went dark at twenty-three after seven. That's only about eight minutes after she left home."

"Kloz, see if you can pull anything from her social media accounts or e-mail," Porter pointed out.

"On it," Kloz replied.

Sophie pulled a folder from her bag and spread the contents on the table. She had pictures of both girls. "Ella and Lili have a similar look, which would suggest an attraction or sexual motive, but the ME said there was no sign of assault with Ella. I'm not willing to write that off as a coincidence just yet."

"Good point. May I?" Porter said, pointing at the photos.

Sophie handed the pictures to him, and Porter taped them to the board. "How old is Lili?"

"Seventeen," Sophie replied.

"Both have blond hair, roughly shoulder length. Ella had blue eyes, Lili has green. They're two years apart. Where did Ella go to school?" Porter asked.

Sophie flipped through her notes. "Kelvyn Park High. She was a sophomore."

"Any reason to believe they knew each other?"

"None that I'm aware of," she replied. "Different schools, different social circles, two years apart. Neither drove."

"What about the gallery?" Porter asked. "Could they have met there?"

"I haven't been to the gallery yet. They don't open until ten."

Porter scratched at his cheek. "I'd rather you and Clair walk to school, then maybe interview her friend, Gabrielle Deegan. Nash tends to scare the children."

Nash smiled. "I can't help if I'm intimidating."

Porter nodded at him. "You and I will check the gallery."

"Love me some art."

"I'll text you the address," Sophie said. "It's on North Halsted."

Porter glanced back at the board. "What else?"

The group fell silent.

"Should we watch the video?" Clair asked.

"Yeah, fire it up."

Clair tapped at the screen of her iPad, then set it in the middle of the table. The image was frozen. A horrible angle on a narrow black-top road. The time stamp indicated 8:47 a.m., February 12.

Clair pressed Play, and the time stamp moved forward in real time. Two cars rolled past—a yellow Toyota and a white Ford. When a gray pickup truck came into view, Clair hit Pause. "I'm going to advance slowly," she said, and the image moved forward a few frames at a time.

When the back of the truck came into view, Porter understood. "Freeze there," he said.

The pickup truck was towing a large water tank, the kind belonging to pool cleaners.

"There's no pool in the park, and pool service during the dead of winter is not in high demand," Clair said. "I think that's how he got the water in."

"Do you have any other angles?" Porter asked.

Clair shook her head. "That's the only camera."

Kloz leaned in. "Not much I can do with it. The image is clear, the angle just sucks."

"Roll back a few frames?" Porter suggested.

Clair pressed Rewind. The image reversed one frame at a time with each touch.

"Stop," Porter said. "What's with that glare, and why such a horrible shot?"

The camera pointed at a severe angle, nearly straight down. Normally they either pointed up a road or down a road, the best possible angle to capture cars either approaching or leaving.

They froze the shot that captured the most of the truck's windshield, but a bright white glare obscured their view inside.

Porter could make out the shape of the driver but nothing that would help them identify the person. "Kloz, do you think you can enlarge this and clean it up at all?"

Kloz chewed on the tip of his thumb. "Maybe—tough to say. I'll give it a shot."

"The park manager said they rarely review the footage. The camera is there as more of a deterrent than anything. At some point either it got loose and pointed down toward the ground, or someone loosened it and purposely pointed it that way. He had no idea when or how it happened," Clair explained. "He said the camera used to point down the road to capture the cars and their drivers as they approached."

Porter turned to Kloz, but Kloz waved him off before he could speak. "Yeah, I know. I'll go back through old footage and see if I can determine when it happened, on the off chance we catch our unsub smiling at the camera holding a wrench."

"Sometimes they slip up," Porter pointed out.

"Yep."

"This is good. At the very least we should get a make and model on the truck. If we cross-reference that against pool cleaning companies, we may get lucky." Porter turned back to the board. "Anything else we can add?"

Again, the room went silent.

Porter capped the black marker and took a seat at the conference table. "I want to get a better handle on the abductions themselves. This unsub works fast and appears to have no trouble taking these girls from public places. That means he either blends in well or possibly gets to know them in advance so they don't feel threatened by him. He couldn't pull them kicking and screaming off the street into this pickup truck without being noticed, so somehow he convinces them to go willingly."

"He may have access to other vehicles," Nash suggested. "Public works or a utility company van. Something that disappears in the background."

Kloz flipped his laptop around so the others could see. The screen had a detailed map of Chicago and the surrounding areas. There was a red dot near Logan Square, one at Jackson Park, and a third on King Drive in Bronzeville. "We've got a distance of about ten miles between the two abduction sites. In a city this big, that's a sizable hunting ground. Jackson Park, where Ella was found, is actually closer to Lili's house than Ella's own."

Porter studied the map for a moment. "So Lili was abducted close to where Ella was found. That may be important."

"Ella drowned in salt water?" Sophie was frowning up at the board. "That doesn't make any sense."

"What about a saltwater swimming pool?" Kloz suggested. "That would fit with the truck."

"Is that a thing?" Nash frowned.

Kloz was nodding. "I've got an aunt in Florida who has one. She's allergic to chlorine. They're low maintenance too, no chemicals to measure out."

"There can't be many around Chicago. Think you can run a list?" Porter asked.

Kloz said, "Maybe I can put something together through building permits."

Porter studied the faces around the table. With the exception of Sophie Rodriguez, he had known them all for years. He retrieved the newspaper from Nash's desk and set it on the conference table. "Watch your backs for reporters. Somebody is snooping around a little too close to camp, and they're not afraid to speculate."

Clair flipped the paper around so she could read the headline. "You don't think one of us talked to the press, do you?"

Porter shook his head. "I think they'll print anything to sell papers. And if they can't get one of us to talk, they'll make something up. When we're ready, I'll make a statement. Until then, aside from the Amber Alert on Lili, we're on a press lockdown."

An uncomfortable silence fell over the group. Sophie was first to speak. "Is anyone gonna eat that last donut?"

Kloz's head dropped to the tabletop, and he let out a sigh. "Take it."

Evidence Board

ELLA REYNOLDS (15 years old)
Reported missing 1/22
Found 2/12 in Jackson Park Lagoon
Water frozen since 1/2 — (20 days before she went missing)
Last seen — getting off her bus at Logan Square (2 blocks from
home/15 miles from Jackson Park)
Last seen wearing a black coat
Drowned in salt water (found in fresh water)
Found in Lili Davies's clothes
Four-minute walk from bus to home
Frequented Starbucks on Kedzie. Seven-minute walk to home.

LILI DAVIES (17 years old)
Parents = Dr. Randal Davies and Grace Davies
Best friend = Gabrielle Deegan
Attends Wilcox Academy (private) did not attend classes on 2/12
Last seen leaving for school (walking) morning of 2/12 @ 7:15
wearing a Perro red nylon diamond-quilted hooded parka,
white hat, white gloves, dark jeans, and pink tennis shoes (all
found on Ella Reynolds)
Most likely taken morning of 2/12 (on way to school)
Small window = 35 minutes (Left for school 7:15 a.m., classes
start 7:50 a.m.)
School only four blocks from home
Not reported missing until after midnight (morning of 2/13)
Parents thought she went to work (art gallery) right after school
(she didn't do either)

UNSUB
- Possibly driving a gray pickup towing a water tank
- May work with swimming pools (cleaning or servicing)

ASSIGNMENTS:
- Starbucks footage (1-day cycle?) — Kloz
- Ella's computer, phone, e-mail — Kloz
- Lili's social media, phone records, e-mail (phone and PC
MIA) — Kloz
- Enhance image of possible unsub entering park — Kloz
- Park camera loosened? Check old footage — Kloz

- Get make and model of truck from video? — Kloz
- Clair and Sophie walk Lili's route to school/talk to Gabrielle Deegan
- Porter and Nash visit gallery (manager = Ms. Edwins)
- Put together a list of saltwater pools around Chicago via permits office — Kloz
- Check out local aquariums and aquarium supply houses

10

Porter

Day 2 • 9:08 a.m.

"Sam, you don't have to do this."

"Yeah, I do."

He rang the Reynoldses' doorbell.

They had driven straight here from police headquarters, lights blazing. Porter raced through at least three reds.

Nash shuffled his feet beside him on the stoop. "The department will send a uniform."

Porter rubbed his hands together. The cold was slowly killing him. With the wind-chill, the temperature hovered at three degrees. "It's after nine. They may have already seen the morning paper. It's probably all over the morning news too."

Porter rang the doorbell again.

The curtain over the glass window to the left of the door moved aside briefly, fell back into place. Someone worked the deadbolt. The door opened a few inches. A woman in her mid-forties peeked out, her eyes red and dark, the skin around them sunken with lack of sleep. Her brown hair looked oily, unwashed for days. She wore a thick brown sweater and jeans. "May I help you?"

Porter unfolded his badge case. "I'm Detective Porter, and this is Detective Nash with Chicago Metro. May we come in?"

She stared at him for a moment, as if the words took a second to register. Then she nodded and opened the door while staring past them to the street. "I think the cold finally scared away the last news van. They were still out there last night."

Porter and Nash stomped the snow from their feet and stepped inside, closing the door behind them. The heat wrapped around them, stifling compared with outside. Porter didn't care. He could stand in a fire pit for an hour, and his fingers would still be numb. He cleared his throat. "Is your husband home?"

Mrs. Reynolds shook her head. "He's not back yet."

"Did he go somewhere?"

The woman took a deep breath and sat on the arm of the leather sofa behind her. "He's been driving around looking for Ella since the day she disappeared. He comes home long enough to eat and get a few hours of sleep, then just goes out again. I went with him the first few times, but it felt so futile. Driving up and down random streets like we're going to spot her darting between houses or something, like a runaway dog. I can't tell him not to go, though. It would break his heart. He tried staying home last Tuesday, and we were both climbing the walls. He went back out again last night after dinner."

"It helps to stay active," Nash said.

She looked at him, her face blank, then went on. "For the first week, I did nothing but make phone calls. All Ella's friends and our family, our neighbors, anybody I could get to pick up. Shelters, hospitals, morgues . . . sitting here, trapped in this house, it feels so . . . helpless. But what else can I do? We've got posters hanging everywhere. Little good they do in this weather. Nobody is outside unless they need to be."

Porter took a deep breath. "There's no easy way to say this—"

Mrs. Reynolds raised her hand, silencing him. "You don't have to. I saw it on the news this morning. The television hasn't been turned off in three weeks. I dozed off on the couch, and when I woke up last night, they were running footage at the park. They never came out and said it was Ella, only that a girl's body had been found in the lagoon. A mother knows, though. I guess I've known for weeks. I think I saw you on TV. You look familiar."

"I'm so sorry."

She nodded and blotted at eyes that looked like they had shed their last tear two weeks earlier. "My Ella wouldn't run away, we knew that from the moment she went missing. I think I lost a little bit of hope with each minute after that. A girl can't just disappear in today's world, not with cameras and the Internet everywhere. A girl disappears completely, and you gotta know something bad happened." She took a deep breath. "How did she die?"

"We think she drowned. We're still waiting on the full report."

"She drowned in the lagoon?"

Porter shook his head. "No . . . someplace else. She drowned and was placed in the lagoon."

"You mean, she *was* drowned. Somebody did this to her, right?"

"I'm afraid so."

Mrs. Reynolds's eyes drifted to the floor. "I want to ask you if she suffered, but I think I already know the answer, and I'm not sure I really want to hear it out loud. I mean, somebody took her weeks ago. Do you know when she drowned? Do you know what this monster did to my baby in all that time?"

Nash's eyes had also drifted to the floor. "At this point, we don't know much more than that. We had hoped to tell you before you—"

"Before I heard it somewhere else? That's very noble of you, but those reporters . . . well."

"Do you have a way of reaching your husband? Maybe we should call him? Tell him to come home?"

Again, her gaze went blank as these words sank in. Porter had seen this before, the disconnect. People who are greatly traumatized sometimes separate slightly from reality; they *watch* the events around them rather than live within them. Mrs. Reynolds nodded and pulled a cell phone from the folds of the blanket on the couch. After a few seconds, she mouthed *voice mail,* then looked to the floor as she left a message. "Floyd? It's me. Please come home, honey. They . . . the police are here. They found her, our baby."

She disconnected the call and dropped the phone back onto the couch.

A back door slammed, and a little boy came marching into the living room, leaving a snowy trail behind him on the kitchen floor.

Bundled in a navy blue snowsuit with a floppy yellow hat, scarf, and black gloves, he couldn't have been more than seven or eight. "Mama? Somebody built a snowman in our yard."

Mrs. Reynolds glanced at him, then turned back to Porter and Nash. "Not now, Brady."

"I think the snowman is hurt."

"What?"

"He's bleeding."

11

Lili

Day 2 • 9:12 a.m.

Lili had been alone, and now she wasn't.

The man came down the steps and just stood there for maybe two minutes, watching her. He held something in his hand, but she couldn't make out what it was.

When he finally spoke, his voice was low, deliberate, and practiced in its delivery. "You didn't drink the milk."

Lili had not drunk the milk, and she wouldn't. She wouldn't eat or drink anything this person planned to offer her. She would sooner starve to death than accept something from him.

"Why not?"

She didn't answer, she only pulled the quilt tighter around her body as she pressed into the far corner of her cage.

"This doesn't have to be unpleasant. Not unless you want it to be. I'd prefer you to be comfortable and relaxed," he said. "Are you warm enough?"

Against the wall to her right stood the HVAC system and water heater for the house. The unit had run on and off since she woke here but was silent now. The vent in the side pointed directly into her cage and was, in fact, very warm. She wasn't about to tell him that, though.

"If you get too cold, be sure to let me know."

He stepped from the shadows at the base of the stairs and approached her cage. Funny, she thought, how she quickly grew to consider this *her* cage. From the inside, it seemed to offer her safety from the threat outside. As he stepped closer, she was grateful for the chainlink and metal bars separating them, the protection they offered. Her free hand reached around behind her, her fingers wrapping around the chainlink mesh and squeezing, the cold steel digging into her skin.

As the man stepped into the light, she got a good look at him. His skin was incredibly pale, the color of paper; she could make out the webs of veins at his neck, tiny roadways on his cheeks and forehead. He wore a black knit cap pulled down tight on his head, covering his hair—if he had any at all. His eyebrows were thin, barely there. When she saw his eyes, she wished she had not. The way he peered at her, a deep gaze from behind cloudy gray. They were the eyes of an old man, lost behind cataracts and film. He didn't look old, though, maybe thirty at the most. The eyes did not fit; they weren't natural. The right eye seemed darker than the left, bloodshot. Lili wanted to look away but didn't want to give him the satisfaction. She wouldn't show weakness.

"I apologize for my appearance. I haven't been well. Today is a good day, though. I promise you it's not contagious. Please don't be frightened," he said, the lisp evident.

Lili squeezed the chainlink, welcoming the pain it brought, the distraction. She set her jaw, firm and defiant.

The man's mouth hung open slightly. She heard a slight wheeze with each drawn breath. "I'm going to let you out, and you're going to do as I say." His eyes flicked to the object in his right hand, a stun gun. He said nothing of it. Lili knew they weren't fatal. She wondered just how much they hurt. Would she be able to push past him and get up the stairs, even if he shocked her?

With his left hand, he slipped a key into first the top padlock, then the bottom, sliding each from the door and hanging them on the chainlink. Then he lifted the latch and pulled open the door.

Lili remained still, her fingers tightening on the back of her cage.

"Please come out," he said quietly. "I could shock you and take you out, but then we would have to wait or possibly start over. It's best that you just do as I say."

His eyes bore into her, those cloudy eyes. There was a bandage on his right hand near the wrist, dirty, stained with dried blood.

"Out now!" he screamed.

Lili jumped and drew in a deep breath.

"Why do you make me shout? Please don't make me shout. I don't want to be loud. I don't want to be mean. Just come out so we can begin, please. The sooner we start, the sooner it will be over."

She didn't want to, Lili knew she shouldn't, but she forced herself to stand and walk toward the man, toward the door of the cage, her eyes looking over his shoulder at the stairs behind him, at the light pooling toward the top.

"Others have tried to make the stairs, but nobody ever has. You can try if you like, but it will only lead to a shock and delays. We would have to start over, but we *would* start over. It's best that you just do as I say," he said again in the most reassuring of voices. She felt his hand on the small of her back through the quilt, guiding her, nudging her toward a large white freezer against the wall with the stairs.

He lifted the lid.

Lili expected a rush of icy-cold air—they had a similar freezer at her house. Instead, warm, humid air rose from inside. The freezer was filled with water. She took a step back, tried to push away from him, but the prongs of the stun gun against her back held her still.

"The water is nice and warm. Go ahead and touch it."

Lili watched her hand reach for the water, operating with a mind all its own. She dipped her fingers into the water. It was warm, far warmer than the air.

"You'll want to take off your clothes. It's better that way."

He said this so nonchalantly, casually, a conversation between two old friends.

"I'm not—" The words slipped out before Lili realized she spoke. She capped them off and shook her head. Her hands gripped the quilt and pulled it tighter around her small frame. She wanted to step away from the water tank, but he was standing behind her. His warm breath drifted over her neck.

His left hand fell onto her shoulder and tugged at the quilt.

Lili screamed, the first real sound she'd made since waking here.

She screamed as loudly as she could, the sound so powerful it felt like a knife grating at the inside of her throat. It echoed off the basement walls and cried back at her in a voice that wasn't her own. This voice sounded like a terrified little girl, like someone who'd lost control, someone who'd given up, someone she didn't want to know.

The metal prongs of the stun gun bit into her neck, two cold metal teeth followed by a pain so intense, it sliced at every inch of her, a blade cutting from her toes to her fingertips. Her eyes rolled back into her head, and her legs gave out from under her. Lili's scream died away in an instant as silence enveloped her.

She awoke on the floor, lying atop the quilt. The man was tugging her panties down. He had removed all her other clothes. Lili tried to reach for the edge of the quilt to cover herself, but her arm wouldn't work. She stared at her fingers, still twitching.

"I didn't want to shock you. I don't want to hurt you. Please don't make me hurt you again," the man said. "You can have the clothes back when we're done. It's better this way, you'll see."

Lili understood what would come next, and she tried to mentally prepare herself.

The man wrapped one arm around her back and the other under her knees and lifted her from the ground. Although he appeared sick, he was surprisingly strong. He lifted her over the freezer filled with warm water and gently lowered her inside. Lili was five-two. Her toes brushed the far side as her legs drifted out, flattening. He held her up at the shoulders, keeping her face above the water.

"Warm, isn't it? Nice."

The warm water was oddly comforting; it felt like slipping beneath the surface of a pool, allowing the water to hold you as you drift along. Lili noticed the feeling returning to her fingers, her arms, the warmth massaging her limbs back to life.

"Close your eyes, relax," he said in a soothing tone, his lisp barely catching. Calm. "Take in a deep breath, a nice, long breath."

Lili did as he said, not because he told her to, but because she wanted to. She allowed her lips to part and pulled in the basement air, allowed it to fill her lungs, a breath like those she learned in yoga class, a cleansing breath, deep and full.

"Now let it out slowly, feel the air leave your body," he said in a whisper. "Feel every bit of it."

Lili released the—

The man pushed at her shoulders and plunged her into the water with such force, her head banged on the bottom of the tank. Her legs kicked and her arms flailed. Her fingers caught at the top edge for one brief second before the smooth plastic slipped from her grasp.

Lili could hold her breath for a long time, almost two minutes the last time someone timed her. But that only worked when she filled her lungs with fresh air first, when she was prepared. She hadn't filled her lungs, she'd emptied them, just as the man asked, and when he pushed her beneath the surface she inhaled instead, her body's attempt at grasping for air. Instead of air, she gulped down water and immediately coughed, expelling it even before her head hit the bottom, expelling the water only to inhale more. The water filled her throat, her lungs, resulting in a pain so severe, Lili thought she might implode. When she stopped kicking, when she stopped flailing, the pain went away, and for one brief second Lili thought she would be okay, she thought her body had somehow found a way to survive on water, and she went still. She saw the man looking down at her from above with those gray, bloodshot eyes, his mouth agape. He was distorted through the water, but she could see him. Then everything went black, and she saw nothing at all.

12

Clair

Day 2 • 9:13 a.m.

Clair and Sophie Rodriguez pulled up to Lili Davies's house on South King Drive and parked Clair's green Honda Civic behind two news vans. Both had their satellite antennae raised, but there was no sign of the reporters or the camera operators.

A light snow filled the air, leaving the sky a hazy white.

"It's colder than a witch's tit out here," Clair said, rubbing her hands together.

"I never understood that expression," Sophie replied, eyeing the vans.

"Witches get no love."

"Oh, I know that feeling."

Clair glanced over at her. "What happened to that guy you were dating, James, John, Joe—"

"Jessie. Jessie Grabber."

Clair chuckled. "Really, that's his name? Grabber?"

Sophie rolled her eyes.

"I'm sorry. It's a bit high school to make fun of a name, but come on, Grabber? No sneak attack down at Lover's Lane with a name like Grabber."

"Well, he was anything but. I think that was part of the problem. I was hoping for a little something, but he was nothing but a gentleman. All the way on through date number four I got nothing but a peck on the cheek. A girl's got needs."

"Like witches."

Sophie nodded. "Like witches."

"I'm still not warm." Clair frowned.

"Me either."

"Witch tit."

"Witch tit." Sophie shivered.

Clair shuffled in her seat, looking up and down the street, then pointed at the graystone beside them. "That's Lili Davies's house, right?"

"Yes, 748."

"And her school is where?"

Sophie pointed out her window. "Four blocks east of here. You can nearly see it."

The snow shifted from tiny flakes to something a little larger than Clair's favorite breakfast cereal, and her body gave an involuntary quiver. She zipped her jacket all the way up, wrapped a heavy-knit purple scarf around her neck, and donned a fluffy pink cap. When she turned back to Sophie, the woman had done the same. "You look like the Stay Puft Marshmallow Man."

Sophie smirked. "You look like Willy Wonka's long-lost sister."

"Perfect. Let's do this." Clair tugged at the door handle and stepped out onto the sidewalk. The snow was about two inches deep and still coming down, flying at her at an angle. She jogged in place for a second as Sophie rounded the car, her breath leaving a white plume in the air. The two women started walking east on Sixty-Ninth Street, hunched against the snow.

They crossed Vernon Avenue, and Clair stopped, staring ahead. "If I wanted to grab a girl, that seems like a good spot."

She stared at the dark tunnels one block up where the Skyway crossed over Sixty-Ninth Street, three lanes of traffic running in each direction. At approximately fifteen feet per lane, that meant she was looking at a space about one hundred feet wide with only a small break at the median in the middle. Although three lights burned under each section, they offered little to break up the gloom.

Clair looked up at the sky, searching for the sun. "What time is sunrise?"

Sophie tilted her head, a line appearing between her brows. "About seven or so."

"So our girl made this walk about two hours earlier in the day, a little after the sun poked out. If it came out at all. This stretch is fairly deserted now, but that may be different closer to school time. Still, though, someone could easily park around here, maybe feign a breakdown, then grab her when she walked by. The tunnel would be my bet; everything else is fairly wide open."

They had reached the start of the underpass. Sophie pressed a hand to the concrete. "This is a good neighborhood. There's not a bit of graffiti on these walls and no sign of homeless activity. I can't imagine someone could stand around very long without getting noticed."

They followed the sidewalk under the Skyway, their footfalls echoing off the walls. When they came out the other side, Sophie pointed. "There's her school."

Wilcox Academy was a private school housed in what appeared to be a repurposed factory or warehouse building. The red brick façade was immaculate. It could have been built a year ago. The parking lot beside it was posted FACULTY ONLY and was full. A public lot sat across the street, most likely utilized by the students.

Clair pulled open the large glass door, and both women stepped inside, a wave of heat wafting out. "This makes me want to hop back in the car and drive straight to Florida."

"Can I help you?"

Clair turned to find an elderly security guard sitting at a table to their left. She took a step forward, and a buzzer went off.

The guard pointed toward the entrance. "Metal detector built into the door frame."

Clair showed the man her badge. "I'm Detective Norton with Chicago Metro, and this is Sophie Rodriguez with Missing Children. We're investigating the disappearance of one of your students, Lili Davies."

The security guard's smile fell away. "Heard about that on the way in. I'm so sorry for her family. She's a good girl."

Sophie's head tilted slightly. "You know her?"

He nodded. "This is a small school, only about two hundred kids total. I see each of them every day, hard not to get to know them. I'm former Pittsburgh PD, retired about six years ago. If there is anything I can do to help, I'm here for you."

"What can you tell us about her?" Clair asked.

"Like I said, never gave me any trouble. Usually got here around seven thirty or so. Many of the students hang out across the street there in the lot until first bell, but not her. She'd try to beat the crowd and get up to class. Not too many friends." He waved a hand. "Don't get me wrong, she was well liked, just a bit of an introvert. Could always tell there were big plans cooking behind her eyes. Always thinking, that one."

Sophie glanced out the window at the cars across the street. "Did she ever ride in with anyone?"

He shook his head. "If she did, I never noticed. If I saw her outside, she was usually coming up the walk the same way you did."

Clair pulled off her hat and scarf. "What about Gabrielle Deegan? Do you know her?"

The corner of his mouth turned up, and he brushed at his chin. "Gabby can be a bit rough around the edges, but she's a good girl too. The two of them are together a lot, a bit of yin and yang thing there."

"What do you mean?"

He looked down the hallway, then turned back to them, lowering his voice. "I have to be a bit hard on her, you know? Being the law here. But I see her for what she is: just a girl looking for some attention. She's not fooling me none. She'd never admit it—in fact, I bet she'd outright deny it—but I think she may be one of the smartest students here. I think she acts out because she's bored, not because she's a troublemaker. She'll come into her own one day. Until then, it's my job to steer her away from big trouble and let her get away with a bit of little trouble, find that balance. Every class has at least one."

"Do you know where we can find her?"

"I'll call upstairs, see if I can get someone to bring her down for you," he replied, reaching for the phone on his table. "Watch your wallets and jewelry." He winked.

13

Porter
Day 2 • 9:14 a.m.

Porter and Nash stood at the Reynoldses' back door, staring out into their yard.

About fifty feet out, toward the left corner under a large birch tree, a snowman stared back at them.

The beady black eyes glistened under a stovepipe hat. The snowman was tall, at least six and a half feet, maybe more, the body thick and wide, glistening with ice, a red rose at his snowy lapel.

The arms were fashioned from tree branches, each capped with a black glove. The right hand held the handle of a wooden broom. A corncob pipe jutted from the corner of its makeshift mouth, and dark blood trickled down from an icy neck.

Snow fell, filling the air with a white haze. The scene was so odd, so picturesque. Porter felt he was looking at the page of a childhood storybook, not a real yard. There was a swing set off to the far right and woods behind the yard.

"Nobody in your family made that?" Nash asked.

Mrs. Reynolds had her arms wrapped around her son. "No."

The single word escaped her lips, but she didn't take her eyes off it, this stranger in her yard.

Porter tugged at his zipper and reached inside his coat, retrieving his Glock.

Brady's eyes went wide. "Whoa, is he going to kill the snowman, Mom?"

"I'm not going to hurt the snowman. I'm worried he may try to hurt me," Porter said quietly. "Did you see anyone else out there? Anybody at all?"

"No, sir."

"How about you and your mother go back into the living room for a few minutes? Think you can take care of your mom while my partner and I check this out?"

Brady nodded.

Porter looked from the boy to his mother. "Go along now."

When they were gone, he turned to Nash. "Stay here and keep a bead on those trees back there."

Nash withdrew his own weapon, his eyes scanning the woods.

Porter stepped out the back door, into the falling snow. From somewhere in the back of his mind, an old children's song began to play.

Small footprints littered the newly fallen snow, crisscrossing the yard near the door, then petering down to a single set ending at the snowman. Porter followed the footprints as best he could, taking small strides so he could place his feet where the child had rather than create another trail. Snow had fallen most of the night, a few inches at least, but it seemed inconceivable that someone could build such a thing without leaving any tracks. His eyes drifted to the broom perched in the snowman's hand. He supposed it was possible that whoever did this used the broom to sweep away their tracks, but that didn't explain how they got the broom back into his hand without leaving a final trail. Porter also noted that their yard was fenced. A four-foot chainlink. The gate leading to the front yard was open.

Porter saw a faint trail leading from that gate to the snowman. Not footprints, more of an indent, as if something heavy had been dragged from the front of the house to the back, to here.

He stood in front of the snowman.

It towered over him by nearly a foot. From this angle, the smile upon its face, made from tiny pieces of a broken branch, looked more like a smirk.

Porter remembered building hundreds of these as a kid—pushing the snowball along until it became a snow boulder, too heavy to push at all. Normally, a snowman is constructed by starting with a large snow boulder at the base, then placing another smaller one on top of that to form the torso, then another at the very top to take the place of a head.

This snowman was not constructed that way.

The snow on this snowman had been packed in place. Someone took the time to sculpt the snow into the shape of a snowman rather than use the far faster traditional method.

All of these thoughts rushed through Porter's mind in an instant as he glanced over the creation from top to bottom, his eyes finally landing on the dark red at the neck—dark red seeping through the white like a giant snow cone.

Porter snapped a branch of a nearby oak and, using the splinted end, carefully plucked at the snow beneath the darkest red spot, where it congealed at the base of the neck. Whoever built this had sprayed the snow with water as they worked, causing it to harden into ice—another trick Porter learned as a child. If made properly, a snowman would be as sturdy as a stone statue, standing tall for the remainder of the winter. If you failed to harden the snow, chunks would break away with the first sun. By midafternoon, half your work would be piled at the ground.

Porter used the stick to break through the ice and to scrape away the packed snow, digging deep enough to reveal the torn neck of the man beneath.

14

Lili

Day 2 • 9:15 a.m.

It hurt.

It hurt so bad.

Lili's body convulsed in one big spasm as her lungs fought to expel water, to cough it out. She inhaled in a quick gasp even though she didn't want to, she didn't want to breathe in more water, she didn't want to die. She did inhale, though, the motion as involuntary as listening, and this time her lungs filled with air. She coughed again, ridding her lungs and throat of more water. This was followed by another gasp.

She was cold.

So cold.

No longer in the water but lying on the concrete floor.

Her eyes snapped open.

The man was above her, his palms pressing down into her chest.

As her eyes met his, he stopped. His eyes went wide, and he leaned in, his stale breath rushing over her face. "What did you see?"

Lili gulped another breath of air and swallowed, then another after that.

"Slow down, you'll hyperventilate." He reached for her right hand and pressed his thumb into her wrist. "Your pulse is still a bit irregular, but it will even out. Lie still. Breathe in through your nose, out through your mouth, calming breaths."

Lili forced her breathing to slow, doing as he said. Sensation returned to her fingertips, to her toes. She was so cold. She began to shiver uncontrollably.

The man reached for the quilt and draped the sour material over her body. "Your body temperature began to drop the moment you died. It will return to normal in a moment. What did you see?"

She tried to blink away the haze from her eyes, but it hurt to try and keep them open. The thin light seemed incredibly bright, hot, burning. When she pinched her eyes shut, she felt a light slap at her cheek.

Died?

"What did you see?" he asked again. He rubbed her arms through the quilt, the friction slowly warming her.

"I . . . I died?" She coughed again, the words scratching at her throat with the last bit of water.

"You drowned. Your heart stopped for a two full minutes before I brought you back. What did you see?"

Lili heard the words, but it took a moment for them to sink in. Her brain was sluggish, thoughts moving slowly, groggily.

Her chest hurt. There was a deep pain at her ribs. She realized he had probably performed CPR to expel the water and kick-start her heart. "I think you broke my ribs."

He grabbed her shoulders and shook her limp body. "Tell me what you saw! You have to tell me now before you forget! Before it goes away!"

The pain at her chest burned like a knife gouging her belly—Lili shrieked.

The man released her, pulled back from her. "I'm sorry, I'm so sorry. You just have to tell me, and this will all be over, just tell me."

Lili thought about it then, her mind jumping back to the moment she plunged beneath the water, the moment she . . . had she really drowned? She remembered breathing in water, consciousness pulling away. She remembered blackness.

She remembered nothing.

"I didn't see anything. I think I passed out."

"You were dead."

"I . . ." Her words drifted off. She didn't remember anything at all.

He was staring down at her, his bloodshot eyes wide and wild, spittle dripping from the corner of his mouth.

"I remember blacking out, then you waking me. Nothing else."

"You must remember something?"

Lili shook her head. "Nothing."

He released her shoulders and sat back, his back pressed against the large freezer. He pulled off his knit cap and scratched at his head in frustration.

Lili gasped.

There was an enormous fresh surgical incision running across his bald head. It started above his left ear and trailed around to the back of his head. It was stitched together with black thread, the flesh raised and purple.

He pulled the cap back down, covered up, and stood, favoring his right leg. Reaching down, he pulled Lili to her feet. The blood rushed from her head, and she swooned, her vision going white. He held her still until she could stand on her own, then led her back to the cage, guiding her inside. He tossed her clothes in behind her and slammed the door, then clicked both locks back in place.

"You can get dressed. We'll try again in a few hours. You will remember next time," he told her.

He started for the stairs, his right leg dragging slightly behind him. "Drink the milk. You'll need your strength."

Lili eyed the glass, now warm. A fly had landed in it and drowned.

15

Clair

Day 2 • 9:17 a.m.

The security guard had ushered Clair and Sophie to the far corner of the school's lobby, then made a few phone calls. There was a small sitting area with a black leather couch, two matching chairs, and a small sign that read: FREE WILCOX WI-FI — PASSWORD AVAILABLE AT SECURITY.

Clair studied the leaf of a large potted tree. "How do they keep this alive indoors? There's no light."

Sophie glanced over. "A ficus? They're like the weeds of the tree world. They'll eat up whatever light you cast on them. This one is probably sucking up the fluorescents overhead and whatever it can pull from the windows by the door back there."

"It's like a frankentree. Looks completely healthy on a diet of artificial junk. I wish I could do that," Clair replied.

"The one next to it is a philodendron. They're easy to maintain too—just water whenever the dirt feels dry. I've got a few at home. They're near impossible to kill."

Clair glanced over. "Oh, I could kill it. My plant love leaves nothing but brown branches and shriveled blooms in its wake. I'm not fit to be a plant owner."

They heard footsteps from above and glanced up to see a teenage girl coming down the stairs with a purple backpack slung over her shoulder. Not very tall, about five feet or so, with shoulder-length brown hair and pink highlights. She slowed as she saw them, eyeing them warily.

"Gabrielle Deegan?" Clair said, looking up at her.

The girl nodded, descended the remaining steps, and rounded the corner to the sitting area. "Are you looking for Lili?"

"We are," Sophie said, gesturing toward one of the empty chairs. The girl glanced at the security guard, who offered a reassuring smile, then plopped down into the seat. Sophie and Clair sat opposite her on the couch. "I'm Sophie Rodriguez with Missing Children, and this is Detective Clair Norton with Chicago Metro."

Clair noted that Sophie didn't mention she was with *Homicide* at Chicago Metro.

"Gabby, call me Gabby. Nobody calls me Gabrielle but that guy over there." She nodded at the security guard. "Captain Law and Order. I should be out looking for Lili, and he's got these doors locked up tighter than his daughter's chastity belt."

Clair exchanged a glance with Sophie, trying not to smile.

"Do you have any leads?"

Gabby wore the traditional school uniform, but Clair noticed her white blouse was untucked and her skirt looked like it had been hemmed up an inch or two from the norm. Her ears, eyebrow, and lip all had piercings, but she wore only a single set of small matching silver loops at each ear. No doubt dress code prohibited anything else —someone seeking individuality in a sea of the same would not be doing so here. Every time Clair entered one of these private schools, she recalled the scene from *The Wall* with all the identical students marching in unison into a giant meat grinder.

"She's been gone a full day," Gabby went on. "She could be lying in a ditch right now or tied to a bed with some crazy psycho telling her to call him Daddy while he jerks off on her chest. If that 4MK guy took her, who knows what he's doing to her. You need to find her."

"When was the last time you spoke to her?" Clair asked.

"Wednesday night. She was working," Gabby said. "She texted me from the gallery."

"What did she say?"

"She didn't say anything, she just sent me a picture of a new Mustang. Cherry red. It was gorgeous. Her dad said he'd buy her a car when she graduates next year, so we've been doing this thing where we send each other pictures of cool cars when we find them. She's not sure what she wants yet. But her dad said if she graduates with straight As, he'll buy her whatever. He's a doctor, so I think he's serious. I told her she should get a Maserati, but she doesn't want to take advantage of him. She's trying to find something cool but still affordable. I keep telling her to break the bank if she can, so she sent me the Mustang pic, and I sent her this one."

She held up her phone. Clair leaned in closer. "What is that?"

"A Tesla Roadster. They don't make them anymore, but it's a way cool car. Fully electric and can do zero to sixty in two point seven seconds. It will even get a few hundred miles per charge. They stopped making them in 2012, but the specs are much better than anything else out there, even the new electric cars. You can find them for around seventy thousand now, even though they went as high as a few hundred when they first came out."

Clair thought about her seven-year-old Honda Civic parked down the street and made a mental note to call her dad and ask for a car. Apparently that route was much more fruitful than saving pennies followed by a visit to the buy-here pay-here lot. "May I see that?"

Gabby handed her the phone.

Clair scrolled through her text messages. No actual words were exchanged with Lili, only photos of cars over the past few weeks.

Gabby went on. "She was hoping to get her license soon and maybe talk her dad into buying the car earlier. She's had straight As since finger painting in grade school. That's not gonna change between now and graduation. We thought it would be cool to drive to school every day, even though it's only a few blocks."

Clair returned the phone to her. "Do you have a license?"

Gabby shook her head. "I don't really need one, not now anyway. I get along fine on the bus or the train. Parking in the city can be a bitch. I figured riding in someone else's car was the way to go." She offered a wry smile. "Particularly if it's a Tesla Roadster."

"Have you ever done that?" Sophie asked. "Ridden in someone else's car to school?"

Gabby shifted in her seat and scratched her elbow. "Sometimes, if the weather is bad. We always see somebody we know on Sixty-Ninth. If it's raining or snowing heavily, we might catch a ride."

"What about yesterday morning? Think Lili caught a ride with someone?" Clair asked.

Gabby thought about this for a second. "It was snowing pretty good, so I guess it's possible."

"We're going to need a list of everyone who might've given her a ride. Do you think you can do that?" Sophie asked.

Gabby chuckled. "You think one of the boys here took her? Not a chance. She'd kick their ass before they got their pecker out of their pants."

Sophie tilted her head. "Would she get in the car with a stranger?"

"No."

"Then . . ." Sophie let the word hang.

Gabby leaned forward, twisting her fingers together. "Right before school, Sixty-Ninth is full of students, driving and walking. If someone tried to pull her into a car or something, somebody would have seen her."

"What about if she got into a car with someone she knows?" Clair asked. "Think somebody would notice that?"

Gabby sighed. "I don't know. Maybe."

"Think you can make that list for us? Anyone you can think of who may have given her a ride?"

Gabby nodded and pulled a notepad out from her backpack.

16

Porter

Day 2 • 10:26 a.m.

They found Floyd Reynolds within the body of the snowman, a deep gash in his neck. Someone had tied him to the metal pole of a large bird feeder, then built the snowman around him, slowly covering him in ice and snow.

Porter and Nash watched in awe as CSI painstakingly removed the snow in bits and pieces, carefully bagging and tagging each one for analysis back at their lab, slowly revealing the man beneath.

"This took time, a lot of time," Nash said under his breath.

"Few hours at least," Porter agreed.

"How can he do something like this completely unnoticed?"

Porter motioned around the yard. "We've got nothing but a tree line at the back here, hedges to the right blocking the view from the neighbors, a wood fence on the left. For someone to really see what was going on back here, they'd have to come through the gate at the front yard. This isn't visible from the street."

"Mrs. Reynolds is preoccupied, and the boy was probably in bed by the time he got started," Nash added, thinking aloud.

Porter's gaze fell to the ground. He started for the front yard.

Nash followed a few paces behind him, careful to duplicate his steps and avoid multiple tracks. He did this more out of habit than necessity. CSI had already searched the snow and found nothing.

Porter pushed through the gate, paused for a second, then went to the silver Lexus LS parked in the driveway. The car was parked at the side of the house, not visible from the front door. Mrs. Reynolds thought her husband had left, but most likely he'd never gotten the car in gear.

The unsub opened the rear door and slipped into the car behind the driver's seat. "He was hiding back here when Reynolds came out, probably ducked down in back. There's a motion light up there. Mrs. Reynolds said her husband left after dinner, so it was probably dark out. He would have tripped the light — only place to hide is the backseat. He waited for Reynolds to get in, maybe get the seat belt around him, and close the door. Then he came up and got something around the man's neck, something thin like a piano wire, judging by the way it cut into his throat." As Porter spoke, he climbed into the back of the car and acted everything out, moving in slow motion.

He looked at the back of the driver's seat. "We've got a shoe print here in the leather. Looks like he tried to wipe it away and missed part. He must have put a foot against the back of the seat for leverage."

"CSI said it's a size eleven work boot. They don't know the make," Nash said.

"It takes a lot of strength to kill a man like that. He'd be thrashing about, fighting back, trying to work his hand under the cord. Reynolds's movement would be highly restricted — the steering wheel would see to that. He might have tried to get the door open, but most likely both hands went to his neck. The power position is in the backseat. Reynolds wouldn't have been able to get the cord off, even if he were the stronger man. The leverage and angles all work against him," Porter said.

Porter climbed out of the backseat and opened the front door. "The blood spatter on the windshield and dashboard fits."

The steering wheel and door were covered in black fingerprint powder. "Our unsub kills him, climbs out, reaches into the front, takes Reynolds by the shoulders, and drags him out, drags him all the way to the back." Again, Porter mimics the movement, his back hunched, hauling an invisible body through the snow until he reached the remains of the snowman. Reynolds's body was completely visible now, all the snow and ice removed. Porter looked at the props on the ground, the stovepipe hat, the black gloves, and the broom. "He must have used the broom to sweep away what he could of his tracks. Last night's snow did the rest."

"We think he walked off into the woods," one of the CSI officers said. It was the same woman Porter and Nash had met at the Jackson Park Lagoon crime scene.

Porter nodded in agreement. "That's how I would have left. You're Lindsy, right?"

"Yes, sir," Rolfes replied. She pointed at the ground leading into the trees. "The snow isn't as thick under the trees, but he brushed it anyway. Looks like he used a branch or something, something not as effective as the broom. We've got a faint trail. It comes out one block over on Hyicen Street. He probably parked his own vehicle there."

"Any tire tracks?"

Rolfes shook her head. "Nothing to identify the unsub's vehicle. Two uniforms are going door to door to see if anyone saw a car parked there last night."

Porter's phone rang. He glanced down at the display. "It's the captain."

"You gonna answer?"

"Nope."

Nash frowned. "Balls. You know what that means."

Porter's phone went silent. A moment later Nash's phone rang.

"Double balls."

"Tell him we're still at the scene. We'll come in as soon as we wrap up here," Porter said.

Nash sighed and answered the call.

Behind them, a woman screamed.

Porter turned to find Mrs. Reynolds standing at her back door. "Christ, I told them to keep her and the boy in the living room. She shouldn't see this," he said.

Nash shrugged his shoulders and walked away from the house, his phone pressed to his ear.

17

Clair

Day 2 • 10:26 a.m.

Clair fell back in the squeaky-wheeled office chair and picked at the cracked green leather on the armrest. She reached for her coffee cup and brought it to her—

Empty.

Dammit.

"Do you want another refill?" she asked Sophie.

Sophie glanced up from the sheet of notebook paper in her hands. "I'm good. We've got two more left. Let's wrap this up so we can get out of here."

After they spoke to Gabby Deegan, the security guard had escorted them to the second-floor administration office and introduced them to Noreen Outen at the front desk. She'd looked up at them with a forced smile from behind glasses thick enough to leave the top of her nose red with their weight. Clair felt a headache coming on just watching her eyes strain.

After identifying themselves, they'd sent her off on two tasks— round up the students on the rather extensive list Gabby provided them (sixteen names in all), then check the attendance records for the twelfth—they were looking for anyone who didn't make it to class that day, any class, on the off chance a student picked up Lili and left with her.

While the woman plugged away at her homework assignment, Clair and Sophie had begun interviewing the students lining up in the hallway outside the office. Now they were fourteen down, two to go. So far, none of the students remembered seeing Lili that morning, either walking to school or in the building.

"Who's next?"

Sophie glanced down at Gabby's notes. "Malcolm Leffingwell and Leo Gunia. Want to flip for it?"

Clair tilted her head back in the chair. "Leo!"

Sophie giggled. "Jeez, Clair. Do you have to shout every name?"

"I love the way kids jump when they hear their name shouted out from the admin office. Every bad thing they've done since wetting their first diaper runs through their head. See? Look how white that kid's face is."

Sophie glanced up at the boy coming through the door. "You're a damn sadist, woman."

"Just keeping them on their toes."

Leo Gunia wore the same white shirt, navy pants, and blue striped tie as all the other boys they had spoken to. His black hair was neatly cropped, and he had the slightest amount of stubble growing under his chin.

Clair suppressed a smile. Why is it all teenage boys think they can grow some form of facial hair? She had yet to meet one who actually could. Instead, they had these bitty shadows and patches of peach fuzz. She was tempted to send each one on his way with a razor and a bottle of testosterone. "Please take a seat, Leo."

Sophie explained who they were and why they were there.

Leo held their gaze, nodding as she spoke. "The whole school is talking about it."

"Really? What are they saying?" Sophie asked him.

The boy shrugged. "Only that somebody might have taken her on her way to school the other day. That 4MK guy."

"It wasn't 4MK," Clair told him.

He shrugged again. "Well, somebody, then."

"Did you see her that morning?"

The boy didn't say anything. His eyes fell to the floor. He shuffled his feet.

"Leo?"

"I should've stopped. It was so cold out, she must have been freezing, but I had to get to class early to try and prep for a test. I had to work the night before and didn't have time to study," Leo said quietly.

Clair leaned forward in her chair. "So you saw her? Where?"

"On Sixty-Ninth, right before the overpass." He glanced up, his eyes watery. "She was hunched over, walking against the cold. It was snowing kind of heavy, and I didn't see her until the last second. I don't know what happened. I thought about stopping, I think my foot even reached for the brakes, but that test came into my mind, and I looked at my clock and I was already five minutes late. That meant I only had about twenty minutes to study—by the time I parked and got upstairs, probably less. Anyway, I saw her at the last second. I couldn't have stopped if I wanted to, and I didn't have enough time to double back. I figured someone else would give her a ride."

Clair glanced at Sophie, then back to Leo. "Did you see anyone else stop for her?"

Leo lowered his head. "No. I'm not sure I would have noticed even if the car behind me did. I wasn't thinking, and with the snow . . . If I would have picked her up, she'd probably be okay right now. This is my fault."

Sophie asked, "What time was it when you saw her?"

Leo sighed. "Seven thirty."

"You're certain?"

He nodded. "I needed an A on that exam, remember? I was counting the seconds all morning."

"What did you score?"

Leo sighed again. "B minus."

Clair took down Leo's contact information and gave him her card. They sent him back to class.

Malcolm Leffingwell had not seen Lili all week.

Noreen Outen poked her head back in. "That the last of them?"

Clair stood up and stretched her back. "Yes, ma'am. Any luck with the attendance records?"

Noreen pushed her heavy glasses back up her nose, then skimmed a small notepad. "We had two students out sick that day, both phoned in by their mothers—Robyn Staats and Rosalee Newhouse. Nobody late to first period, nobody unaccounted for. We have good students here; they wouldn't get mixed up in any shenanigans."

Sophie nodded at the notepad. "Do either of those girls know Lili?"

Noreen said, "Well, let me think. Robyn is a freshman, Rosalee is a junior. It's possible, I suppose, but I don't know for sure."

"We'll need to speak to both of them too," Sophie told her.

Noreen nodded.

Clair fell back into her chair. It felt like they were spinning wheels.

18

Porter

Day 2 • 10:31 a.m.

"Why does the captain want to meet us at my apartment?" Porter asked.

He had both hands on the steering wheel, his knuckles white.

The red and blue lights flashed in the corner of his eye atop the charger, and the siren wailed behind the throaty engine. He was doing eighty-one on I-94.

Beside him, Nash held the Oh Shit handle above the door with his right hand and gripped the seat with his left. "He wouldn't say. I tried to get it out of him. His exact words were 'Get Porter back to his apartment now.'"

Porter pulled the wheel to the left and circled around a gas truck. "Well, did he sound angry? Upset? Worried?"

Nash shrugged. "He sounded like the captain always sounds. I couldn't get a read on him."

"Fuck!" Porter slammed his hand into the horn and held as a blue Prius pulled into his lane. "Damn tree-hugger."

"Is there something at your place I should know about? Why would he want to meet there?"

The Prius's right blinker came on, and the car pulled lazily into the next lane. The moment it passed, Porter dropped the Charger into fourth and flew past, coming within inches of the car's protruding mirror.

"Sam?"

"I don't know."

Nash groaned. "You don't know if there's something at your place I should know about? Come on, Sam. This isn't first grade. I'm your partner. You can tell me. Does this have something to do with Heather's death?"

Porter said nothing.

He took the exit for Lake Shore Drive.

Along with the captain's white Crown Vic, there were three vehicles Porter didn't recognize parked in front of his building—two black sedans and a van. All bore federal plates. He double-parked, blocking in the van, killed the siren, and left the lights flashing as he bound from the car and up the steps with Nash behind him.

They were in the hallway at his door—Captain Dalton, Special Agent Diener, Agent Poole, and Special Agent in Charge Hurless of the Bureau's 4MK task force. There were two federal crime-scene techs Porter didn't recognize.

Dalton saw them push through the door at the stairs and hurried over. "What the fuck were you thinking, Sam?"

"What do you mean?"

"You know exactly what I mean."

Nash stood beside Porter. He said nothing.

Dalton clicked through some images on his cell phone and held the small screen up to Porter. "Did you take it because of this? Are you looking for her?"

Porter glanced at the screen. It was the note Bishop had left for him on the bed in his apartment along with the ear of the man who had killed his wife.

Sam,
   A little something from me to you . . .
   I'm sorry you didn't get to hear him scream.
   How about a return on the favor?

A little tit for tat between friends.
Help me find my mother.
I think it's time she and I talked.
B

"Are you looking for her?" Dalton repeated.

Porter took a deep breath. "I'm trying to find him."

"That's not your job," Dalton said, fuming. "Have you been in contact with him? Has he reached out to you at all?"

"No."

"Would you tell me if he had?"

"Of course I would."

Dalton dropped his phone back into the pocket of his thick brown coat. "I want to believe you. But I'm not so sure I can anymore."

Nash frowned at Poole. "What are you up to?"

Poole raised his hands defensively but said nothing.

Dalton's forehead furrowed. "He didn't do anything. Security caught your buddy here on video sneaking into the FBI's office across from yours this morning."

"He was probably just turning the heat up for them. Always nice to come into a toasty office on a day like today," Nash replied. He jerked his thumb back at Diener. "That pud tugger was sitting at my desk in our office this morning. We're all one big happy family down there. Share and share alike."

SAIC Hurless stepped forward. "Our office is considered federal territory until we vacate. Trespassing is a prosecutable offense, local law enforcement included."

"I pulled the file on Barbara McInley," Porter said.

Dalton rolled his eyes.

Hurless drew closer. "Theft of federal property would be a separate but equally damning charge."

"I'll return the file as soon as I'm done."

"You'll return it now. Then we'll decide if you get to keep your badge," Hurless replied.

Dalton's face went red. He turned to Hurless. "The only person who will decide what happens with Detective Porter's badge is me. You're guests in my house. I can put you and your team out on the street with one phone call."

Hurless stepped closer. "Let's be clear, Captain. We're here because your prize detective let a serial killer walk. That mistake will cost lives. There's a good chance it already has. You've got one girl dead and another missing, two crimes probably attributed to our guy, and you put the same clumsy detective in charge. Now he's stealing files. How much blood do you want on your hands before you decide it's time to fix this?"

"4MK didn't take the girls," Porter said quietly.

"Enough." Dalton grunted.

"I want to know what else this man is hiding. Open the door," Hurless said.

"No fucking way!" Nash blurted out. "Unless you have a warrant, you've got zero business in there."

Hurless began ticking off items on his fingers. "Federal trespass, theft of federal property, impeding a federal investigation, aiding and abetting a wanted *federal* fugitive . . . notice the key word? Losing his badge is the least of your friend's worries right now."

Dalton took Porter by the shoulder and led him back down the hall. "You need to open that door."

"Why?"

"You let them in, let them take a sniff around, and the charges go away. You share whatever you've got cooking in there, and this goes away," Dalton said. "You don't, and I can't protect you."

"Screw them, Sam," Nash said.

Porter glanced back down the hall at the men standing at his door. Poole met his eyes. "All right."

"Sam!"

Porter offered a weak grin at his partner. "It's fine. I really don't give a shit anymore. Maybe it will help catch him."

Dalton drew in a deep breath and steered Porter back down the hall.

Porter pulled his keys from his pocket, unlocked the door, and pushed it open.

Hurless and Diener pushed past him into the apartment, followed by the two crime-scene techs. Poole went in next. His eyes dropped to the ground as he walked past Porter and the others.

Porter followed, with Dalton and Nash at his back.

A whistle from the bedroom. "Holy hell," Hurless said.

"Oh, Christ," Dalton said, his breath catching as he stepped into the room.

Nash said nothing. He stepped up behind the others, dragging his feet.

"What am I looking at?" Hurless asked.

"Every mention of Bishop in the past four months, worldwide," Porter replied. He stepped up to the map, located the yellow thumbtack he had placed at the Jackson Park Lagoon, and pulled it out, dropping it onto the nightstand.

Diener was watching him. "What was that one?"

"Jackson Park. I told you, he didn't take these girls. This is something, someone different."

Poole crossed the room and kneeled down at the laptop, his eyes drifting over the text on the screen. "Google alerts?"

"Every mention of Bishop or 4MK online," Porter replied.

Poole positioned the screen to get a better look, prepared to type, then turned back to Porter. "May I?"

"Sure."

Porter watched as he scrolled back through the messages, scanning the subjects of each, then refreshing the screen to load the previous fifty, repeating. When he reached the end, he looked up at the maps. "Where do you think he is?"

"I have no idea."

Hurless started opening drawers, rifling through his clothes.

Nash crossed the room and stood between him and Porter's dresser. "You seriously going to go through the man's underwear drawer?"

"Step aside, Officer," SAIC Hurless said.

"It's fine, Nash. Let him look at whatever he wants. I'm not hiding anything," Porter said.

Hurless faced him. "Where's the McInley file?"

"In my car, under the driver's seat." Porter tossed him the keys.

Hurless tossed the key to one of the techs. He disappeared out the front door toward the elevator.

"What other files are we going to find in here?" Hurless asked.

Porter crossed the room and sat on the edge of the bed. "That's the only one I have."

"Because you put the others back?"

"Because it's the only one I took."

Poole stood up from the laptop and turned to him. "Why Barbara McInley?"

Porter thought about this for a second, not sure he wanted to say anything, then decided he wasn't helping anyone by keeping his thoughts to himself. "A gut instinct, that's all. Something feels off about that case."

"Off how?" Poole asked.

Agent Diener snickered. "Who cares? He's not Philip Marlowe. Gut instincts only sub for evidence in old black-and-white movies and pulp books."

"Off how?" Poole repeated.

Porter ran his hand through his hair. "She's the only blonde. Eight girls taken, and she's the only blonde."

"You're kidding with this, right?" SAIC Hurless said.

Poole stepped closer. "He took the loved ones of the true criminals in his eyes. The McInleys only had blond children. He didn't have a choice."

Porter shrugged. "Maybe, but the crime doesn't fit, either. Barbara McInley's sister hit and killed a pedestrian. It was an accident. All the other crimes, everyone else he decided to punish, did something premeditated."

Poole thought about this. "That's still thin."

"I never said I had something solid. Just a gut instinct, a hunch. Like your buddy said—just my very own Philip Marlowe moment, nothing more," Porter told him. "If it played out, I would have told you."

The tech returned holding the McInley file and handed it to SAIC Hurless. He waved it at Porter. "What did you find in here? Anything to back this up?"

"I didn't get a chance to look," Porter said. "It's been a busy morning."

SAIC Hurless stared at him for nearly a minute, neither man saying a word, then turned back to the two techs and the other federal agents. He waved his arm at the wall. "I want photos of all this, then bag and tag everything. Bring it all back. Turn over every inch of this place. You find anything at all having to do with this case, I want to know about it."

He turned back to Porter and stood inches from his face. "I find you're holding out, if this guy reached out to you and you're holding back, if you know anything at all you're not telling me, I will not hesitate to lock you up. I don't give a shit what kind of seniority you may have or what your track record is, you're nothing but a fucking thief to me, a thief and a hack interfering with a federal investigation. Now's your chance to come clean, if there's anything at all you haven't told me; now or never. I hear about it in an hour, and you're done. Do you understand me?"

"There's nothing else."

The man let out a breath.

Porter's eyes stayed on him.

When SAIC Hurless finally turned away and crossed the room to root around in Porter's closet, Porter found himself looking at the photo of Heather on his dresser, her bright, reassuring smile, and he had never felt so alone.

One hour and four file boxes later, they were finished.

Porter's wall was once again bare, save for the tiny holes left by the tacks and the paint damaged by roughly removed tape. Agent Diener had the laptop under his arm and was slowly circling the room on the off chance something was missed. In the hallway Porter heard SAIC Hurless mumbling something to Dalton, but he couldn't make out the words.

On his way out, Poole prepared to say something but then changed his mind. Porter watched him slip into the elevator, with the techs behind him, lugging the last of the boxes.

"Diener?" Hurless shouted out. "Let's go."

Agent Diener pushed past Porter and went to the elevator, trailing the scent of an aftershave forgotten since 1992.

The doors opened. Hurless said one last thing to Dalton and ducked inside, his eyes fixed on Porter as the doors creaked shut.

Dalton came back into the apartment with Nash behind him. "I really don't know what the hell you were thinking, Sam. This is a clusterfuck."

"It's not like he was hiding evidence," Nash pointed out.

Dalton went red. "You keep your mouth shut. I seriously doubt all this was going on under your nose and you didn't know."

Porter said, "He had no idea. This was all me."

Dalton spun back to him. "Not only have you compromised the 4MK investigation, now you're impacting our efforts to find this new psycho snatching girls. I can't afford to take you offline right now."

"Then don't."

"Hurless took it to his assistant director, and the AD called our chief. This is completely out of my hands." The captain's eyes fell to the floor. "I'm relieving you of duty, one week. You've got to get this shit out of your head. I find out you didn't drop it, and this will play out much worse. They agreed not to charge you, but the suspension is nonnegotiable."

"Captain, this is just a pissing contest. You can't let politics dictate your actions. Catching this guy has to be our priority, nobody knows more—"

Dalton held out his hand. "Gun and badge."

Porter knew better than to argue. He handed over his Glock and identification.

Dalton dropped both into his jacket pocket, turned, and left the apartment. He pressed the elevator call button.

"This new guy is nasty, Captain. He's escalating fast," Porter said.

Without turning, Dalton replied, "Nash and Clair will handle it. I don't want to hear anything from you for the next seven days. I do, and you'll get another seven. Do we understand each other?"

Porter said nothing.

"Do we understand each other?" the captain repeated.

"Yes," Porter said.

The elevator arrived and Dalton stepped inside, his hand holding the door open. "Nash, you're with me."

Nash looked to Porter but said nothing. Porter offered a slight nod.

Nash stepped inside the car. The doors closed, and Porter found himself standing in the middle of his apartment, his heart pounding in his chest, the silence screaming.

19

Lili

Day 2 • 11:36 a.m.

Lili huddled in the corner of her cage, the thick blanket wrapped around her. She had gotten dressed, but she couldn't get warm. She couldn't stop shivering, even when standing next to the heater vent. She couldn't stop looking at the dark staircase in the corner of the basement or listening to the creak of old floorboards as the man moved around upstairs.

A spider crept across the chainlink a few inches from her foot, and she pulled away, pushing deeper into the corner.

With each footfall upstairs, a tiny bit of dust rained down from the rafters, a thin fog in the gloomy light. Lili tried to pretend this was snow and she was looking out a window. She tried to pretend she was safely back in her room at home, but the illusion broke whenever the man cried out.

He screamed, a lot.

His words were incoherent, a muffled blast of nonsense, and they were followed sometimes by crying, other times by a pain-filled wail. But they broke the relative silence of the home and lingered on the air, somehow living in those tiny bursts of dust drifting down.

Nothing preceded the cries.

Lili's father once hit his index finger with a hammer while trying to help her build a birdhouse for school, and he let out a similar wail but it hadn't lingered—like he caught himself about the scream, realized his daughter was watching, and bit his tongue. The scream came to an abrupt halt, dying somewhere in his throat as his face flushed with red.

The screams from the man upstairs did not drop off so suddenly. He would be silent for a really long time, no movement or noise at all. Then his voice would fill the house with the sharpness of a blade, then linger as they morphed into sobs.

Lili didn't know what brought on his screams. She didn't want to know. She preferred he keep whatever it was upstairs.

He had come down only once in the past hour. He emptied the bucket he had left for her waste, washing it in the utility tub before returning it to her cage. He then eyed the still-full glass of milk with the fly floating on top, picked it up, and carried it back up the stairs, all without uttering a word. He looked sickly pale, though. When Lili met his gaze, she couldn't help but turn away, her eyes unwilling to look upon him—somehow, that had caused him to stay a little bit longer. If she wasn't looking at him, he felt more comfortable looking at her, staring even. Who knew what thoughts ran through his head.

When he came back again, Lili would lock her eyes on him and not turn away, maybe say something about his wound. Maybe that would make him go away sooner.

Lili knew plenty of boys like this.

The confident ones had no problem glaring at her. Some made sure she knew they were watching. The shy boys, though—they may look, but the moment she felt their eyes on her, the moment she looked over at them, they would turn away and lose themselves in something else, pretending she wasn't there at all. Her friend Gabby thought of it as some kind of game, always calling out the shy boys and making them feel all embarrassed whenever she caught one.

There was one boy in their class, Zackary Mayville, notoriously shy. Gabby got partnered with him during science class last week, and just to mess with him, she unfastened two of the buttons on her blouse, just enough so her bra was visible when she bent down over their workbench. He turned bright red every time, looking but trying not to get caught looking, and Gabby managed to get through the entire hour with a straight face. Lili hadn't, though. She couldn't stop laughing and nearly didn't get the assignment done. She had to—

Lili heard footsteps on the stairs. The man appeared.

He had changed clothes. Now he wore black jeans, a dark red sweater, and the same black knit cap from earlier. When he reached the bottom of the steps, he sat, and this time he did stare at her.

Only minutes earlier, Lili had told herself that she would stare back, that she would watch him with an intensity in her eyes, unflinching, unnerving. She would rattle him. She didn't, though. Instead, she looked away. She focused her gaze on the concrete floor and watched him from the corner of her eye.

He sat there for a long time, at least twenty minutes, his breath coming in short, wheeze-filled gasps. When he finally spoke, his voice was low. "I'm sorry if I alarmed you. Sometimes it hurts."

Lili wanted to ask him what he meant, but she didn't. Instead, she remained silent.

"Sometimes," he went on, "I feel like someone's got their fingers around my eyeball and they're squeezing with all their might, not enough to pop it, but almost. I have meds, but they make it hard to think, to focus, and I need to concentrate right now. I need my wits about me."

Lili wanted to ask him about it, find out what was wrong, but kept her thoughts to herself. She wouldn't speak to him.

He reached up and scratched at his cap, then stood. "It's time to do it again."

20

Clair

Day 2 • 11:49 a.m.

Kloz gave his chair a push with his right foot and sent it spinning. "No shit? Sam couldn't stop being a cop? Not exactly a news flash."

Nash sat on the edge of the conference table, Sophie and Clair at the opposite end. "He should have told us."

"It's not like we could have covered for him," Clair said. "Sounds like the captain didn't even give you a chance."

Nash pointed across the hall. "It's those ass clowns over there."

Kloz gave his chair another spin. "This has conspiracy written all over it."

"What do you mean?" Nash asked.

"Someone higher up is covering their ass. We should be working directly with the feds on this. Instead, they scooped up the investigation and cut us out. In what world does that make sense? I'll tell you—in a world where someone higher up wants to distance this department from the case."

"Who? Dalton?"

"Maybe higher. The mayor was friends with Talbot. He took a lot of flak when that all went down. Then you got the press saying Sam let Bishop go . . ."

Clair threw a pen at him. "Sam didn't let anyone go. He saved that girl."

Kloz caught the pen and put it in his pocket. "We know that, but it's a juicier story if he lets him go. The mayor's bestie is a criminal, the lead detective lets the serial killer walk . . . it makes perfect sense for the feds to come in and lock everyone else out."

Clair turned to Nash. "Do you think he's in contact with Bishop?"

"Sam?"

"Yeah."

Nash shrugged. "Dunno."

"Would he do that?" Sophie asked. "Talk to that man on his own?"

Nash shrugged again. "He's been playing things close to the vest since Heather died."

"Who's Heather?" Sophie asked.

Clair tilted her head. "You didn't hear?"

Sophie shook her head.

"Sam's wife was killed in a convenience store robbery a few weeks before all this went down with Bishop. He probably shouldn't have been working, but he had been on 4MK since the beginning, so when we thought he died we had to bring him back in. 4MK was his case. They caught the guy who killed her, and then he escaped police custody. Bishop killed Talbot, Porter saved Emory, then he spent a little time in the hospital recuperating. When he got home, he found a box on his bed. Inside there was a note from Bishop and an ear belonging to the man who killed his wife. Bishop got him," Clair explained.

"What did the note say?"

"Bishop asked Sam to help find his mother," Nash told her.

"His mother? What does she have to do with this?"

Clair rolled her eyes. "We don't have time for this right now. I'll fill you in when we're back in the car. We need to keep moving, figure out how to proceed without Sam." She turned back to Nash. "What happened at the Reynoldses' house?"

Nash loaded up the photos on his phone and slid it across the table to Clair and Sophie.

Kloz leaned in to get a better look. "The same guy who killed Ella Reynolds did this?"

"I don't believe in coincidences," Nash replied.

"But why?"

"That's the million-dollar question."

Sophie swiped back through the images. "That doesn't make sense. If the unsub is targeting the Reynolds family, why would he take Lili Davies? They don't know each other. There's no connection."

"There must be a connection, we just haven't figured it out yet. What do we know about the father?" Clair asked.

Nash stood and went to the whiteboard. He wrote FLOYD REYNOLDS and underlined it, then wrote WIFE: LEEANN REYNOLDS under it. "He worked for UniMed America Healthcare, has for the past twelve years. Sold blanket insurance and health-care policies. According to his wife, he brings home about two hundred thousand a year before bonuses, and they have no debt aside from an American Express card they pay off every month."

Klozowski whistled. "That's some nice scratch. I'm clearly in the wrong line of work."

"We have UniMed," Sophie pointed out.

"They're the number three provider in the state," Nash told them before writing SIZE 11 WORK BOOT PRINT FOUND on the board under UNSUB.

"Where?" Sophie asked.

"On the back of the driver's seat in the Reynoldses' car. A Lexus LS. Looked like the unsub tried to wipe it away but must have been in a hurry. Sam thinks he put his foot there for leverage when he strangled the father."

Kloz's eyes turned toward the ceiling. "Size eleven would put him around seventy-one point five inches, about six feet tall."

"How do you know that?" Sophie asked.

"The average person is six and a half times taller than their shoe size. Any smaller or larger and their feet are out of proportion with their body, which means they'd have trouble walking, standing, balancing," Kloz replied.

"Huh."

"Hang with me, and I'll school you on all kinds of trivia."

"No, thank you," Sophie told him.

Clair said, "I'm not sure I buy the no-debt thing. Maybe they don't have traditional debt, but what about something not so traditional, like gambling or something he may not have shared with the wife? If you owe the wrong person money, I can see them making an example out of Reynolds's daughter."

"They wouldn't take him out, though," Kloz said. "Do that, and there's nobody left to pay."

"What about the wife? Maybe she owes somebody, and they made examples out of her daughter *and* her husband," Sophie said. "Women bet on the ponies too."

"They have time for that between all the cooking and the cleaning and baby making?" Kloz said, raising his notepad to shield his face from flying pens.

He lowered the notepad a moment later to find Clair just staring at him. "You are such a douche-nozzle."

Sophie was shaking her head at him. "I don't like you much."

Nash studied the board. "That's actually a good point."

"Thank you," Kloz said, smiling triumphantly.

"Not you, asshat. Sophie," Nash said. "Clair, ask Hosman to dig into their finances in case things are amiss in suburbia."

"On it."

"Is somebody watching the mother?" Klozowski asked.

Nash nodded. "We left two uniforms there to keep an eye on her and their little boy. There were also three news vans outside when I left. I don't think they'll get much alone time in the near future. Probably a good thing."

Clair was flipping through the images of Reynolds on Nash's phone again. "This doesn't really feel like a collection hit. Those guys tend to work efficiently, a double tap to the head, no mixed signals. They don't build snowmen or spend hours positioning a body under the ice just right. Whoever this is, they're trying to send some kind of message."

"They're not afraid of getting caught, either," Sophie said. "They're spending a lot of time in visible places."

Clair nodded. "Somebody with nothing to lose has no fear, no remorse, they just act. That makes this guy very dangerous."

Nash drew a line between Ella Reynolds and Lili Davies. "These two are connected somehow."

Klozowski's phone buzzed, and he glanced down at the display. "We've got a make and model on the truck from the park footage. It's a 2011 Toyota Tundra."

"See if you can get a list of matches within a hundred-mile radius of the city."

Klozowski was already tapping at his phone. "Yep."

"Any luck enhancing the image of the driver?"

"Nope," Klozowski replied. "I tried before I came down here. The camera is old and doesn't have the resolution."

Nash went back to the board, crossed out the completed items, and studied the remaining list of assignments. "This is getting long, and now we're down a man."

Kloz set down his phone and raised his hand.

"Yes, Kloz?" Nash said, pointing at him.

Klozowski grinned. "See what I did there? Remember when Bishop raised his hand? That's a 'callback.'"

"Do you have something to add?"

Kloz nodded. "Yes, sir. I can go out in the field. I need to run to that Starbucks anyway to tackle their video footage."

Nash glanced up at the evidence board. "What about your other assignments?"

"I'm not running a one-man show upstairs. I've got staff. I'll bring my laptop, and they can feed information to us as they get it," Kloz said.

Nash nodded. "Done. Ladies, let's divide and conquer. You take the art gallery. They should be open by now. Kloz and I will hit Starbucks and tackle some of these other items on the list. At this point, we've got to assume Lili is still alive. We need a break."

Clair stood up and stretched. "Should someone check on Sam?"

"Nope," Nash replied.

Evidence Board

ELLA REYNOLDS (15 years old)
Reported missing 1/22
Found 2/12 in Jackson Park Lagoon
Water frozen since 1/2 — (20 days before she went missing)
Last seen — getting off her bus at Logan Square (2 blocks from
　　home/15 miles from Jackson Park)
Last seen wearing a black coat
Drowned in salt water (found in fresh water)
Found in Lili Davies's clothes
Four-minute walk from bus to home
Frequented Starbucks on Kedzie. Seven-minute walk to home.

LILI DAVIES (17 years old)
Parents = Dr. Randal Davies and Grace Davies
Best friend = Gabrielle Deegan
Attends Wilcox Academy (private) did not attend classes on 2/12
Last seen leaving for school (walking) morning of 2/12 @ 7:15
　　wearing a Perro red nylon diamond-quilted hooded parka,
　　white hat, white gloves, dark jeans, and pink tennis shoes (all
　　found on Ella Reynolds)
Most likely taken morning of 2/12 (on way to school)
Small window = 35 minutes (Left for school 7:15 a.m., classes
　　start 7:50 a.m.)
School only four blocks from home
Not reported missing until after midnight (morning of 2/13)
Parents thought she went to work (art gallery) right after school
　　(she didn't do either)

FLOYD REYNOLDS
Wife: Leeann Reynolds
Insurance sales — works for UniMed America Healthcare
No debt? Per wife. Hosman checking

UNSUB
- Possibly driving a gray pickup towing a water tank: 2011
  Toyota Tundra
- May work with swimming pools (cleaning or servicing)
- Size 11 work boot print found — back of driver's seat,
  Reynolds car (Lexus LS). Used for leverage?

ASSIGNMENTS:

- Starbucks footage (I-day cycle?) — Kloz
- Ella's computer, phone, e-mail — Kloz
- Lili's social media, phone records, e-mail (phone and PC MIA) — Kloz
- ~~Enhance image of possible unsub entering park — Kloz~~
- Park camera loosened? Check old footage — Kloz
- ~~Get make and model of truck from video? — Kloz~~
- ~~Clair and Sophie walk Lili's route to school/talk to Gabrielle Deegan~~
- Clair and Sophie visit gallery (manager = Ms. Edwins)
- Put together a list of saltwater pools around Chicago via permits office — Kloz
- Check out local aquariums and aquarium supply houses
- Hosman to check debt on the Reynoldses

21

Porter

Day 2 • 12:18 p.m.

Porter needed a Big Mac.

Not only a Big Mac but a large fry, chocolate shake, and an apple pie for dessert.

He needed it so badly, the craving drove him to walk steadfast from his apartment, three blocks down Wabash, and directly into the nearest McDonald's, which was hopping this time of day. He ordered, took his meal to a small table in the back, and devoured every bit. Seven minutes later, he found himself staring at an empty tray, his stomach still rumbling.

He desperately wanted to talk to Heather. The immense hole in his heart once filled by the sound of his wife's voice burned.

Heather had been gone for six months now, and it felt like six thousand lifetimes. People told him he would heal with time, the hole would grow smaller, fill with other loves, with life lived. It hadn't, though. Instead, the void only seemed to grow larger, and he found himself missing her more each day.

Heather understood. Heather listened.

Porter wanted to tell her about the past six months. He needed her advice. He needed the sound of her voice.

"You kept me from venturing down the rabbit hole, Button," Porter said quietly. "Now I'm knee deep and sinking fast."

Last month he canceled her cell phone service. Until then, he'd called her regularly, sometimes three or four calls in a day, just to hear her sweet voice on the other end of the line, enough distance to make it sound real, to make *her* sound real. Silly, he knew, but it was all he had. Her presence slowly faded from his life no matter how tight he held on. Her body may have died suddenly, but her spirit lingered. Porter held that spirit's hand with all his might, unwilling to let go at first, finally coming to the realization that he had no other choice. That was the night he turned off her cell phone, and when he called her the next morning, it wasn't her voice that answered but instead a robotic operator telling him the number was no longer in service. At that point, her hand slipped from his and she was gone.

He would kill to have her back.

Even if only for five minutes, to have her back, to hold her, to ask her what to do next.

"I love you, Button," he said quietly.

With a deep sigh, Porter stood up, gathered his trash, and dumped everything into the overflowing can at the door. He stepped out into the icy day, welcoming the numb of it.

Then he wandered.

Twenty minutes later Porter found himself standing in the lobby of Flair Tower on West Erie, a small puddle forming at his feet. He hadn't planned on coming here, and as he pushed through the doors he considered turning right back around, but instead he found himself standing still, his eyes looking out across the lobby but not really taking anything in, dazed.

"Detective?"

Porter hadn't heard her walk up. He hadn't expected her to walk up, a building this size, but there she was, standing in front of him.

"Hello, Emory."

The last time he had seen her was at the hospital shortly after she was rescued from 4MK. Bishop had placed her at the bottom of an elevator shaft in that building on Belmont, used her as bait to lure Porter in. She had been malnourished, gaunt, her skin pale. Her right wrist had been badly damaged by the handcuffs he used to restrain her, and Bishop had removed Emory's left ear, yet she still managed to smile that day. Her hair was longer now, her face fuller, color in her cheeks.

"Detective, are you okay?"

"I'm ... I'm sorry. I'm not really sure why I'm here. I meant to come and see you, you know, after, but things have been so hectic, the time got away from me," he said.

"Let's sit." She took his hand and led him to some couches placed in front of a fireplace in the corner of the lobby. A log crackled, wrapped in thick flames, the heat reaching out and lapping at the air.

Porter tugged off his gloves, his fingers nervously twitching together. "I probably shouldn't be here."

Emory smiled. "That's silly — it's good to see you. I meant to stop by the station a dozen times but couldn't bring myself to go. Silly. I guess it's hard to find the words after something like that. The whole thing feels like a bad nightmare that happened to someone else. Like a movie I watched a few months ago and left at the theater. I can't talk to my friends, they don't understand. Ms. Burrow, either. She tried to coax the story out of me a few times, but I couldn't ... it all made her very uncomfortable. She wanted me to talk for my own sake, not because she wanted the details, and I didn't see the point in burdening her with those details. It was my nightmare. There's no reason for her to suffer too, have those thoughts in her head."

"Did you see a shrink?"

Emory laughed and shook her head. "They sure wanted to see me. I don't know how many dozens of them reached out. I tried to talk to one, but I couldn't stop thinking she planned to write a book about whatever I told her, and the idea of walking past a book at the store, knowing this ordeal was carved in stone for others to read, the idea of all that shut me right up. I couldn't tell her anything."

"I don't think they're allowed to do that. She would have lost her license."

"I suppose."

Emory's hands rested in her lap. Porter could still see a faint scar on her right wrist, but for the most part, the surgeons had done a wonderful job repairing the damage. On her left wrist, a small fig-ure-eight tattoo — Bishop gave her that too.

She raised her right wrist and pulled back the sleeve. "They did a good job, right?"

"If I didn't know what happened, I'd never guess. It's barely noticeable."

"I'm going back in next May. The doctor says he can wipe it out completely, but we need to give it a chance to heal up first," she told him, rotating the wrist. "I still don't have full motion, but it seems like it's coming back."

Porter's eyes inadvertently went to her left ear, hidden behind her long chestnut hair. He caught himself, almost looked away, then figured he wasn't fooling anybody. "How's the ear?"

A wide grin spread across her face. "Wanna see?"

Porter couldn't help but smile back. He nodded. "Is it gross?"

"You tell me?" Emory pulled her hair back, revealing a perfectly natural-looking ear. "Pretty cool, huh?"

Porter leaned in closer. Aside from a small scar visible at the base where doctors had attached the extremity, he couldn't tell it wasn't her original ear. "That's amazing."

Emory rolled up the sleeve of her right arm and showed him a small scar below her elbow. "They grew it here, using cartilage from my ribs. It only took a few months. The surgery was about six weeks ago. The doctor said Bishop removed mine with near surgical precision, so they had no trouble attaching the new one. Usually when they do this, the ear is torn off in some kind of accident and they have to try and piece the mess back together again. I guess I got lucky."

"I think you're a very strong girl."

"You wanna know the best part?"

"What's that?"

She turned her head and showed him her other ear. "Notice something different between the two?"

It took Porter a minute, and then it came to him. "Your right ear is pierced and your left one isn't?"

"Yep." She beamed. "The left *was,* but not anymore. I think I'm gonna leave it that way." She held up her left wrist, showed him the small infinity tattoo. "I'm on the fence about keeping this. I think a small reminder of what happened isn't necessarily a bad thing. Sometimes it's good to remember the bad. It makes other things seem not so terrible."

"You are one remarkable, inspiring girl."

She let her hair fall back. "Why, thank you, Detective."

The two went quiet for a minute, not an awkward silence, but something a little more comfortable. Porter found himself watching the flames as they wrapped around the logs in the fireplace, the wood slowly growing red and white. The crackle they produced was soothing, relaxing. This girl had lost her mother as a child, now her father, and yet she smiled. Porter wanted desperately to smile. He wanted to smile and mean it.

As if reading his mind, Emory leaned in closer. "He wasn't much of a father to me. I barely knew him. If not for the money, the way my mom drafted her will, I'm not so sure he would have wanted me around at all."

"He was your father. I'm sure he cared for you. He just had trouble showing it."

"He was a horrible man," she said quietly. "Not to me but to so many other people."

Porter considered telling her something to the contrary, try to build him up, thought better of it. She was a big girl. She deserved the truth. "It's important to remember he's not you. He never was."

Tears welled up in her eyes, and she fought them back. "That's not what the press says. They say it's worse now than ever. All his assets going to a kid, leaving nobody to run the business. Building inspectors shut down one of his skyscrapers last month, and the press blamed me. Nearly four thousand lost jobs."

Porter knew the building. Talbot had used substandard concrete in the construction. When the shortcut was discovered, he'd tried to retrofit the building (and most likely pay off inspectors), but the project was shut down anyway. The building cost a little over $700 million dollars, and it was set for implosion. Better to end it now, Porter supposed, than let construction complete and the thing topple over down the road. "They're trying to sell papers. How could that be your fault?"

"There's a lot of fighting going on at Talbot Enterprises," Emory explained. "Three of my father's senior officers are contesting his will. They're saying he drafted it under duress, that my mother forced him to leave everything to me. With all of them making grabs for the money, key decisions aren't happening, and things are falling apart. I'm not old enough to assume control, so Patricia Talbot stepped in as interim CEO until somebody can take over full-time." Emory let out a sigh. "She's suing me directly. She claims my father didn't have the right to leave all that he did to me, that everything rightfully belongs to her. Then there's Carnegie . . ."

Porter knew all about Carnegie, Talbot's other daughter. She regularly made the papers before Talbot died. Constant partying and arrests, a fixture on the Chicago social scene, and not a good one.

"She's been badmouthing me on social media and in every interview she does, whenever she gets the chance," Emory said. "She calls me Bastard Bitch. She ends every message with hashtag BastardBitch. I've never met her, and she acts like she'd stab my eyes out with a pen in the street if we were to cross paths."

With that, the tears did come, and Porter put an arm around her.

After a minute or so she wiped her eyes. "I'm being so selfish, going on about me. What about you? How are you doing?" Emory asked. "I heard about those girls. The papers say it's 4MK. That they wouldn't have been taken if it wasn't for you. The *Tribune* actually said you let him go, which is silly, I should know."

"It's not 4MK."

"No?"

"Nope," Porter replied.

Emory shook back the tears and forced a smile. "You'll find them. You found me."

Porter hoped to God she was right.

Nearly an hour had passed. He had to go.

Emory somehow understood. She rose from the couch, and when he did too, she wrapped her arms around him and squeezed. "I can't talk to a shrink. Maybe we can talk sometimes? If you're willing to listen?"

"I think I'd like that."

"Yeah. Me too."

When Porter left Flair Tower, the hole in his heart felt a little smaller.

22

Lili

Day 2 • 12:19 p.m.

"No! No more!" Lili screamed.

The man reached for her anyway, his large hands tugging at the quilt wrapped around her. "We must continue," he said.

Lili scrambled across the damp floor, sliding, her feet slipping, trying to get a grip on the damp concrete. She found herself in the back corner of the cage, unable to go any farther. "Please stop!" No place else to go.

The man raised the stun gun and pointed it at her. He pressed the button, and Lili watched lightning jump across the two metal prongs, smelled ozone in the air. "One more hour, then we can do it again, I promise. I promise." She tried to say this, but she shivered so hard that only a handful of syllables actually came out, fragments of words.

If they did it again, this would be the fourth—no, fifth time. Wait, maybe the third time. She couldn't be sure. Her thoughts didn't want to come together; her string of consciousness had a knot, something that kept her brain from working properly. White flakes whirled across her vision, making it difficult to see what was happening around her, a snowstorm in the basement, that's what it looked like, a whiteout of haze and gray.

He reached for her through the snow, the fingers of his left hand outstretched. "Now, while we're close."

His other hand, the one with the stun gun, drew within an inch of her, the gun nearly touching her neck. Lili couldn't take the pain of another shock. It felt like fire chewing at her bones, gnawing away from her inside out. A pain worse than dying.

She knew what that felt like now too, to die.

He thrust the stun gun at her face, pressed the button again near her eye.

"Okay!" she shouted. At least, she *tried* to shout. Only the sound of the letter *k* left her throat from somewhere behind chattering teeth.

The man pulled back, if only slightly. His free hand scratched at the knit cap, at the festering incision beneath.

Lili tried to stand, but her feet failed her, her legs folded, made of jelly now.

He reached in and offered a hand. His nails were bitten to the quick, the tips of his fingers red and puffy

Lili's fingers wrapped around his. His palm felt cold, clammy. She didn't want to touch him, but she knew she couldn't stand on her own, not now. And she had to stand. She had to do this willingly, or it would only hurt more. He would make it hurt more.

He led her from the cage, Lili putting most of her weight on him to stay upright.

When they reached the water tank, she looked up at him. She looked deep into his cloudy, lifeless eyes. "Thirty minutes, please. Just let me rest."

"We're too close."

Lili stared at him for a long time, the seconds ticking away like hours. Finally, she nodded. Lili released her hold on the quilt around her neck, and the tattered material fell to the ground, pooling at her feet. She hadn't gotten dressed again after the last time. Not after he said they would do it again in a few minutes. Instead, she only curled up with the quilt, the soft green quilt, *her* quilt. She curled up with the quilt in her cage and waited. She saw the clothing he gave her—his daughter's clothing, he had told her—folded neatly in her cage, just inside the door. He put the clothing away sometime after she dumped the articles on the floor beside the tank.

Lili had thought they were alone in the house. The last time, an hour or so ago, Lili screamed for his daughter, but there had been no answer. She pictured a girl her age sitting alone in a small bedroom upstairs, her hands over her ears, unwilling to accept what her father was doing down below. How could she? How could anyone? At first Lili refused to believe the girl knew what was happening, but soon she realized she must; the house wasn't that big. Lili's own house was much larger, and she was certain she'd hear cries from the basement. This girl, this man's daughter. She understood all too well, and she did nothing.

"Get in," the man said.

Lili looked down at the water. She knew it was warm, warmer than the basement, soothingly warm, comforting, but she feared it more than anything else in her entire life—more than the anger of her parents or the pain of a horrible injury, more than this man beside her.

It was death.

"Get in now," he said.

Lili took a deep breath, but it did little to stem the quivers passing through her body, the weakness building deep within and slowly taking hold of her all. She took a deep breath, placed a hand on the edge of the large freezer, and climbed over the side. Then she sank into the water and lay down, the man holding her head above the surface at her shoulders. When her ears dipped below the water line, she lost all the sounds of the basement and heard nothing but her own breathing, the echo of her pounding heart, even the sound of her eyelids snapping shut and open again.

The man lifted her up just a little, enough to bring her ears back into the air. "Remember this time," he said. "Remember it all."

"I will," Lili said.

The man shoved her beneath the surface, pressing her weakened body against the floor of the tank. Lili didn't try to fight him this time, she didn't even suck in one last breath. Instead, she inhaled the water. She choked back the pain as fluid filled her lungs, she fought the urge to cough, and breathed in more. She breathed in more until the wavy image of the man hovering above her faded away, until all went black, until it didn't hurt anymore, telling herself to remember she had to remember.

Lili would not wake up again.

23

Nash
Day 2 • 12:20 p.m.

"You can't possibly expect me to work my magic surrounded by the scent of freshly ground coffee without a venti caramel macchiato in my hand, can you?" Kloz said as he sat behind the manager's desk in the back office of the Starbucks on Kedzie.

The room was cluttered, no more than a hundred square feet, with the desk pressed against the back wall and random boxes of supplies littering every inch of open floor space. With Kloz behind the desk and Nash standing to his right, the manager had to stand in the hall-way outside the office.

"What about you? Would you like something?" the manager asked Nash. He had thinning brown hair, glasses, and about thirty pounds more than his frame was built to carry. He shuffled from side to side, his hands in constant movement. Nash couldn't help but wonder what inhaling coffee fumes for ten hours a day would do to a person. "Can I get a regular large coffee, black?"

"What kind? We've got blond, dark, decaf Pike Place, Caffè Misto, Clover—"

"Regular large coffee, black," Nash repeated.

His shoulders slumped. "I'll see what I can do."

Nash watched him disappear down the hall toward the front of the shop, then turned back to Kloz. "Well?"

Kloz had three windows open on the monitor. He was studying the text on the third with narrow eyes. "This thing is old, at least five years. The drive is only a half gig, and they're running an HD camera setup at 1080p."

"Don't make me hurt you. I need it in English."

Kloz rolled his eyes. "Because the camera is recording a high-end, detailed image, it takes a lot of space to record. This computer doesn't have a lot of space. When the drive runs out of room, the program automatically starts recording over the oldest images."

"How far back can you go?"

Kloz expanded one of the windows and studied the text. "It's not as bad as Sophie said. I can pull all recordings going back for about two and a half days. Full recordings, nothing deleted. When computers overwrite data, they don't do it in a linear, date-based way as we would, they record in bytes. This means when older videos are written over, fragments of that full video can stay on the drive."

Nash leaned in. "So you can pull snapshots older than two and a half days but not full, uninterrupted video?"

A grin spread over Kloz's face. "Now you're getting it."

"So, anything with our girl?"

"I think we're too late for that too. I'm running a program to piece back together the fragments, but so far the oldest image we've got is less than two weeks."

"And she went missing three weeks ago."

"Yep."

The manager returned holding two large cups and handed them to the detectives. Nash sniffed at his, then took a sip. "It's coffee?"

"That's what you wanted, right?" the manager asked.

Nash nodded. "Yeah, I just expected you to come back with some froufrou drink."

Kloz took a slurp from his cup. His lips came away covered in white foam. "I love me a good froufrou drink. This is three hundred calories of yum."

"Are you serious?" Nash frowned. "Three hundred?"

The manager shrugged. "That's a venti, twenty ounces at one hundred fifty calories per ten, so yeah. Three hundred."

Nash set his cup down and stared at it. "How much in mine?"

"Zero, unless you add sugar. It's just black coffee."

Kloz took another drink. "Don't judge me."

The manager glanced at the computer screen. "Any luck?"

"This thing is a piece of shit."

He nodded. "I told that to the detective who came by the last time. Corporate rarely upgrades them unless they break down, and believe me, I've tried to break this one, but it's a workhorse. They really don't care about long-term storage. If we get robbed, corporate wants to capture the event, but there is really no reason to keep more than a day or two's worth of footage."

The manager's phone dinged, and he pulled it from his pocket, read the message on the display, then put the oversize Samsung away.

Kloz was staring at him. "You have Wi-Fi here, right?"

"Of course."

"What kind?"

"A, B, G, N, and AC at 2.4GHz and 5," he replied.

"All the best, right? Your customers probably demand it."

He nodded. "Corporate *does* stay on top of that. Our best customers park themselves here for hours."

"What are you getting at?" Nash asked.

Kloz stood up and began tracing the wires, particularly a thick blue one. He followed the cable behind three cases of cups stacked in the corner. There were shelves behind them. He slid the containers aside, revealing a number of gizmos with flashing lights, nothing Nash recognized. He stopped at one device in particular, a small black box with two antennae sticking out the top. Kloz flipped it over.

"This is their Wi-Fi router and access point. It's a Ruckus Zone-Flex, state-of-the-art. Remember all those people staring at their laptops and smartphones out there? They're all connecting to the Internet through this," Kloz told him. He opened the lid on his MacBook. "See? I've connected to Starbucks Wi-Fi before, so my computer connected automatically. Now I'm on the same network as all the people here." He was pointing at an icon in the corner near his clock.

"How does this help us?" Nash asked him.

Kloz clicked at his keyboard. A new window opened, and data began to fly past much faster than Nash could read. "This is the traffic on their router in real time." He turned to the manager. "You shouldn't keep your username and password on a sticker attached to the router. That's the first place a potential hacker will look if they have access."

He raised both hands. "That's all Corporate. I don't touch that thing."

Kloz went back to his MacBook. "I can see every e-mail, web page, picture, or song accessed by the people out there, right here, right now, by watching this log file."

"I'm still not sure how that helps us," Nash said.

Kloz smiled. "If I were a hot leading lady and you were Tom Cruise, this is the part where you would try to kiss me."

"I'm not going to kiss you, Kloz."

"I'm not going to let you."

"What does all this mean?"

Kloz held up his index finger and began typing again. Nash watched him cut and paste some data from an e-mail into the program he was running. Then he clapped his hands and grinned. "We can't watch Ella Reynolds on video because that is long gone, but we can view everything she did while she was here dating back over a year and ending on January twenty-first. Her phone and computer."

Nash thought about this for a second. "The twenty-first? That's the day before she was reported missing. That means she never made it here on the day she disappeared. That narrows down our timeline a little bit. What else you got?"

Kloz wasn't listening to him. He was busy typing again. He didn't speak for nearly three minutes, then: "Kids will always be one step ahead of their parents."

"What do you mean?"

Kloz had two windows open on his screen. He selected the one on the left. "This represents all the data we pulled from Ella's computer and her online accounts. Her phone disappeared with her, but we have her laptop. Her browser history was nearly nonexistent. She either used a secure browser or encrypted her traffic. Most kids know how to do it—they don't want their parents snooping around. So, I took her Mac address—that's an ID unique to her computer—and ran it through the Starbucks router. That's this window here." He clicked on the box on the right. "The router captures all her activity, encrypted or not. If I compare the two windows, filter one against the other, I can see what she looked at while encrypted. Basically everything she didn't want her parents to find."

"Is it porn?" the manager asked. Nash had forgotten he was still standing there.

"Sadly, it is not porn," Kloz said. He opened another window and turned the computer so Nash could see.

Nash clucked his tongue. "Huh. I wouldn't have expected that."

24

Clair

Day 2 • 12:46 p.m.

"There it is, 3306," Sophie said, pointing out her window at the blue and white awning above the storefront's large picture window, THE LEIGH GALLERY printed in large block letters.

Clair maneuvered her Honda into a vacant space in front, and the two women shuffled across the cold street, careful not to slip on the icy sidewalk.

A tiny bell rang as they pushed through the doorway, and a woman with shoulder-length blond hair and glasses looked up at them from a desk at the back of the store. "Good afternoon, ladies." She smiled. "Let me know if you have any questions or if there is something I can help you with."

Clair took in the store. She had never seen so much color in one place. The walls were covered in paintings from floor to ceiling, every inch of space filled with canvases ranging in size from a few inches to four or five feet big. The works ran the gamut from abstract to landscapes, lit by strategically positioned track lights at the ceiling. Tables filled the open floor space on either side, covered with statues, vases, figurines. Clair couldn't spot a method to the organization. It appeared to be total chaos, yet it was wonderful. If she wasn't working, she could have spent hours here.

Sophie had picked up a small statue from a table on the right. "I love penguins, they're so cute."

The woman stood up from the desk, placed her glasses on top of her head, and walked over. "Those are made by a local artist named Tess Marchum. She crafts each one by hand. I love the way they stand guard at the table, watching over all the other pieces. She made the giraffes and zebras too. Such a talent."

Clair made a mental note to return to this place when she had time to browse. She turned to the woman. "Are you Ms. Edwins?"

"Yes. Please, call me Collette."

Sophie set the penguin back down on the table, patted it on the head. "My name is Sophie Rodriguez. I'm with Missing Children, and this is Detective Clair Norton with Chicago Metro. We'd like to ask you a few questions about Lili Davies."

The woman's smile left her face. "Have you found her? Is she all right?"

"Not yet, but we have a lot of people out looking for her," Clair said. "When was the last time you saw her?"

"The night before last; she closed for me. She was supposed to work last night too, but she didn't come in. When five o'clock came around, I really began to get worried. It wasn't like her. I can't remember the last time she missed a shift, and if she was running late, even only a few minutes, she always called or texted."

"What time was she due in?"

"She usually works the four-to-close shift and locks up," Collette replied.

"The night before last, when she did come in, did you notice anything strange about her?" Clair asked.

The woman shook her head. "Not at all. She got in a few minutes early and was her usual bubbly self. Always smiling, that one. The customers love her." She hesitated for a moment, then lowered her voice. "I saw the paper this morning. Do you think the Monkey Killer took her?"

Clair shook her head. "This isn't the Monkey Killer." She spoke the words aloud but wasn't so certain herself. After the events a few months ago, it felt as if Bishop was finished. His ultimate target had been Arthur Talbot, and he got him. He had no reason to continue. Killers rarely stopped of their own accord, though. If Bishop had just been on hiatus, he'd be itching to come back, and even though these recent crimes didn't fit his usual MO, they reeked of him. Clair could see Bishop's smiling face, and she shook the image from her mind.

"But somebody took her?" Collette asked.

"We think so, yes," Clair told her.

"Have you noticed anyone strange in the gallery over the past few weeks? Someone you didn't recognize or someone who may have paid just a little too much attention to Lili and not enough to the art-work?" Sophie asked.

The woman chewed at the inside of cheek. "Most of our custom-ers are regulars. We do host events here a few times each month and tend to draw in a couple new faces. On a regular day like today, we get our share of browsers too, people I don't know, but nobody in re-cent memory jumps out at me. Usually, Lili gets in at four and I leave around five, so our schedules don't overlap much. It's very possible someone came in after I left. Lili is such a pretty thing, I'm sure she's got her share of male suitors who stop by after I leave. I've caught her friends hanging out in here on more than one occasion, but they're never any trouble. I don't mind it, as long as they don't interfere. It can get quiet in here sometimes, all alone."

Clair eyed the ceiling. "Do you have any security cameras?"

Collette shook her head. "I'm afraid not. This is a nice neighbor-hood, and we don't work with cash, so I've never felt the need to in-stall them."

"You mentioned events," Clair said. "Do they draw a large crowd?"

"Oh yes, we'll get a few hundred people in and out of here when-ever we feature a local artist. We have our regulars, then they invite their friends and fans. There's food and drinks. We try to do them as often as possible," she replied.

Clair turned to Sophie. "If I wanted to stalk a young girl, get close to her, that seems like the best time to do it, right? Large crowd, strange faces. Much less likely to stand out than coming in on his own." She turned back to Ms. Edwins. "Any chance you keep some kind of sign-in sheet for those events?"

Collette nodded. "We do. We gather names, addresses, and e-mails so we can add visitors to our mailing list. We also supply a copy to the featured artist."

"Would it be possible to get copies of those lists?" Clair asked.

At this, Collette hesitated, then reluctantly nodded. "If it will help Lili, of course. Give me a moment."

Clair watched the woman head toward the back of the store and disappear down a hallway behind the desk. She turned back to Sophie. "If our guy came in, I doubt he provided his real name or contact information."

"Then what good will the lists do us?"

"We'll review all the names and isolate the bogus ones—names that don't tie out to the address provided, bad e-mail addresses . . . hopefully that will narrow it down to only a handful of records. Once we do that, we can—"

A scream erupted from the back of the gallery.

Clair tugged her Glock from the holster at her shoulder and ran toward the sound with Sophie behind her. They maneuvered around the desk, down the small hallway, past a dark bathroom, and found themselves in a small storage room. Collette Edwins stood just inside the doorway, one hand still on the light switch, the other pressed to her mouth. She stared at the center of the room.

Clair followed her gaze, her grip on the gun tightening.

Lili Davies's lifeless body hung motionless against a metal shelf, her eyes glossy, empty, her mouth slightly agape. A black electrical cord encircled her neck, the flesh around it purple. She looked horribly pale.

Clair swept the room, holstered her Glock, then went to the girl, her fingers going to her neck in search of a pulse. Nothing. Her skin was cold. The cord around her neck had been tied to the supports of the metal shelf, holding her up.

"Did she hang herself?" Collette choked out.

"No," Clair said. "She was dead before her body was placed here."

"Who else has access to this room?" Sophie asked.

Collette was shaking. "I . . . I was just back here not two hours ago. I had to restock some of the figurines out front. She wasn't here. Nobody was here. I've been alone all morning."

"What about that door?" Clair asked. There was a steel door at the far corner of the room.

"We keep that door locked. It's only opened for deliveries."

Clair reached into her pocket and produced a latex glove, pulled it over her hand, and tested the doorknob. It was locked, as was the deadbolt above it. "Everybody out," she said.

25

Poole

Day 2 • 1:03 p.m.

Special Agent Frank Poole settled into the rusty metal desk he had been assigned in the basement office of Chicago Metro. The boxes of information taken from Detective Porter's apartment were on the table beside him. SAIC Hurless and SA Diener had gone back to the FBI's field office on Roosevelt to check on their other cases after a rushed lunch at a small diner on Wabash. Poole decided to come back here. He expected Hurless to fight him, but instead his supervisor only helped him load the boxes into his car and instructed Poole and the techs to bring everything straight here.

Poole closed the door and switched off the overhead fluorescents, plunging the room into total darkness except for the small lamp burning at his desk.

He opened the file on Barbara McInley and flipped through the contents. He preferred to work like this, in the dark, no distractions. No noise, no bustling office around him, not a single voice except the evidence.

Barbara McInley. Seventeen years old. The Monkey Killer's fifth victim. Bishop took her because her sister, Libby McInley, hit and killed a pedestrian on March 14, 2007. He flipped back to the inside cover of the folder, to the photo of Barbara McInley stapled inside. Beautiful girl. Blond.

He looked up at the whiteboard in the corner of the room, his eyes straining to see the images of Bishop's victims. All brunettes, all but Barbara. He lost himself in those images, and when he glanced back at his watch, he realized nearly ten minutes had passed. He reached for his phone and dialed a number he'd programmed in at the start of this investigation but had yet to use.

The line rang three times before a gruff voice picked up. "Hello?"

Poole cleared his throat. "Detective Porter?"

"Yeah."

"This is Special Agent Frank Poole."

Silence, then: "Okay."

Poole went on. "We're here, on this investigation, because we were asked to be here. You understand that, right? We can't take over a case unless we're invited."

"Who invited you?"

Poole ran his hand through his hair. "If they wanted you to know, they would have told you. I don't think it's my place to communicate that information."

"You called me," Porter said. "What would you like to communicate?"

"If given a choice, I wouldn't intrude like this. I wouldn't want someone else to butt into one of my investigations, and it's not something I want to be party to."

"Yet, here you are."

"Here I am," Poole agreed.

"Someone feels I messed up, and they brought you in to save face —not your fault you're here, just doing your job, is that it?"

"They say you let him go, that you're too close."

"You can believe whatever you want. It's your case now," Porter said.

Poole stood up, his chair squeaking in protest, and walked over to the whiteboard, to the pictures of the girls. "The truth is, I don't care much for the political bullshit of all this. I get the feeling you don't either. You and I, I think we're both after the same thing. We just want to put this monster down."

Porter said nothing.

Poole went on. "My boss and Diener are hoping to make a name for themselves with this case. I think that's their agenda."

"And you don't have an agenda?"

"I don't want this guy to hurt anyone else," Poole replied.

Neither man spoke for a long while. Porter was the first to break the silence. "Why did you call, Agent Poole?"

"Frank," he said. "Call me Frank."

"Why did you call me, Frank?"

Poole returned to his desk, to the file. "Barbara McInley. I got the feeling you were holding something back earlier."

"I told you and your boss, I haven't had a chance to look at the folder."

"But your gut tells you there's something there?"

Again, Porter said nothing.

Poole continued. "My gut is telling me to trust your gut."

Poole heard nothing from the other end of the line. He said nothing either. He'd wait for the other man to speak.

Porter finally let out a sigh. "That day when I got called back into the case, I had been out on leave for a few weeks because of my wife's murder. Nash caught the body, the one we thought was the Monkey Killer. Things moved so fast. We brought Bishop in from CSI because he seemed sharp. We weren't looking for a killer anymore. We thought he was dead. Our entire focus fell on finding Emory. We got back to the war room, all the key players from the 4MK task force were there, and there was Bishop, the new guy. We ran the evidence. It sometimes helps me to run from start to finish to keep it all straight in my head, sometimes it sparks something new, something jumps out. Anyway, we ran the evidence for Bishop but also for the rest of us, a bit of a refresher."

Poole nodded. "You wanted to run the data from a new angle, no longer looking for the man behind the evidence, but use the data to try and piece together who he was, where he would have taken Emory."

"Yeah. Sometimes when you shift focus like that, something comes to you from left field. Something you didn't catch with the first go-around. The case became more about our missing girl," Porter said.

"As we reviewed the evidence, Bishop weighed in. And I swear to God, even looking back now, that little shit seemed like all of this was new to him. He stared at the boards not only with a straight face, but I could see the gears turning in his head, I could see him thinking through the evidence, connecting dots, making things fit, and generating theories. I've played it over and over in my mind, and not once did he do anything to tip us off to the fact that he was really our killer. He played the part of Paul Watson CSI so well, I think even he forgot who he was—he looked like he wanted to catch 4MK as much as we did. I know you probably think I'm just making excuses, that I was sloppy, that someone should have seen through the ruse, but his character was that complete. He not only wore a mask, he became that mask."

"He's a sociopath," Poole said. "In that moment, he may have been Paul Watson. People like him, when they don't have a conscience of their own, they're like a blank canvas, an empty vessel. They can drop a personality into that space and it takes over, fills that void. I've seen others like him. In some, the personality takes over completely, and in others they're all somehow in there together, aware of each other."

"Well, like I said, in that moment he was Paul Watson, and Paul Watson looked like he wanted to catch 4MK. As we reviewed the evidence, as we went over each victim's story, he paused at McInley. He made a point to mention she was the only blonde. At the time, it just seemed like a rookie comment. I mean, we obviously all knew she was the only blonde, we'd stared at these photos for five years. But he lingered there, if only for a second. As a rookie comment, I let it pass, but now—"

"Now you're replaying that scene, you know you were in the room with 4MK, and 4MK lingered on Barbara McInley," Poole summarized.

"Yeah."

"That's not much."

"I think I've said that a few times now. Nothing solid, only my gut," Porter said. "There is the crime itself too. McInley's sister killed a pedestrian in a hit-and-run, it was an accident. With all the other victims, Bishop played off the fact that someone related to them com-

THE FIFTH TO DIE • 125

mitted an intentional crime. Something premeditated, thought out, and orchestrated. A hit-and-run doesn't fit."

Poole looked back to the file. "According to the arrest report, she hit a pedestrian who was crossing the street against the light. He stepped out into traffic into the path of her car."

"If she wouldn't have run, she wouldn't have been charged. Not for something like that," Porter said. "There's the similarity to the way Jacob Kittner died too. Don't forget, Bishop paid that guy to step out into traffic. I don't believe in coincidences."

"Me either," Poole replied. "Give me a second." He pulled up Libby McInley's record on his laptop and reviewed her file. "According to records, she was charged in March 2007 and convicted of man-slaughter for the vehicular death of one Franklin Kirby in July 2007, sentenced to ten years, of which she served seven and a handful of months. She was released on parole six weeks ago."

"What was the name of her victim again?"

"Franklin Kirby. Why? Do you know him?"

Again, Porter went quiet.

"Porter. If the name means something to you, you need to tell me," Poole said.

"You should check on her. Let me know what you find."

"Why?" Poole asked, but Porter had disconnected the call.

26

Porter

Day 2 • 1:04 p.m.

Across town, Porter stood at his mailbox in the lobby of his apartment building, his cell phone in one hand and the *TV Guide* in the other. He was staring down at the floor, at the picture that had fallen from the pages of the magazine when he freed it from his cluttered mailbox.

Porter knelt, leaned in closer.

The photo was five-by-seven, black and white, on matte paper. A picture of a woman in a prison jumpsuit being led through an outdoor chainlink walkway, one guard in front, another behind her. Her hands were cuffed behind her back, and her head hung low, her face barely visible in the shadows. It appeared to be a distance shot, grainy, as if enhanced with software beyond the capabilities of the original lens. Porter could make out ORLEANS PARISH PRISON on the wall behind her in block letters.

Porter dropped the *TV Guide* to the floor beside it, picked up the photograph with his gloved hand, and flipped it over. On the back was one simple sentence written in black ink.

I think I found her.

B

27

The Man in the Black Knit Cap

Day 2 • 1:14 p.m.

"Did she see?" the voice on the line said.

The man in the black knit cap pressed the phone against his ear. "No, she did not."

He sat at a small desk made of pressboard and black plastic, the top littered with paper, colored markers, and drawings. So many drawings. The desk was under a window overlooking the street. Outside, his neighbor walked his dog, a small white Lhasa apso dressed in a red and green sweater. The dog lifted its back leg and peed in the snow. The man in the black knit cap watched the yellow stain grow, a stain besmirching his yard. His neighbor lived ten feet over, yet he walked his dog here every day to pee. The dog finished its business, scratched at the edge of the sidewalk with its stubby back legs, then tugged toward their house.

The wound on the side of his head itched, and he scratched at it, the knit cap shifting position under his fingers, slipping on his bald head.

"The next one will see," the voice on the other end of the call said. "She will be the one."

"I hope so."

"Did you put her where I told you?"

"Yes."

"Did anyone see you?"

"Nobody sees me anymore."

"Did anyone *see* you?" the voice repeated.

"No."

"Good."

"Yeah."

The man picked up a green marker and began coloring one of the drawings on his desk. His hand began to shake, the ink crossed the lines, and he threw the marker across the room.

He heard a sigh through the phone. The man behind the voice could see him, somehow—he could always see him. "Sooner or later, they all see. It's just a matter of time." He was talking about the girls again.

The man in the black knit cap missed the girls. The house seemed so quiet without them. He picked up a red marker, held it to the drawing, and watched his hand begin to shake. He put the marker down, and the shaking stopped. He stretched his fingers out, made a fist, stretched again. The movement felt good, felt normal. He stopped. His hand wasn't shaking. He picked up the marker. His hand wasn't shaking. He touched the marker to the paper. His hand did not shake. He began to color. The small lines he made grew longer, wider, the marker taking on a mind of its own, scribbling, the hand shaking. He pressed harder, but it did no good. The ink crossed the lines. The red ink spread over the green he had tried moments earlier, the color turning a muddled brown. The lines of the drawing disappearing under these involuntary scribbles, the image slowly dying under his touch.

He dropped the marker and turned in the chair, facing the room.

His daughter's red sweater lay crumpled on the floor behind him, her tiny shoes beside the bed.

"I want to get the next one now, before it gets dark," he said.

"You must be patient."

He knew the voice was right. The voice was always right.

He scratched at his head again, his nails digging into raw flesh, his fingers coming away moist with blood. "But you'll tell me when?"

"I will."

"I'm ready."

"I know."

The line went dead then.

The man in the black knit cap turned in the chair, again facing the desk, and set the phone down. He looked out the window. The dog was gone, his neighbor was gone, and the stain in the bright white snow remained.

He picked up a yellow marker and began to color the drawing.

28

Porter

Day 2 • 2:17 p.m.

Porter had spent the last hour sitting on his couch, the photograph on the coffee table before him. He had brought over the reading lamp from his bedside, removed the shade, and swapped out the bulb for a hundred-watt. The light was bright, unforgiving. He leaned over the picture, studying every inch, every pixel.

His mind raced.

Libby McInley killed Franklin Kirby. Barbara McInley died for the crime.

Of course, he knew the name.

Bishop told him that name right before he pushed Arthur Talbot into the elevator shaft. The name Franklin Kirby was etched into his skull along with all the loose strings surrounding 4MK. Franklin Kirby was the real name of the man who ran off with Bishop's mother and neighbor, a lover to one, possibly both. He killed his partner, the man Bishop called Mr. Stranger in his diary. The man Bishop later told him was really named Felton Briggs. Briggs had been some type of security officer or private investigator employed by Talbot. Neither name had ever turned up in the various databases Porter searched.

Ghosts, just like Bishop.

Until now.

He looked back at the photograph. His eyes fixed on the woman.

He sat there for a long while, unmoving.

When he looked up, he eyed his apartment. The feds had made a mess of the place, pulling down books, emptying cabinets, dumping drawers. Heather's picture stared up at the ceiling, knocked over in their search.

He didn't want to be here.

He couldn't be here.

Not now.

Porter stared at the photograph on the coffee table.

Ten minutes.

Twenty minutes.

"Fuck it."

He stood, went to the bedroom closet, and pulled out his suitcase. Five minutes later the bag was packed and sitting at the front door.

He went to the freezer, removed the foil package labeled *ground beef*, peeled it open, and removed the contents—nearly three thousand dollars in cash at last count. He folded the bills, shoved them into his pocket, and returned to the living room.

He surveyed the room again, then went over to his La-Z-Boy, his favorite chair. He picked it up by the base and turned the chair on its side. The loud *bang* as it hit the hardwood echoed through the otherwise quiet apartment.

Porter slipped his fingers under the material at the bottom and tugged. It came away, held only with Velcro.

Bishop's diary was duct-taped to the wood frame under the cloth. He never did log it into evidence. He pulled the small book free, removed the tape, and slipped the black and white composition book into his pocket with the money. Returning to the table, he retrieved the photograph from Bishop, his hand no longer gloved, and pocketed that too.

Porter took out his cell phone, switched it off, and placed it on the coffee table.

At the front door, he took one last look at his apartment, at Heather's fallen picture, then picked up his suitcase and left, locking the door behind him.

29

Clair

Day 2 • 6:23 p.m.

Clair handed Nash a cup of coffee and fell down into the chair beside him. "This guy is like a ghost. You could have heard a pin drop in that gallery, and somehow he managed to pick the back-door locks—two of them, mind you—get into the storeroom, and position Lili's body, all without making enough noise to get the attention of the manager, who wasn't more than ten or fifteen feet down the hall."

Nash took a drink of the coffee, his nose wrinkling. "This is horrible."

"It may have been sitting in that pot a while. It looked a little crusty around the edges."

He looked down into his cup, shrugged, and drank some more.

Eisley had agreed to perform an emergency autopsy on the body of Lili Davies; they'd been waiting in his office at the Medical Examiner's Office for a little over an hour. Aside from Lili's body, no evidence was found at the gallery. Not a single fingerprint or shoe track. The unsub most likely wiped everything down on his way out. There was only the girl.

Eisley had ordered she be brought straight here so he could get to work.

Clair and Nash agreed to wait for the results, while Klozowski checked in with his IT team. Sophie Rodriguez went straight to the

Davies home. They didn't want the family to learn about all this on the news, like the Reynoldses had.

"So Ella Reynolds was looking at cars?" Clair asked.

Nash had told her what they found in her browser history at Starbucks.

He took another drink of the coffee, forcing it down. "Cars R Us on Pulaski Road. For about two weeks she searched their inventory nearly every day. Then she seemed to find something she liked, a 2012 Mazda2 Sport for $7,495, bright green with cloth interior, 1.5-liter engine, automatic transmission, and seventy-five thousand miles."

"That's high mileage."

"Yeah." Nash forced a smile. "That was my first thought too."

"You said the searches were encrypted, right? Why would she hide something like that from her parents?" Clair asked.

Nash shrugged. "Maybe they didn't want her buying a car yet. She was only fifteen. Maybe they thought she was too young."

"Seems weird to be looking at cars when you're not even old enough to drive."

"Hell, I was ready to buy when I was eight years old," Nash replied.

"At fifteen, girls are usually interested in guys with cars, not buying their own car."

"Not all girls."

"Guess not."

"Kloz and I planned to head there next, when you called about Lili," he told her. "We'll drive over when we're done here."

Clair remembered something Gabrielle Deegan said. "You know, Lili Davies's best friend, Gabby, said that Lili was in the market for a car too. For the last few weeks, all she texted were pictures of cars, trying to figure out what she wanted. Her dad said he'd buy her one when she graduated."

She watched Nash take another drink of his coffee, mulling this over.

"Any chance she visited this dealer? Maybe that's our link."

"Our unsub is a used-car salesman?"

Nash stood and slowly paced the office. "He'd have easy access.

Think about how that process works. Somebody like Ella or Lili finds a car they like, they go down to the lot, and they're met by our unsub. It's unthreatening, they're going to him instead of the other way around. He shows them the car they came to see, or shows them other cars on the lot. They spend some quality time together. When was the last time you got off a car lot in less than an hour? They rope you in. They ramble around with the salesperson, get to know each other, maybe go for a few test drives. All of these things are disarming. Girls like Lili and Ella may have their guard up when a guy approaches them on the street, but a scenario like this? Hell, they'd be trying to get on the unsub's good side, so he puts in a word with the finance guy."

Clair's eyes went wide. "When you go for a test drive, they take a copy of your driver's license, all your personal information. He'd have that when they left."

Nash shook his head. "Neither girl had a license yet, remember?"

"Maybe they had to fill out a form or something."

"Maybe."

"It's worth checking, for sure."

"Yeah."

Eisley pushed through the double doors, drying his hands with a paper towel. He tilted his head back toward the examination room. "Come on."

Clair stood and followed him back inside, with Nash behind her. She popped a piece of gum into her mouth and offered one to Nash.

He shook his head. "I think I'm getting used to the smell."

"In this office, the day you get used to the smell is the day you retire," Eisley told him.

Lili Davies's naked body was laid out on the table, her chest still open with a large Y incision that began at her shoulders and ended above her pubic bone. When she came into view, Nash went pale and reached out a hand to Clair. "I'll take that gum now."

Clair snickered and handed him a piece. She leaned over the body. Lili's face looked so peaceful.

Eisley tilted the large light above the table, focusing the beam on the open chest cavity. "Normally, I would have closed her up, but I wanted you to see this." He reached inside, pointing beneath her ribs. "See these marks on the lungs?"

Clair followed his finger to dark streaks across the pink surface. There were dozens of them on both lungs. "What are they?"

"When the lungs fill with fluid and strain against the pressure, it can sometimes cause bruising," Eisley told her.

"So, she drowned? Like Ella?" Nash said.

Eisley nodded. "In salt water, just like Ella."

Clair leaned in closer. "I thought our bodies don't bruise after the heart stops pumping. If she died from drowning, should there be bruising?"

"It's normal to find both pre- and postmortem bruising on the lungs from drowning," Eisley told her.

"Then why are you showing this to us?"

Eisley leaned back in, his finger tracing the girl's lungs. "See how some of the marks are much darker than others, like these here?"

Clair nodded.

"This indicates multiple traumas. Some are older than others."

"You mean, she drowned more than once?" Nash said.

"From what I am observing, this girl drowned six, maybe seven times over a twenty-four-hour period."

Clair frowned. "How is that possible?"

"I think your unsub drowned her, then revived her," he said. "If you look closely at her ribs, you'll see micro fractures. I think he performed CPR on her. I also found multiple electrical burns from a stun gun, so he used one either to subdue her or to revive her."

"Would that work?"

Eisley shook his head. "No. The electricity would dissipate across her skin. It would need to be directed to the heart. Maybe if he placed a metal plate under her when he did it, but I'm skeptical even that would work. CPR, though, he could have brought her back with CPR."

"Multiple times," Clair said.

"Six or seven, at least."

"My God."

Nash lowered his head, scratched at his eyebrow. "So he drowned her repeatedly until he was unable to revive her."

"That would be my conclusion as well, yes," Eisley said.

Clair stepped back from the table. "Why . . . why would . . ." she said, more to herself than anyone else.

Eisley frowned. "I'm afraid there's more."

Clair watched as he crossed the room and pulled back the sheet covering a body against the wall.

Ella Reynolds.

"I reexamined 14982F and found the same marks. The near-freezing and thawing of the body damaged her cells, making this condition less pronounced. I should have noticed regardless. I have no excuse—it slipped by me. I focused primarily on the drowning aspect itself, and my attempts to minimize damage from the conditions in which you found the body."

"Ella," Nash said softly. "Her name is Ella."

Eisley raised his left palm. "Well, yes. Ella. Of course."

"He drowned and revived her over and over again too?" Nash asked.

Eisley nodded grimly. "In her case, it appears this took place over a much longer period of time. Sometimes days between each event, whereas with 149 . . . with Lili, only an hour or less elapsed between each. There is a clear escalation in your unsub's behavior. Had Lili been permitted more time to recover, she may have been able to survive. Unfortunately, the human body can only take so much. She wasn't given a chance."

"What about Ella's father?" Clair asked. "What did you find there?"

Eisley gently replaced the white sheet covering Ella's body, then crossed the room to the metal drawers built into the wall. He tugged one open and gestured for them to come closer. "I've been trying to call Porter, but I'm getting voice mail."

"Sam had to take a step back for a little while," Nash said.

"Everything okay?"

"Just a personal matter."

Eisley looked like he was about to press further, then changed his mind. The body of Floyd Reynolds was encased in a thick black body bag. He slid the zipper down from the head to midsection, then spread the plastic so they could see inside. The skin was pale white save for the thick purple and black cut at his neck. It was worst at the center, above the Adam's apple, and grew thinner and lighter as it spread out across his neck, ending at about the ears.

Eisley followed the line, with his finger hovering about an inch above the surface. "This is from a very thin wire, piano or electric guitar string, most likely. They sell thin cable at most hardware stores, but to me this appears thinner than what you would find there. Like I said, resembling string from a musical instrument. Porter had mentioned finding a footprint on the back of the car seat. That fits with what I'm seeing here. The unsub got the string around this man's neck, then pulled at it with tremendous force. Because the back of his head was cradled against the headrest, the unsub had tremendous leverage. If you look closely at the center here, you'll see the string cut nearly to the windpipe. The trauma lessens at the sides, consistent with strangulation from behind."

"So, definitely the cause of death?" Nash asked.

Eisley nodded. "I'm confident of that. I found nothing else."

Clair's cell phone vibrated. She plucked it from her belt and read the text. "Randal Davies just suffered a major stroke."

30

Clair

Day 2 • 6:51 p.m.

Clair and Nash fought the tail end of rush hour traffic and pulled into the emergency room drive of John H. Stroger, Jr. Hospital about thirty minutes later. They found Sophie Rodriguez sitting in the corner of the waiting room with Grace Davies, Lili's mother.

Sophie spotted them as they came through the automated glass doors and quickly walked over to meet them. "We were in their kitchen. I broke the news about Lili, and they took it about as well as could be expected. He was holding his wife, then his body just went limp. She tried to hold him up, but he's a big guy. He fell to the floor and began to convulse. I dialed 911 immediately, and the paramedics arrived about four minutes later. The convulsions stopped by that point, but his breathing was labored and his heart rate was very low. I had trouble finding a pulse, but when I did, I only recorded about forty beats per minute."

"Does he have any kind of history?" Clair asked.

Sophie shook her head. "Nothing, according to his wife. He exercises daily. Even with all this going on, he was prepping for a run when I got there, said it helped him clear his head."

"His daughter is missing, and he wanted to go for a jog?" Nash said.

"People cope in strange ways." Sophie glanced back at Grace Davies. "She lost her daughter, and now her husband is in ICU. I can't imagine what she's going through."

A doctor pushed through the double doors at the back of the ER, scanned the crowd, and started toward Grace Davies. Clair, Nash, and Sophie rushed back over.

"I am so sorry, Grace," the doctor said. "This is the last thing you need in your life right now."

"You know each other?" Clair asked.

The doctor's eyes went narrow. "And you are?"

"I'm Detective Clair Norton, this is Detective Nash, and Sophie Rodriguez with Missing Children."

His face softened. "You're helping to find Lili." He nodded, then: "She's such a sweet girl. I've known her her entire life. Who would do such a thing?"

Grace's face went white, and her red, puffy eyes again filled with tears. Sophie put an arm around her.

Clair told the doctor Lili had been found. His eyes were on Grace Davies the entire time. When she finished, he took a deep breath. "This is horrible." He went to Grace and wrapped his arms around her, whispered something at her ear.

"How do you know the Davies family?" Clair asked.

"Randal works here in Oncology. I've been head of ER going on six years now, we're a tight group at this hospital," the doctor said. "Randal and I both completed our residency at McGaw."

Nash took a step closer. "What is Dr. Davies's condition? Is he going to pull through?"

"He's stable for now, but the stroke may have caused permanent damage. I'm waiting for the results of the CT scan to come back." He released Mrs. Davies and took a step back. "Grace, how long has Randal been taking lisinopril?"

The woman's forehead puckered. "What's lisinopril?"

"It's used to regulate high blood pressure."

"Randal doesn't have high blood pressure."

The doctor placed a hand on her shoulder. "Is it possible he had high blood pressure and didn't want to tell you? Maybe he didn't want to worry you."

Mrs. Davies shook her head. She pulled her phone from her purse and began tapping at the screen. "He doesn't have high blood pressure. We both test a few times each week with this Bluetooth cuff he brought home from a conference last year." She handed him the phone. "See, it records our results."

The doctor scrolled through the readings. "These are all normal."

"Randal exercises daily," she told him. "At his last physical, the doctor told him he was as fit as a thirty-year-old."

"If that's the case, we have a serious problem," the doctor said, stroking his chin.

Clair had remained silent through all of this. Something was wrong. "What is it?"

At first the doctor didn't speak, lost in his own thoughts. Then: "We found a concentrated level of lisinopril in his blood. If I had to guess, he took a rather large dose—three, maybe four hundred milligrams."

"What's considered normal?" Nash asked.

"Anywhere from two-point-five milligrams to forty, no more than that."

Clair turned to Sophie, but before she could ask her a question, Sophie started nodding. "I'm thinking, I'm thinking . . . we were in the kitchen. I had a glass of water, Mrs. Davies was drinking—"

"I was drinking orange juice," Mrs. Davies said. "Randal made a pot of coffee. I don't drink coffee. It tends to keep me up at night."

"You think someone spiked the coffee?" Nash said to Clair.

Clair began to speak, then pulled him aside, outside of earshot. "Our unsub killed Ella Reynolds's father," she said in a low voice.

"He strangled and nearly removed the head of Ella Reynolds's father with piano wire," Nash said. "This a drug overdose, hardly the same MO. Maybe Dr. Davies had high blood pressure and was self-medicating to manage the condition, hiding it from his wife for some reason. Who else takes their blood pressure on a regular basis at home?"

Clair raised her wrist and showed him her Apple Watch. "This thing tracks every step I make during the day, monitors my heart rate, it even tells me when I've been on my ass too long. Everyone is tracking their health stats these days." She poked his oversize belly. "Everyone should be, anyway."

"I'm comfortably plump, Clair-bear. I don't need some gizmo on my wrist to remind me of that four times per day."

"If a normal dose is two-point-five milligrams to forty, and he had ten times that, it's no accident. Someone tried to kill him," Clair said.

"It could be a suicide attempt," Nash pointed out.

"Only one way to find out," Clair said. She pulled out her phone, dialed Metro. "I'm getting CSI out there."

Nash nodded reluctantly. "I'll ask Mrs. Davies where she hides the spare key."

31

Poole

Day 2 • 7:04 p.m.

Special Agent Frank Poole parked his red Jeep Cherokee on the 300 block of Mckeen Road in Downers Grove a few houses down from 317 on the right. Barbara McInley's file lay open on the passenger seat.

This was the only known address for Libby McInley, noted in her file by her parole officer upon her release six weeks earlier.

He shouldn't be out here.

He knew better.

A late-eighties Ford Taurus sat in the driveway. By the looks of it, the car had sat there for some time. The color appeared to be a faded burgundy or brown, hard to tell in the remaining trickle of evening light. There were no tracks in the driveway, snow piled high on top. Substantial rust, low tire pressure, neglected, forgotten. Long blades of brown grass and weeds poked out of the fresh white layer of snow, winter's attempt at covering up an unkempt lawn, failing. The house was a single-story box of a thing, no real discernible style. Four walls and a roof with an attached one-car garage. White paint had long ago given up its hold on the siding, and dark wood shone through from beneath where it had peeled away. The roof was in need of replacement, visibly sagging over what was most likely a very small living room.

Lights began coming on in the surrounding houses, but 317 remained dark, lifeless.

You want to take a look, a voice at the back of his mind whispered. *Just a quick peek, and you can be on your way. No harm, no foul, nobody will ever be the wiser.*

Poole *did* want to take a peek. He wanted to talk to her. Porter had been right. Something felt off about her sister's death. It nagged at him, and Poole knew if he didn't do this, he'd spend the next two weeks thinking about doing it. The only way to get it out of his system was to walk up to that house, ring the bell, and have a few words with Ms. McInley.

After hanging up with Porter, Poole had run a detailed search for Franklin Kirby, McInley's hit-and-run victim. He came up blank. The man had been identified by the driver's license in his wallet. There was a photo of it in the McInley file but no record of him in the driver's license database. The number on the license was assigned to a woman named Lesley Carmichael, forty-six, living in Woodlawn—*not* Franklin Kirby. Libby McInley hit and killed a man carrying false identification, although still a name Porter clearly recognized.

Poole stepped from the Cherokee out into the cold evening wind, closed the door behind him, and crossed the street to 317. Neither the public sidewalk nor the stone walkway leading to the front door had been shoveled. The front porch was also lost beneath a layer of at least four inches of snow. He pressed the bell with a gloved finger, heard the double chime inside, and waited.

Nothing.

He rang again, glancing back at the driveway.

Poole turned back to the door.

No sound from within.

No lights.

Libby McInley might have spotted him, killed the lights. She wouldn't be the first person on parole to hide from a cop on their doorstep. There was no current employment information listed in her file. She probably had little reason to leave the house. Hell, he wouldn't be out in this weather if he didn't have to be.

He knocked on the door, three loud raps. "Ms. McInley? I'm Special Agent Frank Poole. I know you're in there. Open the door."

He had no idea if she was in there, but the ruse typically worked.

Poole blew into his gloved hands. He felt like he was standing in a tub of ice water. His breath fluttered through the air and dissipated.

Poole stepped off the porch and over a small hedge, then pressed his face to the large picture window. The glass was cold, covered in frost. He couldn't see inside.

If the heat were on, you'd feel it at the glass, right? Who doesn't have their heat on in this kind of weather?

He stepped back and began to circle the house, attempting to look in each window as he went. If one of the neighbors saw him, they'd surely be dialing 911 right now. At the side of the house he nearly tripped over a rusty bicycle, an old red Schwinn lost beneath the thick snowdrift. There were also the remains of potted plants, long since dead, and random lengths of garden hose, coiled and forgotten for the winter.

Around back he found a wood deck. A black Weber BBQ lay on its side, lost to slumber, lawn chairs piled up around it, no rhyme or reason. He stepped up onto the deck, the boards creaking under his weight, popping noises.

Could be rotten. Might fall through.

He carefully made his way to the back door.

The screen was cut.

A straight cut, about five inches long, enough for a man to get his hand inside the door.

Enough to unlock the screen door, get to work on that deadbolt with a lock picker's kit.

Poole tried the doorknob. Unlocked.

He reached inside his coat, unsnapped and removed his Glock 22, held it low, against his hip, pointing at the ground. A small LED flashlight was attached to the barrel. He flicked it on with his forefinger.

He gave the door a little push. It protested, frozen in the frame. Again, with more force. When it finally opened, it did so with a loud thwack.

The smell hit him first, the sweet, sickly odor of something turned, something gone bad. It wafted out, warning him off, telling him to get back into his car and drive away.

"Ms. McInley? This is Special Agent Frank Poole. I'm coming inside."

The wood door opened into the kitchen. Poole gave it a push with the toe of his shoe while sweeping the room with the barrel of his gun, the light. Dishes were piled high at the sink, the counter buried under them. There were also pizza boxes and cartons from Chinese takeout, empty soda cans and water bottles.

The heat was off.

As he approached the sink, he realized the dishes were frozen in a block of ice. A thin coat of frost covered everything.

Still, the smell.

Poole walked past the kitchen counter into a small dining room. Boxes and paper littered the table—job applications, copies of a résumé, "Elizabeth McInley" printed in bold font at the top. There were newspapers, unopened bills, clothing—a woman's blouse and bra, all haphazardly tossed about.

"Ms. McInley? Are you in here?"

Poole's breath floated through the cold air. He spotted the thermostat on the wall and glanced at it. The heat was switched off, the dial turned to the coldest position.

An open doorway stood to his left. Poole followed it into the small living room, the gun and flashlight pointed forward now, leading him. To his right stood the front door, along with the picture window he had tried to peer into, as opaque from this side as it was from the front yard. On his left, a couch lined the wall, facing a small television propped up on milk crates. There was a cheap pressboard table in front of the couch. Someone had shoved the contents to the floor— magazines, a remote, a few utility bills, and some advertising circulars.

Sitting on top of the table, spaced evenly, centered, were three white boxes tied off with black string. The white of the boxes was riddled with specks of brown and crimson, a spatter of sorts.

There was a small bathroom directly across from where he stood, and another door to the left of the television, most likely a bedroom.

Poole stepped forward and swept his eyes over the bathroom. The white tub was ringed with brown, the sink covered in dry toothpaste.

A moldy towel was on the floor, bunched up and shoved to the side near the toilet. Someone had wiped at a spot in the middle of the mirror; Poole's hazy reflection stared back at him.

He backed out of the bathroom into the living room, his gun now pointed at the bedroom door. He saw the boxes on the table from the corner of his eye. He tried not to look at them. Poole approached the open bedroom door with a wide arc, preferring to enter the room straight on rather than sliding against the wall and going in from the side. The beam of his flashlight dancing over the walls revealed a ratty dresser, the bed.

A woman's body was tied to the bed at all four corners. Her clothing had been cut away, the tattered remains scattered about the floor. Her flesh was covered in tiny red cuts, thousands of them, every exposed inch. The eyes were gone, two black sockets. Her mouth was filled with dry, crusty blood. Poole knew that beneath her matted hair her ear was gone too. He'd find those things in the boxes.

He removed the flashlight from his gun and holstered the weapon.

He stared at the remains of Libby McInley.

32

Poole

Day 2 • 7:12 p.m.

Poole stood perfectly still, his breath caught in the air before him, thin wisps of white curling about.

The room felt so still.

When you enter a room with at least one person already present, you know they are there. The human body somehow feels this person on an instinctual level. Your sense of caution, self-preservation, these things heighten. There is a subtle surge of adrenaline as the body takes in the sight and sound of this person, the body language and demeanor. Nearly instantaneously, the brains jumps to judgment— am I attracted to this person or repulsed? Indifferent or taken aback? Our body, our minds, come to all these conclusions in less time than it takes to blink an eye.

If the person in the room is alive.

When you enter a room occupied only by the dead, there is none of this. Without the soul, the body is just a husk, a shell, and somehow the mind knows that too. Different signals are sent: How did this person die? When did she die? Is whoever or whatever killed her still here? Could that something hurt me?

Poole looked down at the body of Libby McInley, and he felt nothing but a profound sense of loss, one that caused his heart to ache.

He stepped closer to the bed, the beam of his flashlight slipping over her body.

Her fingers and toes had been removed. He found them lined up neatly on the nightstand, a pair of stained lobster shears beside them.

Bishop had never done that before. He was escalating.

Poole tried a lamp beside the bed. The bulb had been removed.

With 4MK's previous victims, the kill room always eluded them. He staged the bodies when he wanted them to be found. Not once had they learned where he actually killed them. SAIC Hurless suspected that he killed them in the tunnels beneath the city, but Poole always felt differently. Poole believed Bishop had a kill room, someplace secluded, meaningful to him, someplace he could work without disruption, someplace that could eat the screams before they escaped.

Libby McInley died in immense pain. She died slowly. And she died here, alone.

There was blood everywhere. The beam of Poole's flashlight traced it up the walls behind the bed, across the sheets, to the green shag carpet beneath his feet. He shouldn't be stepping here, not like this. He was most likely contaminating potential evidence, but something told him they wouldn't find anything here—nothing useful, anyway. They'd only find whatever Bishop wanted them to find.

Poole leaned in close to the body, his flashlight over her spoiled flesh, the tiny cuts.

Razor blade.

Each no more than a half inch. So many, her skin covered in dried blood.

Poole removed his glove and reached out to her, his fingers brushing over her forearm.

She was cold but not frozen. The heat had been turned off in the house long before she died—days, maybe a week earlier. She had died recently, within the past day or two.

It was then that he saw something in the cuts. He hadn't seen it at first, probably because of the direction he faced. He didn't see it until he looked down at her arm from the head of the bed.

Words.

He had not just cut her with a razor blade. He had written upon her, her body a canvas under his brush. Tiny words, barely visible under the blood. The arms bled less tied to the bedposts. They were above her heart.

You are evil — You are evil — YOU are evil — you

The same phrase, over and over again, every inch of exposed skin.

She had been alive when he did these things. The small pools of blood at each cut told him so. He started at her feet and worked his way up. He could tell that too from the amount of blood at each wound. She finally died somewhere near the rib cage. He continued beyond that point, but the cuts were swifter after.

He hadn't enjoyed it after she died. He needed to finish his work, though.

This was violent, this was revenge.

"Who was Franklin Kirby to you?" Poole asked aloud of both Libby McInley and Anson Bishop. Neither answered.

Ten minutes later he retraced his steps back out of the house, back to his Jeep Cherokee. He climbed inside, started the engine, and placed a call to SAIC Hurless. He considered calling Detective Porter too but changed his mind. He wanted to see his face when he talked to him about this. He needed to understand exactly what Porter knew.

33

Porter
Day 2 • 10:04 p.m.

Detective Sam Porter arrived in New Orleans at a little after ten, following a two-hour layover in Dallas, the only flight he could book same day. While in Dallas, he attempted to eat at a McDonald's in the terminal, but his stomach was a mess. He couldn't keep anything down.

From the New Orleans airport, Porter took a cab directly to the Orleans Parish Prison on Gravier Street. He told the driver to circle the prison until Porter spotted the chainlink-surrounded sidewalk and the sign from the photograph. There he asked the driver to stop and wait for him.

Porter got out of the cab and crossed the street, sweating in his heavy coat even at this late hour. He had never been outside of Chicago during the winter. The difference in temperature this far south was amazing. The air was thick, humid, filled with the distant stench of a city that felt used, abused, and hosed down nightly.

He approached a guard stationed near the gate. The man told him visiting hours started at nine and went until six, no exceptions. The warden would be in at seven. Take it up with him.

The guard didn't recognize the woman in the photograph, but he did recognize the guard walking in front of her. "That's Vince Weidner. He's on days, gets in at eight."

Porter thanked him and returned to the cab.

"You got someone in there?" the driver asked, and Porter pulled the door closed.

"Someone, yeah."

"I spent my share in that place, probably be in there now if my cousin hadn't hooked me up with this gig. Tough to make a living around here. The jobs pay just this side of shit, and all the tourists drive up the real estate. A regular joe can't afford to live in the city on what you get. Got to live in one of the outer parishes and commute. Or you got to find a way to augment your income."

"That how you ended up in there? Augmented income?"

The driver let out a chuckle. "My other cousin taught me the fine art of pickpocketing. He can separate just about any man from his wallet."

"If he's so good, how'd you get caught?"

"Didn't say *I* was good at it. I think Cousin Mic may have left out a step or two during training. I got nabbed on my first attempt. Had my fingers in some man's back pocket, he grabbed my wrist and snapped it. I yelled so loud, three cops came over to see what all the ruckus was about. I shouldn't have picked such a big son a bitch for my first mark, but I figured he wouldn't feel much with all that bulk in the way. I was very wrong."

"How long did you get?"

The driver let out a sigh. "Three long weeks and a day. Time served by the time I made it to trial. That was enough for me, though. I got no interest in seeing the inside of that place again, no sir. My butt is perfectly happy right here in this seat. Speaking of which, where are we heading?"

Porter's eyes were locked on the building. Beige stone, narrow windows. She was in there somewhere. "What can you tell me about the warden?"

"Not a damn thing. I got in there and kept my head down, didn't speak to damn near anybody. I did my few weeks in my lonesome, washed the stink off when I got out. I saw the warden for all of two minutes when I first came in off the bus, and he didn't speak a word, just watched the guards drive the fresh cattle into their stalls," the driver said. "Hard-looking man, that one. Comes with the job, I suppose." He looked at Porter in the rearview mirror. "Probably none of my business, but what's your friend in there for?"

"Dunno."

"Reason I ask is the minimum-security prisoners are housed in the other building at the east wing. We get a lot of drunk and disorderly around Orleans—most of the rides I take out here are to pick someone up who had one or ten too many the night before in the Quarter and ended up getting hauled off for a sobering night in the tombs. The east wing is on the other side of the prison. This here side is for the hardcore criminals. The ones who need a little more than a one-night scare to get them right with God. You gotta go into the right building, or you'll waste an hour getting to the front of the line before you find out you're in the wrong place," he explained.

"She's in this building."

"Oh, well, that's too bad."

"Is there a hotel near here?" Porter asked.

"Shit, no place you'd wanna stay. Why don't we head back to the strip and get you something nice on Bourbon."

"I need someplace close."

The man drew in a long breath. "Well, we got the Traveler's Best up the block, but I didn't even let my cousin stay there, and that was after he got me busted."

"That's fine," Porter said.

The driver rolled his eyes and slipped the car into gear. "Your vacation, spend it the way you like. Fair warning, though—you throw beads from your balcony at someone in that part of town, and they're likely to empty a .22 on you."

The hotel was not in the best of neighborhoods. Only a few blocks from the prison, the squat pink building sat atop a parking garage, two stories of rooms beneath a large fluorescent sign that read TRAVELER'S BEST VALUE INN HOTEL — VACANCY. Half the lights were out, and two of the bulbs flickered from behind the dirty white plastic.

The driver slipped the cab into Park at the side of the building. "You sure about this?"

Porter was already halfway out the door. "They take cash, right?"

"You could probably trade a pack of Luckys and a bottle of Ripple for a room in that place. I'm sure they welcome cash."

The meter read $51.23. Porter pulled three twenties from his wallet and handed them to the driver. "Keep it."

They quickly disappeared in the man's shirt pocket. "I'm Hershel Chrisman, by the way. You need a ride anywhere, you give me a ring and I'll be right over, even here." He nodded at the hotel, handing Porter a business card with his phone number printed in big block letters. "Walk through the parking lot along that concrete wall. The office is on the other side of the elevator, opposite end of the building. You change your mind and decide you want a room at the Hilton on Bourbon, you give me a ring. You want to see the sights, you give me a ring. Been here all my life, I know this town inside and out." He lowered his voice. "If you can't spring your lady friend, I know a few places where you can find yourself a brand-new lady friend. Just give me a ring."

Porter nodded and slipped the card into his pants pocket. "Thanks for the ride, Hershel. Take care of yourself."

The cab pulled away, and he found himself standing there alone, the distant sound of sirens and loud voices drifting in from the dark.

Porter followed the cinder-block wall through the parking garage, which reeked of rotting garbage, and found the office beyond the elevators. There was no door or friendly lobby, only a thick glass window stained and smeared with God knew what. A man in his late fifties, pudgy, with a balding gray head and black-rimmed glasses, watched Porter as he approached, first on a small computer monitor, then from the window.

Porter stepped up to the glass. "I'd like a room, please."

The man licked at his cracked lips. There was something at the corner of his mouth. It looked like a crumb of Doritos, orange and moist. "I'll need to see two forms of identification and a credit card."

Porter pulled out his wallet. "No ID. I'm paying cash."

The man shrugged. "Twenty-nine nighty-five per night, plus a hundred-dollar security deposit. We need to protect our valuables."

Porter fished five twenties out of his wallet and shoved them through the small slot at the bottom of the window. "That's a hundred bucks. If I decide to stay longer than three nights, I'll be back."

The manager scooped up the bills, hit the side of an ancient cash register with a balled-up fist to open the drawer, and slipped the bills inside. "What about the security deposit? Can't have you walking off with our sheets or towels."

"I recently redecorated, so I'm all set. No need to worry. I won't even touch the minibar."

The manager narrowed his eyes, studied Porter, then must have figured it wasn't worth the fight. He slid a clipboard through the slot in the window. "Sign in, please."

Porter scribbled *Bob Seger* on the next available line and passed the clipboard back to him.

The man studied the name, then pulled a key from a pegboard at his side and dropped it into the metal tray under the slot. "I've got you in our penthouse suite. It's located on the east side of the building with a wonderful view of the city. Our continental breakfast can be found in the vending machines located at the end of each hall. Enjoy your stay."

Porter reached for the key, not one of those credit card keys but an actual key on a plastic ring, with 203 stamped on it in faded black letters. He dropped it into his pocket, picked up his bag. "Thanks."

The manager had returned to the security monitors. He waved a noncommittal hand at him, the fingertips orange from chip dust.

Porter walked past the elevators to the stairs, followed them to the second floor, and located 203. If he had any neighbors, he couldn't tell. All the windows appeared dark.

He fumbled with the lock a bit to get the key to turn. When it did, he pushed the open, stepped inside, and flicked on the light.

A queen-size bed stood at the center, with a scratched light-oak dresser on the opposite wall. There was a sign beside the television remote that read FREE HBO! but there was no television—only an empty space where one once sat, evidenced only by the scuff in the wood. A faded brown stain took up much of the floor. There was no discernible pattern to it. Someone had tried to scrub the green Berber with some kind of cleanser and only made it worse. A scratched desk and chair filled the far corner.

The room had a bathroom, but Porter couldn't bring himself to take a look. He'd build up to that. Instead, he dropped his bag onto the bed and crossed the room to the window. He pulled back the thick curtain. The lights of the prison were visible in the distance, thin, slotted windows lit up randomly at this late hour.

34

Clair

Day 3 • 4:56 a.m.

The phone rang.

Clair's eyes snapped open. The room was sideways. Her head was down on the cold metal of her desk, floating in a pool of her own drool.

"Fuck me," she muttered, glancing up at the clock. It would be light out soon. After the hospital, Nash had gone to the Davies house to supervise, and she had come back to the war room to work the boards.

She reached for the phone and accepted the call. "Yeah?"

"Detective Norton?"

"Speaking."

"This is Lindsy Rolfes in the crime lab. I've been trying to reach you, but your voice mail is picking up."

"It does that when I sleep on the job," Clair told her. "What's up?"

"I e-mailed our preliminary findings on the Davieses' house to you and Detective Porter about twenty minutes ago. We found a concentrated dosage of lisinopril in the remaining coffee. There were also some scratches noted at the deadbolt on the door in the mudroom. They were inconsistent with marks made by a key or normal use," Rolfes said.

"So someone broke in?"

"That is our conclusion. They picked the lock, came in through that door, and most likely poured a liquefied version of the drug into the water tank of the coffeemaker. Even if Davies filled the tank to the top, this dosage was so high it would not dilute to safe levels." She hesitated for a moment, her voice wavering. "I called the hospital to review the results of Randal Davies's toxicology screen with his doctor, and I was told Randal Davies passed away at ten thirty-four. He suffered a severe stroke, and they weren't able to bring him back."

Clair drew in a deep breath. The two girls, now their fathers.

"There's more," Rolfes said from the other end of the line. "We positively identified the clothing Lili Davies was found in as belonging to Ella Reynolds. There were trace elements of skin tissue and hair from both girls in the material. We also found a small amount of vomit on the sleeve, which matched Lili Davies. I included those findings in my e-mail as well."

"Anything to indicate when the unsub was in the house?"

"Nothing. We found no evidence that the unsub went beyond the kitchen, either. I get the impression he knew exactly what he had planned before entering, got in and out fast."

"Thanks for tracking me down. Let me know if you find anything else," Clair told her.

"Get some rest, Detective."

The call ended, and Clair set the phone down on her desk.

She couldn't rest, not now.

Standing, she stretched and walked up to the whiteboards. Under LILI DAVIES she wrote—

Found in Ella Reynolds's clothing
Drowned and resuscitated multiple times—salt water

Then she added a column for Randal Davies, followed by:

Doctor, John H. Stroger, Jr. Hospital
Father to Lili Davies
Wife = Grace Davies
Overdosed—lisinopril (blood pressure medication)

She looked at the list of assignments, crossed out the ones that were complete. Not much left. They needed another lead.

Four dead.

She wondered if Kloz had gotten anywhere on the list of saltwater pools, the local suppliers, or the aquariums.

Clair found herself glancing at the coffee machine in the corner of the room, then quickly changed her mind. She'd get something out of the vending machine instead, something in a sealed, lisinopril-proof package would do nicely.

35

Nash

Day 3 • 6:43 a.m.

"The heater in this clunker is for shit," Klozowski said, rubbing his hands together in front of the vent.

They were parked across the street from Cars R Us on Pulaski. According to the sign, the dealership wouldn't open for another hour—two hours earlier than normal, for some kind of Valentine's Day sale. Red streamers hung all around the lot.

After spending most of the night at the Davieses' house supervising CSI, Nash found just enough time to run home, shower, and change clothes, before picking up Kloz at his apartment downtown. He found him sitting on the stoop outside chugging Red Bull.

Nash patted the dashboard. "Connie has seen better days, but I'll get her back to prom-queen status. It's just going to take a little work."

Kloz's hands stopped moving, and he stared at him. "You're creeping me the fuck out right now. I'm serious. I'm getting a Christine vibe from you, and that didn't end well for anyone, not even the car. Why don't you trade this hunk of scrap in on a nice Toyota or Honda? Something with airbags and a CD player. That's an eight-track player, Nash. A fucking eight-track player. Where the hell are you going to find an eight-track?"

"Oh, ye of little faith," Nash said. He reached over and banged a fist on the glove box. It popped open and fell against Kloz's knees.

Eight-track tapes rained down to the floor well. "Pop one of those bad boys in."

Kloz stared at the puddle of tapes at his feet. "This car has officially been upgraded to legendary status." He reached down and plucked up one of the tapes. "Hell yeah." He slipped the cartridge into the eight-track player with a satisfying clunk. A moment later the opening riff of Neil Diamond's "Sweet Caroline" started crackling through the blown speakers with a wheezy trill.

Nash drummed his fingers on the steering wheel while Kloz began to sway back and forth to the beat. "John Lennon had nothing on this guy. Pure genius."

Kloz started humming.

Nash reached over and ejected the tape.

"What the hell?" Klozowski frowned.

"If I let you play that, you're going to start singing, then I'm going to start singing, then we're going to have some kind of moment, and when it's over things will be weird between us. I'm not ready to sing Neil Diamond with you. That's a big step. You haven't been in the field long enough," Nash said.

"You would sing with Clair or Porter, though, wouldn't you?"

"That's different."

"Different how?"

"Just different."

"I think I have partner envy. We don't sing in IT."

Nash peered out across the street. "We've got movement."

A man in a thick blue winter coat climbed out of a red SUV and darted through the snow for the squat gray building at the center of the lot. He struggled with the key in his gloved hands, got the door open, and slipped inside.

"Must be the manager or the owner," Kloz said. "You were right. He came in early to prep for the sale."

"Let's go," Nash said. He unfastened his seat belt and pushed open his door. Icy wind nearly knocked him over, and he fought for footing on the ice. He reached for the collar of his coat and held it tight around his neck. He wished he had a hat.

When the traffic broke, he crossed the street as quickly as he could without falling down. Klozowski followed behind him.

Cars R Us was a small lot, a half acre at the most, surrounded by a high black fence and tall yellow floodlights set to illuminate the selection of late-model used cars in the best possible light. Each vehicle was tagged with a bit of text beneath the inflated price: Low Miles! No Rust! Great Value! Clean!

Nash hustled past them and stopped outside the office door.

Kloz almost lost his balance on a patch of ice on the sidewalk. He quickly looked around to see if anyone had noticed. Nash stared at him.

"I'm moving to Florida or LA when this is all over. Plenty of work for an IT guy in warm climates," Kloz said when he finally got to the building.

"You do that, and you'll be shunned by Cubs fans. Warm-climate teams are the worst—no fan base. People are too busy driving around the beach all day in search of a parking spot or out playing golf. They don't have time for real sports."

Kloz tapped himself on the chest. "Me, IT guy. Do you think I know the first thing about sports?"

Nash shook his head. "I will never sing with you."

"Whatever."

The door to the small office building was locked, but Nash could see the man moving around inside. He knocked at the glass and held up his badge and identification. The man inside turned from a file cabinet in the far corner, a coffee scooper in his hand. He had no trouble displaying his annoyance at the interruption and made a show of dropping the scooper back into a Costco-size can of coffee before shuffling over to the door. He still wore the blue coat, now unzipped halfway down his large belly. A green sweater poked out from beneath.

The man studied the badge through the dirty glass door. "What do you want?"

"That's no way to greet public servants," Kloz said.

"We're with Metro PD. We need to speak to you," Nash shouted back, competing with the howling wind.

The man gave a longing look back at the coffeemaker, then twisted the lock in the door and pushed it up, ushering them in. "Hurry up, don't let the heat out."

Nash and Kloz slipped inside, and he locked the door behind them. He looked back at the coffeemaker.

"You seem pretty intent on getting that thing going," Nash said.

He sighed. "Sorry, I quit smoking last year and quit drinking the year before that. Caffeine is the only vice I have left."

"Go ahead," Nash said.

They watched the man hustle back over to the file cabinet and carefully measure out ten scoops of coffee grounds and fill the machine's reservoir from a small sink in the corner of the room. He pushed a button and the coffeemaker came to life, hissing and popping as the water heated. He turned back to them and finally relaxed. "I'm Mel Cumberland. What can I do for you fine officers of the law?"

"I'm Detective Nash, and this is Edwin Klozowski." He pulled his cell phone from his pocket, tapped at the screen, and held it up. "Do you know this girl?"

Cumberland's hand shot over to the desk at his side, and Nash nearly reached for his gun before he realized the man was only retrieving a pair of glasses. He heard Kloz snicker behind him.

Cumberland slipped the glasses on and stepped closer. "May I?"

Nash handed him the phone.

He brought the phone to about an inch of his face, tilting his head slightly to get a better view through the glasses. "Should I know her?"

"There's the car," Kloz said from behind him. Nash turned and followed his pointing finger to a bright green Mazda2 parked in the side lot.

"Oh, her," Cumberland said, handing the phone back to Nash. "Listen, I go through this with parents all the time. There is no law that says a kid can't buy a car. They're just not allowed to drive it until they get their license. She had no credit, so I told her she can't take it off the lot until she's made at least ten payments. She'll be sixteen by then, so no harm, no foul. If her parents are going to call the cops on me, I suggest they review the rules and regulations before they start wasting taxpayer money. I'm sure you've got better things to do with your time. I know I do."

Behind Cumberland, the coffeemaker sputtered. With practiced care, he swapped the pot with a stained mug, held it there, then swapped them again when the mug was full. Printed across the front in faded black letters were the words: NO FUNNY SAYING HERE, JUST SOMETHING TO HOLD MY CAFFEINE (AND SOMETIMES WHISKEY).

"I wouldn't mind a cup of that," Klozowski said. "Maybe in one of those, though." He nodded at a sleeve of Styrofoam cups lying on the side of the cabinet.

Cumberland filled two cups and handed them to Kloz and Nash. "She made the first two payments on time, but she's late on the third one, nearly two weeks now. Kids have no sense of responsibility these days. Probably blew her money on a prom dress or some shit and didn't think to stop by and say she'd be late. I usually cut the kids a break and waive the late fee the first time around, try and get them to understand the importance of timely payments, but rather than fess up, some of them hide. They do it twice, and we got a problem."

"She's dead," Nash said, watching the man's face for a reaction.

There was no reaction, only: "Well, I didn't do it."

"No?"

Cumberland set his mug down on the filing cabinet and raised both hands. "I'm not sure what you're thinking, but all I did was sell her a car. I've seen her maybe four, five times tops. She came in, looked around the lot a few times, settled on the Mazda, then set up an in-house payment plan, that's it. Like I said, she's two weeks behind on the latest payment. Last I saw of her, it was right after the first of the year. Technically, she didn't even buy that car. She needed to build up ten percent down before we could make it official."

"So you haven't seen her since January?" Nash asked.

Cumberland walked around to the other side of the desk and hit a few keys on his computer keyboard. "Ella Reynolds, right? She last came in on January third and put down three hundred and twelve dollars. I told her she only needed to do two hundred, but she didn't want someone to buy that car out from under her, so she paid extra to try and get the deposit together. Month before that she paid two hundred seventy-three. That was on December second."

"Wonder where she was getting the money," Kloz said. "We don't have a record of her working."

Cumberland scrolled through his file. "According to her application, she tutored other students. That's what she wrote for employment, anyway."

"She might not have told her parents about that," Klozowski said. "I used to tutor too and I never told Pops. He would have cut my allowance. I kept my mouth shut and collected from both."

"I'm sure you were a stellar example of a child," Nash replied. "Tutoring explains all the Starbucks visits. Aside from browsing for a ride, she might have been meeting students there."

"Starbucks and the library, that's where I always did it," Kloz agreed.

Nash scrolled to a photograph of Lili Davies on his phone and showed it to Cumberland. "How about her? Have you ever seen her here?"

He peered at the tiny display, squinting behind his glasses. "Nope. Her I do not know."

"Could she have come in and met with another salesman?"

Cumberland shook his head. "Even if she did, I'm always here. I make it my business to know every face that comes through the gate. Some of these younger sales guys are good, but I'm better. Somebody may walk away from them without buying, but not me. I always get the sale."

"We're going to need a list of all your employees," Nash said.

"That's easy. There's me, Brandon Stringer, and Doug Fredenburg. Doug's my mechanic. He's been out sick the past two days with the flu. Brandon is due in at eight."

"Did either of them have contact with the Reynolds girl?"

"Not that I know of," Cumberland told Nash. "The first time she came in, Brandon was with another customer. She was a determined little thing, gave the Mazda a quick once-over outside, then came right up here into the office and told me she wanted to buy it. No test drive or nothing. Not that I would have let someone without a license test-drive, but I would have taken her for a ride in it."

"Where was the other guy? Fredenburg?"

Cumberland tapped at his computer again. "Looks like he was under a Pontiac in the garage, changing out a master brake cylinder. He rarely has contact with the customers. You're more than welcome to wait for Brandon to get in. Maybe take a look around the lot?" He nodded at Nash's Chevy Nova parked across the street. "Your car's got the potential to be a sweet ride, but do you really have the time and resources to get it there? How about trading it in on something nice, something turnkey."

"Something with working heat and maybe a stereo without a crank on the side," Kloz said. "Your car is so old, you have to feed the horses under the hood."

Both men stared at him.

"Come on, that was funny."

"No, son, it really wasn't," Cumberland said.

Nash and Kloz climbed back into the Chevy. Snow swirled over the windshield.

Nash started the car and glanced back across the street. "I don't think the coffee king is our guy."

"I'll defer the actual detecting to you detectives, but I'd have to agree, he doesn't fit. Grabbing a girl from his own lot seems downright stupid, and frankly, he doesn't seem motivated enough to pull something like that off."

"He's too old," Nash said. "These kind of crimes tend to have a sexual motivation typically reserved for the thirty-five-and-under set. Even if there is no actual sex, it's the driving factor. Cumberland's easily in his fifties. Overweight. A teenage girl would beat the hell out of him if he tried to offer her candy and flowers. He's got no shot of kidnapping out in the open like this. We're looking for someone younger, stronger, someone with motivation."

"It could still be one of his employees," Kloz pointed out. "Just because he said Lili Davies didn't come in doesn't really make it so."

"Both girls were in the market for a car. This is the closest thing to a lead we've got. We'll wait for them to get in."

Kloz reached for the power button on the stereo.

"Don't."

36

Poole

Day 3 • 6:44 a.m.

They had been there all night.

CSI moving in and out of Libby McInley's battered house in thin plastic suits, at least a dozen of them in all. Poole watched from the driver's seat of his Cherokee. Careful as they were, he tried not to think about what all that traffic was doing to his crime scene.

SAIC Hurless was on the front stoop, his cell phone pressed to his ear. Special Agent Diener was somewhere inside.

Poole watched as Hurless disconnected his call and crossed the street to where Poole was parked.

He rolled down the window.

"She's been dead a few days, according to the ME. We think he started . . . we think she was bound to the bed around this time Wednesday, and he took his time with her, ten to twelve hours from the first wound to the last. He started with her toes, finished with her fingers. The eyes, ear, and tongue were somewhere in between."

"What about the cuts?"

"The ME says he did those as he went along. Probably alternated between cuts and removing appendages," Hurless explained. "He kept her in the bed. She urinated and defecated in place. The bindings at her right ankle cut clean through to muscle."

Poole wouldn't close his eyes. He knew if he did that, he would see all of this play out. He would see Bishop tying this woman to the bed and torturing her for the better part of half a day as her screams went unanswered. "This seems sloppy . . . for him. For Bishop."

"He's evolving. We know who he is now. He doesn't have to be as careful as he was before," Hurless said.

"Maybe."

"You think it's something else?"

"Something, yeah."

"That's a bit cryptic."

Poole said, "He never cut a body like that. The toes and fingers, that's all new."

"Like I said, escalating."

"I suppose."

Hurless shuffled his feet. His breath hung around him in the icy air like a smoker's cloud. Snow had begun falling again, thick, heavy flakes. "You followed Porter's bread crumbs out here, didn't you."

This was more of a statement than a question. Poole nodded. "He's got good instincts."

"Good instincts? He worked with this guy for the better part of a week and had no clue. Then, when he had the chance to bust him, he let him go. Let him walk right out from under half of Chicago Metro. He should have caught Bishop five years ago, we shouldn't be here, and that woman"—he nodded back at the house—"should still be breathing. Keep this in perspective."

Poole said nothing to this, his eyes on the house. The broken-down car in the driveway, the bike on the side. "She was isolated here, a shut-in. When we check with her parole officer, I think we're going to find he couldn't get her out of the house at all. He came to her."

It was Hurless's turn to go quiet. A year ago he might have jibed Poole for such a statement, but Poole had proven himself time and time again. He requested his assignment to this task force for precisely that reason.

Special Agent Diener came out onto the front stoop of the house, saw both of them, and waved. "There's something you need to see," he shouted.

Poole got out of the Jeep and followed Hurless back across the street, his head low to block the flakes that had taken on the feel of ice and sleet.

Inside, the power was still off. CSI had set up a generator in the backyard, and orange extension cords snaked through the hallways and rooms. Double halogen floodlights on yellow metal stands were positioned around the residence, filling every inch with bright light and harsh-lined shadows. Hurless and Poole followed Diener from the front door to the back bedroom, where Libby McInley still lay. A photographer slowly made his way around the bed, capturing every inch of her horror. Poole could hear her screaming from that frozen, blood-filled mouth.

Another tech was dismantling the 3D imaging camera set up on a tripod at the center of the room. When operating, the camera spun at the top of the stand and took a full image of the room from all angles, stills and video. The camera would then be moved to another room to repeat—images would be captured from the entire house, and possibly outside. A computer would stitch the images together, and agents could virtually walk the crime scene from anywhere at any time, as it appeared today. Poole had no need for this technology. For better or worse, he had near-perfect retention, eidetic memory. He wouldn't be able to cleanse his mind of what he saw here if his life depended on it. The sights, scents, and sounds all burned into his brain.

Four of the halogen lights illuminated the bed. They were bright, but the photographer's flash was brighter. Poole looked away.

Diener stood next to the dresser, in front of an open drawer. He held a small Mag-Lite, the beam pointed inside.

Poole followed the light, peered down into the drawer.

"Any one of those things could send her back to prison. Why risk it?" Diener said.

Poole pulled a pair of purple latex gloves from his pocket and slipped them on, then reached into the drawer. He removed a driver's license and passport, both with Libby McInley's photograph, both with the name Kalyn Selke. He set the fake identification down on the top of the dresser, then reached back inside, retrieving the gun, a matte-black .45. "It's loaded."

"Doesn't look like she even made a play for it," Hurless pointed out.

"She wouldn't have had a chance," Poole said. "Bishop would have taken her by surprise, subdued her. The ME will find something in her toxicology, some kind of sedative, propofol or Nubain. He's used both in the past."

Hurless turned to Poole. "You said she was a shut-in. This looks like she was planning to run."

"You only have to stay ahead of the demons. An inch outside their grasp will do," Poole said under his breath.

"What the hell is that supposed to mean?" Diener scoffed.

"Just something I read once, in a Thad McAlister novel," Poole told him. "I don't think she was agoraphobic. She was hiding from someone. She was scared."

"Bishop?"

"He killed her sister, maybe he somehow got a message to her in prison, threatened her in some way. I think this Franklin Kirby person she killed was important to him somehow. That's why the scene is different. He didn't kill Libby McInley because of Talbot or in relation to the crimes Talbot was involved with. I think this is some kind of revenge killing. He wanted her to suffer, to feel pain," Poole said.

He spotted something poking out from beneath a folded brown sweater. Poole reached inside and took it out. It was a Polaroid of two women in bed, naked. The edges were frayed, the color muted.

"I'm beginning to like this girl," Diener said.

"It's old. Fifteen, twenty years, I'd guess. Nobody uses Polaroids anymore."

"There's something else in there." Hurless was pointing at the edge of the sweater, under the opposite corner.

Poole saw it. He reached inside. It was a lock of blond hair about six inches long, held together with nylon-covered black rubber hair ties on each end.

37

Larissa

Day 3 • 7:21 a.m.

Larissa Biel stood on the corner of West Chicago Avenue and North Damen. Every time someone opened the door to Pierre's Bakery behind her, she fought the urge to run inside and eat her weight in cookies, cake, and other assorted yummies. Was it even legal to vent that smell out into the streets? The Valentine's Day dance was tonight at school, and she had to fit into her dress. It was tight as is, and one or two donuts would push her over the edge. Kevin Dew would be there, and she knew the moment he spotted her in that strapless black dress he'd forget all about chasing Kiesha Gerow and ask her out instead.

The bakery door opened again, and an old guy wearing a fluffy blue coat and green scarf with little elves climbing on Christmas trees came out eating a breakfast sandwich. Steam rose from the thick bagel with eggs and bacon, and her mouth began to water.

No!

No more. She walked a couple more feet down the sidewalk, closer to the corner. The icy wind reached around the building, and she shivered.

Where was this guy?

She stomped her feet and began running in place. Ten minutes ago she would have cared what the other people on the sidewalk thought, but not now. Now she was freezing her butt off, and if she didn't keep moving, she'd become a human Popsicle.

She saw him then.

He pulled to the curb directly in front of her, sliding between a FedEx truck and a beat-up SUV with the flashers on.

Larissa tugged at the door handle and pulled the door open the moment he stopped moving. She dropped down into the seat and shut the door behind her, holding her hands up to the heater vent. "You're twenty minutes late. I almost left."

He scratched at the side of his black knit cap. He looked like he was bald, but it was hard to tell under the hat. "Do you have your paperwork?"

Larissa nodded and handed him a printout from her pocket. "So, how does this work?"

He offered her a thin smile as he attached the paperwork to a clipboard and tossed it onto the backseat. "The contest you won entitles you to one free lesson. If you decide to continue, the cost is four hundred dollars. That will buy you thirty hours of in-class instruction as well as eight hours behind the wheel—the minimum the state of Illinois requires in order for you to obtain your license. We have other programs ranging up to seven hundred dollars if you have trouble with something specific like parallel parking or questions on the written exam."

"And you can pick me up here each time?"

He nodded. "We pick up students all over the city. We can drop you off anywhere within city limits too. Ultimately, you'll be doing the driving."

Larissa smiled politely. The instructor had trouble saying the *s* in *students* and the *c* in *city*. She thought it was kind of cute, reminded her of Kevin.

"Shall we get started on your complimentary lesson?"

Larissa tugged the seat belt across her chest and snapped it into place. "I'm ready when you are."

She watched as he placed a Student Driver placard on top of the dashboard before pulling back out into traffic. This seemed a little silly, considering it was painted all over the outside of the car too.

38

Porter

Day 3 • 7:33 a.m.

Porter sat on a wooden bench just outside the warden's office deep within the concrete bowels of Orleans Parish Prison. He'd walked from his hotel and quickly determined this part of town was better viewed at night.

The city of New Orleans had an odd smell to it. Even in the best parts of town, it hovered an inch or so above the roads, just enough to drift up to your nostrils and remind you of where you were. Near the prison, that scent didn't bother to hide. You could almost see the fumes, an oily residue on every surface, dripping from the streetlights and sewer grates. Every alley and vacant lot had its share of residents, not only locals but tourists who drank their fill and wandered off from the lights, music, and action of the main drag to this place, somewhere behind Oz's curtain.

When he arrived at the main gate, the guard had met him with tired indifference. Before Porter could talk, the man went into a canned rant about visiting hours and the locations of the visitor gates. Porter handed him one of his Chicago Metro business cards and told him why he was here. The guard had not asked to see his badge, and when he passed through security, he told them he'd left his gun in his hotel room safe. He ran the risk of someone calling Chicago Metro to check his story, but he had little choice. He wouldn't get access as a civilian.

The corridors of the Orleans Parish Prison were walled in cinder block and painted a dull white. He was led through a series of hallways and switchbacks until he had no idea what direction he faced. The air felt stale and stagnant, and the echoes of their shoes gave the impression of being deep underground. The guard escorting him said this was a shortcut to the warden's office, passing through the belly of the beast. Porter had never been claustrophobic, but if he spent too much time here, that particular condition might be in the cards. He couldn't imagine working here, spending every day here. At each steel door, they had to pause and wait for someone to buzz them in. He felt the cameras' blank stares. They encountered one every twenty feet or so.

At the end of the corridor they passed through a series of doors spaced only about ten feet apart, reminding Porter of an airlock or a decontamination chamber in an old sci-fi movie. On the other side stood the administrative offices. While also cinder block and steel construction, the space had been sparsely decorated with a worn rug and plastic fern, a bit of civilized oasis in the barrens.

The guard pointed at the bench. "Warden is here but making rounds. Should be back soon. Sit tight."

That was nearly thirty minutes ago.

No fewer than six cameras covered the room from the various corners, some moving, others stationary, all watching.

"Detective Porter?"

Sam hadn't heard anyone come in, yet this man was standing not four feet from him. "Yes."

"I'm Warden Vina. What brings you to our little slice of paradise?"

"I need to see one of your prisoners."

"I haven't worked in visitation for over a decade, but last I checked, visiting hours still start at nine, and it's fairly easy to follow the signs outside to the line. Not much of a need for me to be involved. I tend to like it that way."

The warden was a few inches shorter than Porter, standing around five foot eight. His hair looked like it had gone gray some time ago, and he kept it shaved close to his skull. His small eyes were set close together over a nose that looked like it had been broken and reset multiple times. There was a scar on his neck, thin and pink. It disappeared beneath the collar of his blue shirt. He was stocky and sure of himself, and his gaze didn't falter. His eyes remained locked on Porter's, a prisoner's stare.

"We have reason to believe this particular prisoner may be connected to 4MK."

"Oh, you're *that* Detective Porter."

"Yep. I'm that Detective Porter."

"I've been following the case on TV. Crazy. Connected how?"

"I'm not at liberty to say."

"Well then, I guess I'm not at liberty to let you see one of our prisoners."

"I could come back with a warrant," Porter said.

The warden shrugged. "Please do. And when you come back with that warrant, show it to the guard at the visitors gate." He turned and started for his office door. "Enjoy your time in New Orleans, Detective."

"She may be his mother," Porter said. "I need to keep this visit under the radar. If the press gets wind, they could burn the only lead we've got. I need your help, Warden."

The warden stopped short of his door, shaking his head. "I really hoped for a nice, quiet weekend. Helping you does not sound nice or quiet."

"You can save lives, Warden. I just need to speak to her."

The warden turned back to him. "What's her name?"

Porter fell silent for a moment. He had the guy on the hook; he couldn't lose him. "I'm not sure. I have no idea what she was charged with, either."

The warden smirked. "Detective, we've got around two thousand prisoners here, but we've had as many as sixty-five hundred, before Katrina. Some are awaiting trial for felony, and some are here on lesser charges like traffic, D&D, or municipal. The rest are here on behalf of the Louisiana Department of Corrections or the federal government for a long-term stay. How exactly do you expect to track her down without a name?"

Porter pulled the photograph from his pocket and handed it to the warden. "This is all I've got."

The warden took the photograph, then pulled a pair of glasses from his pocket. He flipped it over, read the message on the back, then turned back to the grainy image. "That's the west gate," he said, studying the image.

Porter pointed at the guard walking in front of Bishop's mother. "That is—"

"Vincent Weidner," the warden said. "I recognize him."

"Maybe he remembers her?"

The warden let out a deep sigh. "Come on," he said, nodding toward his office door. "Let me see what I can do."

39

Clair

Day 3 • 8:13 a.m.

Clair's cell phone rang from the corner of her desk in the war room. She snatched it up and pressed the Accept button. "Detective Norton."

"Detective? This is Sergeant Dawn Spiegel. I run the 911 desk."

"What can I do for you, Sergeant?"

"One of my operators took a very odd call a few minutes ago. I think it may be related to your case. Can I play it for you?"

Please don't let this be another missing girl. "Yeah, go ahead."

"Hold on for one second. I'll have to put you on speaker," the sergeant said.

Clair heard a slight rattle as the woman set down the phone on the other end. "Here it is."

"Nine one one, what is the nature of your emergency?" she heard the operator ask.

A slight hesitation, then the voice of an older woman, slow, papery: "He died twice."

"I'm sorry, ma'am, I didn't understand you."

"He died twice," the older voice said, louder this time, more urgent.

There was an audible sigh from the operator. "Who, ma'am, who died twice?"

"Floyd Reynolds."

Clair stood and went to the evidence board.

FLOYD REYNOLDS
Wife: Leeann Reynolds
Insurance sales—works for UniMed America Healthcare
No debt? Per wife. Hosman checking

Beneath the existing text, she wrote:

Strangled with thin wire (piano?) outside of own home (in car)
Body hidden in snowman
Father of Ella Reynolds

"Who, ma'am?" the operator asked.

This time it was the old woman who sighed. "Floyd Reynolds. He died last week, and he died again yesterday. He's in today's obituaries."

"Ma'am, do you understand that making a false call to emergency services may result in charges of a class four felony?"

"Nobody dies twice."

"A class four felony is punishable by one to three years in prison and a fine of up to twenty-five thousand dollars. Making false calls to 911 can put our law enforcement officers and emergency responders in serious jeopardy while also straining public resources," the operator told her.

"If you are not the correct person to alert, perhaps you should transfer me to the proper department."

There was an audible click, and at first Clair though the operator hung up on the woman, but she came back a few seconds later. She must have muted the call.

"Floyd Reynolds is a common name, ma'am. I'm sure it's just a coincidence. I don't want to see you get into trouble, so I'm going to hang up now. I advise you not to call back with this. If you do, you will most likely be charged."

"The name is the same. The birth date is the same. The address is the same. This is the same man. He died twice," the woman insisted. "Take a look at today's *Chicago Examiner*."

At this point the call dropped.

Clair heard Sergeant Spiegel pick up the phone and take it off speaker. "After the operator disconnected the call, she alerted the other operators of what she believed to be a crank. Our normal procedure is to log the false call and initiate charges with Metro if they call back repeatedly. I recognized the name from the blotter, so I pulled up the newspaper online. Floyd Reynolds does, in fact, appear in the obituaries twice. There is an entry today and one last Wednesday. All the identifying information matches up. Same guy."

Clair frowned. "How is that possible? He died yesterday."

"What is your e-mail address? I'll send you the links."

40

Porter

Day 3 • 8:16 a.m.

"Is that . . . ?"

"Nicolas Cage, yeah," the warden said, leading Porter into his cramped office. The framed mug shot hung on the wall to the left of his desk. "He was our guest in April 2011, after getting wrapped up in a fight at a local bistro. Even busted a window. Them Hollywood types sometimes forget when the camera stops rolling. He enjoyed his stay so much, he stopped back a month later after a couple too many drinks. He got into a loud argument with his wife in the middle of the French Quarter. We would have let it pass, but he kept pushing the officers. They had no choice but to arrest him. Great actor. I loved him in *Con Air.*"

"Is that the one with Sean Connery?"

The warden held up a finger and picked up his phone. "CO Weidner to the warden's office, CO Weidner to the warden's office," he said into the receiver. A moment later Porter heard his words echo through the prison's intercom system.

"The film with Sean Connery is *The Rock,*" the warden told him, hanging up the phone. He gestured to one of the empty seats in front of his desk. "We get our share of celebrities through here, being a bit of a party town. We let them sleep it off, just like the college kids who get a bit too rowdy, and put them out the door the next day. Unless there's property damage or someone gets hurt, there's not much need to push charges. If we charged every D&D who passed through the Quarter, the prison would be full inside of a week, and there'd be nobody for the women to flash their tits at."

A knock at the warden's door.

Porter looked up and immediately recognized Vincent Weidner from the photograph. His dark hair was a little longer than most prison guards', hanging above his collar, and he had a close-cropped goatee. There was a scar on his neck, about two inches long, below the base of his chin. Porter figured it to be a few years old. It was ragged, not a professional incision but an injury resulting from a knife or broken glass. Porter thought about the scar on his own leg, where Bishop had stabbed him in the thigh. It itched in return, and he fought the urge to scratch.

Weidner's eyes fell on Porter for a moment, and then he turned back to the warden. "Good morning, sir. What can I do for you?"

The warden pointed to the other vacant chair, and the guard sat, moving slowly. Prison guards always seemed to move with caution, running every possible scenario before making a move—at least the good ones did. The rest tended to get hurt. Considering the scar, Porter wasn't quite sure which camp Weidner fell into.

"This is Detective Sam Porter with Chicago Metro. He's chasing down a lead and asked for our assistance," the warden explained. He nodded at Porter. "Do you have that photograph?"

Porter pulled the photo from his jacket pocket and handed it to the guard. "He pointed at the woman walking between the two guards. "Do you recognize her?"

Weidner tilted his head a little to the right. "She's a doe."

"A what?"

"A doe. Unidentified. Jane Doe number 2138, I believe," Weidner said, returning the photograph. "What's this about?"

The warden pulled his computer keyboard closer and typed with both index fingers. "Jane Doe number 2138. She joined us on January eighteenth of this year, a little over three weeks ago. She's been arraigned, pled guilty, and is awaiting sentencing. Picked up for grifting down on Bourbon."

"I guess your catch-and-release policy doesn't apply to petty theft?" Porter said.

The warden scrolled through the screen. "She stole the wallet of a man from Jersey, and it contained . . . oh, that's rough."

"What?"

"He had five hundred and twelve dollars in his wallet," the warden said. "Theft of anything over five hundred in Orleans Parish carries a felony charge. If the man had bought one more hurricane, she would have most likely been tagged with a misdemeanor and would be heading home soon. As it stands, she's looking at a minimum stay of two years, maybe longer, if this isn't her first offense."

"Ouch."

"Yeah. Well, if you're gonna play, though, you gotta be ready to pay," Warden Vina said. "Apparently, she had three other wallets on her person. None of the identification matched her, and she hasn't given her name."

"What about her prints?"

Vina shook his head. "Not in the system, ours or national. She has one identifying mark, a small tattoo on her wrist." He turned the monitor around so Porter could get a better look.

Porter's eyes widened. He leaned over the desk. It was a small figure eight, identical to the one found on the wrist of Jacob Kittner, the man killed by a city bus and originally believed to be 4MK. Bishop branded Emory Connors with the same tattoo. "I need to see her," he said.

The warden turned the monitor back around. "We'll need to get permission. She's lawyered up."

Porter frowned. "How'd she get a lawyer without providing a name?"

Weidner cleared his throat. "I was there for that. It happened on intake during her initial interview. She didn't say a word from the moment we took her off the bus until more than an hour after we sat her down in Interrogation. She just stared at the detective running the questioning, Detective Dunleavy. She had this grin on her face the whole time. After an hour or so, she leaned across the table and said three words: 'Lawyer, Sarah Werner.' Then she leaned back in her chair, folded her arms, and smiled again. I don't know how Dunleavy kept his cool. I sure as shit couldn't." He caught his language and glanced at the warden, who waved him off.

"Who's Sarah Werner? A local?" Porter asked.

"You'd have to ask Dunleavy," Weidner replied.

The warden put his phone on speaker and dialed a number.

A gruff voice answered. "Yeah?"

"Dunleavy? This is Warden Vina at the OPP. I'm here with a detective from Chicago and one of our guards. What can you tell me about that Jane Doe from a few weeks back? Represented by Sarah Werner?"

"Oh, hell. That bullshit again?" Dunleavy sighed. "Not much to tell about the crime. She got caught grifting the wrong pocket. He said he'd been pickpocketed in the past and had a habit of checking his wallet sporadically when he walked in public. She gave him a light tap walking past, his fingers went to his pocket, discovered the lack of wallet bulge, and he grabbed her arm. She countered with a mean scratch to the side of his face and started screaming at him, random shit like 'I'm not coming back, you've got to let me go! I'm not gonna let you hurt me anymore, I've had enough!' That got the attention of a couple local boys who had been partaking in happy hour at the Crooked Broom. They came stumbling out, pulled the two apart, and proceeded to beat the hell out of the guy."

"Crap," the warden said.

"Broke two ribs, knocked out three teeth, and blackened up both his eyes real good. Could have been much worse, but the man's wife came out of the bar at that point, saw her husband at the wrong end of the shitkickery, and screamed." Dunleavy took a breath and went on. "Scream number two was enough for the local boys to snap out of caveman mode, and one of them grabbed our little grifter before she could disappear in the crowd. A tourist saw the local grab her, thought he might hurt her, and nearly got into a fight of his own pulling her away from him. PD showed up at that point and pulled everyone off everyone and sent them to neutral corners in zip-tie cuffs until they could sort things out." Dunleavy covered the phone and shouted something to someone. Porter couldn't make it out. He came back a moment later. "I didn't have the privilege of meeting Ms. Doe until they got her back to HQ and set her up with accommodations in one of our interview rooms. At that point the conversation was decidedly one-sided. I worked her for a bit, got absolutely nowhere, and then she played the lawyer card."

"Sarah Werner."

"Yeah, Sarah Werner."

The men went quiet. The warden looked at Porter, who nodded, then glanced down at the phone. "Thanks, Rick. If we need anything else, we'll be in touch."

"Wonderful, you do that."

The line went dead, and Warden Vina pressed the Off button, leaning back in his chair. "Getting you in to see her will be tough. As a civilian, you'd have to have her agree to meet with you and put you on her visitors list. As a detective, you can't be allowed in to see her unless her attorney clears it first. Either way, there is some hoop jumping in your immediate future."

Porter said, "Where can I find Sarah Werner?"

41

Larissa

Day 3 • 8:53 a.m.

Black murk, tiny flecks of color and dust spinning through the air, dancing in her vision. Larissa Biel rolled over, reached for her quilt to pull it over her head.

Saturday.

No class today.

No class meant sleeping in. No school meant she could burrow under her thick quilt and sleep until midmorning, maybe later if she wanted to. Her mother was working today. The house was empty, quiet. Then she remembered her appointment with the driving school. She'd set an alarm. The alarm would go off soon. Until then, though, she could sleep. She reached for her quilt, and her hands found nothing.

Her room sounded funny. An unfamiliar electric buzz, equipment running.

Larissa had already gotten up.

She had left the house.

She remembered walking to the corner in the cold to meet the instructor, getting into his car.

Her mattress was cold and hard. Her bedding smelled awful.

"Would you like milk? I brought you milk."

The voice was soft, hesitant, a stranger. Larissa fought back the sleep, willed her eyes to open. When they fluttered open, so heavy and tired, a pain wrapped around them, like someone had beat around in her head with a golf club and squeezed.

"It might be warm now, but warm is good. I like warm milk."

He'd stabbed her with something, the instructor. Right after she fastened the seat belt, there was a prick at her thigh, a sharp pain. She remembered looking down, seeing the needle, seeing him push the plunger on the needle.

Nothing then.

The dim basement came into view, the shadow sitting on the stairs at the opposite wall, chainlink between them.

Larissa sat up and nearly fell back over, her vision filling with a quick white light before leveling back off. The room was dark. The only light coming from somewhere at the top of the staircase.

"The milk will help get the drug out of your system. I'm sorry I had to do that to you, but you wouldn't have come if I hadn't."

The man in the black knit cap, the instructor.

She was in a cage, a chainlink cage, wrapped in a filthy green quilt on a concrete floor. Her head snapped around, taking in her surroundings. A water tank, heater, workbench. There was an old white freezer against the wall with the stairs, but it must have been broken—the freezer made no sound and the lid was open, leaning against the wall.

At the base of the freezer there was something on the floor covered with a painter's tarp. She saw herself under that tarp, being found under that tarp.

"What's that?" she said, her voice hoarse.

He stood up from the steps, fast, angry. "Never mind that. You never mind that."

She heard him shuffle closer, one leg dragging slightly behind him. He stopped about three feet away and scratched at his knit cap. Larissa saw his eyes now, dark around them, sunken in his face. They looked gray, listless, the eyes of a much older man. They were bloodshot, and dried tears crusted in the corners.

"Don't look at me, not like that." He took a step back, backlit now by the light at the top of the staircase, his features obscured.

Larissa forced herself to her feet, every muscle in her body protesting, weak and tight. The filthy green quilt fell to the floor. Her jacket was gone. She crossed her arms at her chest, pulled the sleeves of her sweater down, and curled her hands up inside. "If you let me go, I won't tell anyone about this. It can be our little secret." She thought about the dance tonight, she thought about Kevin Dew. She couldn't be here, this wasn't real. "My parents know where I am. They know I met you for lessons. If I'm gone too long, they'll report me missing. They'll call the police. Do you want that? If you let me go, it won't come to that. I'll forget all about this."

This was a lie. Her father had left early for the construction site, and her mother had planned to go into the office. She liked to work on Saturday afternoons because nobody else was there. Her parents planned to go out to dinner tonight, and both knew Larissa was going to the Valentine's Day dance. When they got home from work, they'd just assume she was at a friend's getting ready—they wouldn't expect her back until midnight, maybe later. Nobody would be looking for her. Nobody would miss her.

"Are you of clear mind and soul?"

He had trouble pronouncing the word *soul,* and he made a strange grunt afterward, as if angry with himself.

"I don't understand."

He leaned forward for a moment, caught himself, and slipped back into the shadows. "To see, you must be pure. To be pure, you must be of clear mind and soul." He began to rub his thumb and forefinger together in a circular pattern, some kind of nervous tic. "The last one, she wasn't of clear mind and soul, and I think that's why she couldn't see. It will be different for you. I'm certain."

Larissa's eyes went back to the tarp on the floor.

"The sooner we start, the sooner you'll be free. You want to be free, don't you?"

"Yes, I want you to let me go."

"I can set you free, but I'm afraid I can never let you go."

She crossed her small cage and went to the gate, secured by a padlock at the top and another at the bottom. She gripped the gate with both hands. "Let me go, you crazy fuck! Let me out of here!"

Aside from the rubbing of his two fingers, the instructor didn't move, a shadow against darker shadows. He licked at his dry, chapped lips.

Larissa screamed.

She screamed as loud as she could, a scream so loud, her throat burned. She stared him directly in the eyes and screamed until every ounce of air had left her, and then she sucked in another breath and screamed again. When she finally stopped, the room fell into a deep silence, nothing but the hum of electrical appliances and a slight ticking noise from the water heater.

"I sometimes scream too. Screaming makes me feel better," he told her. "Nobody ever hears me, and they won't hear you either."

He started for the stairs, pausing at the foot. "Drink your milk. You'll need the strength. I'll be back soon, and we'll get started."

She watched as he climbed the steps, favoring his right leg. When he reached the top, she heard a door close. He left the light on.

The glass of milk sat in the corner of her cage, just inside the door. Larissa picked it up, poured out the milk onto the concrete, and wrapped the glass in the green quilt before dropping it to the floor and stomping on it with her shoe. Then she unwrapped the quilt and carefully selected the sharpest shard, a piece about three inches long, holding it in her shaking hand. "Let's get started, fucker."

42

Clair

Day 3 • 8:59 a.m.

Clair heard Nash and Klozowski in the hallway a few seconds before they came through the door. They were arguing, something about Neil Diamond.

She shook her head.

When Nash walked into the war room, she tossed a pen at him. He caught it mid-flight.

"What the hell, Clair-bear?"

Kloz ducked past him and shuffled to his desk. "Didn't Porter instigate a 'no throwing stuff at the other detectives' rule?"

"Porter's on suspension, so that rule is null and void," she told them. "I've got something. This could be big."

Nash sat on the edge of the conference table. "Good, because we struck out at the car dealer. Turns out Ella Reynolds was paying off a Mazda behind her parents' backs. We talked to all three employees. Brandon Stringer, one of the sales guys, recognized Ella from her photo, but that was the extent. He was with another customer when she first came in. Cumberland, the owner, handled her from there. None of them knew Lili Davies outside of the news. There's a mechanic on site, Douglas Fredenburg, but he's not our guy. He's got a wife and five kids at home. He wouldn't have the time to orchestrate a poker game let alone multiple kidnappings and murders. Besides,

Cumberland gave him a full alibi. None of them seem right for this. More dead ends."

Clair had a number of printouts laid out on her desk. She picked one of them up and handed the page to Nash.

"What's this?"

"Read."

Nash held the page up and read aloud. "In loving memory of Floyd Bernard Reynolds, May 11, 1962—February 13, 2015. Please join us Monday, February 16, 2015, at 5:00 p.m. at Saint Gabriel of the Sorrowful Virgin Catholic Church for a memorial service honoring Floyd, who was a loving husband and father. There will be a reception immediately following in the church hall." Nash lowered the page. "It's the obit for Reynolds, so what?"

Clair retrieved another printout and handed it to Klozowski.

He gave her a sidelong glance, then cleared his throat. "In loving memory of Floyd Bernard Reynolds, May 11, 1962—February 13, 2015. Father of lies, husband of death, finally found peace among the roses. No more flowers please, send only your blessings."

"That's a bit dark," Nash said.

"That's ex-girlfriend dark," Kloz agreed, handing the sheet back to Clair.

Clair turned back to Nash. "The one you read appeared in this morning's *Chicago Examiner*. This one"—she shook the page in her hand—"ran last Wednesday, before Reynolds died, also in the *Examiner*."

Nash reached for the paper. "Let me see that one—"

Clair ignored him and went to the whiteboard. She taped both pages up beneath Floyd Reynolds's information.

"Or not," Nash said under his breath.

Clair went back to her desk. "There's more."

She snatched up another sheet and read aloud. "Dr. Randal Frederick Davies, husband of Grace Ann Davies, father of Lili Grace Davies, has left us with bated breath, smelling of lavender and cat's claw at both the end and start of his wasted journey as he walks in hand to the light."

"Not exactly ringing of sunshine and rainbows either," Kloz said.

"Davies died?"

Clair nodded. "Late last night. He suffered a severe stroke. A complication from the drop in blood pressure."

"They got the obit out that fast?"

Clair walked back to the board and taped the page up under the name Randal Davies. "Whoever ran it didn't wait for him to die. His obituary ran four days ago, also in the *Examiner.*"

"So this guy is running obituaries in advance for the people he plans to kill?"

"Yep."

"What about the girls?" Kloz asked, pulling his laptop from his bag.

"I looked, but I couldn't find anything on the girls, only the fathers."

Nash walked over to the whiteboards and studied the printouts. "Do we know who ran them?"

"That's the odd part."

"*That's* the odd part?"

"I just got off the phone with the woman in charge of obits at the *Chicago Examiner.* She's been there for forty-three years, says she personally reads every obituary before they go to print because, in her words, 'common folk have no respect for grammar,' and she swears she has never seen the two messages that appeared last week. She did remember the one from today—she even recalled the corrections she made before going to press. When I read her the other messages, she scoffed at them, said she would have flagged both. Apparently obituaries are submitted via a form on the *Examiner*'s website, and they get their share of false deaths, mainly kids playing pranks. Normal practice is not to run anything without verification. She usually gets a copy of the death certificate or confirms with the funeral home. There is also a charge." She crossed the room and sat back at her desk. "Obits are big moneymakers for the papers. In all three cases, credit card data was provided. The card used for both of Reynolds's obituaries is the same and belongs to his wife. The card used for the false obituary on Randal Davies was Grace Davies's American Express. On the false obits, somebody submitted the data online, then immediately hacked their system and coded them as 'approved'—they essentially bypassed this woman and the paper's safeguards by sending them directly to print without any verification."

"I'm looking at the code behind the *Examiner*'s web form. Their system captures information the user cannot see. Their operating system, IP address . . . a few other data points," Kloz said, his eyes scanning the text rolling across his screen.

"The woman I spoke to at the *Examiner* sent me a file of all the submissions in the past thirty days. It should be in your inbox," Clair told him.

"Got it, reviewing the data now too."

Nash studied the false obituary for Randal Davies. "If this ran four days ago, that puts it before Lili Davies disappeared."

Clair nodded.

"So who was the real intended victim? The father or the daughter?"

Clair had spent the past hour puzzling over that exact question, and she didn't have an answer. "I think he's going after both but for different reasons. He's drowning the daughters, over and over again. That was consistent with both girls. He takes his time, revives them, and repeats until their bodies finally give out—weeks for Ella Reynolds, days for Lili Davies. With the fathers, he killed them in completely different ways, and he killed them fast, almost like an afterthought."

"Not an afterthought, not if he's planting the obituaries," Nash said.

"Okay, not an afterthought. More of a statement," Clair said. "What he's doing to the girls, the drowning, that serves some kind of purpose for him."

"Like he's trying to learn something."

"Like he's trying to learn something," Clair agreed.

"So his focus is the girls, and the fathers are some kind of smoke-screen?"

Clair pressed her fingers to her temples. "No, they're more than that. I'm not sure why, not yet."

"Fathers, daughters . . . this is beginning to sound a lot like 4MK," Nash pointed out.

"Drowning doesn't fit, and Bishop made it a point to not kill the parents. He felt they suffered more alive after the loss of their child."

"Maybe he evolved, or devolved."

"Why would Bishop change his MO?"

"I found the records," Kloz interrupted. "In all three cases, the IP addresses originated at the homes of the victims. That means the obituaries were either sent from each home or made to look that way."

"Can something like that be faked?"

Kloz touched a finger to the top of his laptop screen, thinking. "It would be tricky. You can't really fake the incoming IP on a form. The string is captured after the data leaves the host machine."

Clair launched a pen at him. He hadn't seen her pick one up. She was getting fast. The pen bounced off Klozowski's shoulder and fell to the floor beneath his desk.

"Hey! I don't mind you throwing things at Nash, but I gotta draw a line when you try to hit me," Kloz said.

"Keep it in English, and you can avoid the hurt."

Kloz crouched down, putting the laptop screen between him and Clair. "To send the message with their IP address, the request would have to originate within their house, from their router. There are a few ways to do this." He ticked them off on his fingers. "One, hack into their computer from a remote location. This is fairly difficult. The unsub would need to gain access by sending them malware to open a backdoor or finding a hole in their OS. If they don't update their OS on the regular, this gets easier, but it's still a crapshoot because you wouldn't know if and how you can get in until you try—risky. Two, hack the family's Wi-Fi. This is a bit easier. It can be done from the street outside their home and only requires a few tools anyone can download off the web."

"Getting so close sounds dangerous too," Nash pointed out.

"He's sending these messages before he's taken or hurt anyone. Nobody would be watching for him. He could be in and out in a few minutes, particularly if the family doesn't update the firmware on their router."

"Nobody updates their firmware. We learned that at that Starbucks."

"Exactly." Kloz nodded. "There's also the newspaper itself. That would be option number three. The unsub would need to place the ads via the web form, then hack the data stored on the newspaper's servers. Once he got in, he'd have to change the IP addresses. This would be the most difficult. If it were me, I'd go after the Wi-Fi."

"Would that leave some kind of footprint? Like what you found at Starbucks?" Nash asked.

Again, Kloz nodded. "The newspaper didn't capture Mac addresses in their data, but the routers at each location would. I just need access."

"Would you need to go inside their houses?" Clair asked. "With all they're going through . . ."

"I could do it from the street, same as the unsub. No need to disturb the families."

Nash said, "The list the newspaper sent over of all the submitted obituaries, can we run the names? Look for obits on people without a death certificate on file? Maybe we'll get lucky and find his next target before he hits."

"It will be tricky without social security numbers or something concrete to rule people out, but I can give it a shot," Kloz said.

Clair read over the assignments on the whiteboard. "Any luck putting together a list of saltwater swimming pools around the area?"

"If I tell you yes, will you promise to stop throwing things at me?" Kloz said.

"No."

"You're an evil woman," Kloz said. "File sent. You should see it in your inbox. We can rule out saltwater swimming pools. The water Eisley found in the girls' lungs had too high a salt content. Pools are kept around three thousand parts per million, and the water we're looking for is around thirty-five thousand, on par with ocean water. That in mind, I found eighteen aquatic stores selling saltwater fish and supplies. I sent you that list too."

Clair stood up from her desk and updated the board. "Okay, I'll check those first thing. The two of you do a drive-by at the victims' houses and get what you need from their routers. Then we'll touch base."

"Sam would make me get a warrant for the router data," Kloz said.

Clair leveled another pen, ready to throw. "I'm gonna pretend you didn't say that out loud."

Evidence Board

ELLA REYNOLDS (15 years old)
Reported missing 1/22
Found 2/12 in Jackson Park Lagoon
Water frozen since 1/2 — (20 days before she went missing)
Last seen — getting off her bus at Logan Square (2 blocks from
  home/15 miles from Jackson Park)
Last seen wearing a black coat
Drowned in salt water (found in fresh water)
Found in Lili Davies's clothes
Four-minute walk from bus to home
Frequented Starbucks on Kedzie. Seven-minute walk to home.

LILI DAVIES (17 years old)
Parents = Dr. Randal Davies and Grace Davies
Best friend = Gabrielle Deegan
Attends Wilcox Academy (private) did not attend classes on 2/12
Last seen leaving for school (walking) morning of 2/12 @ 7:15
  wearing a Perro red nylon diamond-quilted hooded parka,
  white hat, white gloves, dark jeans, and pink tennis shoes (all
  found on Ella Reynolds)
Most likely taken morning of 2/12 (on way to school)
Small window = 35 minutes (Left for school 7:15 a.m., Classes
  start 7:50 a.m.)
School only four blocks from home
Not reported missing until after midnight (morning of 2/13)
Parents thought she went to work (art gallery) right after school
  (she didn't do either)
Found in Ella Reynolds's clothing
Drowned and resuscitated multiple times — salt water

FLOYD REYNOLDS
Wife: Leeann Reynolds
Insurance sales — works for UniMed America Healthcare
No debt? Per wife. Hosman checking
Strangled with thin wire (piano?) outside of own home (in car)
Body hidden in snowman
Father of Ella Reynolds

RANDAL DAVIES
Doctor, John H. Stroger, Jr. Hospital
Father to Lili Davies

Wife = Grace Davies
Overdosed — lisinopril (blood pressure medication)

UNSUB

- Possibly driving a gray pickup towing a water tank: 2011 Toyota Tundra
- May work with swimming pools (cleaning or servicing)
- Size 11 work boot print found — back of driver's seat, Reynolds car (Lexus LS). Used for leverage?

ASSIGNMENTS:

- Starbucks footage (1-day cycle?) — Kloz
- Ella's computer, phone, e-mail — Kloz
- Lili's social media, phone records, e-mail (phone and PC MIA) — Kloz
- Enhance image of possible unsub entering park — Kloz
- Park camera loosened? Check old footage — Kloz
- Get make and model of truck from video? — Kloz
- Clair and Sophie walk Lili's route to school / talk to Gabrielle Deegan
- Clair and Sophie visit gallery (manager = Ms. Edwins)
- Put together a list of saltwater pools around Chicago via permits office — Kloz — Clair to visit
- Check out local aquariums and aquarium supply houses — Clair
- Hosman to check debt on the Reynoldses

43

Poole

Day 3 • 9:23 a.m.

Poole stood in the center of the room loaned to them at Chicago Metro headquarters and stared at the wall.

Agents from the Chicago field office had spent the night recreating the wall of data from Porter's apartment here, using photographs taken from the scene.

Detective Porter had been extremely thorough. It didn't take long for Poole to determine the meaning of each colored thumbtack. Red represented a sighting of Bishop, blue for the location of the reporter or local media outlet reporting the story, and yellow for the home of anyone who went missing or murdered with a method similar to those used by 4MK.

There was a yellow thumbtack at Jackson Park, where the body of Ella Reynolds was found. Porter insisted Bishop had nothing to do with her disappearance or death, yet he'd felt the need to mark it on his map, then tried to remove the marker. Poole found this interesting. He was aware of at least three other homicides in the Chicago area over the past two months that had not been flagged on Porter's map, so why Ella Reynolds?

There was no thumbtack for Lili Davies. There was a good chance Porter had fully intended to put one up and never had the chance.

Poole hadn't seen his own apartment in nearly two days. He knew

Porter's wife died recently. The detective might not have been home between the time of the disappearance and the FBI seizing the data.

But still.

He walked over to the new whiteboard, commandeered from somewhere else in the building. He didn't ask where. In the top left corner, he wrote the name LIBBY MCINLEY, added her mug shot, numerous photos from the crime scene at her home, and his notes.

Bound to bed.
Toes and fingers removed.
Ear, eyes, and tongue removed.
Numerous cuts—torture.
Revenge.
Fake identification (license/passport, name of Kalyn Selke)
.45

They ran the name, Kalyn Selke, and learned she was a seven-year-old child killed twenty-four years ago in Woodstock, Illinois. If she had lived, she'd be only one month younger than Libby McInley. The various forms of identification they found weren't fake, they were real government documents. This means McInley somehow obtained a copy of Selke's birth certificate and social security card and used them to obtain a passport, then used these three documents to apply for and receive a driver's license in the false name. This was a time-consuming process but one she could have easily learned while in prison. He supposed she may have even worked on this from behind bars, but she would have needed help. She had access to computers and the Internet, so the research would have been possible, but someone on the outside would have had to write the letters and mail them.

Beneath the information on Libby McInley, the final item listed was the lock of blond hair. He drew an arrow from the text to a photograph of the hair that was taped at the top of the next column. He had hoped CSI would find DNA attached to one of the strands, but that was not the case. The neat band of hair had been clipped from the owner's head, not torn. There was no identifying information. An analysis of the hair told them the owner was a habitual smoker of both tobacco and marijuana. This person had also been taking Xanax, a very common anxiety medication, at the time of this particular hair growth. They could not tell whether the hair came from a male or female. The lab estimated the age of the hair to be around twenty years. They were quick to point out that this meant the hair sample itself was twenty years old. They had no way to determine the age of the person from which it came. It was cut from someone's scalp approximately fifteen to twenty years ago, they said. The two black bands holding the hair together on either end were common elastics manufactured by a company called Goody, available in nearly every drug and grocery store.

"Where do you want this?"

Poole turned to find Diener holding a large white file box—the box of paperwork discovered by Detectives Nash and Norton at the apartment on La Salle, staged by Bishop four months ago. "Set it on the table there."

Diener dropped the box with a heavy thunk. "Everything here has been indexed and imaged. You can see it on your tablet. What do you need the originals for?"

"Scrolling through pictures doesn't work for me. I need something tactile."

"Yeah, well, you better do it fast. Hurless said you're wasting your time digging through this. He wants us to talk to McInley's neighbors and her parole officer."

"Why don't you do that?"

"Yeah?"

Poole nodded. "Start with the uniforms. They already spoke to most of the neighbors. Revisit the few surrounding her house. I placed a call to her parole officer. As soon as I can secure an appointment, I'll call you and we can meet there."

Diener hated to be cooped up in the office, and Poole knew he'd bite at the chance to get out in the field, even in this weather. Poole also knew talking to the neighbors wouldn't go anywhere. He didn't care. He just wanted Diener out of his hair.

Diener made a beeline for the door, grabbing his coat off one of the chairs. "Hurless will probably be back from the field office in an hour. You'll want to be out of here before he shows up."

Poole gave him another quick nod and returned to the box. He wasn't worried about Hurless.

He began removing the bound stacks of papers and placing them on the table in neat rows.

44

Porter
Day 3 • 9:33 a.m.

"I gotta tell you, for a man on vacation, you're doing it all wrong," Hershel Chrisman said from the front seat of the taxicab. "Most tourists don't set foot in this part of town, and when they do, they go running back out. Better to mess with the juju priestesses and peddlers around the strip than the gangbangers around here. People are so poor around these parts, they eat their cereal with a fork to save on milk. They gotta take the bus to do a drive-by."

Porter smiled for the first time in two days. At first glance, the area didn't look so bad. They were parked in front of a series of shotgun homes that had been converted into businesses along South Broad Avenue, some of the same kinds of businesses he'd find on California Avenue back in Chicago near Cook County Prison—bail-bond offices, lawyers, check-cashing stores. In Chicago those places had graffiti on the walls and bars on the windows. Here each office masked the ugliness behind a bit of New Orleans charm—brightly colored paints, ornate architectural design; the bail-bond office next door even had a porch with two wicker chairs placed around a knee-high table ready for morning lemonade. They were parked at a white and green converted shotgun house with a small plaque on the door that read SARAH WERNER, ATTORNEY AT LAW.

"Might be a while," Hershel said.

"I don't mind waiting."

He shrugged. "Your dime. What did you think of Traveler's Best?"

The night before, Porter hadn't been able to decide what would be worse—sleeping under the sheets in the bed at his hotel or sleeping on top of them. The last time a cleaning crew passed through that room, Reagan was probably president. He spent the night in a straight-back wooden chair with his feet up on the desk—best to stay off the floor. "It was wonderful, a slice of home."

Hershel snickered. "I told you that place was a shit hole."

Across the street a man wandered out of the alley, came to the sidewalk, and dropped his pants. Porter couldn't help but watch as the man urinated while whistling a tune he didn't recognize, then zipped up and walked back into the alley, a hand over his mouth as he yawned. In the dank shadows of the alley, Porter saw at least three other people shuffling around, another lying on a rumpled sleeping bag. A large cardboard box was propped up against the side of the dumpster. One of the shadows ducked inside.

"He ain't from around here," Hershel said.

"No?"

"People of New Orleans may not be rich, but we respect the city, even the dirty parts. This here is a magical place." He nodded back toward the alley. "People like that ain't Louisiana bred. He's probably a tourist passing through, got stuck along the way maybe. The city will get 'em out, run 'em right on out. Ain't no place for that here."

"You told me this was a bad part of town, that I shouldn't be here."

Hershel waved his hand. "Ain't the part of town that's bad. Would you shoot your dog 'cause he has some fleas? This part of the dog happens to have more fleas than most, that's all."

A black BMW with dark tinted windows pulled up beside them and parked. "That's a lawyer car, if ever I seen one," Hershel said.

Porter watched the driver's side door open. A woman with shoulder-length brown hair and sunglasses far too large for her face stepped out, glanced around the block, and closed the door, starting for the office.

Porter leaned into the front seat. "What do I owe you?"

Hershel glanced at the mirror. "$16.75."

He handed him a twenty and waved off the change.

"You want I should wait for you?"

Porter watched as the woman unlocked the front door of the law office and slipped inside, closing the door behind her. He handed the driver another ten. "Wait five minutes, if I'm not back out by then, go ahead and take off. I'll call you if I need you."

Hershel took the money and dropped the bill into his shirt pocket. "This woman of yours must be something special to go through all this trouble. Most men move on rather than deal with the likes of this. I hope she realizes she's got something good in you, remembers that when she gets out."

Porter stepped from the taxi and gave the roof a tap before turning and heading up the steps to the office.

An alarm chimed as he opened the door and made his way inside. The air conditioning hit him like a wave. He hadn't realized how hot and humid it was outside, even at this early hour.

"Take a seat, make yourself comfortable. I'll be right out," a female voice called from the back. "I just got in and was about to boil a pot for tea. I'm useless without caffeine."

The office wasn't very large, only about ten feet wide and maybe fourteen feet deep. Although an attempt had been made to convert the space, Porter still got the impression he was standing in the parlor of an old home more than a law office. The ceilings were high and edged with crown molding, the center finished with an intricate pattern of tin inlays. Wainscoting covered the walls. There was a fireplace beside a large leaded window to his right, with a small couch and two chairs placed in front. The wall on his left was lined with built-in bookcases and texts that looked as old as the house. At the back of the room stood an antique wood desk with two more chairs, all three covered with stacks of books and papers. Behind, a doorway led into a bright hallway. In his mind's eye, he pictured this place as it once was: a sitting room here in the front, with the kitchen and a less formal family room toward the back. He could hear shouts of children calling from one end of the house to the other, haunted voices long lost.

"Feel free to clear off one of the chairs at my desk. Just put that stuff on the floor," she called out from the back room. "Sorry, I wasn't expecting visitors today."

There was a second floor. He could tell from the outside.

He wondered if the additional space had been converted into an apartment at some point, and he wondered if Sarah Werner lived here. Like the façade of the former house turned office, this place seemed out of touch with the vagrants outside, a sanctuary from the dark cloud hanging over this part of the city, a place caught up in time and out of sync with the happenings beyond the thick doors and plaster walls.

Porter crossed the room to the desk, lifted the stack of paperwork from a chair, placed the documents on top of the pile on the other chair, and took a seat.

Several framed degrees hung from the wall beside the desk. Ms. Werner had earned her undergraduate at Penn State and her law degree from the University of Pennsylvania Law School in Philly in 1998. Porter hadn't gone to college. He joined the force shortly after high school. He considered obtaining a criminal justice degree, but after he'd spoken to several police officers, it quickly became apparent that such a degree would do nothing but saddle him with debt. If he wished to advance beyond the role of detective the force might require additional college credits, but he had no desire for that, never had. Those working above him carried a load of stress on their backs and spent their days behind a desk worrying about budgets and staffing. His mind required the challenges reaped by working in the field.

"I am so sorry I kept you waiting."

Porter turned to find a woman standing in the hallway behind the desk, a cup of steaming tea in each hand.

"I brought one for you," she said. "Figured it would be rude not to, and I prefer not to drink alone." There was a sparkle in her brown eyes, a hint of mischief when she said this. "Oh, but I forgot to ask if you need milk or sugar?"

Porter reached for the cup. "This is perfect, thank you."

She had a bit of an accent, carefully trained away and refined, but still present. Didn't sound local, not Cajun.

Sarah Werner smiled, handed him the cup, and gracefully lowered herself into the chair at the desk, cradling her own cup at her lips with both hands. She wore a dark gray skirt suit with black stockings over finely tuned legs, something Porter guiltily noticed before they disappeared under the desk. He glanced back at the degrees on the wall, did the math. If she'd gone straightaway into college, that would make her around forty-five, about a decade younger than him. He would have never guessed. If he ran into her on the street, he would have assumed mid-thirties at the most. Aside from the tiniest of lines at the corners of her eyes, her skin was flawless. Her brown hair fell to her shoulders in gentle waves. He could smell the faint scent of lilacs.

"I suppose I should ask who you are," she said, smiling.

Porter pulled himself back into the moment. "I'm sorry, it's been a crazy few days." He handed her one of his cards. "I'm Detective Sam Porter with Chicago Metro."

She studied the card for a moment, then set it on the corner of her desk. "The Four Monkey Killer?"

"You know the case?"

She set his card atop a pile near her phone. "I'm a criminal defense attorney, Detective. I'd be the first to admit, my fascination with the criminal mind may border on obsessive. I follow all the high-profile cases as closely as I can. How can I help you? Do you think he's found his way to New Orleans?"

Porter took a drink of his tea, then set the cup down on the desk. "What I am about to show you needs to remain between us. You can't discuss it with anyone, you understand? We haven't gone public with this and can't risk this information getting out yet."

"Of course."

Porter reached into his jacket pocket and took out the photograph, set it on the desk, and turned it around so she could get a better look.

Sarah's eyes remained fixed on his for a moment, then she looked down at the image. "Is that . . . ?"

"Your client, yes. I believe so."

"But what does she have to do with the Four Monkey Killer?"

Porter turned the photograph over and showed her the note written on the back.

"I think I found her. B," Sarah read aloud. She frowned and looked back at him. "I don't follow. Found who?"

"That is Anson Bishop's handwriting. He believes your client is his mother."

Her expression remained neutral. "And what do you think?"

Porter shrugged. "I don't know what to think. At this point I'm just following a lead. What can you tell me about her?"

Sarah slid the photograph back to him and pulled a manila file from the stack of papers at her right. She opened the folder, revealing a photograph of a mug shot clipped to the left side and a handful of documents bound on the right.

"Jane Doe number 2138. Aside from that designation and her list of charges, I know nothing about her. I've met with her twice, and she hasn't said a word."

"Not even to you?"

"Not even to me."

"The warden's office told me she specifically requested you. Her only words were your name."

It was Sarah's turn to shrug. "And I don't have the slightest idea why. I don't know where she even got my name. I advertise quite a bit locally, so most likely she saw one of my cards or flyers. Maybe she heard I take on pro bono work. Maybe she picked me at random from the phone book, who knows. The first time I met with her, I explained that she could speak to me freely. Nothing between us would be passed on or shared. I gave her the full attorney-client privilege speech. We sat there for thirty minutes, and she only stared at me." She took another sip of her tea, then went on. "The second time I went down there, I reviewed her charges, explained how serious they were. She still said nothing. She signed my legal representation paperwork, though, so I know she comprehends what I tell her. I know she can read, she just refuses to speak."

"Has she been to court yet?"

Sarah rolled her eyes. "What a shit show that was. Judge Kobrick has seen just about everything around here, and he's not one for playing games. He threatened to enter a guilty plea when she wouldn't speak at the arraignment. I convinced him to give me a two-week stay. We're set to reappear on February nineteenth, which gives me less than a week to sort this out. I'm heading down there today, and if she won't talk to me, I may have to call in a psych consult."

"I can get her to talk."

Sarah finished her tea and turned the cup slowly between soft, manicured fingers. "Then what? Charge her with something in Chicago? I'm not sure that's in my client's best interest."

"I'm after her son, not her."

"What makes you think she knows where to find him? Even if she does, why would she tell you? I'm only aware of one instinct stronger than self-preservation," Sarah said. "That's a mother's instinct to protect her young."

"I can get her to talk. I can help you." Porter leaned into the desk. "Please, let me see her."

She smiled, closed the folder, and finally nodded. "All right."

45

Larissa

Day 3 • 10:06 a.m.

Larissa found herself staring across the room at the painter's tarp in front of the freezer, at the bulk underneath it. He had said "the last one," the instructor. Larissa knew he was talking about another girl. He had done this before. He was too prepared, too systematic about it all for this to be the first time.

She'd clutched the shard of glass in her palm a little too tightly and had already cut herself twice. Nothing serious, but enough to draw blood. She wiped her palm on her jeans and held her hand there until the pressure sealed the wound and the bleeding stopped. Then she gripped the shard again, willing herself not to squeeze. With each passing second, though, her grip tightened, her fingers tightened, they pressed against the razor edge of the glass until she again felt the warmth of blood. This time she didn't attempt to stem the flow. Instead, she focused her mind on the pain. The pain awakened her senses, made her alert, helped her concentrate on her surroundings.

She checked every inch of the cage.

The metal frame was bolted into the concrete, and there wasn't enough room at the top to climb over and slip past, no more than two inches. The padlocks on the door were both heavy-duty, with MAS-TER stamped across the front. They were round, designed to prevent the use of bolt cutters, not that she had any bolt cutters. If she had a pin or a paper clip, she could try to pick them, but she had neither of those.

Her cell phone was gone. No doubt he took the iPhone and smashed it. Even she knew the police could track her down from the signal.

A loud scream came from upstairs.

A man's scream.

Larissa almost dropped the shard of glass, now slick in her hand.

The instructor sounded like he was in great pain.

The cries lasted for about a minute and died away, going from a shriek to muffled sobs, then nothing at all.

Was somebody here to rescue her?

Had somebody hurt him?

Larissa closed her eyes, tried to focus her mind on listening, to hear what was happening upstairs.

The house dropped into silence again, nothing but the ticking of the heater and the occasional pop of the structure settling.

"Help me! I'm down here!"

Her voice sounded small and weak against the newfound wall of silence.

She heard the handle of the door at the top of the stairs. First it rattled, then the door opened, squeaking as someone pulled it wide.

Light from above reached down the steps, bright fingers extending to the bottom of the stairs before the basement shadows pushed them back.

Larissa gripped the shard of glass, felt blood trickle down the side of her hand and drip to the ground at her feet.

Footsteps on the stairs.

She tensed.

When she saw the instructor, when he came around the corner and his gray eyes found her, she willed herself not to look away. She glared at him, her jaw tight. With her fingers, she drew the shard of glass farther up against her palm, concealing it. She pressed her hand against her jeans so he wouldn't see the blood. She'd get him the moment he opened the door. She'd launch herself at him and dig the glass deep into his neck and twist it just to be sure.

He carried something in his hands. When he drew nearer, she realized he held a neatly folded pile of clothing. He set it on the ground near the door.

"I have a daughter your age. These are her clothes."

Larissa looked down at the pile. Black leggings, socks, underwear, and a red sweater. The sweater looked old, worn, the color faded.

"Do you like them?"

She said nothing.

"You will put them on when we are done."

"You have a daughter?"

The instructor's face was blank. "I'll tell her that you like them. She'll be happy to hear that."

"Where is she? Does she know I'm here?" Larissa took a step back. *Help! Your father's fucking crazy! Help me!*

He lowered his gaze to where the glass of milk had been. "She doesn't come down here. She doesn't like the basement."

From the corner of her eye, Larissa saw the painter's tarp. She turned away. She couldn't look. She needed to stay strong.

He stared at the place the milk had been, and then he spotted the puddle of milk toward the back of her cage, partially mopped up with the quilt. "About half the girls break the glass and try to hurt me. The other half do not. He told me you'd be a fighter. A fighter is good. That strength is good."

The instructor touched the pile of clothes with his shoe. "You will put these on when we're done. You'll be pretty then. You'll feel pretty. This is her favorite sweater. There's a pony on the front, see?"

He unfolded the sweater, held it up.

"When we're done with what?" The question came out before Larissa realized she'd spoken, and she wished she could take the words back. She didn't want to know the answer.

The instructor continued to hold up the sweater, her words lost on him. He looked at the pony on the front, smiled, then carefully folded the garment and placed it atop the pile. "You need to remove your clothes."

Larissa shook her head slowly, her grip tightening on the shard. She backed deeper into the cage. "No. No way."

The man's mouth was open just a little, as if he were breathing through it rather than his nose. His tongue slipped out, licked at his cracked lips, and disappeared back inside. He produced a stun gun from his back pocket, held the little black device up, then pressed the trigger. Lightning jumped between the two poles. "You will set down the piece of glass in your hand, you will put it on the concrete, then you will undress so we can get started. Then you will see. Once you see, everything will be okay."

Larissa almost slipped on what was left of the milk. The cut in her palm deepened as she tightened her grip. Blood dripped to the floor.

The instructor's eyes widened. "Do not hurt yourself! Drop the glass!" He pulled a set of keys from his pockets and fumbled with the locks.

Larissa held the shard of glass against her own neck, pressed into her flesh. "Stop, or I'll cut myself. I'll slice my own throat. So help me God, I'll do it." She tried to sound calm, collected, she tried to sound as if she were in charge, but instead the instructions came out at a high pitch, choked by waiting tears.

She backed deeper into the cage, slipped on the quilt, and fell against the back wall. Her free hand tried to steady her but instead landed on the remains of the glass, tiny shards cutting her palm in a dozen places.

The instructor had the first lock off and was working on the second one.

Her breath caught in her throat. She couldn't get enough air. Her eyes locked on this man, this monster, as the second lock opened. He wiggled it from the door and tossed it aside, stepping into the cage, coming toward her. He stepped on her arm, the one with the shard of glass, pinning her to the concrete while simultaneously lunging with the stun gun.

Larissa's fingers gripped a handful of the glass from the concrete with her other hand, little diamonds of glass, and without a second thought, she got them to her mouth, as many as she could, and she swallowed. Five, ten, twenty, she didn't know how many. She thought they would hurt as they slipped down her throat, but they didn't, like swallowing a pill or a piece of an ice cube.

The instructor wrestled the large shard of glass from her hand. He tossed the makeshift weapon out through the door of the cage, causing it to shatter into several smaller pieces when it hit the concrete. By the time he forced her other hand from her mouth, it was too late. She swallowed. He threw her back against the floor, tossing her like a discarded rag doll as a scream erupted from his own throat, a scream louder than any she could have managed. He screamed for nearly a full minute before finally backing out of the cage and securing the locks.

"What have you done?" he growled.

Larissa felt the tiniest of pains in her belly, nothing more than a pinprick.

46

Nash

Day 3 • 10:07 a.m.

"Why the hell are they still here?"

Nash slowed to a crawl and parked his Chevy about two blocks from the Davieses' house. Two news vans were parked across the street from the home. One had its large antenna extended into the sky. There was no sign of the reporters or cameramen. Most likely they were inside the vehicles, sheltered from the cold.

"We need to get closer," Kloz said beside him, his face buried in his laptop. "I can't see their Wi-Fi from here."

Nash wasn't sure it mattered. When Klozowski logged in to the Wi-Fi at the Reynoldses' house, they discovered that the logs on the router had been wiped clean. The unsub had cleared all records after sending the obituaries.

"Fuck it." Nash pulled back out into the street, passed the vans, and parked in front of the first one.

Kloz chuckled.

"What's so funny?"

"They named their Wi-Fi network 'FBI Surveillance Van.' Anyone trolling the local Wi-Fi signals would think the FBI is camped out somewhere nearby."

"That doesn't seem to be scaring away the media."

"Most people just use their last name or their street address, which is a bit silly. Why tell the bad guys which house the Wi-Fi belongs to? That's like putting your address on your house key," Kloz said.

Nash eyed the news van behind them. The back door had opened the moment they parked. "We've got about thirty seconds before the sharks ascend."

"That's going to be a problem."

"Why?"

"I've got the make and model on their router, but it looks like they changed the default password when they changed the name of the Wi-Fi. I'm running a brute-force attack on the password," Kloz explained.

"How long?"

"Minute, maybe two."

The cameraman was out of the van, pulling the hood of his coat up over his head to shield himself from the snow. He reached inside for his camera and rested it on his shoulder.

Nash glanced toward the house.

All the blinds were closed. If anyone was inside, he couldn't see them. A woman climbed out of the van wearing a thin trench coat that highlighted her figure but couldn't have done much to protect her from the cold.

Lizeth Loudon from Channel 7.

She said something to the cameraman and looked toward Nash's car, one hand holding a microphone, the other fixing her hair.

Someone stepped out of the second van, a man in a suit. Nash didn't recognize him. He started for their car too. A cameraman jumped out and followed behind him. "Shit."

Kloz's eyes remained fixed on the screen.

A knock at the window.

Lizeth Loudon.

She made the universal sign for *roll down your window*. Nash waved at her. "Now would be a good time to finish up."

"Almost got it."

The second reporter walked past her, barked out an order to his cameraman, and pointed at the space in front of Nash's car, directly in their path. The cameraman unfolded a tripod and started walking there.

"Oh, hell no," Nash said. He dropped the Chevy into gear and pulled forward with a lurch. The cameraman jumped back, the bumper nearly clipping the tripod.

"I'm in," Kloz said. "Careful, don't pull out of range."

Nash reversed and came within an inch of the van. When the cameraman again started for the front of the car, he dropped the Chevy back into first and pulled forward. This time he did hit the tripod, and the cameraman slipped on the ice and dropped into the snow, his camera beside him.

Another knock at the window.

Loudon was shouting at them.

Nash smiled, waved back at her. The red light on the camera behind her came on. "Now would be a *great* time to finish up," he said, grinning through clenched teeth.

"Got it," Kloz said. "Go!"

Nash floored the accelerator. The Chevy skidded and fishtailed as the back wheels spun, attempting to gain traction. Snow flew up in all directions, covering the reporters and their equipment. The car shot forward, a cloud of white smoke behind them.

47

Porter

Day 3 • 10:36 a.m.

Sarah Werner parked her BMW in a side lot, and Porter followed her across the parking lot to a small side entrance about two hundred feet down from the line of people at the main visitors center. Two guards searched her thin leather briefcase and patted them both down after a pass with a handheld metal detector. Porter was asked to provide his driver's license, then remove his belt and shoelaces. The license was returned, the other items placed in a locker behind the guards. He was handed a key with a numbered tag. Werner wore no belt, and she had swapped her heels for flats before leaving her office. Their photos were taken and printed on large red identification stickers with the word VISITOR across the top.

A female officer waited for them on the other side of Security, summoned automatically when Werner had said they were here to see Jane Doe #2138. She nodded at both of them. "This way, please."

A buzzer sounded at a heavy metal door, and they stepped into the stale air Porter remembered from earlier.

The walls in this portion of the prison were downright cheerful compared with the warden's offices — a muted aqua with beige border and an off-white ceiling. Cameras positioned at all corners followed as they passed, blank, all-seeing eyes that swiveled slowly on their bases. The officer led them through three other doors before they entered a large room filled with tables. Most of the tables were occupied with inmates on one side and their visitors on the other. Noise was deafening, echoing off the cinder-block walls. Along the west wall were individual rooms. The officer handed an envelope to Werner, then opened the door to the second one and ushered them inside; the door closed behind them with a clack.

Werner dropped her briefcase onto the aluminum table and sat at one of the four chairs bolted to the ground. She opened the envelope and scanned the text on the single page inside. "Holy hell."

"What is it?"

"Ms. Doe got herself into a bit of an altercation last night. One of the other inmates tried to stab her with the business end of a modified toothbrush. Before the guards could get the two women apart, Jane Doe wrestled the toothbrush from the other inmate's hand and stabbed her three times—once in the neck, and twice more in the thigh. Then she dropped the toothbrush and stepped back with both hands up. She managed to miss all the major arteries, but she still put the woman in the prison's infirmary. The first woman claims our Jane started the little scuffle, but two other witnesses say inmate number one struck first and Jane was defending herself. Depending on the results of the investigation, additional charges may be filed against her." She set the paper down on her briefcase and swore. "Nothing like attempted murder to start the morning."

"I'm guessing Jane Doe still isn't talking?"

Werner nodded at the door. "I guess we'll see in a second."

A loud buzz sounded, and the door swung open. One guard in front, another behind her, Jane Doe #2138 shuffled into the room.

Her feet were shackled together, and a chain connected those restraints to similar handcuffs at her wrists. This forced her to bend awkwardly forward, her long brown hair covering her face and trailing down over her red jumpsuit. The guards led her to one of the chairs and fastened her restraints to an eyehook in the table. She raised both hands to her head and brushed the hair back out of her eyes. Porter caught a glimpse of the figure-eight tattoo on her inner wrist before it disappeared back into her sleeve.

"Hello, Jane," Werner said. "I brought a friend today. This is Detective Sam Porter with Chicago Metro PD."

Porter watched the woman's eyes lift and land upon him. He fought the urge to look away. She tilted her head slightly and leaned back in the chair, interlacing her fingers. There was no smile, no frown, nothing but her dark, piercing stare. Porter took the seat beside Werner, across from the woman. He reached into his pocket, took out the photograph, and set it on the table between them.

Her eyes flicked down to the picture, then settled back on him.

Porter turned the photograph over. "Your son sends his regards."

If she looked back down, Porter didn't see it. Her eyes remained on him. She steepled her index fingers and leaned against them, pressed them to her full lips.

Her sleeve drifted down. Porter pointed at the tattoo. "Why don't you tell me about Franklin Kirby? Did he have one of those tattoos too?"

At the mention of Kirby's name, the corner of her mouth drew up in a slight smile. She forced it away with another tilt of her head.

Werner let out a frustrated sigh. "Do you want to tell me what happened last night? You've got zero chance of getting out of here if you're gonna pick fights with the other guests. The wrong witness statement, and you'll find attempted murder charges on your sheet. A grifting charge is one thing, but laying out bodies is sure to tie you up for a bit."

Jane Doe's eyes remained on Porter.

Werner continued. "Look, you can keep up the silent treatment as long as you want, I don't care if you talk to me or not, but keep in mind you're not helping yourself with this, you're just digging a deeper hole. We've got less than a week to work out some kind of defense, or at the very least poke some holes in what happened so we can plea down to a lesser charge, and I can't do anything without your help."

While she didn't speak, Porter could see the intelligence behind her eyes, something in the sparkle at the corners. Her breathing was slow, steady. No doubt her pulse beat at a measured pace. No anxiety, no worry—she wouldn't allow those things. The shackles, the locks on the door, this place, all an illusion to her, meaningless, a hindrance at best.

Porter thought of Emory Connors and all the people who had died at Bishop's hand. He thought of the little boy raised by this woman, the little boy shaped by this woman.

An anger welled up inside him. He leaned forward. "Calli Tremell, twenty years old. Elle Borton, twenty-three. Missy Lumax, eighteen. Susan Devoro, twenty-six." He ticked them off on his fingers, one at a time, slowly, deliberately. "Allison Crammer, nineteen years old. Jodi Blumington, twenty-two. Gunther Herbert, Arthur Talbot, Harnell Campbell. All of them dead. The attempted murder of Emory Connors. Because of your son, your child. Who else? How many others?"

Porter had purposely left Barbara McInley off the list, watching her expression closely as he skipped over the name. She betrayed nothing, though. He might as well have been reciting a grocery list.

Jane Doe #2138, Bishop's mother, this evil woman, she leaned back in her chair, rolled her fingers across the top of the table with a steady tap, then laced them back together.

Porter wanted to strangle her.

He stood, retrieved Bishop's diary from his pocket, and dropped the small book down on the table at her hands. "I know exactly who you are," he told her. "I know exactly what you are."

Porter crossed the tiny room and banged twice at the door, her eyes burning at his back.

48

Nash

Day 3 • 10:40 a.m.

Nash pressed the End Call button on his phone and dropped it back into his pocket. "I'm getting nothing but voice mail for Sam. His line's not even ringing."

Klozowski didn't look up. His gaze was fixed on his center monitor, a 27-inch surrounded by four 22-inch screens.

Nash felt like he could get a tan standing here. Although Kloz had his laptop in the car, he insisted he could analyze the data faster at his desk at Metro.

"You said we shouldn't call him," Kloz said in a distant voice as he scrolled through text. "He made his bed and all that."

Nash pulled his phone back out of his pocket and dialed Porter's home number. "It's not like him to go silent." Four rings, then an answering machine picked up. He hung up. "Maybe we should swing by there."

"I think I've got something." Kloz studied the screen.

Nash leaned in, carefully avoiding the Batman memorabilia and candy bar wrappers scattered haphazardly around Klozowski's desk. The screen was filled with strings of numbers and letters paired off, separated by colons. "What am I looking at?"

"See this here?" Kloz pointed at a series of dates. "Notice how the data starts on February ninth?"

"Yeah."

"Well, the data should go back much further than that. Months, maybe years. The data writes to this file until it runs out of room, and then old data is purged for new data. Thing is, they never run out of room."

"So if it starts on February ninth, that means our unsub wiped the file like he did at the Reynoldses' house, right? So we've got nothing?"

Kloz pointed at the screen with a pen. "We've got something. See this first one?"

He indicated a line that read:

02-09-2015 21:18:24 a8:66:7f:04:0c:63

"The first part is the date, the second part is the time, and this last section is a Mac address. I combed through the entire file, and this particular Mac address only appears one time—right here, the very first entry," Kloz explained.

"What does that mean?"

"I think our unsub wiped the router data and disconnected, but not before the new log recorded his or her presence for one second. I've accounted for all the other Mac addresses listed during this forty-eight-hour period. Every one ties back to a device at the house but this one."

"Can you trace it?"

Kloz shook his head. "Sort of. The ID is unique to this computer. Mac addresses are built into the hardware so nobody can change or modify the string, but you can't trace it across multiple networks to find a current location. Not like an IP address, anyway."

Nash let out a sigh. "Then how does this help us?"

"It's still a bit like a fingerprint," Kloz said. "I ran this unique Mac address through the data we pulled from the Starbucks and found a record in the log. The unsub was connected to that network for a total of thirty-three minutes with the same computer." Kloz leaned back in his chair. "Chicago has a pretty hefty public Wi-Fi system. We've got towers in the parks, the libraries, the trains—they're everywhere. On February twelfth, this same Mac address connected to the public system at Jackson Park for nearly an hour and a half in the morning."

"When he hid Ella Reynolds in the water."

Klozowski nodded. "The activity appears to be passive, occurring at intervals rather than randomly. This tells me the unsub probably had his laptop in the truck we saw on that video, but he didn't actually use the computer. The traffic I found is most likely automated tasks like e-mail, just his computer working in the background. One hit every minute. If he had actually used it to browse the web, we'd see more random hits."

"Why would he connect to the Wi-Fi and not use it?"

"I don't think he purposely connected this time," Kloz said. "Most likely, he connected the laptop to the public network at some time in the past and didn't delete the connection. By leaving the entry in the system, his computer would automatically connect whenever he's in range of that same network again, like mine did at Starbucks. It's a time saver. In this case, anytime he's within range of the city Wi-Fi."

"So back to my original question—can you trace it?"

"Back to what I said earlier. An IP address is a bit like a landline telephone installed at a house. The number is always the same and always on, so it can be traced back to a static physical location. A Mac address is specific to the device, in this case a laptop. That laptop can be switched on or off and connect to a million different networks. It can move from one to the next or go dark for an indefinite period of time. This means we can't trace it, but we can watch for it."

"How?"

"When the city planners rolled out free public Wi-Fi, they built in a backdoor for law enforcement. I can write a bot and put it out there. If our unsub's laptop connects to the public system, we would be alerted. At that point, we'd be able to narrow his location down to the specific hub he's attached to. That's going to be a much wider grid than an IP would give us, though—the towers have about a quarter-mile radius."

"A quarter mile of city blocks might as well be different countries," Nash said.

"We'll know where he is in the city. It's a start. Maybe we'll get lucky and it will cross with something else."

49

Porter

Day 3 • 10:42 a.m.

Sarah Werner followed Porter out into the hallway. The guard closed the door behind them, locking Jane Doe in the interview room.

Werner glared at Porter. "What was that you gave her?"

"A diary Bishop left for us at a crime scene a few months back. It details specific events from his childhood. If that's really her, she should recognize those events."

She frowned. "You say *recognize* and *events,* and all I hear is *implicate* and *crimes.* You told me if I let you see her, you wouldn't do anything that would lead to additional charges."

"At best, the information in that book is circumstantial."

"How did you get it past the guards, anyway?"

"Down the back of my skivvies."

Werner's eyes narrowed. "For future reference, as her attorney, I could have given it to her. No need to smuggle in contraband—"

"Good to know. I'm prone to chafing."

". . . and as her attorney, I'd appreciate a heads-up before you share anything with her."

"Noted. How long will they leave her in there?"

"Until lights out, if that's what I tell them to do," Werner said. "Why?"

"Can we observe her?"

The attorney locked eyes with him. Porter knew she was upset. She had every right to be. But he didn't think she was *that* upset. This was more about setting a pecking order, putting him in his place.

Porter gave her his best poker face.

She clucked her tongue as she thought it over, then shook her head and turned toward the door to their left. "Come on."

The small observation room was little more than a narrow hallway. Judging by the doors, similar rooms were placed between each of the interview rooms. There was a large one-way mirror window on the wall to the left overlooking the interview room. There was also a small desk with a computer monitor. On the monitor was a close-up of Jane Doe sitting at the table from the angle of the camera in the corner of the room.

A single chair stood at the desk. Porter offered it to Werner, but she declined, opting to stand.

Jane Doe hadn't moved. She faced them, the small book in front of her on the table, her fingers drumming over the cover. Her eyes were fixed on the mirrored side of the glass, yet Porter still felt she could see them.

Five minutes passed, then ten. Porter was ready to go back in when she sighed, flipped the cover open with a finger, and began to read. His body relaxed, and he leaned on the desk. Werner stood beside him, the envelope bouncing against her thigh.

"Has she been in other fights?"

She stopped tapping the envelope, crossed over to the desk, and sat on the corner. "This prison is horrible, one of the worst I've seen. The staff turnover is so high—more than fifty percent just in the past year—I have yet to see the same guards twice. There's a revolving door on this place. Most of the inmates know the facility better than the guards at this point. Many of those inmates are lifers with absolutely nothing to lose and an axe to grind on any surface presenting itself."

"Like a new prisoner who refuses to speak?"

"Like a new prisoner unwilling to play by any of the rules. She keeps to herself in the yard. If someone tries to talk to her, she walks off. You send those kind of signals in a place ruled by hierarchy, you're bound to piss someone off." She raised the envelope. "Now, with this, she's declared hunting season. I'm worried other prisoners smell blood and they might gang up on her. They'll join just about any cause to help break up the boredom."

"Can you confine her to isolation?"

She grunted. "Sure, if there's room. Violence is at a record high, and prisoners see those spaces as the only reprieve. It's gotten so bad, the feds are considering taking over management of this prison from the City of New Orleans and the sheriff's department. Who knows if that would even help. A report came out last month—in the past twelve months there have been over two hundred inmate-on-inmate crimes, forty-four uses of force by the staff, three reports of sexual assault—who knows how many others unreported. They've had sixteen suicide attempts, twenty-nine inmates transported to a hospital with injuries too severe for the on-site infirmary. Here's the real kicker, though—when the feds published their findings, they said these numbers were seriously understated."

"How so?"

"They keep a log in the infirmary, a *handwritten* log. Only the warden has access. The log listed one hundred and fifty incidents of assault since last January. One hundred and nineteen of those were never reported by the Orleans Parish Sheriff's Office. Broken bones, stitches . . . traumatic injuries, all swept under the proverbial rug. Prisoners are supposed to be housed based on a classification system—risk factors like mental health, past violence both outside and inside. The guards don't seem to take any of that into account. I wouldn't be surprised if some of them get off on the violence. I've heard rumors of backroom betting and purposeful placement of problem inmates together to get something going. Internal investigations are a joke, just memos between staff and management, the warden. Nothing concrete gets to the files."

She must have realized Porter was staring at her. She looked down at her feet. "Sorry, I get a bit passionate about this. I've seen some relatively good people go in here over the years and come out not-so-good people."

Porter smiled. "It's nice to know someone is passionate about something. This isn't an isolated problem. We've got the same issues in Chicago. Sometimes the only clear difference between an inmate and a guard is the side of the bars they happen to be standing on that particular day."

Werner stood up and turned back to the one-way window. "I don't know what to make of her yet."

Jane Doe turned the page, the faint sound of her chains clanking through the observation room's speakers.

"Ask the guard to remove her restraints," Porter told her. "Let her get comfortable."

50

Poole

Day 3 • 11:02 a.m.

"Oh, holy hell. I'm gonna catch shit for this." Vernon Bedard plopped down into the wooden chair behind his desk and let out a slow breath. "I was supposed to check on her last Wednesday, a 'surprise' visit, and I never had the chance. My caseload is bullshit."

Libby McInley's parole officer had called Poole back about an hour ago, and he met Poole and Agent Diener in the lobby of the Cook County Adult Probation Department downtown, not far from Metro HQ.

Bedard had spotted them both the moment he stepped off the elevator. A pudgy man with thick hands and even thicker glasses, he wore a yellow button-down shirt and brown slacks that looked about two sizes too small. He escorted them to his office on the third floor — a small box with a single window overlooking the parking lot. Stacks of files covered his desk and the cabinets lining the far wall.

Three staplers sat on his desk. Poole found his eyes drifting to them as the man spoke.

"Gave me a bad feeling, that one."

"When did you see her last?" Diener asked.

Bedard swiveled in his chair, dug through yet another stack of files on the credenza behind him. "Here we go." He turned back around and opened McInley's file. His thumb slipped down a log attached to the inside flap. "January ninth. She was quiet and adjusting well after release," he read, his voice tapering off.

"You seem hesitant. Is that not an accurate assessment?" Poole asked.

Bedard leaned back in his chair, pulling the file with him. His index finger flicked at a yellow Post-it note in the corner. "Here's the thing. Many inmates have trouble when they first get out. Five years or more seems to be the magic number, in my book. When they're incarcerated for more than five years, the prison lifestyle tends to feel more normal to them than life on the outside. I think it's the structured routines—meals at the same time every day, yard at the same time, lights out, lights on. Every day they spend in there with someone else driving the car, they get a little more dependent on the structure, a little more of their free will dies off. This is great while they're in prison. They become easier to control over time but they also forget what it's like to be self-sufficient. When they get out, some of them are overwhelmed by all the decisions, the choices. Little things we take for granted, like where, when, and what we're gonna have for lunch, can become monumental, staggering problems."

Poole leaned forward and studied the log in Libby McInley's file. "So she wasn't 'quiet and adjusting well after release'?"

Bedard studied both men for a moment. "She was neither of those things. She was a mess."

"Then why write it?"

"I'm here to help these people put together a life on the outside. Hold their hand, teach them how to take care of themselves again while also avoiding all the temptation and problems that landed them in prison in the first place. It isn't easy, for me or them." He laid a hand on the file. "My files are easily accessible by nearly everyone in the system, not by just my superiors. Certain employers—government jobs mostly—educators with work release, government-controlled housing landlords . . . law enforcement." He eyed them both. "I write the wrong thing in a file, and I create a problem for this person, a handicap that follows them for a very long time. I write Libby McInley is experiencing problems adjusting on the outside, and before you know it, she's denied educational opportunities because another parolee seems better suited. Work release may gloss over her. Before you know it, she can't function at all out here."

"Is that what the yellow Post-it note means?" Poole asked. "Some kind of internal code so you know what's really happening regardless of the notes?"

Bedard nodded. "Green means all good, red signifies problems. Blue means adjusting but slowly."

"Her tag is yellow."

"Yellow means she wanted to go back. I've seen parolees commit a felony, then turn themselves in to the nearest police station just to get back inside." Bedard glanced down at the photo of Libby McInley in the file. "I was hoping to get her into a halfway house. She was on the list for an opening. If that didn't work, I would have pushed her to take on a roommate or two. Sometimes the extra contact helps."

Poole found himself looking at the three staplers again. He forced himself to turn back to the parole officer. "Mr. Bedard, I'm going to ask you a question, and I want you to think about your answer very carefully." He leaned forward, an elbow on the man's desk. "In your opinion, did Libby McInley want to go back because she wasn't self-sufficient and couldn't take care of herself or because she feared something on the outside and felt safer in prison?"

Bedard frowned. "You mean like was she in danger? Somebody could have been after her?"

"Yes."

Bedard drew in a long breath, let it out slowly. "That's tough. She didn't communicate anything to me. The last time I saw her, she seemed frazzled. She got me a glass of water from the sink, and I noticed her hands were shaking. Her eyes were dark and puffy from lack of sleep. She appeared thin to me, she had dropped weight, probably wasn't eating well. Nothing to indicate she thought she was in danger, though. I think I'd pick up on that. I see it a lot with gang members."

"Do you ever search a parolee's residence?" Agent Diener asked.

"Sure, if there is probable cause."

"Did you ever search Libby McInley's residence?"

The parole officer shook his head. "She was in on a hit-and-run. Not drugs or weapons. Even in prison, she steered clear of those things. Drug testing is mandatory while on parole, and she passed every time. I never had cause to search her house. What are you boys getting at? Was she mixed up in something?"

Bedard shifted in his seat.

Poole knew what the man was really asking. *Was she mixed up in something I should have caught? How much trouble am I in here?*

"Does the name Kalyn Selke mean anything to you?"

"No."

Diener leaned in closer. "Are you sure?"

Bedard turned to his left, located his computer keyboard under a few sheets of notepaper, and keyed in the name. "I don't recognize the name. She's not one of my parolees. I don't see her in the system, either."

Poole said, "We found a driver's license and passport in Libby's house, both in the name of Kalyn Selke, but with Libby McInley's photo."

"Real or fake?"

"Real."

"Not easy to put that together."

Poole went on. "The real Kalyn Selke died at age seven. She was hit by a car while riding her bike. That was twenty-four years ago."

"Probably got a birth certificate and used it to get a passport, then used both of those for the driver's license," Bedard said, thinking aloud. "If she did this while in prison, she had help. If she did it after she got out, she still had help."

"What makes you say that?"

Bedard shrugged. "It happens more than you think. Like I said earlier, starting over for these guys is tough. Some of them feel they have a better shot under a new identity. About ten years ago, a guy doing life at Ohio State Pen was busted for running an ID assembly line. He'd isolate prisoners closing on release, sell them on the benefits of starting over, then sell them again on package deals. The prisoner would arrange for payment through someone on the outside to this man's cousin, also on the outside, then the cousin would set up the ID and it would be waiting when the prisoner got out. You can't do this from the inside, there are too many phone calls to make, letters to write. You need a physical address to receive the documents. They won't mail them to the prison care of your inmate number."

"I suppose not."

Bedard scratched his neck, looked at his finger. "This ring in Ohio? It was believed they were pulling in nearly two hundred K a year running identities. I wouldn't be surprised in the least if someone was doing it up at Stateville Correctional where she was housed. Probably somebody at every prison. Maybe multiple somebodies. As the technology improves, the business becomes more specialized and more profitable."

"We also found a .45 in the same drawer," Diener said.

Bedard sighed. "Could have got that from the same guy. They sell a la carte—identification, weapons, travel plans. The right amount of money and you can buy whatever life you want, I suppose."

Poole said, "Did she have money?"

Bedard skimmed her file again. "Her parents are both deceased. 4MK took care of her only sibling. I don't see any visitors during her last year. You'd have to check with the prison to go back further. No phone log, either. The way I understand it, she did her time alone, stayed out of trouble. What kind of resources did she have before she went in?"

Diener glanced down at the notes on his phone. "She owed twelve thousand on her car, forty-eight thousand in student loans, and her checking account had thirty-two dollars in it. The funds were eaten up by bank fees over the years, until the account eventually closed."

The parole officer spread his hands. "Well, there you go. No scratch. There are two types of payment in prison: cold, hard cash and favors. If she didn't have money to pay for this, I'd look into the latter. She may have agreed to do something for someone once she got out in exchange for the identification. Maybe a hit—that would explain the gun."

"You had contact with her. Did she seem capable of something like that?" Poole asked.

"After a few years in prison, I think anyone could go there, even an innocent girl from the suburbs."

Ten minutes later, they stood outside next to Poole's Jeep. The snow had lessened into light flurries, and everything was white. Poole wiped the windshield clear with the sleeve of his coat. "Any luck with the neighbors?"

Diener shook his head. "The uniforms learned a whole lot of nothing. I canvassed the houses four deep on either side. Not a very savory lot. The only one who remembered seeing her at all was this old woman across the street. She spends her day planted at her picture window with her nose firmly in everybody else's business." He glanced down at his phone. "Name is Roxy Hackler. Said she saw Libby a total of three times since she moved in. The day of the move, a cab dropped Libby off with a single duffel bag. The next day, Roxy spied her walking back from the grocery store with an armload of bags. Then last week, she said Libby came outside and paced the sidewalk, talking on a phone. She thought it was strange on account of the weather. Who goes outside in this to make a call?"

"Any idea who she talked to?"

"No record of a phone in her name. We didn't find one at the house."

"Could the house be bugged?"

Diener kicked at a small pile of blackened snow at the curb. "Doubtful. The techs didn't find anything, and they've been through the house top to bottom and bottom to top several times now. Doesn't mean she didn't think the place was bugged, though. Wouldn't be the first person to get out of prison and think someone was watching or listening in."

"In this case, somebody might have been."

Diener blew out his cheeks, his white breath lingering in the air. "Bishop never went back after a second family member. She's the first. She knew he was coming and tried to run. He was faster."

Poole nodded. "That's how I see it. We figure out why, and we get closer to Bishop."

"So what's next? I'm freezing my balls off out here."

"I'm heading back to Metro. I need to finish going through the box Bishop left behind. Why don't you work on the IDs? Try to determine where Libby got them. We need to know who was helping her."

"Should we be watching the families of his other victims?"

Poole didn't have an answer to that one.

51

Larissa

Day 3 • 11:21 a.m.

Larissa Biel rolled over on the cold concrete, her legs pulled to her chest. From the corner of her eye, she saw a puddle of vomit beside her head, flecked with red. She had lost count of how many times she threw up in the past few hours. Her throat hurt terribly. She couldn't swallow, she couldn't speak.

She'd thrown up some of the glass. She saw that too, sparkling among the bits of red and yellow. But her stomach ached something fierce, so she knew she had not gotten it all.

After she swallowed the glass, the instructor had grabbed her by the hair and dragged her to the freezer, then forced her head inside. She hadn't been prepared for water, and it filled her nose and throat, her coughing causing her to suck in more.

"Drink!" he shouted.

She couldn't breathe.

He wouldn't let her breathe.

The water burned at her eyes, tasted of the ocean. She tried to spit the salt water out, but he forced her mouth shut and pinched her nose until she swallowed. He repeated this three more times before the vomiting began. Then he tossed her back to the ground in the cage and locked the gate.

Larissa had not felt the glass going down, but the shards came up like razor blades, and when she cried out, it hurt even more.

The instructor watched her now.

He sat a few feet away on the concrete floor outside her cage, his dark eyes fixed. She heard him breathing, deep, ragged breaths. He held his right hand in his left; the fingers twitched.

A moan escaped Larissa's lips, and she rolled over again. She couldn't face those eyes.

"And fear not them which kill the body, but are not able to kill the soul, but rather fear him which is able to destroy both soul and body in hell," the instructor whispered behind her in a voice so low, at first she wasn't sure she heard him at all. After a few seconds of silence, he repeated the words, the *s* in *soul* dragging out with the hiss of a venomous snake.

Her stomach clenched and she tried to cry out, but the pain in her throat stifled the sound before it escaped, turning it into a muffled wheeze.

Larissa focused on the glass.

She didn't want the glass to come up. She wanted it to cut right through her stomach and into her other organs. She wanted the glass to end this. She would swallow more if she could.

The pain meant she was still alive. When the pain stopped, she would find peace. The pain didn't stop, though. She felt a burn at her belly like a hot knife from inside. Larissa clenched her knees and let out a silent scream.

Behind her, a cell phone rang.

A distant voice on the other end of the line, not on speaker but loud enough to hear. "Swallowing glass may not prove to be fatal. She may still see."

The instructor let out a watery sigh. "She's damaged, she's been compromised. She can't see. She'll never see."

"You need to try."

"I need another."

The basement dropped into silence again as the call ended.

The instructor let out an angry grunt.

Quiet.

Still.

Dark.

"And as it is appointed unto men once to die, but after this the judgment," the instructor said, inches from her ear.

Larissa jumped, pain burning in her belly.

He was right behind her. She hadn't heard him come into the cage.

Did she pass out?

How long?

She felt his hot breath on her neck. Smelled the stink of it.

She must have thrown up again, but she had no memory of it. Her hair was sticky.

Larissa turned to face him, the pain unbearable.

The cage was empty. The basement empty.

Alone.

The corner of the green quilt was bunched up under her head.

The house creaked around her, otherwise silent as a tomb.

52

Clair

Day 3 • 12:23 p.m.

Clair pushed through the door of Tanks A Lot Aquarium and Fish Supplies on Fifteenth and felt a wave of hot, humid air wrap around her. She stomped the snow from her boots and unzipped her jacket.

Rows of blue tanks lined each wall of the narrow shop, with three aisles of various goods filling the middle of the store.

A man with long, gray hair looked up from the counter behind the register, his finger holding a place in the paperback he was reading, the latest Jack Reacher. "Can I help you?"

Clair had visited three similar stores this morning. Each had proven to be a bust. She shuffled over to the counter and showed the man her badge.

He set the book down on the counter and frowned. "Did you find it?"

"Find what?"

"So you didn't find it."

Clair narrowed her eyes. "I'm not sure what—"

"If you didn't find it, you shouldn't be standing here. You should be out looking. You're wasting time." He let out a frustrated snort. "My deductible is five thousand dollars. It's only worth a fraction of that, so I can't claim it, can't afford to buy another one. I need you to find the bastard who took it and bring it back here."

Clair held up her hands. "I think we need to start over. I'm a homicide detective with Chicago Metro, and—"

"Homicide? Why would a homicide detective be searching for my stolen water tank?"

"Someone stole your water tank?"

"Isn't that why you're here?"

Clair dug her phone from her pocket and pulled up the picture Kloz isolated from the security camera at the park. "Is this it?"

The man took the phone and studied the picture, pinching the screen to zoom in closer. "Hard to say, that's a crappy picture. Could be. I think so. Where did you find it?"

"Do you recognize the truck?"

"Nope."

Clair retrieved her phone and dropped it back into her pocket. "When was your water tank stolen?"

"When I filed the report. Shouldn't you know this already?"

"Let's pretend I don't."

"You clearly don't."

Clair had never beaten an elder, but the prospect was growing increasingly enticing. "When was your water tank stolen?"

He drummed his long fingers on the countertop. "Week after Christmas. Busted into the warehouse at the back and ran off with it."

"Was anything else taken?"

"Twenty bags of salt."

"Can you show me?"

He folded over the page in his paperback and gestured for Clair to follow. The fish watched as they walked past, and Clair tried not to look. Fish had always creeped her out. Some of these were large too. She pictured tiny little teeth in their mouths. How people swam in open water, she'd never understand.

A door at the back of the shop opened into a cluttered warehouse. The walls were lined with metal shelves and racks. Old glass tanks cluttered the corner to her left, stacked precariously atop one another like a clear game of Jenga. Three metal barrels overflowed with plastic pipes and tubes of various lengths and sizes.

To her left, a large machine churned with a sound not unlike a broken clothes washer. The contraption stretched on for about ten feet, with piping flowing from box to cylinder to tank. Smaller pipes disappeared into the wall, no doubt leading back into the front of the shop.

"That's my water filtration system. All those tanks out there are salt water, which is far trickier than fresh. One slip with the pH, too much salt, not enough salt—any little thing can throw off the ecosystem, and they're all dead. Doesn't take long, either, couple hours at the most." He stepped over, studied one of the gauges. "I had a large pufferfish a few years back, thing was damn near a foot long. Something spooked him, and the little guy blew up to the size of a basketball, released its poison, and took out almost half my inventory. I swapped out the old filter for reverse osmosis after that and haven't had a problem since. Still need to keep an eye on levels, though."

Clair didn't care to hear about the life and times of pufferfish. "Can you show me where they got in?"

The shopkeeper gestured toward the back of the warehouse. "My guess is they used the door."

There was a large overhead garage door with a smaller metal door to the left. The second door had two deadbolts and a slide bolt. The overhead door was electric. "Which one?"

"Dunno."

"There was no sign of forced entry?"

His face pinched, turned red. "Like I told the first officer, the door is always locked. The overhead is always closed. I check them when I get in, and I check them again when I leave. They got in this way for sure. If the cops aren't smart enough to figure out how, that's on them, not me."

Clair went to the smaller of the two doors, unlatched the deadbolts, pulled back the slide, and opened the door. The cold air rushed in, and she held her jacket closed with her free hand while studying the edge of the metal door. There were no scratches or dents. The door hadn't been pried open. The deadbolts were both heavy-duty Medecos, tough to pick but not impossible. "You're sure this slide bolt was latched?"

"You'd be hard-pressed to find a time when it's not. I only use the big door, and that only opens with the remote in my truck or this button here." He pointed toward a glowing button on the wall.

Walking back to the center of the room, he spread his arms out wide. "The tank was right here. I disconnected it from my truck the night before and filled it from the hose on the filtration system. Got it set up for the next day."

"What was happening the next day?"

"I maintain sixteen large aquariums around the city, makes up nearly twenty percent of my business's revenue. Think I can do that if I can't haul water? Water evaporates, gets dirty, has to be replaced. I haul the tank on my runs so I can do a swap or replenish whenever necessary."

Clair looked up at the garage door opener, a Craftsman 54985, according to the large decal on the side of the motor housing. A ladder leaned against the wall to her right. "Do you mind?"

He brought the ladder over and set it up under the opener. Clair pulled her car keys from her pocket, then climbed up and studied the back of the device. She found a yellow button, pressed it, then pressed the button on the remote for her own garage. The light bulb in the opener blinked as the unit memorized the signal.

When she pressed the button on her remote again, the motor above whirred to life and the door began to open. She pressed it again, and the door reversed.

"I'll be damned."

Clair climbed down off the ladder. "Who else has access to this space?"

"Just me."

"No vendors, employees, landlord?"

"I hired a girl a few weeks back to help out up front, but she only showed up for a day. Nervous little thing. I don't think she liked to be around people much." He lowered his voice. "She was in Stateville Correctional for manslaughter, just got out. She told me what happened, and it sounded like an accident. Seemed like she was having trouble finding work, so I figured I'd give her a shot. We don't do a lot of cash business here, and I didn't see her walking off with a handful of fish. I'm a pretty good judge of character, and no alarm bells went off when I interviewed her, so why not, right? I'd been thinking of putting an ad in the paper anyway to get some part-time help."

Clair's eyebrows furrowed. "She applied for a job you hadn't advertised? Not even a sign in the window?"

He shoved his hands in his pockets. "She came in on a busy day, saw I needed help, and offered. Like I said, I'd been thinking about advertising."

"What was her name?"

"Libby. Libby McInley."

Clair took out her cell phone and dialed a number from speed dial. Straight to voice mail: "This is Detective Sam Porter of Chicago Metro, I'm—"

She disconnected.

Dammit. She'd meant to dial Nash.

53

Poole
Day 3 • 1:18 p.m.

Ah, my friends!

It is good to know you finally found your way here! I had hoped to be there with you when this moment came, but alas, it was not meant to be. I take solace in the fact that this material has found itself into your capable hands, as I am sure you will take it to your compadres in financial crimes so they may add it to the mounting pile of evidence against Mr. Talbot and company. While I believe this box contains more than enough information for a substantial conviction, I'm afraid I couldn't wait for the trial portion of the program and went ahead and passed a sentence I believe to be more than fitting for the crimes at hand. Much like his longtime business partner, Gunther Herbert, Mr. Talbot will meet with justice face-to-face today, and he will answer for his actions on the swiftest of terms. Perhaps I will allow him to give his daughter one last kiss before goodbyes are said? Perhaps not. Maybe it's best they just watch each other bleed.

Truly yours,
Anson Bishop

Poole smoothed the edges of the paper, studying the handwriting — neat and readable, yet oddly disturbing.

The note had been in the box found at an empty apartment by Detectives Clair Norton and Brian Nash days after Bishop kidnapped

Emory Connors, hours after he kidnapped her biological father, Arthur Talbot. The apartment address appeared on employment documents Bishop completed as part of his fake identity and immersion into the Chicago Metro crime lab as Paul Watson. Bishop wanted the information found and had orchestrated a plan (one of many) to ensure it was found no earlier or later than he wished. He knew they'd track the address once his cover was blown but no sooner.

Poole had laid out the contents of the box in neat rows on a folding table before leaving to visit Libby McInley's parole officer.

Reams of paper all bundled together, twelve in total.

The first seven bundles contained information centered on Arthur Talbot, specifically his real estate transactions and financial holdings. The Financial Crimes divisions of both Chicago Metro and the FBI were still unraveling the details, but to date they had seized more than fifty million dollars in assets believed to be derived from criminal activity. Due to the large size of Talbot Enterprises, most assets were frozen, but the courts allowed the company's operating accounts to remain funded. Ultimately, they wished to sort this mess out without jeopardizing the thousands of legitimate jobs created by Talbot's endeavors. Emory Connors's trust had also remained untouched, as it was entirely detached from Talbot, something he apparently insisted upon.

Poole set these bundles aside.

The next four bundles were also tied to Talbot but branched out to include two organized crime families operating in and around Chicago, as well as twenty-three individuals. The crimes ran the gamut from gambling and money laundering to drugs and prostitution. This data led to six arrests, with many more in the pipeline.

Poole slid these bundles aside as well. It was the last one that interested him.

The final bundle held about three hundred pages of paper. The topmost sheet was lined in green and white with tiny, concise handwriting. The first line read:

163. WF14 2.5k. JM.

Attached to the bundle was a manila envelope containing twenty-six Polaroid pictures of teenagers in various stages of undress, both male and female. Each Polaroid was numbered. The handwriting did not match Bishop's. According to the report Detective Nash filed, the envelope hadn't originally been attached to this bundle but had been at the bottom of the box. While the two were most likely connected, Poole preferred to leave evidence exactly as found to preserve the findings. Attaching the two items based on assumptions was careless and could lead to false conclusions.

Poole ran a finger over the first line of text:

163. WF14 2.5k. JM.

The number 163 was believed to tie out to a specific child—a white female fourteen years old, either sold for 2.5K or bought for that amount, most likely dollars but possibly another form of currency. Bitcoin was the currency of choice for most human traffickers.

Poole knew Bitcoin well. The currency had been a thorn in the side of law enforcement since 2008, since criminals could trade it online like cash, leaving no way to trace just who was trading it and what it was being traded for.

If the line meant 2,500 Bitcoins, that would set the value at about 2.6 million US dollars. That was highly unlikely. A fourteen-year-old white female in good health typically sold within the United States for under $25,000. *K* was sometimes used to abbreviate Bitcoin. If that were the case, then 2.5K would be equal to approximately $2,600, which was far more likely.

The idea that a human life could be bought and sold at any amount disgusted Poole, and he forced the thought from his head. He had to focus on the evidence.

163. WF14 2.5K. JM.

Child number 163, a white female fourteen years old, sold or was for sale at a price of $2,600. The initials JM could belong to the child or possibly the individual buying or selling the child. There was no way to be sure.

Poole flipped through the Polaroids. None were numbered 163.

Someone had matched the other photographs to specific line items;

yellow Post-it notes had been placed beside each corresponding entry. Nineteen girls and seven boys.

Poole counted the lines on the first page—twenty-six. With close to three hundred pages, that meant there were almost eight thousand children listed here. Correction: there were almost eight thousand *people* listed here. If the number appearing after the code for race and gender was, in fact, age, many of the entries were older, although the highest number he found was twenty-three.

Chicago ranked third in the country for the highest levels of human trafficking. Recent studies estimated there were at least 25,000 victims in and around the city. If this list was to be believed, it represented nearly one-third of them. Poole had no reason to doubt Bishop's intel. All his other data had panned out.

The Cook County Human Trafficking Task Force, the Chicago Regional Human Trafficking Task Force (CTTF), and the Illinois Task Force on Human Trafficking all received copies of the data, but they hadn't made any headway determining the exact meaning. Should they figure it out, the data might lead to the largest human trafficking bust in US history.

Poole stood up and stretched his legs. He picked up one of the Polaroids and walked over to the whiteboard, held the picture up against the one they discovered in Libby McInley's house. He had initially hoped they came from the same camera. A long shot, to be sure, but he needed a common thread, something to connect all the pieces.

The pictures had not come from the same camera.

Analysis indicated the photos of the children were taken with 780 Turbo Polaroid film, while the photo discovered at McInley's house had been taken with PX 680 Color Shade FF. He also learned that Polaroid cameras were much like the barrel of a gun. Each camera left a unique pattern on the photos printed, a series of fine lines too small for the human eye to distinguish but enough to identify pictures taken with the same camera with the aid of a microscope. All of the photos Bishop provided in that box had been taken with one camera. Serial numbers embedded within the film traced back to manufacturing dates and told them that the pictures had been taken over a two-year period sometime in the late nineties.

Poole's phone rang, and he shuffled back to his desk.

Diener.

He pressed the Accept button.

"Frank? I've got something. You were right."

"The IDs?"

"Yeah. Illinois Vital Records received a request for a replacement birth certificate about a year ago, April 10, 2014, through their on-line portal."

"While McInley was still in prison."

"Yeah. The request was submitted by Kalyn Selke—well, someone pretending to be Kalyn Selke. They supplied all the necessary information: name of the hospital at birth, city and state of birth, mother's maiden name, father's full name. They stated the reason for the replacement as 'lost in fire.' They even submitted a photo ID with Libby McInley's picture. It was bogus, but nobody bothered to run it. The replacement went out on May 2, 2014. About a week later, on May 8, 2014, a passport application was received using the birth certificate and three utility bills—electric, phone, and cable—all for the same address, the same place the documents shipped to—a residence in Brighton Park. I'm heading over there now."

Poole's chest tightened. "Text me the address. I'll meet you there."

54

Clair

Day 3 • 1:31 p.m.

"How long is this going to take?"

Klozowski raised a hand and waved her off, his eyes fixed on his computer monitor. "I'm trying to find a good camera angle. Tell me when you spot something that—"

"That one!" Clair shouted out.

"Hell, Clair-bear, how about using your inside voice?" Nash said from over her shoulder.

Clair leaned in and touched the monitor. "That's the back door of the fish store. What street is this?"

Kloz clicked on the information tab next to a graphic of a CCTV camera. "Corner of Sixteenth and Mortimer."

"Can you get in any closer?"

"I'm at full zoom right now. What day do we need?"

"He said the tank was stolen about a week after Christmas," Clair said. "He didn't file a report until January fourth. Maybe start with December twenty-seventh to be sure?"

Kloz let out a breath. "That's a big window."

"Better to cast a big net."

Nash leaned in on the other side. "I thought these things let you search by make and model?"

Kloz leaned back in his chair. "How about a little personal space? You smell like radishes."

"I had a salad for lunch," Nash said, stepping back. "I'm trying to make a conscious effort to eat healthier."

"You had a McDonald's salad for lunch, and it was swimming in ranch dressing. That's one of the most fattening things on the McD's menu."

"Bullshit."

"I shit you not."

"Focus, gentlemen!" Clair said. "Can you search by vehicle type?"

Kloz shook his head. "Not exactly."

"That's *not exactly* an answer."

"The cameras can't identify make and model of a vehicle, but they do read and record all the license plates. I can cross-reference that information with DMV records and—"

"So as long as our unsub didn't swap plates on the vehicle, you can search the plates captured by the cameras and isolate all 2011 Toyota Tundras passing through this intersection without the need for a time or day," Clair interrupted. "Do it."

Kloz began typing. "I work better with coffee."

"You find something, and I'll buy you Starbucks for a month."

"That's wonderfully generous of you, but it doesn't solve my current situation."

Clair rolled her eyes at Nash. "Go get him something to drink."

Nash opened his mouth, prepared to argue, then thought better of it. He headed toward the small break room in the corner of the IT department.

Clair lowered her voice, leaned in closer. "Have you talked to Sam?"

Klozowski's gaze remained fixed on his monitor. "We're not supposed to contact him. I would never consider violating a direct order."

"I've tried him three times. I keep getting voice mail."

"Nash called too, a few hours ago. Same thing," Kloz said quietly.

A list appeared on Klozowski's screen. He selected a number of items and clicked Enter. "Look, the last thing I want to do is sound like the only grown-up in the room. Porter's my friend too, but he fucked us. The feds swooped in and took over the 4MK case, I'm good with that. That's how things happen in the real world. I washed my hands of it and moved on. You did. Nash did. Porter should have too." He stopped typing, his shoulders slumped. "You did back off, right? You don't have a secret crime-fighting lab somewhere?"

He started typing again before Clair could respond, then went on. "I like my job. I wish to succeed at my job, so I do what I'm told. Maybe that makes me a little weird, but I sleep like a baby, not a worry in my head. Oh, boy."

"What?"

"Toyota Tundras are popular."

"How many do you have?"

"Six hundred and twelve between December twenty-third and twenty-eighth."

Nash returned, carefully balancing three Styrofoam cups. He set one down next to Kloz and handed another to Clair.

Clair looked down at the screen. "Can you sort the list by the number of times they appear? Libby McInley working at this fish shop for one day is not a coincidence. If she's somehow working with our unsub and scouted the place out, that means our unsub didn't have to, so passes by this camera were probably limited. Higher numbers might be regular traffic patterns, like the same people coming and going from work every day."

Kloz adjusted some of the entries at the top of his screen, then hit Enter again. "Okay. Highest number of passes is fourteen. One hundred and six single passes, ninety-three doubles . . . I'm gonna sort from lowest to highest, then pull up static pictures."

Clair watched as the list disappeared, replaced with a dozen images of trucks, all taken from the same angle. "We're looking for someone towing a water tank."

Their eyes drifted over the pictures. After a few seconds, Kloz clicked Next at the bottom of the screen. The images were replaced with a new set. They studied the photos, then he clicked Next again, and again after that. They were twelve screens in before they found it. "There you are," Kloz said.

"Definitely the same truck we saw on the Jackson Park camera," Nash said.

"We need to run the plate and pull a name and address," Clair said. "Can you zoom in on the driver?"

"Yep." Kloz slid a toggle with his mouse, and the image expanded to take up the entire monitor. He double-clicked on the windshield until the driver's face came into view.

"Oh, balls," Nash muttered.

"Is that . . . ?" Kloz leaned back in his chair, his mouth open. He rubbed at the back of his neck.

"That's Bishop," Clair said softly.

55

Porter
Day 3 • 1:35 p.m.

"My chiropractor is not going to be happy with me," Sarah Werner groaned. She was lying on the desk in the observation room, the computer monitor and keyboard pushed to the side.

Guards had checked on them regularly about every thirty minutes, and Werner waved them off each time.

Porter slid back up in the chair. His everything hurt too.

He glanced at the clock hanging in the corner. "It's been about three hours. What's she doing in there?"

Sarah turned her head and looked back through the one-way window. "Still reading. We should have gotten lunch."

Porter's stomach grumbled in agreement. "I want to be here when she finishes. Best not to give her time to digest."

"No words related to food, please."

"Sorry."

Porter raised his arms over his head and stretched. He fought back a yawn. "You don't have to wait with me if you've got something else to do. I don't want to hold you up."

Sarah did yawn, covering her mouth. "I've got absolutely nothing else to do today."

"No significant other in your life?"

Sarah laughed. "I'm a criminal defense attorney in one of the country's most dangerous cities. I made the mistake of selecting an office with an apartment above it, which means my work literally comes home with me within just a few steps. Not that location matters, because I spend eighty hours or more a week with my head buried in case files regardless. If I'm not planted at my desk, I'm here or at the courthouse, sometimes the police station. Every decision I make sabotages any chance I may have at a life." She rolled her head and smiled at him. "This is the closest thing I've had to a date in about four months."

Porter felt his face flush. "Really? How am I doing?"

Sarah turned her gaze back to the ceiling and studied her fingernails. He noticed that they were not too long. If she wore polish, it was naturally toned. "You get points for originality, that's for sure. Your choice of venue is a bit subpar, though better than some."

"Maybe I could take you to dinner? Make it up to you?" The words slipped out before Porter realized he said them, and he wished he could take them back.

It was Sarah's turn to blush. She nodded at his hand. "Maybe you should clear that with home, Romeo. I may be hard up, but I'm not ready to go there yet. I don't even own a cat."

Porter's thumb slipped over the edge of his wedding ring. He looked down at the band. "My wife passed away last year. I probably shouldn't wear it anymore, but my finger doesn't feel right when I take it off."

Sarah turned back to the ceiling. "Our date just officially turned awkward. I'm sorry."

"I'm out of practice. In high school, I could turn a date south in under four minutes."

"Oh, big man on campus, were you? I can't imagine what you were like in high school."

Porter had to think for a minute, the distant memories teasing at him, barely visible through a long tunnel. "Sometimes all that seems so long ago. Then at other times it feels like yesterday."

"The type of memory designates the appeared distance in time."

"What does that mean?"

Sarah let out a shallow sigh. "Oh, something I read in a psychology text as an undergrad. The brain perceives happy times as recent activities when recollecting them. Horrible memories, though, they are pushed way back, sometimes forgotten or blocked altogether. Some sort of defense mechanism, I suppose. Surround yourself with the good, put some distance between you and the bad, that sort of thing."

"Maybe I should be the one lying down, Doctor."

"Want to trade?"

"The chivalrous gentleman in me would never subject a lady to this chair. The damn thing is nearly barbaric." Porter shifted his weight, the cold wood digging into his hind end. "If it was in the interrogation room, I'd get it—keep the suspect on their toes, but in here? Some poor guard probably spends a good chunk of his life in this chair."

"This desk is sorely lacking a memory foam pad too. *No bueno.*" She turned back to him, resting her head on a hand. "What do you remember?"

"From high school?"

She nodded. "Did you spend a lot of time getting shoved inside lockers, or were you the one doing the shoving?"

Porter chuckled. "I'm sure someone would have locked me in if I fit. I was a bit chubby."

"You?"

"Oh yeah. One fifty and five-two as a freshman."

"That's not too bad. You obviously grew out of it."

"I was *the* number one target whenever we played dodgeball. Then, junior year, I shot up nearly a foot. Looked like someone grabbed my head and stretched me out. Felt like that too. I remember it hurt like hell, and I lost all coordination for a while there. My arms and legs seemed too long. I'd trip over myself walking down the hall. I was a mess."

"I bet nobody screwed with you then, though. You were tall for high school."

Porter shrugged. "They didn't really mess with me before. I was a bit of a class clown. Someone tried to pick a fight, I'd crack a joke, all would be well."

"Too bad you couldn't hold on to that humor as an adult." Sarah grinned, her eyes twinkling in the dim light.

"Thanks."

She swung her legs off the desk and sat up on the edge, smoothing her gray skirt. "What's your best memory of high school?"

Porter thought about that for a second, drew a blank, then sat back up straight in the chair. "Oh no, I shared something with you. Now it's your turn. You're a pretty girl. I bet school was a breeze for you."

"Huh. I'm not sure what I should read into more. The fact that you called me *pretty* or called me a *girl*."

"Hell, you clearly didn't skip a single session of that psychology class, did you?"

"Not a one."

"I'm sure at some point we all became men and women, but I'm not quite sure at what age that occurs. I still feel like a kid, think of myself as a boy," Porter told her.

"I think it's around the time we get a mortgage, a real job. When we stop being the responsibility of others and take on responsibilities of our own."

"When we become fully visible," Porter said quietly.

"What?"

"Just something in Bishop's diary. He felt little children were invisible to the rest of the world and become less transparent with age. We're fully visible as adults, then fade again as we get older until society no longer sees us anymore," Porter explained.

"Huh. That's a bit profound. I think I'll keep it," Sarah said.

"I prefer not to collect my psychological and spiritual guidance from psychopaths."

"Yet you recalled the words verbatim."

The bang at the glass caused her to jump off the desk with a yelp. Porter stood up, his eyes fixed on the one-way window.

Jane Doe stood there, inches from the other side. The diary pinned against the window beneath her outstretched palm.

56

Poole

Day 3 • 1:35 p.m.

Special Agents Frank Poole and Stewart Diener sat in Poole's Jeep Cherokee about half a block down a quiet residential street from 519 Forty-First Place.

Poole studied the property through the lenses of Zeiss 526000 binoculars, heavy but extremely effective.

The house was small, probably two bedrooms, maybe one bath. Single story. The light-green paint was faded and chipped. A chainlink fence surrounded the property. A FOR RENT sign hung sideways at the gate, held in place precariously by a single black twist-tie in the corner. The sidewalks, yard, and driveway were all buried under at least a foot of snow. Nobody had shoveled here in some time. There was no car in the driveway. Heavy drapes drawn over the windows prevented him from seeing inside.

"Both the birth certificate and passport were shipped here. Security footage at the DMV has Libby obtaining the driver's license herself using the false docs three days after she was released from Stateville Correctional," Diener told him.

"Looks abandoned. No footprints in the snow leading up to the house. Can't see inside, curtains are drawn." Poole lowered the binoculars. "Probably some kind of drop house. Whoever helped her get the documents used this place for the address, nothing more."

Poole zipped up his jacket and wrapped a scarf around his neck. "I'm going to get a closer look."

Diener eyed the falling snow. "When's this shit supposed to let up?"

Poole didn't much mind the snow. Sometimes the ugly of the world was better left under a blanket of white.

The Jeep door groaned as he swung it open. Poole slammed it behind him. Sometimes the driver's side door didn't close well in the cold. He heard Diener get out and round the car, his shoes crunching in the snow.

They followed the sidewalk until they stood across from the property, then crossed the street. Poole had yet to see another car. Traffic appeared limited to only residents. That would make this a bit of an odd choice for a mail drop. Most preferred high-traffic areas. People tended to notice strangers in quiet neighborhoods, and those utilizing mail drops did not like to be noticed.

Images of Libby McInley's house flooded Poole's mind, specifically images of what he'd found inside. A sour taste filled his mouth. He wished he could forget such things, but his mind was rather insistent on keeping them at the forefront.

There were two mailboxes, both on a post at the edge of the property's sidewalk. The one on the left was meant for newspapers, had no door, and was empty. Poole opened the metal box beside it and extracted the few pieces of mail. "Publishers Clearing House addressed to Libby McInley and a veteran's donation card addressed to Resident, both postmarked this week. Somebody's watching this box," Poole told Diener before putting them back inside.

Diener glanced around the street. "About half the driveways have been shoveled recently. Once we check the house, we should speak to the neighbors. Quiet street like this, we're bound to find someone with eyes on this place."

The gate in the chainlink fence was frozen shut, and Poole had to beat on it a bit before the latch snapped open. The gate swung with reluctance through the thick snow, and they followed the sidewalk to the front of the house.

"Frank." Diener said his name quietly, a gloved hand pointing at the door. The deadbolt was missing, nothing but a gaping hole where it once was. The doorknob looked loose. The top was scratched and dented. Someone had hit it with something. Scuff marks marred the frame.

Poole unzipped his jacket and reached inside for his gun before trying the door. He pointed a finger at Diener, then at the side of the house. Diener drew his own weapon and disappeared around the corner in search of a back door.

Poole reached for the doorknob. Although it turned, he had to hold it steady. The bolts tasked with holding the assembly together had been either removed or unscrewed, and the entire cylinder felt like it might fall apart in his hand. The latch released with a click. He gave the door a gentle push.

The door opened on a small living room. Someone had taken a knife to the cushions of a dilapidated brown leather couch. Piles of stuffing floated through the room, tumbleweeds of white. The heat was off.

"This is the FBI. I need you to step out into the open!" His voice echoed through the house, the kind of sound that only came from an empty, forgotten place.

He stepped inside.

Graffiti covered the walls. Multicolored gang tags, names, and random sayings—Dasha Loves You, Little Mix, and X-Train Chirps. Poole had no idea what half of it meant.

Across the house, a back door popped open with a loud crack. Diener entered the kitchen with his weapon drawn, barrel pointed at the ceiling. He nodded at Poole and turned to the hallway at his right. He pulled a small flashlight from his pocket, switched on the beam, and held it under his gun, sweeping the light down the hall.

Poole crossed the room and followed him. The drywall in the hallway had been either kicked or punched in—there were dozens of holes from top to bottom. Someone looking for something buried in the walls or kids messing around, there was no way to know for certain. Once gold, now a soiled brown, the carpet stank of urine.

In the first bedroom, they found a mattress on the floor surrounded by empty food and beverage containers. A blanket was bunched up in the corner. Someone had taped newspapers over the windows beneath the drawn drapes. The bathroom had been used recently, but since the water was off, the bowl overflowed with a frozen mess Poole refused to think about. The bathtub had not fared much better. The vanity doors were gone, exposing cracked plastic pipes.

They moved on to the second bedroom.

No mattress here, only a torn sleeping bag and a battered gas camping grill. Someone used it either for cooking or to keep warm, or both. The room reeked of stale pot.

They returned to the living room. There was no basement. The house was deserted.

"I think we've got some homeless people flopping here, or maybe it's a hangout for local kids. Makes sense as a mail drop." Poole holstered his weapon. "How long has the house been vacant?"

Diener was back in the kitchen going through drawers and cabinets. "More than a year." He stared down into the sink drain. "Someone poured concrete in here."

"Kids do that sometimes," Poole said, studying the graffiti on the living room wall.

Diener went on. "I couldn't find much information on the property. The original owner passed away, and the house went to his three kids. They all live out of state. It's been on the market. I think they tried to rent it too—no takers though." He pulled a dead mouse out from under the sink, holding it by the tail, and tossed it across the room. "I don't understand why. The place is charming."

Poole ignored the mouse as it thudded against the floor near his feet. "There could be something here." He traced the graffiti with the beam of his flashlight.

Diener came over, stepped into the light. "Looks like more kid crap. Vandals, gangs, that sort of thing."

Poole pointed to a small block of text written in black marker.

Because I could not stop for Death,
He kindly stopped for me;

The carriage held but just ourselves
And Immortality.

"That's not kids, it's a quote from 'The Chariot' by Dickinson. And this one." He located another block of text written in the same hand.

A telling analogy for life and death:
Compare the two of them to water and ice.
Water draws together to become ice,
And ice disperses again to become water.
Whatever has died is sure to be born again;
Whatever is born comes around again to dying.
As ice and water do one another no harm,
So life and death, the two of them, are fine.

"That's from Hanshan, a Chinese poet dating back to the Tang Dynasty," Poole said.

"How the hell do you know that?"

"I had a girlfriend in college who was into Buddhism. She quoted from this book of poems all the time; this was in there."

"Figures. Why the underlining?"

Poole thought about it for a moment and shook his head. "I don't know."

Diener moved a few feet down the wall. "I've got another one over here, same handwriting."

Let us return Home, let us go back,
Useless is this reckoning of seeking and getting,
Delight permeates all of today.
From the blue ocean of death
Life is flowing like nectar.
In life there is death; in death there is life.
So where is fear, where is fear?
The birds in the sky are singing "No death, no death!"
Day and night the tide of Immortality
Is descending here on earth.

Poole frowned. "I think that one is Tibetan, but I could be wrong. I'm not sure why these words are underlined here either, *Home*, *fear*, and *death*."

Diener scratched at the back of his neck. "Smart kids but still kids. I don't think this has anything to do with Libby McInley."

Poole pulled out his phone and prepared to take pictures of the wall. "Why don't you go talk to the neighbors? I want to document this just in case."

The agent snorted. "Oh no, I canvassed the neighbors at McInley's murder scene while you sat nice and toasty back at Metro. If anyone is going back out in that cold on a door-to-door, it's you."

Poole looked reluctantly at the wall.

"Don't worry, I'll get every inch of it," Diener assured him.

With a nod, Poole pushed back out through the front door, into the icy air.

57

The Man in the Black Knit Cap

Day 3 • 1:35 p.m.

The man in the black knit cap pressed his fingers to his temples and squeezed. His thoughts pounded from inside, trying to get out, and it hurt. It hurt so much. He didn't realize he'd screamed again until the sound trailed off from his lips, a bit of saliva dripping down to the collar of his sweatshirt. He opened his eyes and the light from the window pushed in, sliced at his pupils, his retinas, a new pain on top of the old.

He fumbled with the lid of the prescription bottle in his left hand, the childproof white top slipping under his bloody fingers three times before he finally got the bottle open. He shook out two tablets, placed them in his mouth, and swallowed them dry, the chalky tablets gritty on the way down.

The bottle dropped to the top of his desk, and the remaining pills spilled out across his drawings, some clattering to the floor. He didn't care.

He looked down at his left hand, at his bloody fingers. He scratched at the incision on his head until he drew blood, yet even that wasn't enough. The moment he stopped, there was a second of relief, maybe two. Then the itch started again, beginning at his left ear and trailing to the back of his head like a thousand insects on a death march below the surface of his skin, burrowing deep into his head.

The insects ate his thoughts. He knew that now. They fed on his memories. That was why he had so much trouble remembering. They fed and multiplied, and the itch grew with their numbers—only a couple at first but now so many.

He reached for the phone, missing the first time. He grabbed at it and hit the first programmed speed dial, *his* number. The only number. The line rang once, twice, three times—

The mailbox you have reached has not been set up by the user and cannot accept incoming messages at this time. Please try your call again later.

He hit End Call, then the speed dial again. Three rings—

The mailbox you have reached has not been set up by—

He hung up. He wanted to throw the phone across the room. He wanted to watch the cheap plastic shatter into a million pieces as it hit the wall. He didn't though. He couldn't.

He needed another girl.

He needed the man to get him another girl.

Someone who would see. Someone who would see soon.

His vision cleared as the pill began to work, and he looked down at the drawing spread out in front of him. He remembered sketching this particular image, his daughter riding a bike along the sidewalk outside their house. It hadn't been that long ago, only last fall, about the time the first leaves began to drop. The drawing was wrong though, because the bike should be red. His right hand squeezed around the soft material of his daughter's sweater. He didn't remember picking it up, but there it was, bunched up in his hand, his index finger poking through the small collar.

He raised her sweater to his nose and smelled.

Nothing.

He wasn't quite sure when his sense of smell deserted him but knew it had been recently, probably in the past few days.

She was disappearing along with his senses, with his thoughts, his memories, as the insects feasted.

Shuffling through the contents scattered over the top of the desk, he found the red marker and removed the cap. He carefully lowered the tip to the paper, aiming for the metal frame of the bike. He knew the shakes would come, and he anticipated them, his face hot with blood as the anxiety built beneath his flesh. The tip of the marker found the page, and his hand remained steady as he cautiously moved the felt side to side. Tears came as he colored the image, as his hand moved like it once did, sure and steady. Tears came and fell upon the picture, his daughter on her shiny new bike.

From the basement came a muffled cry, but he ignored it.

He hated that girl for what she had done.

Damaged.

Unable to see.

Useless.

She would suffer for her sins. She would burn.

The bike colored, he moved on to color her sweater, identical to the one he held in his hand. The red sweater, always the red sweater. He colored the garment with the careful strokes he possessed in the time before all this, back when everything was right.

Even the itch had gone. Not entirely, but lessened, and he told himself he wouldn't scratch at the incision anymore. He wouldn't risk reopening the wound.

Another groan from the basement, this one louder than the last.

The itch tingled, just for a second. Not enough to require scratching. He wouldn't scratch at it.

He finished with the sweater and retrieved a blue marker, going to work on the sky. The fall skies in Chicago were usually marked with gray, but this bike ride was a happy time, and happy times called for blue skies.

He was so into his work, he didn't see the person cross the street through his window, he didn't see him approach his front door. He didn't notice him at all until he heard the knock, the heavy-handed knock downstairs.

The incision itched as the insects scattered for cover on tiny little feet.

58

Porter

Day 3 • 1:36 p.m.

"I think she's done," Sarah said, her fingers pressed to parted lips.

"You think?" Porter let out a breath.

Jane Doe stood there, her body frozen, the diary pressed between her palm and the window, the bang still reverberating through the room.

Sarah started for the door. "Give me a second. Let me talk to her before you go back in?"

Porter nodded, his eyes fixed on the woman on the other side of the glass. He knew she couldn't see him, but that didn't change the feeling that she was looking directly at him. Her eyes were filled with rage, dark and haunted, yet her breathing appeared measured. He couldn't get a read on her. Her heart could be racing, or possibly slow and steady. He imagined the latter. During the course of his career, he had encountered many people who could control their bodies, these physiological responses, to a certain extent, train themselves to remain calm when pressed with detrimental emotions. Their eyes though—there was no such filter on the eyes.

Sarah appeared on the other side of the glass, and Jane seemed not to notice her at first. She remained still. It wasn't until her attorney took a seat at the table that she finally turned. She crossed the room and sat beside Sarah, placing the book on the table.

She leaned over and whispered in Sarah's ear.

Sarah looked up at this, startled, maybe the first time she had heard her client speak. She said something too low for him to hear in return, then stood and went to the camera controls in the far corner. Porter watched as she flicked two wall switches. The first disabled the video feed, the second shut down audio. The observation room became deathly quiet as Sarah looked toward him from the other side of the glass, her eyes landing a little to his left, unsure of his actual location, before she returned to her seat beside Jane Doe.

The woman smiled at him then — subtle, to be sure, but a smile nonetheless. Then she turned back to her attorney and leaned in close.

Porter watched their lips move, a silent movie playing out before him, their hands and bodies telling a story he couldn't quite make out. Jane referred to the diary more than once, flipping to specific pages, her finger running along the text as she mouthed the words to the other. Through all this, Sarah Werner listened. She nodded, she shook her head, she frowned. She read parts of the diary as the other woman pointed them out. Porter wanted to pick up the chair, throw it through the glass, and climb into that room. He wanted that more than anything.

Finally, nearly thirty minutes later, Sarah stood and left the room. Her client buried her face in her hands.

The door to the observation room opened, and Sarah's head poked inside. "Come on, she's willing to talk to you now."

Porter realized his hands were trembling. The observation room couldn't be more than sixty-five degrees, yet a sweat had broken out on his brow.

"Are you all right?"

He nodded and started for the door.

She led him around the corner back to the interview room. The guard in the hallway had been replaced by another. Younger, Hispanic. He eyed them with indifference before returning his gaze to an interesting spot on the floor.

Porter entered the interview room and took the seat across from Jane again. Sarah sat beside her. The guard closed the door behind them.

Jane slid the diary back across the table to Porter, her fingertips lingering on the black and white cover. "This is not how it happened."

He wasn't sure what he had expected her voice to sound like. Harsh and authoritative, he supposed. It was anything but. The words slipped off her tongue with the smoothness of a bow on a violin. There was none of the anger he expected. She was calm, collected. He detected a slight southern accent.

"No?"

Her fingers left the diary. She folded them on the edge of the table, her head tilted slightly to the left. "Anson has always had a bit of an imagination, a leaning toward self-indulgence."

Sarah sat quietly across the table from him, her eyes first on the diary, then on him.

Porter leaned in closer. "Do you know where I can find him?"

Bishop's mother rolled her fingers, her nails tapping against the aluminum.

"Do you know where he is?"

The smile was there again, although she tried to suppress it, a hint at the corner of her lips. "Give me a pen."

"I don't have one."

She frowned. "I suppose not. They worry someone like me might plant it in your neck. So mistrustful, the powers that be." She kicked her feet beneath the table. "And me, all unshackled, ready to spring."

"Give her a pen," Porter told Sarah, his eyes fixed on her client.

Sarah's eyes narrowed. "Sam, I don't think—"

"Please."

Her posture stiffened, the tone of his voice taking her aback. She let out a breath and reached down into her briefcase, retrieved a blue ballpoint pen, and set it on the table in front of Jane.

The woman picked it up and removed the cap. Her free hand flew across the table, and Porter pushed back in his chair, almost toppling over. He regained his balance as her hand took the diary and pulled it back to her with a soft giggle. "No need to be jumpy, Sam. I don't usually bite."

Something about hearing his name come from her mouth sent the fingers of a dead hand over his spine.

She opened the cover of the diary and wrote on the first page. When she finished, she capped the pen and handed it back to Sarah, who quickly returned it to her briefcase.

Porter reached across the table and retrieved the diary, opened the cover. "What's this?"

She smiled, then stood. "I'd like to go back to my cell now."

She stood and went to the door and knocked twice at the glass.

The guard's face appeared in the small window, and a little door opened at waist height. She turned, facing them, and placed both hands in the opening. The guard locked a pair of handcuffs on her outstretched wrists and tightened them with a click behind her back. She stepped forward and the door swung open. The guard took her by the shoulder. "We'll talk again soon, Sam. I'm looking forward to it." Pausing at the door, she added: "Look to the place where the monsters hide, Detective. That's where you'll find answers."

With that, the guard led her away, the sound of her soft shoes shuffling down the hallway.

Sarah turned to Sam. "What did she write?"

He flipped the diary around so she could see the page:

12 Jenkins Crawl Road
Simpsonville, SC

59

Poole

Day 3 • 2:03 p.m.

Poole knocked again, louder this time.

The icy wind numbed his cheeks and neck, and he cursed himself for not wearing a scarf.

His knocking at the house on the left side of the abandoned property had gone unanswered. He'd peeked in the windows, and it didn't look like anyone was home. A dog spotted him, looked up from under a blanket on the floor, then went back to sleep without a single bark.

A neighbor had been home at the house on the right of the abandoned property, but she offered little in the way of useful information. The woman answered the door in a huff, her fingers clasping her thick pink robe tight around a rather rotund body. Golf blared from the seventy-inch television behind her at an ungodly volume. The display seemed completely out of place, much too large for the small living room and outdated décor. Empty Amazon boxes were stacked precariously just inside the door next to a coat rack dripping with at least a dozen coats, hats, and scarfs. Two small dogs sat on the couch and began yapping the moment he knocked, their agitation increasing as the door swung open and he came into view. The house smelled like cheese.

The woman frowned at him, yellow teeth behind chapped lips. "What?"

Poole held up his badge. "I'm with the FBI. I'd like to ask you a few questions about the house next door."

She ignored the badge, her stare fixed on him. "I don't know nothing about next door." She turned back to the dogs. "Shut the fuck up! The both of you!"

They hushed long enough to regain their breath, then started again.

"Have you seen anyone enter or exit the house in the past few weeks?"

"The owners don't give two rat's asses about that place. Since Hector died, his kids have let it go to shit, the ungrateful lot. He should have let me have the place. I was the one who took care of him when the cancer began to eat him up and he couldn't go to the store no more. I was the one."

Poole could only imagine the caregiving skill set this woman possessed. "What about after Hector passed, who was in the house?"

Her hand shot up and scratched her cheek, leaving the dry skin pink. "Ain't nobody been over there but maybe kids. Better they hang out there than in the streets, so nobody says much about it. If Hector's kids don't want them in there, they should install a better lock. Maybe put some paint on the place. Hector wouldn't have let his house go like that."

"What about the mail? Is someone keeping an eye on the mail for Hector's kids? I didn't see anything piled up, so someone must be collecting it."

"Man across the street took to collecting the mail. Nice fellow."

"Which house?"

The woman pointed. "The green one there."

When she released the robe, the frayed terry cloth fell open enough for Poole to get a glimpse of the happenings underneath, and he wished he hadn't.

Poole now stood at the green house across the street.

He knocked again.

60

The Man in the Black Knit Cap

Day 3 • 2:04 p.m.

Knocks.

So loud.

The damn incision on the side of his head ached with the noise, and he wanted to shout out, tell them to stop, put an end to it. But the knocks came again and again, each louder than the last until he found himself sitting at his desk with his hands pressed to his ears, the marker falling from his fingers to the floor at his feet.

He stood up.

He stumbled for the door of the small room, for the stairs, nearly tripping over his daughter's clothing strewn about.

He descended the stairs carefully, releasing his ears only long enough to steady himself on the railing.

Each knock echoed in his head.

The pain was worse than a migraine. Worse than a knife to the eye.

He wanted it to stop.

Needed it to stop.

He reached the bottom of the stairs and stumbled across the foyer to the front door. When he reached it, when his fingers slipped over the brass doorknob, he drew in a deep breath. He forced the breath into his lungs, into his muscles, his flesh. He forced the calming air to fill his body and relax the pain. He felt the burning at his cheeks dissipate. He felt the pain begin to lessen. His thoughts cleared.

He forced a smile onto his face and opened the door.

61

Poole

Day 3 • 2:04 p.m.

When the door opened, Poole was looking down at the badge in his left hand, his right hand about to knock again.

When the door opened, Poole didn't realize it was Anson Bishop doing the opening. He didn't look up into the other man's face until a moment after the man spotted his badge.

He had time enough to register his mistake before Bishop's fist wrapped around the collar of his jacket and pulled him inside the green house with the strength of a man running on pure adrenaline. He had time enough to hear four words slip from Bishop's lips before he pulled him inside and threw his body against a small table in the hallway, sending him crashing to the floor.

"You're not Sam Porter."

62

The Man in the Black Knit Cap

Day 3 • 2:04 p.m.

He opened the door.

Two people stood on his porch. Teenagers, a boy and a girl of about sixteen.

The boy was the first to speak. He wore a white shirt and black tie beneath a heavy down coat. "Good afternoon, sir. We are visiting you and your neighbors today to spread the truth. Mind if I ask what religious beliefs you follow? Are you Protestant? Catholic?"

The girl was staring up at the wound on his head, an uneasy smile on her face.

He tugged the black knit cap down tight, covering the inflamed incision as best he could. He returned her smile. "I . . . I recently had surgery. I'm sorry, I usually keep it covered. It can be . . . offensive."

The boy glanced over at the girl, then turned back to him. "If you are still with us, the Lord clearly meant to spare you. Scars are not offensive. They are a sign of healing, proof of faith, as are the trials that lead to them."

The man in the black knit cap found himself nodding, the pain and itch all but gone. "Would you like to come in? Get out of the cold?"

The girl shuffled her feet. She weaved her fingers into those of the boy at her side.

The boy smiled. "We'd love to."

63

Poole

Day 3 • 2:05 p.m.

The small table shattered, and Poole's shoulder burned—he crashed to the floor with pieces of wood raining around him.

Bishop grabbed him by the knee with one hand and just below the shoulder with the other, picked him up, and threw him against the opposite wall of the hallway with a half spin. Poole felt his head impact first the wall, then the hardwood floor with a deep thud. A burst of white light filled his vision, followed by a pain so intense, he thought he might black out. The pain started at his shoulder, right below his neck, and traveled down the length of his arm.

Poole crashed to the floor in a puddle, the butt of his gun digging into the sensitive flesh under his arm.

Bishop kicked him in the ribs.

A new pain, harsher than the first.

Through cloudy vision, he saw Bishop take a step back and pick up one of the broken legs from the table. He knelt beside Poole. "You'll have to forgive me—I wasn't expecting guests. Had I known you were coming, I would have picked up something nice from the bakery down the street. They make these delicious scones, not too sweet. I believe the chef adds a dab of honey, although she's a bit tight-lipped about it."

Bishop raised the table leg and brought it down on the base of Poole's neck. All went dark.

64

The Man in the Black Knit Cap

Day 3 • 2:05 p.m.

The man in the black knit cap ushered his two visitors inside and offered to take their coats. The boy removed his and handed the coat to him. The girl did not. She didn't so much as lower the zipper.

He smiled at them both. "I was about to make hot chocolate. Why don't you join me? Nothing better on a cold day than a cup of hot chocolate. Let's get comfortable in the kitchen, and you can tell me all about your cause."

Without waiting for a reply, he turned from them and proceeded down the short hallway to the kitchen. The boy followed him, the girl behind them both. It was her footfalls he listened to, the hesitancy in her step. Her boots had hard soles.

In the kitchen he pulled two chairs out from the table. "Please, make yourselves comfortable. This will just take a minute."

"You're very kind," the boy said.

From the corner of his eye, the man in the black knit cap watched the boy pull out the chair a little farther for the girl. She gave him a look and sat down. A soft thank-you from her lips.

"Please tell me, what are your names?"

He retrieved a deep copper pot from the cabinet above the stove, poured in some milk, and set the pot atop the gas burner. The blue flame licked across the bottom.

"My name is Wesley Hartzler, and this is my friend Kati Quigley," the boy told him, setting some reading materials on the table before folding his hands.

The Watchtower and *Awake!*

"Jehovah's Witnesses?"

"Are you familiar?" the girl said. Her hands were on the table too, but she still wore thick gloves, her fingers a blur of nervous motion.

Her voice was sweet. It held the ring of a crystal bell.

He retrieved a large wooden spoon from the drawer at his left and began to stir the milk. "I am familiar with God's word in many forms. I have to say, though, when Witnesses come calling, they're usually much older than the two of you."

"We're sixteen, sir. Plenty old enough to spread the word," the boy said.

"Wesley, is it?"

"Yes, sir."

"I couldn't help but agree. There is so much to be learned from to-day's youth, and you are so often disregarded."

He fetched three mugs, located the tin of Godiva hot cocoa mix he kept above the stove, and scooped a large helping into each mug. When the milk began to simmer, he poured equal portions into each mug, then added a drop of vanilla. "My mother used to make cocoa like this, with vanilla, and even after all these years I haven't been able to shake the habit. Vanilla adds just a bit of mystery, a hint at some-thing special."

He placed a mug in front of each visitor and returned to the table, cradling the third. He sat and smiled at them both. "I imagine spread-ing the word is a difficult task in today's world. So many people are lost. It must be frustrating."

"What religion do you follow? Mr . . . ." Kati Quigley asked. She removed her gloves and wrapped her fingers around the mug. He noted that she did not drink.

"You may call me Paul." He smiled at her and sipped his cocoa.

"Like the apostle," Wesley said, before drinking from his own mug.

"Just like the apostle." He wiped his lips on the sleeve of his sweat-shirt. "I suppose I'm a bit of a searcher when it comes to religion. I've pulled a little from here, and some from there. I've found that discovery can be just as enlightening as scripture."

"Our hall is less than a mile from here. You should join us. We have open meetings every Saturday beginning at eight in the evening, and they only go for an hour or so. I'm sure everyone would love to hear your views." Wesley took another drink of his cocoa. A drop of chocolate stuck to the corner of his mouth. "This is delicious."

At his side, Kati jumped, narrowing her eyes at him.

Had he kicked her under the table?

Wesley went on. "After the meeting, there is usually cake and refreshments. Maybe you can share your hot chocolate recipe."

"That sounds like a splendid time."

Kati raised her mug to her lips. He watched her sniff at the steaming beverage. She took a short, hesitant sip. "Mmm, this is wonderful." She placed the mug back on the table in front of her, turning it several times before dropping her hands into her lap.

"I'm glad you like it."

"Do you have a family, Paul?" Kati said.

"I have a daughter your age. She can be a little shy too."

"Oh, I'm not shy."

"No?"

Kati shook her head, sampling the hot chocolate again. He couldn't tell if she was really drinking or only raising the mug to her lips in an attempt to appear like she was drinking.

"Kati can be very talkative once she gets to know you," Wesley chimed in.

"Where is your daughter? Is she home?" Kati's eyes darted over the small kitchen.

"She's resting, upstairs. She hasn't been feeling well lately."

"Is there a Mrs. Paul?"

The man in the black knit cap lowered his gaze. "I'm afraid we lost her when my daughter was born. There were . . . complications."

"God works—"

He waved a hand at her. "I'm very familiar with his mysterious ways."

"These are trials. He's testing you. Testing your faith," Wesley said.

"That may very well be true, but it makes such things no less painful. Have either of you ever lost someone you care about? Someone who means the world to you?"

Wesley and Kati exchanged a glance, then shook their heads.

"You're both so young. Let's hope you don't have to experience such things for a very long time. Let's hope God has no reason to zero in on either of you. If he does, hopefully you'll catch him on a good day."

"Every day is a good day with the Lord in it," Wesley said.

"Yes . . . I suppose it is."

"Will you bring your daughter to the Kingdom Hall?" Kati asked.

He smiled at her. "I'm sure she would like nothing more than to attend."

Wesley finished off his hot chocolate and made a bit of a show of setting the empty mug back on the table. "Well, Paul. I think it's time we get going. We have many others we would like to touch today." He slid one of the pamphlets across the table. "The address of our hall is on the back. Like I said, not very far from here at all. We'd love to see you. You and your daughter."

The man in the black knit cap finished his hot chocolate and scratched at the wound on the side of his head. A slight throbbing began behind it again. "Tell me, Wesley, what do Jehovah's Witnesses believe happens to the soul after death?"

Wesley had begun to rise from his chair. He glanced over at Kati, then sat back down. "Well, we believe the soul dies with the body as punishment for sins committed by Adam and Eve."

"So, no heaven? No hell?"

"Oh, there is a heaven, but God only permitted the souls of 144,000 to join him there, to rule under Christ, to help create a heaven upon earth."

"What becomes of the rest of us, then?"

Kati crossed her arms. "According to Genesis 3:19, God said, 'You will return to the ground, for out of it you were taken. For dust you are and dust you will return.'"

"So, no hope then." He gestured around the room. "All this, and we are nothing more than dirt. All those we love, nothing but food for worms and trees." He heard an anger brewing in his voice and stomped it back down. "I suppose we should strive to be one of the righteous so we can hope to become one of the 144,000, then."

Wesley edged the pamphlet closer to him. "Joining us, spreading the word, that offers the best hope. It is never too late."

The man in the black knit cap wrapped his fingers around his empty mug. "Oh, I don't know. For some of us, it just may be."

With a wide swing, he brought the mug up and bashed it into the side of Wesley's head. The ceramic cracked with the impact, and the little loop handle dangled from his index finger for a second before falling to table. Wesley toppled sideways and crashed to the floor, his chair dropping with him.

Kati took a moment to process what had just happened, her eyes wide and fixed on the boy on the floor at her side. She watched like someone engrossed in a television program, her brain unwilling to accept what she had just seen.

The man in the black knit cap took this moment of hesitancy to leap up, his fingers seizing the collar of her coat.

Kati swatted at his arm, breaking his hold, and threw the remains of her hot chocolate in his face before spinning away and running back down the hallway toward the front door.

The liquid burned his eyes, the soft flesh beneath them. He didn't care. He didn't feel it. He scrambled over the chair and chased after her. "Kati! Sweetie? Hasn't anyone ever told you it's rude to leave the table before you're excused?"

She reached the front door and tugged at the knob, fumbled with the deadbolt.

He had the key in his pocket.

She banged on the door with both fists. She screamed. He could barely hear her. Her cries were muffled, underwater cries. Kati turned, her back against the door. "Please . . ."

He reached for his wound. His fingers came away wet with fresh blood. He imagined the blood seeping down through newly turned dirt in some forgotten graveyard.

"Please don't . . ."

Her head made a satisfying clunk as he slammed it against the hardwood door, his fingertips leaving bloody streaks on her forehead.

65

Porter

Day 3 • 2:06 p.m.

"What does it mean? Is that where she's from?" Sarah Werner asked.

They were in line at the lockers, waiting their turn to check out of the prison.

"You can't go," Porter said flatly.

Sarah frowned at him. "I didn't say I wanted to go. If I did want to, I would."

"There's something brewing behind those eyes of yours, and I don't like it."

"She's my client. I have just as much a right to go as you do. Whatever is there may give me some insight into this case, something I can use to help her."

"Whatever is there is part of the ongoing 4MK investigation."

"I want to read that diary too."

"That's evidence."

Sarah smirked. "Evidence that is not tagged and you are carrying on your person without gloves or any regard for chain of custody."

They reached the front of the line. Porter slipped the key into his locker, opened the small door, and retrieved the contents: his belt, shoelaces, wallet, a disposable cell phone, and a knife—a Ranger Buck knife with collapsing blade.

Bishop's knife.

"Do you want to grab a late lunch?" Sarah asked.

Porter shoved the various items into his pockets and relaced his shoes. "I need to get to the airport."

"We need to talk about this. You can book your flight from the restaurant." She tilted her head to the side, her dark hair falling over her shoulder. "You can't run off on an empty stomach, and I don't think TSA will let you pass once they hear you didn't try any genuine Creole cooking during your visit to the Big Easy."

"You're a hard girl to say no to," Porter said, the weight of the knife pressing against his thigh.

Thirty minutes later they sat at a small table in the corner at Dooky Chase's on the corner of Orleans Avenue and Miro Street. Porter had three plates in front of him—one with shrimp and lima beans, another with cheesy potatoes, and the third holding a sandwich.

There was a direct flight from New Orleans to Greenville, South Carolina, leaving in a little less than two hours. He'd have to rent a car and drive from there to Simpsonville, about twenty minutes away.

"When exactly was the last time you ate?" Sarah asked, staring at the food in front of him. She had a bowl of gumbo and sipped from a tall iced tea.

Porter had to think about that for a second. "Candy bar yesterday, I think." He looked down at his plates, his eyes jumping between the various offerings. "Poor boy or shrimp, poor boy or shrimp, poor boy or shrimp . . ."

"It's po' boy, not poor boy. You're gonna get shunned by the locals before you take your second trip to the buffet."

Porter dug into the shrimp and followed with a forkful of the cheesy potatoes. His eyes lit up. "This is amazing."

"Leah Chase has been cooking here for seventy years. She's in her nineties now. Still has the best fare in the city," Sarah told him. "I've seen Ray Charles in here. Martin Luther King, Jr., used to stop by whenever he was in town. Barack Obama is even a fan. You gotta try this gumbo."

She held a spoonful out to him. Porter hesitated for a second, a flash of Heather feeding him passing through his mind—their anniversary two years ago at Carl's Steakhouse.

"Sam?"

Porter snapped back, took the spoon, and tried the gumbo. Delicious.

"Are you okay? I lost you there for a second."

The sun streamed in from a window beside their table, the rays glinting in Sarah's eyes. The thumb of Porter's left hand passed over the surface of his wedding band. He flexed his fingers, moved his hand to his lap.

"We had a secondary development back at the prison," he said, digging back into the potatoes. "I've been on the fence about telling you, but I think you should know."

"What?"

He reached into his left pocket, pulled out the burner cell phone, and set it on the table. Then he reached into his right pocket, extracted the knife, and placed it beside the phone. "I didn't have a knife or a phone with me when I arrived at the prison. Someone put these in my locker while we were talking to your client."

Sarah's eyes went wide. "We should go back, tell the warden."

Porter shook his head. "That would be a bad idea. He would probably confiscate the phone, start some kind of investigation. He arrests whoever did it, and I lose an avenue of contact with Bishop." He flicked the knife with his finger, the blade spinning on the table. "Bishop mentioned a knife like this in his journal. This might be the same one."

"You think Bishop gave you those things?"

"Not personally, but someone working with him, yeah." Porter looked down at the display. The phone was switched on and fully charged.

"Can I see it?"

Porter handed it to her.

Sarah scrolled through the various menus. "It's not a smartphone. The call log is empty, no stored contacts, no text messages. I don't think it's been used before." She gave the phone back to him. "So now what? We wait for him to call?"

Porter bit into his sandwich. "Now you go back to your office, and I head to the airport."

"Do you really think I'm going to let you do this on your own?"

"I don't recall extending an invitation."

"She's my client. I deserve to know where this leads."

"I'll call you."

"From your burner phone?" She leaned across the table. "How many cops travel on official business without a gun or a phone of their own? How about you show me your badge? All I've seen are business cards. You could have made those down at the QuickCopy."

"Lower your voice."

She did lower her voice, and yet it cut him harder than when she shouted. "How do I know you're not some kind of psycho pretending to be a cop?"

"Let me see your phone," Sam said calmly.

"Why?"

"Sarah, please."

She drew in a deep breath, then pulled her iPhone from her purse and handed it to him.

Porter opened a web browser and typed in his own name. Dozens of articles came up, along with several pictures not only of him but of Anson Bishop and a few of 4MK's victims. He handed it back to her.

Sarah glanced down at the display, scanned the headlines, then shut the phone off. "You need to level with me, Sam. You can trust me. I want to help you."

So he did.

He told her everything.

66

Poole

Day 3 • 2:23 p.m.

Poole's eyes fluttered. He caught a glimpse of the hallway, tried to stand, and blacked out again.

He wasn't sure how long he had been out the first time or when he woke again. When he woke for the second time, he stayed down. He scanned the hallway through watery vision. He tried to listen to the house, but the sound of his own blood pounding in his ears fought him, drowning out nearly everything else.

He lay there for minutes, perhaps seconds. Time and consciousness weren't fluid anymore but instead became a rope ladder without a top, without a bottom, something he only tried to cling to.

The drumming at his ears faded, replaced with the steady tick of a grandfather clock down the hall. He could see the side of it, but the face was turned the other way, the sweeping hands pointing toward something else.

He freed his right hand and tugged his Glock from the shoulder rig.

There was no sign of Bishop.

Poole sat up slowly, first to a crouch, waiting for the dizziness to leave. His left hand found the tender spot on the back of his neck where Bishop had struck him. There was a lump the size of a fist back there. No blood, though. He might have a concussion but couldn't be sure. Poole found his feet and forced himself to stand. A wave of white washed across his vision, and he steadied himself on the wall to keep from passing out.

The gun felt heavy and almost fell from his fingers. He gripped tighter, purposely pressing his finger into the sharp corner of the trigger guard, the bite of pain helping him focus.

Poole started down the hall, his arms outstretched in a double hold, the gun's barrel pointing at the ground ahead of him.

The entrance hallway led to an open-concept dining and living room with a kitchen set into the back corner, all sparsely furnished. He swept all three spaces, then focused his attention on another hallway on the far side of the house, to the left of the living area. Unlike the one at the front door, this hall was narrow. He found a small bathroom at one end and a single bedroom at the other. The sheets atop the double bed were pulled taut. Bishop had made the bed.

There was a dresser along the far wall. Three of the drawers stood open, all empty. Back in the bathroom, he found a wet sink but none of the typical toiletries.

He got the feeling Bishop had been here for a little while, that it was some kind of sanctuary. He hadn't expected a federal agent to show up on his doorstep. He got spooked and cleared out fast.

Poole reached for his phone. It was gone.

He returned to the hall, thinking he dropped it during the struggle with Bishop, but it wasn't there either.

Diener.

Poole went to the door, tugged at the knob.

Locked.

Bishop had taken the time to lock the deadbolt on his way out.

Poole fumbled with the thumb latch, his movements still not entirely his own.

The winter wind rushed inside.

Across the street, the door to the abandoned house stood open.

Poole darted across the road, still holding his gun out in front of him, partially aware of the curtain falling back into place at the neighbor's house, her body highlighted by the large green display behind her as the golf tournament cut to a car commercial.

He didn't realize he'd shouted Diener's name until the sound of his own voice echoed back at him from the otherwise silent house, nor did he spot his body at first, propped up against the corner of the living room wall, his neck, coat, and shirt all soaked with blood.

67

Poole
Day 3 • 2:26 p.m.

The blood was warm.

Poole pressed his index finger against Diener's neck, already knowing what he'd find but compelled to check anyway. One of Diener's lifeless eyes watched him, staring out from a narrow slit. The left eye had been removed, leaving a black void. Diener's left ear and tongue were also missing.

Bishop had punctured the retromandibular just under Diener's chin, then sliced with a downward motion, opening the vein. Diener's hand and arm were covered in blood. He'd apparently tried to stem the flow, but the effort proved futile. Most likely, he had bled out in under a minute.

Poole could see the butt of Diener's gun still secured in his shoulder holster. Bishop somehow surprised him—no time to retrieve the weapon. Diener probably heard the front door and assumed it was Poole returning.

There was little blood at the missing ear and eye, suggesting they had been removed post mortem.

Poole didn't have much trouble finding these missing appendages.

Portions of the graffiti had been cut out of the drywall, four squares in all. Bishop had cut out the poems written in black marker and placed Diener's eye, ear, and tongue in three of the four dark openings.

Poole's heart thudded wildly in his chest, and the bump at the back of his neck ached. He bent back over and searched Diener's body for his phone.

Gone.

When he stood back up, the sudden movement caused his balance to falter. He reached for the wall, his fingers feeling the dirty grit of it.

Ten minutes would pass before he'd find the strength to get to the house next door and call for help.

68

Clair

Day 3 • 2:30 p.m.

"Why would Bishop be working with Libby McInley?" Clair asked.

"More importantly, why would Libby McInley work with Bishop? He killed her sister, for Christ's sake," Nash replied.

They were back in the war room.

The image of Bishop in the truck had been blown up and printed and was now taped to one of the whiteboards at the front of the room.

"We need to share this with the FBI," Kloz said from the conference table. "These cases are connected to 4MK. They need to know."

Both Clair and Nash stared at him.

He raised both hands defensively. "What? We can't hold this back."

"Where is Libby McInley now? She's out of prison, right? Does she have a parole officer or someone keeping tabs on her?" Clair asked.

Klozowski pulled his laptop close. After a few keystrokes, his face turned white.

"What?"

Kloz's eyes went wide, quickly scanning the text. "This is not good."

Clair shook her head, crossed the room, and turned the laptop screen so she could read.

"Go ahead, I wasn't reading that," Kloz said.

She raised a hand, silencing him.

Kloz pushed back from the table on his wheeled chair.

"Fuck, fuck, fuck," Clair finally spat out, turning the display back to him.

"Yeah," Kloz said.

"What is it?" Nash asked, crossing behind them.

"Libby McInley was found dead last night by Poole and friends. Eyes, ear, and tongue removed. Tortured too," Clair replied.

Nash frowned. "If Libby and Bishop were working together, why would he kill her? That doesn't make sense."

"Does anything about Bishop make sense?" Clair glanced toward the door, the room across the hall occupied by the FBI. "Why didn't those guys tells us?"

Kloz blew out a breath. "Two seconds ago you wanted to withhold what we learned about Bishop, and you're wondering why the FBI cut us out of the loop?" He spread out both hands. "Their case, our case. Different cases."

"Until now," Nash said.

"Until now."

Clair crossed the room and looked out into the hall. "I haven't seen those guys since yesterday, have you? Their door is closed."

"I haven't seen any of them since Porter's apartment," Nash said.

Clair turned to him. "We should try Sam again."

Nash took out his phone and dialed. A moment later he shook his head. "Still voice mail, no answer."

"We need to go over there," Klozowski said. "Something's wrong."

"I thought you were afraid of getting in trouble. Thought he needs to take his medicine, got to follow orders," Clair said.

"That was an hour ago. Now it feels like something is wrong."

Nash was still staring at his phone display. "The kid's right, this feels off. Sam doesn't just drop off the radar like this. He'd answer for one of us."

Clair let out a breath. "All right. We figure out our next move, and we hit his apartment while we're out."

Nash nodded. "Yeah, that works."

Clair walked back over to the whiteboards. "Okay, let's focus here. We need to connect these dots. How does Bishop play into this mess?"

There was a knock at the door, and all three turned to find Sophie Rodriguez standing there.

Clair felt her face go slack. "Oh no."

Sophie stepped inside. There were bags under her eyes. Her arms hung limp at her sides. "I took the call ten minutes ago. Larissa Biel. About the same age as the others. She was supposed to attend a school dance tonight. Her mother wanted to surprise her, so she bought them a spa day. She went into the office for a few hours this morning, and when she got home, Larissa wasn't there. She started calling around to her friends. None of them had seen her either. Because of the girls in the news, she got panicked and called Missing Children." Sophie paused for a second. "I don't know, this could be premature, but something feels wrong."

"When was she last seen?" Clair asked.

"Her mother said she was still sleeping this morning when she went to work. That was six thirty. Her father said there is no sign of a break-in and her room looks 'normal,' his word. Her boots, coat, and phone are gone."

Nash reached for his coat. "We need to secure the parents. If this is Bishop, they could be in danger like the others."

Sophie frowned. "What makes you think this is Bishop?"

"We'll tell you on the way." He turned to Klozowski. "Kloz—"

He was back at his computer. "I'm already on it. Checking all obituaries published in the past two weeks for Biel. What are the parents' first names?"

"Darlene and Larry," Sophie said.

"Do you have Larissa's cell phone number? I'll start a trace on that too."

Klozowski's phone dinged.

"I texted it to you," she told him. "Their home address too."

"Get uniforms over there—tell them we're on our way," Clair shouted over her shoulder as the three of them raced down the hallway.

69

Poole
Day 3 • 5:18 p.m.

Poole stood in the center of the green house, Bishop's house, with an ice pack pressed to the back of his neck. Federal agents had taped off this property as well as the abandoned home across the street and now swarmed over both. He watched them take out Diener's lifeless body on a stretcher about an hour ago, only after all evidence was collected and the scene was properly documented.

The woman in the pink robe moved a chair to her picture window and watched the activity with a mug in her hand, golf long forgotten. Agents interviewed her upon arrival but got nothing beyond what she had told Poole.

Special Agent in Charge Foster Hurless stood beside him, his usual scowl etched on his face. "Tell me what happened again."

"I didn't see a car in the driveway. He left on foot. He might still be close. I'm not doing any good standing here," Poole said.

"Medical needs to clear you, and we have a dead agent. I've got people going door to door. The only footsteps in the snow outside are on the walkway and the driveway. There's no garage," Hurless told him. "This place is small."

"Well, I'd remember a car."

"He could have parked on the street. There are cars up and down this road."

Poole said nothing.

"Tell me again."

"There isn't much to tell. We traced the fake identification to a mailing address—the abandoned house across the street. We cleared the house. I drew the short straw, and Diener opted to photograph the interior, particularly the walls with the graffiti, while I talked to the neighbors. The woman across the street said the man living here collected the mail, so I came here next. I didn't expect Bishop to open the door. He took me by surprise. We struggled. He bested me when he got ahold of the table leg. When I woke, I cleared this house, then went back across the street and found Special Agent Diener."

"So you knew someone used the house across the street as a mail drop, you knew that someone came from here, and you still came over without backup?"

Poole felt his face flush. "I had no reason to believe there was any danger. I most definitely didn't expect Bishop."

"And he was expecting Sam Porter? The Metro detective?"

"His exact words were, 'You're not Sam Porter.' I'm not sure what that means."

"It means he wouldn't have been surprised to find Porter on his doorstep."

Poole shook his head. "I know what you're thinking, but Porter is a good cop. He made some mistakes, but he's not mixed up in this, not like that. He wants this guy found, that's all."

Hurless touched his chin. "Maybe, maybe not. I just learned there was a diary on the body they found a few months back, the bus victim they thought was 4MK. Apparently it was Bishop's diary. Porter never checked it into evidence. It's mentioned in the report, but Metro doesn't have possession, never did."

"Why would he withhold evidence?" Poole asked.

"Why would Bishop expect him on his doorstep?"

Poole grimaced, pressing the ice pack harder against his neck. "Why mention the diary in a report if he planned to withhold?"

"The diary is in Detective Nash's report, not Porter's. Porter doesn't mention it once in forty-three pages of typed text."

A crime scene tech approached and stood silently beside SAIC Hurless, waiting for a break in the conversation. They looked at her and she raised her voice. "Sir. We've completed our preliminary of this residence. There are no prints. We found traces of latex residue on many of the surfaces, so he most likely wore gloves while here. Other surfaces have been wiped clean."

"What about the table leg he hit me with?"

"Wiped," she said.

Poole nodded toward the bathroom, regretting the motion the moment he did it. "What about the bathtub or shower. Maybe he bathed here?"

"The bathtub was dry and covered with bleach stains. We think he cleaned it after each use—same with the sinks in both the bathroom and the kitchen. He removed the traps on the plumbing as well. We're taking all the remaining pipes with us in case something got caught up inside. We're also vacuuming all surfaces. We'll find something," she assured them. "Nobody can hide completely."

"Any way to tell how long he was here?" Poole asked.

She shook her head. "He was ready to bug out on a moment's notice. Probably got out in less than ten minutes. He could have been here for days or months."

"The woman across the street said she remembers seeing him as far back as six months ago," Hurless said.

"So Bishop put this together as a safe house before he was outed as 4MK."

"Looks that way. According to property records, the house is owned by a subsidiary of Talbot Enterprises. They've been buying up houses in this area for about two years and turning them out as rentals. They keep the utilities on to prevent the pipes from freezing while they're vacant. The whole neighborhood is a hotspot for the homeless and squatters. Once he jimmied the lock, he'd be able to come and go as he pleased. It's not tough to run a disguise in weather like this. Everyone's got multiple layers on. He wouldn't stand out."

"If he set up this safe house in advance, most likely he has others."

"That would be my guess."

Poole turned back to the tech. "What about the cell phones? Bishop took mine and Agent Diener's."

"Both went dark at twenty-four minutes past two this afternoon," she replied.

Poole lowered the ice pack and turned back to SAIC Hurless. "Can we go back across the street? I want to get a better look at that wall."

Diener's body was gone, but the dark red stain remained. Poole could still hear the man's gruff voice, the shuffle of his gait. He half expected him to come walking out from a back room followed by one of the remaining crime scene investigators.

SAIC Hurless motioned toward the graffiti wall. "What can you tell me about these cutouts?"

Diener's eye still sat precariously on the edge of the dusty drywall, a tag with the number 37 placed beside it.

Poole traced the opening with the tip of his finger. "There was a poem here—Dickinson. Written with a black marker or a Sharpie. It said:

Because I could not stop for Death,
He kindly stopped for me;
The carriage held but just ourselves
And Immortality."

He crossed over to the second hole, where Diener's ear now lay, tagged number 38. "This one was Hanshan." He recalled the poem verbatim:

"A telling analogy for life and death:
Compare the two of them to water and ice.
Water draws together to become ice,
And ice disperses again to become water.
Whatever has died is sure to be born again;
Whatever is born comes around again to dying.
As ice and water do one another no harm,
So life and death, the two of them, are fine."

At the third hole, Diener's tongue now lay in silent reflection of the words that had been here earlier, the number 39 beside it:

"Let us return <u>Home</u>, let us go back,
Useless is this reckoning of seeking and getting,
Delight permeates all of today.
From the blue ocean of death
Life is flowing like nectar.
In life there is death; in death there is life.
So where is fear, where is <u>fear</u>?
The birds in the sky are singing 'No death, no <u>death</u>!'
Day and night the tide of Immortality
Is descending here on earth."

He motioned toward the opening, toward invisible words. "Home, fear, death, were all underlined. The poem is Tibetan, old."

It was the fourth hole that intrigued him most, higher on the graffiti wall and off to the right. Nothing sat within it, only an empty space in the drywall, but clearly cut away by Bishop with the same careful technique he used on the other spaces—nearly a perfect square missing.

Poole had not studied whatever was here as he did the others. With those, he read the words, took in the measured handwriting. He could see each letter with perfect clarity in his mind's eye. This hole was different. At best, he had glanced at this portion of the wall.

"What about this one?" Hurless said. "What was written here?"

Poole raised a hand, silenced him, then closed his eyes, concentrated, focused on what he saw when he first walked the abandoned house. He had seen this wall, but he hadn't *seen* the wall. He hadn't made a conscious effort to memorize it, to take it in. The haphazard artwork and words were nothing more than a smear in his memory, a Pollock painting slightly out of focus.

Are you trying tell me something, Bishop, or are you hiding something? Poole thought.

He pictured the wall, every inch of the wall. He visualized himself walking past, his eyes taking in every speck of color, his eyes glancing over this very spot, this missing spot. The same black handwriting, the blocky letters. He could see them, but they were out of focus, like the background of a photo with a subject front and center and all else blurred. He concentrated on those black words, on the blur, not so much the meaning of the words but the image of them. He concentrated until they came into focus, one letter at a time, and only then did he read, speaking them aloud: "You can't play God without being acquainted with the devil."

70

Kati

Day 3 • 5:20 p.m.

Kati Quigley woke with a start. It had begun slowly, her ascent from sleep, but that last moment when her consciousness climbed out of the well and burst through the opening at the top came fast, and it caused her to jump.

Her hands were tied behind her back. Her feet were bound too. Her eyes covered, some kind of blindfold. The ground felt damp beneath her. The air smelled of waste—feces and urine and something else.

"Hello?"

The sound of her own voice seemed thin, a stranger's voice. A pain throbbed against her temple, and for a moment she couldn't remember why. Then the memories of what happened came flooding back, a horrid onslaught of images ending with the man with the disgusting wound on his head chasing her down the hallway, bashing her into the door.

Oh God.

"Wesley?"

A shuffle beside her, only a few feet away.

A thin light crept through the cloth over her eyes but not enough for her to really see—only vague shapes and shadows, strange monsters dancing in the distance.

"Wesley? Is that you? Are you okay?"

She remembered the ugly man diving across the table and slamming his cocoa mug into Wesley's head, the terrible cracking sound it made followed by Wesley falling to the floor. She ran then. She should have tried to help him, but instead she ran, thinking of nothing but herself as the ugly man came after her.

"I'm sorry, Wesley," she said quietly, sobs threatening to choke her words.

A groan then, again, only a few feet away—not Wesley. This was a girl's voice. Even though it was muffled and faint, she could tell.

"Who's there? Who are you?" Kati pulled her knees to her face, tried to slide the blindfold from her eyes with her knee. It didn't work, though. The cloth was secure, too tight.

She forced her body to shuffle toward the voice, like an inchworm, using her legs to push the rest of her. The pain on the side of her head cried out with each movement, rushing over her with waves of nausea. She didn't stop, though. She forced herself toward the voice until her arm brushed against something soft, something warm.

The other girl jerked as their skin came in contact, and then she pulled some sort of blanket or quilt up between them.

"Who are you?" Kati said again, feeling the squirm beside her.

"She wasn't pure, she will never see. Instead, she has cast herself into the fiery lake to drown in her own blood."

Kati jumped at the voice, a shiver rushing over her body like fingers across a coffin lid.

A man's voice, the man with the wound. He had trouble with the letter *s*. He said the words at just above a whisper from only a few feet away, from the direction she had just moved.

Kati shuffled closer to the warm body next to her. She felt the body twitch beneath the blanket. "Where are we? Where's Wesley?"

The man coughed, his breath catching, sounding wet. "Your friend Wesley is there with you. He is not doing well."

Kati thought of the smells—feces, urine, and something else. She didn't want to think about that something else. "The people at the Kingdom Hall, they know where we are. They know we were on this street, what houses we planned to visit. If you let me go, I'll tell them it was an accident. I'll tell them Wesley fell and you tried to help him."

"I don't care if they come for you. I don't care if they come for me. We'll be done by then."

His voice drew closer now. Kati could hear him crossing the floor, the slight drag of one of his feet. She could hear it, something wrong with the way he walked.

A rattling noise, metal on metal. A door opening.

"Will you see for me?"

Beside her now. She could feel his hot breath on her neck.

"Will you tell me what you see?"

Kati screamed, and the moment the sound left her lips, he shoved something into her mouth, a rag or cloth. It tasted like dirt and something sour. Then his arms were around her—he lifted her off the ground and carried her. A hand came out from the blanket beside her and wrapped around her arm for a brief second before falling away.

"You are a believer, a follower. You *will* see."

Dropping then.

The man let her go, or lowered her, she couldn't be sure. She felt the water first, then his arms were gone, and she sank deeper into it, whatever *it* was. She sank until almost completely submerged, all but her face, her blindfolded face reaching for air from the highest point. Her hands and feet touched bottom, and if she tilted her head, she could keep it above the water line.

The water was warm, nearly hot.

Had Kati been able to see, she would have watched the man in the black knit cap as he pulled the tarp from the stack of car batteries wired in a series next to the freezer converted into a water tank. She would have seen him pick up both ends of the jumper cables attached to the last battery in the series. She would have seen him drop both ends down into the water.

Kati didn't see any of those things.

Kati saw nothing at all as the electricity caused her body to spasm with such strength, she broke the zip ties at her hands and feet.

She saw nothing but the brightest of white lights.

71

Clair
Day 3 • 5:43 p.m.

"I'm not going to sit in here, locked up like a common criminal, while some maniac has our daughter," Larry Biel spouted. He continued to pace the small hotel room—they had been there for nearly two hours, and he had yet to stop moving.

"Larry, this isn't helping. Please come here and sit next to me," Darlene Biel said from the bed.

Clair watched them both from the small table just inside the door.

Uniformed officers had arrived at the Biel household within four minutes of Clair's call. Both were found safely inside their narrow three-story home on West Superior Street. Darlene Biel was on the phone cycling through her daughter's friends for the fifth time, while her husband, Larry, sat at Larissa's computer, digging through the data. He knew his way around a computer and had installed a parental monitoring program called KidBSafe on her PC two years earlier. He reluctantly handed the laptop off to Clair, who in turn had it rushed to Klozowski's team back at Metro.

Clair then explained that while they had no reason to believe their current unsub had their daughter, particularly since it had only been half a day since she was last seen, she would like to place them both in protective custody anyway while they ruled it out. It took twenty more minutes for her to convince them to leave their home. Darlene moved fast. She was in pharmaceutical sales, spent a lot of time on the road, and kept a travel bag packed and ready. In less than five minutes she was at the front door. Larry was not so fast. He lingered in each room as if expecting his daughter to appear from some shadowed corner, an extended game of hide-and-seek, until finally Darlene packed a bag for him and helped get him into a waiting cruiser.

Although Chicago Metro owned three safe houses, Clair opted to take them to a hotel downtown, one she picked at random and paid for with cash. If Bishop was somehow involved, she had no intention of leaving a paper trail. Only Nash knew her location. He and Sophie Rodriguez remained at the Biel house to supervise the search. Undercover cars were parked a few houses down on both ends of the block, ready if the unsub made an appearance.

"Larry, you're making me nervous, please sit down," Darlene said again.

Larry Biel crossed the room one more time, then dropped onto the bed beside his wife, his red face turned to Clair. "How many girls did you say this guy has grabbed?"

"At least two others that we are aware of. But let me stress, we have no reason to believe this person has your daughter. You said yourself she could be with one of her friends. We're just taking every precaution."

"She's not with any of her friends," Darlene Biel said. "She planned to go to Carrie Ann's house to get ready for the dance, and Carrie Ann hasn't heard from her all day. None of her other friends have heard from her today either. She doesn't disappear like this, never. She always tells me where she's going. We don't keep secrets from each other."

"And this guy killed the girls' parents too?" Larry Biel said, ignoring his wife. "The man they found in his backyard packed in snow, is that what happened to him? Is that who you're talking about?"

"I can't comment on an open investigation."

"The reporter said his throat was cut so bad, his head almost came off."

"You're safe here. We're not going to let anything happen to you."

Larry ran his fingers over the pressboard nightstand, tapping them nervously. Clair was beginning to think the man was better off pacing.

There was a knock at the door, and Larry jumped up.

Clair held up a hand. "I got it, please stay there."

With a hand on her gun, she looked through the small peephole, relaxed, and opened the door. She had ordered a patrol officer to pick up pizza.

He handed both boxes to her and held his hand out, hoping for a tip.

Clair closed the door on him, secured the deadbolt and the inner latch, then placed both boxes on the table. "We've got plain cheese and pepperoni."

"I can't eat anything," Larry said.

"Hopefully this will be over quickly, but it's always best to keep your strength up," Clair told him.

Darlene pulled a slice of plain cheese and sat on the corner of the bed. Although she appeared calm, her hand was shaking. A clump of cheese slipped off the side of the slice and splatted on the carpet. "I'm so sorry, I'm a bit of mess right now."

Larry stood up and resumed pacing. On his third pass, he took a slice of pepperoni. "We should be hanging posters, we should be talking to the media. I can get a bunch of guys from the construction site to help comb the neighborhood. I can't sit here like this. I can't do nothing while some psycho has my baby girl. This guy's not gonna hurt me. I'll tear him apart if he tries to hurt me. I'll kill him if he touches my baby."

Larry was a big guy. His job kept him in shape. But Randal Davies had been more than six feet tall and exercised regularly. Floyd Reynolds too. Both were dead now.

Clair's phone rang.

"Hey, Kloz, did you find something?"

Darlene stood up from the bed, looking at her hands. Both were covered in pizza sauce. "I'm gonna clean up."

Clair nodded at her and watched her disappear into the bathroom. Larry continued his pacing.

"I found the obituary. It ran two days ago in the *Sun Herald*," Kloz said from the other end of the line.

"So not the *Chicago Examiner*?"

"Either our guy is branching out, or he's been placing ads in multiple papers and the *Examiner* was just a lucky break."

"What does it say?"

"I texted it to you. Did you get it?"

Clair's phone dinged. "Yeah, hold on." She glanced down at the display:

DEALER OF DOPE
MOTHER AND WIFE
DARLENE BIEL FINALLY FOUND PEACE
AT THE BUSINESS END OF DEATH'S KNIFE.

A crash came from the bathroom, the sound of a body hitting the floor.

72

Clair

Day 3 • 6:04 p.m.

Larry was the first to the bathroom door. He jiggled the handle—locked. "Darlene?"

"Get back!" Clair shouted, her foot missing him by less than an inch as she kicked the door just below the lock. The frame protested but didn't give.

Larry plowed into the door, shoulder first, hitting hard, and Clair heard the splinter of wood as the frame cracked.

Darlene was on the bathroom floor, her body spasming, a white foam dripping from her mouth down her cheeks and chin. Her eyes were open wide, all white, rolled back into her head.

Larry dropped down beside her, cradling her head against the tile floor. His hand was covered in blood, as was the tile beneath her head.

Darlene's body shook. Her toothbrush snapped with a loud crack between her convulsing fingers.

"Turn her on her side! Make sure her tongue is clear, don't let her choke!" Clair shouted out, scanning the room.

Toothbrush in two pieces.

Toothpaste tube open on the counter.

Mouthwash.

The white foam at Darlene's mouth pooled on the floor as Larry turned her on her side.

Clair grabbed the liquid soap dispenser from the wall and tore it loose from the plastic mount, then dropped down beside Darlene. "She needs to drink this!"

Larry's eyes went wide, and he pushed her away. "Hell no—that will kill her!"

Clair fought him, turning Darlene's head. "She's been poisoned, something fast-acting, like cyanide. Most poisons are acidic. Soap is a base. It will neutralize the poison, cause her to throw up."

Before Larry could object, Clair had twisted the cap off the soap and poured the thick, pink liquid into Darlene's open mouth. Then she held the woman's mouth closed and pinched her nose, forcing her to swallow.

Darlene's body jerked with a terrible force, and Clair lost her grip. The woman's head twisted and her arms flailed out. She kicked at the air.

"You're making her worse!" Larry shouted.

Clair forced more soap down her throat, forced her to swallow. It came back up a moment later with a gurgling cough, spewing over the wall and tile. Clair made her drink more. She threw up a second time, then a third. Her body finally stilled, and Clair checked her pulse.

Beside her, Larry's face was white and long. "You killed her! Oh my God, you killed her!"

Clair tried to draw in a breath, but every muscle in her body fought her. "Go call 911."

73

Porter

Day 3 • 8:06 p.m.

Porter and Sarah Werner had landed in Greenville, South Carolina, at 7:25. The sun had vanished over the horizon about midway through the flight. At that point Sarah closed the plastic blind. Porter wasn't aware that she'd been looking out the window at all. Her eyes seemed transfixed on Bishop's diary in her hands. He had watched her finger slide down each page as she read, taking in every word.

At the airport, she had paid for the tickets. At that point she understood Porter was trying to fly below the radar, and the fewer hits on his credit card, the better. He offered her cash, which she refused, citing this trip as a business expense, and she had no problem covering the cost from Uncle Sam's usual cut of her earnings.

She had finished the diary shortly before the flight landed.

In Greenville the rental car, a well-equipped red Hyundai Sonata, had gone under her name as well.

Sarah plugged the address from Bishop's diary into the GPS app on her phone and drove off in relative silence with Porter in the passenger seat.

Once they left the airport property and eased onto the highway, Sarah was the first to speak. "Maybe we should get a hotel and go in the morning, when it's light out. We'll have a hard time seeing anything in the dark."

It *was* dark.

In the city, light found its way into every corner. Streetlights, traffic lights, offices, businesses, there was always light. Out here there was nothing. The sky was pitch black, dotted with distant stars. Along the edge of the highway, Porter could see maybe thirty feet before the darkness blotted out their headlights. Within minutes of their leaving the airport, civilization seemed to drop away, replaced by sprawling fields and nothingness.

Porter glanced over at the GPS. "According to your thingama-gizmo, we're only thirteen minutes away. I'd rather scope it out, see what we can see tonight, and maybe go back in the morning."

"Don't you ever sleep?"

"I slept during police school."

"I find that hard to believe. Where else would you learn a fancy term like *thingamagizmo*?"

Heather.

He had learned it from Heather. One of her favorite non-words.

His thumb drifted to his wedding band.

Sarah caught him looking at it. "Tell me about her?"

Porter felt his face flush. "You don't want to hear about my wife."

"I do," she said. "I'd really like to."

He hadn't really talked about her much since her death. He had tried with both Nash and Clair, the two of them loading him up with alcohol not long after Emory was found and he returned to duty. Although they were his friends, he was technically their superior, and he'd always had a problem showing emotion. There had been plenty of private moments after Heather's death. He still found himself talking to her a couple times a day. Every day as he got dressed, he lingered a bit too long at the closet, his fingers brushing her clothes. Her death left a void in him, a big empty space. He missed her dearly, every second of every day.

"Her name was Heather. She was killed in a botched convenience store robbery a few blocks from our apartment about six months ago. They caught the guy, just a kid really. Harnell Campbell." Porter went quiet for a second, his gaze drifting to the window. "Somehow, he es-caped. He should have stayed in jail, because Anson Bishop tracked him down. Killed him, we think. His body never turned up. Bishop left the kid's ear sitting on my bed like some kind of gift. I guess in a way it was. I sure as hell wanted to kill him. The idea of him spending a few years in prison and getting his freedom back while my Heather was lost ate at me. I came home, and there it was: her killer's ear in a neat little white box with a note."

"What did the note say?"

"It said—

Sam,

    A little something from me to you . . .

    I'm sorry you didn't get to hear him scream.

    How about a return on the favor?

    A little tit for tat between friends.

    Help me find my mother.

    I think it's time she and I talked.

    B."

"Wow."

"Yeah."

"So that's why you're here? That's why you came to New Orleans? To help him find his mother?"

Porter shook his head. "I'm here to catch him, *period.* She's a lead, nothing more. Him killing Campbell, that was a one-sided deal. I don't owe him anything other than a comfortable cell."

"But he could be in New Orleans too. He might have been watching the entire time," Sarah pointed out. "He can't enter the prison without risk of getting caught, but he probably followed your every move."

"Maybe."

"So he could be here, following us."

Porter hadn't thought about that. He assumed Bishop kept tabs on him in New Orleans, but here? "I don't know about that. He couldn't have known what was said between us and his mother. Nobody has seen what she wrote in the diary but us, the address."

"There are cameras in the interview room. It's possible one of them caught a good angle. Somebody on the inside slipped you that cell phone and the knife. He could have followed us to the airport.

Hell, he could have been on our plane. Somebody high profile like him, to be able to hide as long as he has, he's got to be good at disguises, blending in. I think I've seen his face on the news every day since you ID'ed him. To not get caught, with all that heat . . ." She let the words trail off, reached up and brushed an errant hair from her eyes, then glanced up at the rearview mirror. "He's not out here, though. I haven't seen another car in a while. Of course, he could be driving with the headlights off. That's what I'd do."

"I don't think he'd follow us. I think you're right, he's good at hiding. I also think he's smart enough to stay hidden. If I had to bet, he's hunkered down somewhere, waiting for things to cool off a little bit. People have short attention spans. I'm surprised the press has stayed on it this long. As soon as some other big story hits, he'll get put on the back burner. If he plans to make a move, he'll do it then."

"I see what you're doing," Sarah said.

"What?"

"You completely changed the subject. I asked you about your wife, and somehow you managed to turn the conversation to Bishop. I'm not having that. I need answers. I'm a sucker for a good love story. Tell me how you and Heather met. And if you try to weasel out of it and go on about Bishop again, I'm gonna pull over and beat you with the tire iron. I see plenty of places to hide a body out here."

"You are one scary girl."

"Woman. Scary woman and proud of it. Now, tell me about Heather."

Porter sighed. "We met at the hospital, of all places."

"The hospital? What happened?"

"I was a rookie cop, not far from here actually, near Charleston. I took a bullet to the back of the head. She was one of the trauma nurses lucky enough to be working the ER when they brought me in."

Sarah's eyes went wide. "You got shot in the head?"

Porter reached to the back of his head and found the scar, a small bump to the left of center. "It was a peashooter, a .22. My partner and I were trying to take down a petty dealer, mostly dirty heroin and some crack. On the street, they called him Weasel. We cornered him in an alley. I came up from behind him, and my partner circled around the block so he could come in from the other side. He saw my partner first, spun around, and panicked when he saw me standing behind him. He was wired on something, real jumpy. He had the gun in his hand and pulled the trigger by accident. He didn't mean to shoot me, the gun wasn't even pointing at me, it was more of a reflex than anything else. The bullet hit a dumpster behind me and ricocheted, and I caught it in the back of the skull."

"Holy hell. How are you still alive?"

Porter shrugged. "My thick head, I guess. The bullet lodged in place, got caught in the bone. It didn't make it into my brain but got real close."

"Well, that was lucky."

"Yeah, I guess. They think the ricochet is what saved me. A direct hit, and I would have been done. There was still damage, though. Pressure started to build up almost immediately." He paused for a second, recalling. "It's funny, I actually remember the hit. It was like a hard slap to the back of the head. It didn't knock me off my feet like it does in the movies. I stood there like an idiot. Thought I could get back to the car and drive myself to the hospital. I touched it, saw the blood on my fingers, and took about two steps before I passed out. I didn't wake up again for nearly a week."

Sarah slowed as a small animal scurried across the road and disappeared in the bushes at the side. "Were they able to remove the bullet, or is it still in there?"

"No, they got it out. Then they put me in a coma until the pressure finally reduced." His finger found the small scar again. "The bullet went in from a weird angle, came in low on the left. Most of the pressure was centered above the hippocampus region."

Sarah held up a hand. "Wait, I know this. That's the portion responsible for emotions and memory."

"Give that girl a gold star." Porter grinned. "It also runs our autonomic nervous system and handles spatial recognition. They knew my nervous system was intact even while I was in a coma, but until I woke, they weren't able to tell if anything else had been impacted. When I opened my eyes, Heather was standing over me, this beautiful smile on her lips, and I knew I was in love."

74

Clair

Day 3 • 8:07 p.m.

Clair stood in the hallway outside room 316 at the Piedmont Hotel, her hands balled up in fists and her stomach in knots. CSI had arrived ten minutes earlier and sealed off the room.

"Clair-bear?"

She turned to find Nash stepping off the elevator, unfastening his thick coat. "What the hell happened?"

Clair shook her head. She was still trying to piece everything together. "He poisoned her. At least, I think he poisoned her. I forced her to throw up. She was stable when the paramedics took her away. Still unconscious, though."

"But alive?"

"Yeah. Still alive." She took a couple of steps, her back to him. "How is this happening? How is this bastard able to stay ahead of us like this?"

"We'll get him."

When she turned back around, there were tears in her eyes. "I was supposed to protect her, and he got right past me. Tried to take her out right under my nose."

Nash wrapped his arms around her, gave her a hearty squeeze. "This is *not* your fault, Clair-bear. There is absolutely nothing you could have done differently."

"I should have seen this coming. With Randal Davies, the unsub got into their house and poisoned his coffee with lisinopril. The unsub knew only Randal Davies drank it, and he targeted him. Somehow he got poison into something belonging to Darlene Biel, either her mouthwash or toothpaste . . . she traveled regularly for work. He got into her travel bag and set his poison. After Randal Davies, I should have seen that coming, I should have . . ." Her voice trailed off. She pressed her face into his shoulder.

"Detectives?"

Clair pulled away from Nash, wiped at her eyes, embarrassed. "Yes?"

CSI Lindsy Rolfes stood at the hotel room doorway. She averted her eyes as Nash released Clair from the hug. "You were right. The field test came back positive for cyanide."

"Toothpaste or mouthwash?" Clair asked.

"Toothpaste. We found a small puncture hole in the tube. It looks like the unsub injected it into the toothpaste tube with a hypodermic needle about an inch down from the top. Because of the toothpaste consistency, she may have used it for days without encountering the poison. Honestly, toothpaste makes an excellent delivery method— the paste acted as a primitive timer. If the unsub would have placed the poison lower in the tube, he could have bought weeks rather than days before she encountered it. I'd keep that in mind—most likely he wanted it to hit around this time."

Clair drew in a deep breath and let the air back out before speaking again. She wasn't going to let this guy get the better of her, no way. "Anything else?"

Rolfes pushed her glasses up the bridge of her nose with a gloved hand. "That's all so far. We're still testing her personal items. I'll finish up at the lab."

"So nothing in the husband's belongings?" Nash asked.

"Nothing that we've found. I'll call you if we turn up something else." She turned and disappeared back into the hotel room.

Clair massaged her chin, walking in slow circles around the hallway. "The obituary was Darlene Biel. She was the target. That means this guy isn't going after only the fathers, he's going after a parent.

There's a thread connecting them—connecting the girls and connecting the parents. We just need to find it."

"You need some rest," Nash told her. "You've been running on empty for two solid days. You can't think straight like this. Neither can I, for that matter." He lowered his voice. "When I got here, I tried to climb out of my car and forgot to take off my seat belt. I actually sat there for a second or two, trying to figure out why I couldn't get up. My brain is toast. We all need to get some rest and regroup."

Clair was shaking her head. "I'm going back to Metro. I need to work the boards, see all the data. There's something there, I know it. Their daughter is still out there, and she may still be alive. She's only been missing a day."

"We have half the force out looking for her."

"I'm going back to Metro," she said defiantly.

Nash must have known this was a losing battle. "Okay, but under two conditions. One, you try to get some sleep on the couch in the war room. And two, you let me drive you. You shouldn't be driving. You're still shaking from the adrenaline, and when you crash, you're going to crash hard."

"And I'm supposed to entrust my life to a guy who can't work a seat belt?"

"I'm all you got."

"God help us."

Clair's phone buzzed. She pulled it from her pocket and read the text. Her heart sank. "They found the truck and the missing water tank. We've got another body."

75

Porter

Day 3 • 8:07 p.m.

The GPS chimed, told them to make a right turn, and Sarah slowed, following the sign toward Simpsonville.

Porter's gaze had returned to the window. "After I saw Heather standing over me, I saw my partner. He was getting up from a chair in the corner of the room. My captain showed up about an hour later. It was weird at first. I recognized him, my partner. I didn't realize anything was wrong. I remembered chasing the dealer, I remembered the shot, all of it was fresh. Heather asked me my name, I promptly told her I was the love her life, she asked me for the name of the current president, and I told her. Then she asked me for the name of the last president, and I drew a blank. There was no other way to describe it, like someone had taken an eraser and smudged it out. I could picture the guy's face, but his name was gone. The testing started after that, a lot of testing."

"Some kind of amnesia?"

"Fluid elicit retrograde amnesia, that's what they called it. My mobility wasn't impaired, which was lucky. Most of my memories were intact—my childhood, teen years, even recent events, that was all there, but there were these big blank spots, entire months and years missing." He paused for a moment, his finger tapping against the window glass. "Heather used to make me do this exercise where she'd have me write down the bullet points of my life in chronological order, date them as best I could. We'd do it every day, start with a blank piece of paper and fill in everything I could remember. For the first few days, the list got longer with each attempt. There was progress. After about a week or so, that ended. I didn't lose anything else, but those blanks held tight. The doctors assured me the memories would return in time. Some have, I suppose, but to this day I'm still missing time."

"Through all this, Heather stuck with you?"

Porter nodded. "She refused to go out with me on an official date until I was out of the hospital and had resumed a normal life for at least a month. We both felt a spark, knew there was something there, but apparently it's common for patients to fall for their caregivers during prolonged hospital stays, and she was wary that's all it was. I knew it was more than that, but my word didn't hold a whole lot of water in that particular discussion. We still met every day to run my list—that's what she called it, 'running the list'—but she wouldn't go out on an official date. When they finally reinstated me on the force, about three months after I landed in the hospital, she agreed to go to out—dinner and a movie. We saw *The Princess Bride*. We were married four months later."

"Aren't you bothered by this missing time?"

Porter shrugged. "My best memories are with Heather. I remember all of our time together. I don't need anything else."

"And what about the police force? Was it difficult to go back to active duty?"

"Yeah, that was a little rough. I didn't think it would be. Aside from the memory issue, I was fine. Physically, I had no problem—a few written and physical exams, then an interview, and I was back on the streets. New partner, though. My last one transferred to narcotics full-time. That shot took something else from me, in a way. Charleston was ruined. The city felt a bit darker, dirtier. I felt uneasy anytime I was near the alley where it all happened. I began to feel like this anxiety could get me hurt, distract me at the wrong moment. Heather and I talked about it quite a bit and decided to make the move to Chicago, get a fresh start someplace new. I made the transfer to Chicago Metro patrol, and when there was an opening in Homicide, I took it. Hell, that was all so long ago, I was just a kid."

"You never had children?"

"We considered having kids, talked about it more times than I can count, but the timing never seemed to be right. Heather was a bit of a rising star at Chicago General, and I was doing well at Metro. You tell yourself next year will be a better year for it, things will slow down, finances will get in order, so you put it off and you put it off. Before you know it, it's too late. I don't regret not having any, though. I don't think there is a single moment of my life I would change."

"Not even getting shot in the head?"

"Not even getting shot in the head. Hey, pull in there." Porter pointed toward a small Stop-N-Go gas station coming up on the right.

"What for? We have a full tank."

"Supplies."

Sarah slowed and maneuvered the car off the narrow two-lane highway and into the gravel parking lot. A beat-up Ford pickup was parked in front of the store. Aside from that, the place was deserted. She pulled up next to the truck and slipped the car into Park. She held up the diary. "Go ahead. There are a few sections in here I want to give a second glance."

"Be right back." He unfastened his seat belt and climbed out of the Sonata.

An electronic chime went off as Porter pushed through the doorway, and a clerk behind the counter looked up at him for a second before returning to a copy of *Autotrader*.

There were only five aisles in the store, and Porter hit each of them. He picked up two flashlights, a package of C cell batteries, a box of Ziploc bags, a box of latex gloves, a cheap digital camera, and a large bag of Cheetos. He carried everything to the front and dropped the supplies onto the counter.

The cashier looked no more than sixteen or seventeen. He had a large pimple on his pink chin and a nose that was much too large for his narrow face. He set down his magazine, nodded at Porter, and began scanning the items. He scanned the box of gloves four times before it took. Porter was curious if he even knew how to ring something up manually.

"Twenty-three forty-eight," the kid said, looking over the items. "Starting a proctology office?"

"The brain surgeon thing didn't work out, so I figured I'd try my hand at something new."

Porter handed him a twenty and a five and bagged everything himself while the cashier counted out his change.

"Have a nice night, Doctor."

"Yep."

Back in the car, he retrieved the Cheetos and dropped the rest of the bag onto the floor. Sarah held the diary against the steering wheel as she maneuvered back onto the road, her index finger marking her place.

"You've made it through that entire book without so much as a word about it. What do you think?"

She blew out a breath. "I'm not sure what to think. Part of me feels sorry for the kid. Then I think about all the people he's hurt, all the lives he's ruined, and I remind myself that he's a monster. Then there's his mother. She said, 'This isn't how it happened.' What did she mean by that? None of it? Some of it? We just flew six hundred miles because a convict scribbled an address into this book."

Porter said nothing.

She tossed the diary into his lap. "Give me some of those Cheetos."

Porter opened the bag and held it out to her.

Sarah plucked out a Cheeto and dropped it into her mouth. "If my client really did half the things in this book?" She shook her head and licked her fingers. "I can't represent someone like that. No way."

The GPS spoke up, advising them to turn left on Jenkins Bridge Road in one thousand feet. Sarah clicked on the blinker.

Porter thought it was dark after they left the city. It was even worse out here. Not a single house or car anywhere, nothing but roads and farmland.

Sarah made the turn, and though Jenkins Bridge Road was paved, it was rough. She swerved left to avoid a large pothole in the middle of the street, then immediately swerved back right to stay out of another one. At the sides of the road, nature had begun taking back the land. Weeds and foliage ate away at the blacktop, leaving the pavement cracked and ravaged. "BFE," she said, slowing down.

"What?"

"Bum Fuck Egypt."

"I'm not sure what that means."

"It means we are in the middle of absolute nowhere, and I'm about three minutes away from second-guessing many of my recent life choices."

The GPS instructed her to turn left in one hundred feet. Sarah turned on the high beams. "Do you see a turn? 'Cause I don't see a turn. I don't see much of anything."

Porter leaned forward. "There it is. Right after that big rock."

Sarah turned left, and the road turned to a combination of gravel and grass. "If you kill me out here and leave my body in a shallow grave, can you at least find a nice home for my fish?"

"You have fish?"

"I have *a* fish. His name is Monroe. He's an excellent listener and only slightly judgmental."

The farmland had given way to trees—dogwood, oaks, evergreens —that loomed over the car, the branches reaching across the narrow road and twisting above like dozens of interlaced bony fingers.

"Your destination is ahead in one hundred feet," the GPS told them. "It will be on the right."

Sarah frowned. "I don't see anything, do you? Do you think she lied?"

"I don't know what to think."

The GPS played a happy little melody, then: "You have arrived."

Sarah hit the brakes and stopped the car. "There's nothing here. She played us."

Porter stared out the windshield. Up ahead, the road petered out, ending in an overgrown mess of wild bushes and trees. He saw nothing at all around them but dense woods.

He unfastened his seat belt, opened the door, and stepped out into the chilly night air.

Sarah killed the motor and got out too.

Porter's shoes crunched in the gravel as he walked toward the side of the road. The energy drained from his body, his shoulders slumped. "I'm an idiot," he said. "I should have known better."

Sarah rounded the car and stood beside him, placing a hand on his shoulder. "You're a good cop. You chased a lead. They don't always pan out."

Something scurried through the bushes a little to their left. Porter turned to find shining eyes staring up at him. They paused for a second and disappeared into the growth. "What's that?"

"I think it was a raccoon."

Porter took a few steps to the left. "Not the animal . . ."

He reached up, his fingers wrapping around a thick vine growing over—

"Is that a mailbox?"

He tugged at the weeds and shrubs, freeing the crooked post and the cracked white box fastened to the top.

His eyes fixed on the faded word scrawled on the side in black paint, barely visible in the thin light.

Bishop.

76

Poole
Day 3 • 8:07 p.m.

Frank Poole stepped into the basement office at Metro and flicked on the light switch. The fluorescents buzzed to life, casting a yellow glow over the space. His nose crinkled at the strange odor permeating from the far back corner. They had yet to figure out what it was but traced it to an oval stain on the carpet under an old desk.

Poole removed his coat, scarf, and hat and dropped them onto a table by the door. He crossed to the center of the room and sat on the edge of a desk, his eyes locked on the whiteboards at the front of the room.

He should go home.

He should sleep.

He couldn't, though.

Poole knew the moment he closed his eyes, Libby McInley would be there waiting for him, desperately trying to tell him what happened, but unable, silenced.

Diener had left his scarf on the floor near the door.

Stewart, his first name was Stewart.

Poole hadn't known him well. He remembered seeing him around the Chicago Bureau office a number of times, but this was the first case they'd worked together. He wasn't married. No girlfriend. At least, he didn't mention one. Poole knew nothing about his home life.

He didn't know where the man grew up, went to school, whether or not he had any brothers or sisters. SAIC Hurless said he would personally reach out to Diener's family, but he hadn't said who that was.

Poole knew at some point, as the last person to see him alive, he would also have to reach out to that person or persons, that someone special to Stewart Diener. He wished he'd taken the time to learn just who that was.

"Goddammit, Diener," he muttered, shaking his head.

He went to the whiteboards and cleared a spot on the far right and wrote:

Green House—518 41st Place
Bishop—hiding there since?
Wiped—no evidence left behind—planned for fast escape

Drop House—519 41st Place
Libby McInley's fake IDs shipped there—Bishop organized?
Why would Bishop help Libby McInley? Why would Libby agree
    to help? Killer of sister, Barbara McInley?
Why would he kill Libby McInley?

Poole paused at this one. It didn't make sense. Why would he kill Libby McInley if he was somehow helping her? Maybe they had some kind of falling out? That would mean they had a relationship to begin with. What kind of relationship could they possibly have had? He killed her sister. He *tortured* and killed her sister. Did they somehow know each other? If that's the case, did they know each other before Barbara was murdered, or did they somehow get in touch while she was in prison? There would be a record. Not a single piece of mail, phone call, or visit goes unrecorded.

He wrote STATEVILLE CORRECTIONAL on the board.

He'd have to pull all her prison records. Somehow, Bishop had been able to correspond with her. Finding those messages would be key.

Finding the *how*.

Poole cleared another spot on the board and wrote out the three poems and the sentence excised by Bishop from the drop-house wall.

Had Bishop taken their cell phones because they took pictures, created a record of this writing? Originally, Poole assumed he took the phones to slow them down, to give him a head start before Poole could get somewhere and call for help. Now he wasn't so sure.

Bishop expected Detective Sam Porter to find the house, not federal agents. That meant he wanted Porter to find the writing. He wanted Porter to try and figure out the meaning. He and Diener had spoiled that, shown up first, ruined whatever timeline Bishop may have had in place. Poole had taken out his phone to photograph the wall, but Diener had stepped in, stopped him before he got a single picture.

Had he killed Diener because he saw the wall? Photographed it? Would he have seen the images on Diener's phone? Bishop hadn't found any pictures on Poole's phone—maybe that's why he let him live? Figured he hadn't seen the writing?

It was possible.

Poole had seen the writing, though. He remembered every word.

He stared up at the poems, particularly the underlined words:

Ice
water
Life
death
Home
fear
Death

"You can't play God without being acquainted with the devil," Poole muttered.

Death was the only repeated word. He circled both, then wrote *Death x2* at the bottom.

The knot at the back of his head ached. The paramedic said he probably had a mild concussion. He needed sleep but probably shouldn't. He didn't really want to. He wanted to keep working the problem.

Sleep would clear his head.

He went back to the desk and ruffled through his briefcase, found a bottle of Advil, and dry-swallowed three of them.

The contents of the boxes he'd sifted through earlier were still spread out. Polaroid pictures and spreadsheets were strewn about on the desk beside him.

He glanced back up at the boards.

Poole had never believed in coincidences.

This was all connected.

77

Porter

Day 3 • 8:07 p.m.

Porter stared at the mailbox.

It seemed familiar to him—the name Bishop scrawled on the side in a childlike hand, the mailbox itself, this place. He didn't recall a specific mention of it in the diary, yet there was a sense of déjà vu here.

"Sam? Are you okay?"

Porter had closed his eyes. He didn't remember closing his eyes. When he opened them, he found Sarah watching, concern across her face, barely visible in the pale moonlight.

She put a hand on his shoulder. "I lost you again, like back at the prison. I really think we should get a hotel and come back here when it's light out. We both need some sleep, and we can't see anything out here now anyway."

Porter's heart thudded in his chest. He couldn't sleep, not now. "I'm fine . . . I . . . I bought flashlights."

He turned back toward the car, nearly stumbled as he crossed the gravel road. He braced himself on the frame of the vehicle.

Sarah was at his side again. "You're not fine, Sam. You look like you're gonna pass out. Sit down in the car for a minute, catch your breath. You're pale as a ghost."

Sam rubbed at the back of his head, the scar, his other hand still on the car. "I'm okay."

The words came out harsher than he'd hoped. Sarah took a step back.

He took a breath. "I'm sorry, I didn't mean to sound like . . ."

"Like an ass?" she finished for him.

"I didn't expect this to be real." He nodded at the diary, still on the front seat. "I didn't expect *that* to be real. I . . . I can't leave now. I need to look. I need to see what's here. I'm afraid if I leave, this place won't be here in the morning. I know that sounds silly, and probably is, but I need to stay. You don't have to if you don't want to, but I do. I don't think I have a choice."

She reached up, put her hands on either side of his face.

He was grateful for her touch. He *needed* her touch.

"I'm not gonna leave you to stumble around alone in the dark. Whatever this is, we do it together, but I'm going to make one thing very clear. When we get back to civilization, you owe this lady one hell of a dinner."

"Deal." A smile edged across Porter's lips. "I think I saw some old Arby's coupons on the backseat."

They stood there like that for almost ten minutes while Porter's strength returned and his head cleared. At some point Sarah slipped her hand into his. He didn't remember the moment it happened, and he wished he had. These were the moments worth remembering, not some of the other thoughts that rattled around in his head. He gave her hand a squeeze. "I think I'm okay now. I guess I just got a little overwhelmed."

Porter let go and reached inside the car for the bag from the convenience store. He placed it on the roof, removed the flashlights from their packaging, and loaded batteries in each, handing one to Sarah. He put the diary in his pocket.

Sarah flicked on her light and ran the beam up and down the deserted road while Porter read the instructions on the digital camera.

"There's a gravel driveway here, or maybe it's an old road. I can't tell, the weeds took it back." She stood about five feet away from him, near the mailbox. "There's something else too. Looks like there used to be another mailbox next to this one that says *Bishop*. I found a post, but it's busted off about two feet out of the ground."

"It would have said *Carter*. They lived next door to the Carters."

"Oh yeah, from the diary."

Satisfied he had the camera under control, Porter loaded the gloves, Ziploc bags, and camera back into the bag, closed the car door, and went over to her. Her beam was still on the remains of the post. When she saw him beside her, she ran the light up and down the gravel she found. "This is what I was talking about. I don't think anybody has been down there in years."

Porter followed the beam of light, watched it bounce over the rough gravel strewn with weeds and dirt. Watched it dance over the trees, waving silently in the moonlight. He watched the darkness engulf the light at the edge of the flashlight's reach. Then he took Sarah's free hand and started toward that darkness, not another word between them.

78

Clair

Day 3 • 8:15 p.m.

Clair spotted the flashing red and blue lights as they came down Ashland Avenue. She pointed out the windshield. "Over there."

"I see it," Nash replied, turning into the Walmart parking lot.

They followed the signs around the side of the long building to the loading docks at the back. As they rounded the corner, they came upon two patrol cars with a barricade set between them blocking the road. The officer on the left picked up the side of the barricade and ushered them through, replacing it behind them. Nash pulled up between one of the CSI vans and an ambulance. Both paramedics were standing at the back of the vehicle smoking cigarettes, little for them to do here but wait.

"Do you smell gas?" Clair asked.

"That's just Connie," Nash explained. "When she's in Park, the smell comes up from somewhere underneath. I need to get her checked out."

"This car is a death trap, you know that, right?"

"Don't knock my baby while she's down. She'll fix up nice. Isn't that right, Connie girl?" He reached up and ran his hand over the dashboard, then blew a kiss in that direction.

"Bishop's got nothing on you. You're one crazy fuck." Clair

climbed out of the car into the cold air and slammed the door behind her, her hands deep in her pockets. Nash followed, nearly slipping on a patch of ice.

A gray Toyota Tundra pickup truck with a water tank hitched to the back was parked on the ramp leading up to the loading dock. CSI surrounded the truck with large halogen floodlights. The perimeter was roped off with bright yellow tape. At least half a dozen uniformed patrol officers stood around the site, keeping the growing crowd at bay. They were mostly Walmart employees—the store was open twenty-four hours. They must have called in friends, though, because a few of the onlookers weren't in uniform, and a car approached from the opposite side of the parking lot, heading directly toward the lights and crowd. Clair knew, once word got out, it wouldn't take long for this crowd to double or triple in size. It would be even worse once the press arrived.

Clair counted three CSI investigators. All stood inside the parameter awaiting orders.

Lieutenant Belkin saw them and approached from the crowd, shuffling over. He wore a puffy navy coat with his badge affixed to the outer lapel and CHICAGO METRO stamped across the back in large white block letters. "We sealed off the scene as soon as we got here." He pointed at a semi idling about fifty feet away. "That truck arrived a few minutes before eight and called inside—the pickup was already on the ramp, blocking his path. The warehouse supervisor came out, saw someone inside the truck, went to tell them to move, then backed off and called 911 when he realized . . . well, you'll see. He touched the door frame. We took his prints for eliminations, also took a cast of his shoe to rule out his prints around the vehicle. There's a second set in the snow, but they're pretty muddled from this weather. CSI got casts of those. Probably your unsub. They circle the vehicle a few times. Might get something. The supervisor's name is Willis Cortese, and we're holding him inside the building. You can talk to him, but I don't think he's got much else to offer."

Nash pointed at the security camera above the loading dock. "Any footage?"

Belkin shook his head. "There are three cameras back here. Some-one knocked them out last Tuesday. Maintenance hasn't had a chance to replace them yet."

"Knocked them out how? They're mounted pretty high up."

"Cut the video line and bashed the cameras with something good and heavy. They don't know exactly, but the cameras are a mangled mess. Whoever did it had a good handle on the cameras' capabilities. They came in out of the viewing angle. According to Security, the feed is live, then goes black, no shot of the person or persons who did it. I've got one of my guys looking over the hardware and footage in case they missed something."

Nash gave Clair a quick glance. They were both thinking the same thing—Bishop.

Belkin pointed a thumb back at the truck. "That's a fucking mess. I've never seen anything like it."

"Show us," Clair said.

Belkin nodded and turned back toward the truck. He ducked un-der the yellow tape and held it up for Clair and Nash. He approached the driver's side door. The window was open. "Best we can tell, your unsub took the hose from the water tank and emptied the contents into the cab, close to five hundred gallons. It would have taken some time. Twenty, thirty minutes, maybe longer. When I got here, the tem-perature was seven degrees, with a wind-chill of negative two. The CSI folks are still trying to figure it out, but they said whoever did it would have had to spray for a few minutes, then pause for five to ten, then spray again. They said this was done in layers. Even at temps this cold, to do something like this, they had to build it. If they emptied the tank in one shot, it wouldn't look like this. This took patience and one large set of brass balls, particularly out in the open like this."

Clair tried really hard to listen to Lieutenant Belkin as he ex-plained what they were looking at. He went on with additional de-tails about the thickness of the ice, the consistency. She heard Nash ask if it was salt water. She heard Belkin explain that it was not. Salt water wouldn't freeze at this temperature. She heard all this while her brain tried to wrap around what she was looking at.

Inside the cab of the truck was a person. That person was wearing a seat belt and had both hands on the steering wheel. Gaze fixed forward, locked on some nonexistent object off in the distance.

The body was encased in rough ice, thick and crusted all around—thin around the face and head, thick at the seat and floor.

The face stared ahead in a frozen dead gaze.

It was a boy. A teenage boy.

79

Porter

Day 3 • 9:10 p.m.

It was the house they saw first.

What was left of the house.

Porter and Sarah stopped in the driveway, the beams of their flashlights playing over the vine- and weed-covered boards.

There had been a fire, no mistaking that. The roof was gone, and what remained of the walls was charred and black. Most of the structure had collapsed, either with the fire or sometime later.

Porter took out the camera and handed it to Sarah. "You're in charge of pictures."

"Anything in particular?"

"That thing stores a thousand shots, so don't hold back. I want to capture everything. We don't know what might be important."

Sarah held up the camera, looking through the viewfinder at the structure.

The house had been small.

Porter could tell that much from the footprint. Maybe eight or nine hundred square feet, at the most. As in the diary, there was a porch but not what Porter expected. When he read the book, his mind's eye drew a large wrap-around porch surrounding a fairly large home. This place was neither of those things. The porch was only about six feet wide and four feet deep, balanced precariously on old cinder blocks. There were two wooden steps, but he didn't trust either under his weight. Rot had taken them long ago.

"I thought the house would be bigger," Sarah said beside him. "The way the diary described the place."

The camera made a tiny click whenever Sarah snapped a picture. Funny how people hold on to the past, Porter thought. There was no need for a digital camera to make any noise, yet someone took the time to build in the sound.

"The eyes of a child, I suppose. Everything looks a little larger through a kid's eyes."

"I guess."

Porter put a tentative foot on the porch, stepping over the damaged boards. The beam of his flashlight found the place where the front door had once stood, now just a gaping hole.

"You're not going in there?" Sarah said.

"I need to see the basement."

Sarah's flashlight bounced off the two remaining outer walls and the open space where the roof should have been, finally landing on what was left of the floor. "That can't possibly be safe to walk on."

Porter took another step forward. The boards protested beneath him, groaning and aching.

"If you fall through, you could get seriously hurt. We're in the middle of nowhere out here."

Porter's flashlight landed on what was left of an old refrigerator and stove about twelve feet deep into the mess. A rusty padlock dangled from the refrigerator door.

> Promptly at nine, she would latch the refrigerator closed and fasten the door tight with a shiny new Stanley padlock. It would remain locked until lunchtime, and the process would repeat again for supper. While I was perfectly capable of fasting until the noon hour, something told me a little sustenance in my belly would help with the lingering effects of the previous night's bender and possibly set me right for the remainder of the day.

Partial two-by-four walls stuck up in random places like large, blackened toothpicks growing from the floor. An old bathtub was buried under rubble toward the back.

Porter took another careful step and kneeled down at a large hole in the floor where the living room had probably been. The flashlight picked across debris that had fallen through to the lower level long ago, impossible to make much of anything out. For a second he thought he'd found the metal stack pipe the Carters had been handcuffed to but realized it was a tree that had somehow taken root in the cracked concrete floor and grown almost tall enough to reach outside for light.

"Do you see anything?" Sarah asked.

"We'll have to excavate the entire site. This place has been falling apart for years."

"No bodies, though, right?"

"They would have been hauled out of here a long time ago." Porter told himself that was true, yet his mind had no trouble seeing them, dozens of dead bodies wrapped in the tattered remains of this house, flesh burned and black. The place reeked of death.

"Hey, can you toss me the camera? Don't get too close—I don't want you walking out here."

Sarah hesitated, took a practice swing, and lobbed the camera to him underhanded.

Porter caught it with the tips of his fingers. "Thanks."

Careful not to drop the camera, he lowered it down into the hole, his finger on the shutter button. He snapped about a dozen shots, sweeping back and forth, the bright flash illuminating every corner.

"Hey, I found a car!" Sarah called out from somewhere behind him.

Porter took one last look at what remained of the basement and retraced his steps until he was back on solid ground. Sarah stood about twenty feet from the house, her flashlight pointing into a tangled mess of weeds.

He didn't see the car at first, not until he was almost standing on top of it. Sarah was busy stomping down the tall grass. "I think it's a Volkswagen. Hard to tell."

"A Volkswagen? That doesn't make sense." Porter saw the rusted pile of metal then, the cracked windows. The interior had become the home of some woodland creature, the seats covered in matted grass. He walked around the car, carefully inspecting the frame. When the beam of his flashlight landed on the rear bumper, he paused, leaned in closer. "I'll be damned."

"What?"

When Sarah knelt down beside him, he pointed at the bumper sticker, faded, barely legible. She read aloud, "POOR MAN'S PORSCHE."

Father drove a 1969 Porsche. It was a marvelous machine. A work of art with a throaty growl that rumbled forth with the turn of the key and grew louder still as it eased out onto the road and lapped up the pavement with hungry delight.

Oh, how Father loved that car.

"It's a Volkswagen Bug. I think this was Bishop's father's car." Porter stood up and ran the beam of his flashlight over the visible parts of the vehicle. "See how the hood and trunk are both open? The smashed windows and lights? All the damage is consistent with the diary, it's just not a Porsche."

"A poor man's Porsche."

"Yeah."

Porter rounded the back and took a picture of the dirty license plate: expired in October of 1995.

Sarah stood up and pointed off to the right. "There's another house."

Porter followed her gaze, then took a few steps forward. "That's not a house, it's a trailer."

He handed the camera back to her.

"I believe the politically correct term is 'mobile home,'" Sarah said.

He pushed his way through the tall weeds, crossing what was once the Bishop front yard, and Sarah followed. When he reached the trailer, he turned in a slow circle, his flashlight illuminating the surroundings. When he was once again facing the small structure, he stood still, his mind racing. "This must be where the Carters lived. There's nothing else out here."

The screen door at the back of the Carters' house had been left open. The wind owned it now, banging it against the white-paint-flaked frame. I reached for the handle and held it still for Mrs. Carter. She walked past me into the dark kitchen. She hadn't said a word the entire walk back. Neither of us had. If it hadn't been for the sound of her sniffling, I wouldn't have known she was behind me.

Sarah climbed the concrete steps and tried the door, one hinge cracked and separated from the metal frame. "It's open."

The windows, at least the two facing the front, were gone. Frail curtains swayed in the wind, fluttering against the dark interior.

"Let me go first," Porter told her, stepping past. "Stay close."

He moved through the doorway into a small kitchen—a tiny Formica table and bench built into the wall on one side and rusted appliances on the other. The floor was covered in mud, the elements having taken their toll. The refrigerator door was open, shelves bare. Most of the cabinet doors were missing. All the windows in the room were either busted out or standing open, air whistling in. Immediately following the kitchen was a tiny living space with a couch, the material so faded and eaten by rot there was no way to determine what it once looked like. Graffiti covered every flat surface, brightly colored images and shapes interspersed with blocks of text, random names, and various tags.

"Can you get pictures of all this? We'll review them later."

"Must be some kind of hangout for the local kids," Sarah said, raising the camera. "Every teenager needs a respectable place to put away their alcohol and get laid in peace."

Porter moved past the small living space and kitchen, past a tiny bathroom with a dry, stained toilet and a shower curtain balled up in the corner of the bathtub. As his flashlight traveled over the cracked mirror, Porter saw his own face staring back at him. His mind returned to the diary, to a little boy taking this same walk down the narrow hallway.

I began down the hall, with my knife hand pressed against my chest, the blade facing forward. Father taught me this particular grip. If necessary, I would launch the knife forward with the full strength of my arm muscles and the accuracy of a loaded gun. Unlike an overhand thrust, a jab would be difficult to block. This hold also allowed me to go directly for the heart or the stomach, with either an upward or downward motion, respectively. With an upper-hand grip, coming from above, you could only strike down — such an attack was more likely to glance off your victim than penetrate deeply.

Father was very skilled.

He could see Bishop behind him, feel his eyes on the back of his neck. When was the last time he was here? When he was a boy? All those years ago? Or had he returned? Had he returned and walked this same hall again?

"Two doors at the back. Must be the bedrooms," Sarah said from behind him.

Both doors were closed.

Father once told me if you sneak up on someone, you have a second or more to attack before they are able to react. The human brain processes this activity slowly; your victim freezes for a moment as they try to comprehend the fact that you're standing there, particularly in a room where they believe they are alone. He said some victims will continue to freeze, just watching you as if they were watching a television program. They stand there, waiting to see what happens next. Sometimes, not knowing what comes next is better.

Porter wished he had his gun. Why didn't he buy a shotgun locally? No waiting period on those.

His hand went to his pocket, wrapped around the hilt of Bishop's knife.

He reached for the doorknob on the left.

Behind him, Sarah screamed.

80

Kati

Day 3 • 9:11 p.m.

"Wake up!

"Wake up!

"Wake up!"

Muffled.

Words spoken through a wet towel.

A girl's voice.

"Please, wake up . . ."

The words right in her ear. Warm breath. A heavy whisper.

When Kati's eyes opened, they felt so heavy with the effort, they almost slammed shut again. Consciousness returned. With it came pain, washing over her like a hot liquid from inside, burning at her muscles and bones.

The blindfold was gone.

Her hands and feet were no longer bound.

A girl of about her age bent over her, faces nearly touching. Kati's head in her lap.

When Kati's eyes focused on this other girl, the girl pressed a finger to her lips. "He can't hear us," she breathed. "We can't let him hear us. I don't want him to come down here."

Something was wrong with her voice. She sounded like someone getting over a bad cold. It pained her to speak. Kati could see it in her eyes. Dried blood crusted her lips.

Kati tried to sit up, couldn't, fell back into the girl's lap.

The other girl brushed at her hair. "I changed your clothes. It was me, not him. He left clothes for you. Your clothes were all wet. You'll catch cold down here, so I couldn't leave you like that. You don't want to get sick. You need your strength. We need to get out of here. Can't do it alone. Need to work together."

The girl spoke in ragged breaths, each word a struggle.

Kati vaguely remembered the water tank, falling into it.

Then nothing.

"He tried to electrocute you. He *did* electrocute you, I saw him do it. He put you in that big water tank over there and dropped jumper cables down into the water. There was this loud bang, then I smelled . . . I smelled . . . something burning. I think it might have been your hair. I can't tell. Your hair is still wet. He took you out of the tank and gave you CPR. He gave you CPR for a long time, then you coughed, but you didn't wake up. He watched you for a while, then he put you in here. He put you in here with me and went upstairs. He hasn't been back down. Not yet. We need to be quiet so he doesn't come back down. If he realizes you're awake, he'll come back down, I know he will."

The girl coughed.

She grimaced in pain.

When she took her hand away from her mouth, red spittle covered her palm. "I . . . I swallowed glass, to keep him away from me. It worked, he didn't touch me." A weak smile. "Guess I showed him, huh?" She wiped her hand on the green quilt wrapped around her body. "I'm Larissa."

"I'm Kati," she managed, her own throat dry, needing water. "Where . . . where is Wesley?"

"Who?"

"I . . . I came here with Wesley Hartzler. He was with me."

"I haven't seen anyone else, only you. He only brought you down here."

"I came here with him," Kati repeated.

At this, Larissa's eyes lit up. "Could he have gotten away? Maybe he went for help?"

Kati saw the strange man leap across the table, saw him smash his cocoa mug into the side of Wesley's head. Wesley falling to the floor. "I don't know, I think he hurt him. I think he hurt him really bad."

"Maybe he didn't hurt him so bad. Maybe he got away. Otherwise, I think he'd be down here with us. He would have locked him in here."

Kati looked up at the girl holding her, watched her eyes dart desperately around the room before they fixed on the ceiling. "How long have you been down here?"

The girl's gaze turned back to her, a quick, animal-like movement. "I . . . I'm not sure. A day, maybe? I passed out after I swallowed the glass. It's been hard to keep track of time. What day is it?"

"Saturday," Kati said, forcing herself to sit up. Her head was spinning. She touched her left temple and winced.

Larissa's face fell. "He took me this morning. It hasn't even been a day. God, it feels like I've been here a week." She coughed again, more blood.

Kati tried to stand, fell back over. Larissa helped to steady her. "Be careful, I'm sure you're still weak."

Kati nodded, drew in a deep breath, tried to stand again, this time pulling herself up with the chainlink. Once on her feet, she started to circle the cage, checking every seam, every little opening.

"I've been over it a dozen times. He welded all the seams and bolted the frame down into the concrete. There's no room to get out at the top, and he's got two padlocks on the gate. There's no way out of here."

Kati rounded the corner and came to the door. She studied both locks. "Where does he keep the key?"

"On a chain around his neck. Do you know where we are? Where the house is, I mean?"

"You don't know where we are?"

Larissa shook her head and told her how he had abducted her.

"This house is on Lowell. There are neighbors all around. Wesley and I came here recruiting for the Jehovah's Witnesses."

"Does anyone know where you are?"

Kati frowned, dropping the lock. It clattered against the metal frame. "No. There was a large crowd of us at the start, roughly two dozen, but we all left the hall early this morning and split up to cover the most ground. We were gone hours before we got to this house. I lost sight of the others. We go in small groups to stay safe. I stuck with Wesley because he said he knew the neighborhood, he knew this street."

Kati crouched back beside Larissa. "You said he didn't touch you or me. Is that why he took us? Did he take us for sex?"

A tear formed at Larissa's eye, and she wiped it away with a dirty hand. "At first, I thought so, but with you . . . he asked if you would see for him, if you would tell him what you saw, before he put you in the water, before he electrocuted you. When he was trying to revive you, he kept telling you to come back from the light, come back to him. He was frantic. He didn't want you to die, but he tried to kill you. I don't—"

A door opened at the top of the stairs.

Heavy footsteps.

Larissa lay back down, covered herself with the quilt. "Pretend to be sleeping still. He'll leave you alone," she whispered, closing her eyes.

Kati didn't, though. She stood there, she stood there at the door as the man with the black knit cap came down the remainder of the steps to the basement, his right foot dragging slightly behind him.

"You're awake." He approached the cage. "My daughter's clothes fit you well, that's good. I wouldn't want you to catch cold. I should have removed your clothing before I put you in the tank. It's better that way, but I wasn't thinking clearly."

He wrapped his fingers through the chainlink, gripping the metal. "You must tell me, what did you see?"

Kati looked at his hands. His fingernails were dirty, his skin covered in small colored lines, smudges from markers or pens. On the side of his head, his large incision was partially visible at the edge of the cap. The wound was red and inflamed against his pale skin, flaked with dried blood, scratched raw.

"What did you see?" he said again. The *s* drawn out, a lisp. He watched her anxiously with unblinking eyes.

Kati reached up, brushed her finger over his, then clasped at his filthy hand through the chainlink, holding him within her grasp. She leaned close, her face inches from his. "I saw something amazing," she told him. "I saw the face of God."

81

Porter
Day 3 • 9:13 p.m.

The raccoon scrambled out of the bathroom, down the hall, and disappeared out the front door, which still hung open at the front of the mobile home.

Sarah jumped back, an embarrassed look on her face. "Come on, that didn't scare you? Not even a little?"

"I'm trembling on the inside," Porter told her, trying to suppress a smile.

He reached back for the doorknob, twisted, and opened the door on the left side of the narrow hallway.

A small bedroom.

Empty, but for some broken beer bottles piled up in the corner. The window was boarded over, busted out like the others at the front of the house.

Porter turned to the door on the right. "If there's another raccoon, I'll protect you."

"My hero."

He opened the door.

Another bedroom, this one furnished.

A full-size bed flanked by two nightstands occupied the left wall. On the opposite wall was a closet with what were once mirrored doors. Both had been smashed long ago, the pressboard beneath covered in graffiti. The drawers from the nightstand had been removed. Two were missing. The other two were in the closet, stacked in the corner. The mattress on the bed was stained an assortment of colors, none of which Porter could identify. The room smelled of mold and mildew, stale air.

"Nobody has been in here for a long time," Sarah said. "That mattress might even be too gross for kids."

"Never underestimate the power of a teenage boy's hormones. This is like a penthouse when you're sixteen."

"I can't imagine someone actually living here. This was someone's home at one point."

Porter went to the drawers in the closet, lifted the one on top—both empty. The dresser on the wall beside the door had been ransacked too. Three of the drawers were missing. His mind drifted back to the diary, to Bishop's mother pulling out these same drawers in search of something.

He said, "Look to the place where the monsters hide, Detective. That's where you'll find answers."

"What?"

"That's what she told me, back at the prison."

"Monsters hide under the bed," Sarah said.

Porter lifted the mattress, forcing it up and leaning it against the wall with a grunt. The cloth of the box spring beneath had either rotted or been carted away by something for nesting. There was little left but ragged edges along the wood frame. "When I was a kid, I used to hide all the good stuff under my mattress, monsters or not."

Sarah ran the beam of her flashlight over the box spring. "By good stuff, if you mean dust bunnies and more beer bottles, you've struck gold. What exactly are you looking for?"

"I'm not sure," Porter admitted. "In the diary there was a large beige metal box under here."

"Well, it's gone now."

Porter lifted the box spring and leaned it up against the mattress on the wall, then knelt. He ran his fingers over the floorboards, under the beam of his light. "The floorboards are uneven."

"This whole place is uneven."

"They've been pulled up, then put back."

Sarah crouched down next to him. "I think the bad guys in the diary would have checked that, don't you?"

"Maybe it was done later. I need a screwdriver."

"If you think I packed a screwdriver before heading out on this little outing, you clearly don't know me. I'm thrilled when I remember my iPhone charger—something I just realized I left on my desk."

Porter pried at the boards with his fingers but couldn't get a good grip. "What about the car keys?"

"Those I do have." Sarah pulled the keys from her pocket and handed them to him.

He set his flashlight down on the floor, and Sarah pointed her beam at the boards as he worked the key into the small space between two of them. At first there was no give, then they both heard a pop as the first of three boards separated from the floor. He pulled it out and set it aside, then tugged at the next board. This one came out easily, as did the next. He removed five in all, creating an opening about two feet square.

Porter took his flashlight and shined the beam down into the hole. "What do you see?"

He reached inside, pulled out a sleeping bag, and handed it to Sarah. "Looks like camping gear. There's another sleeping bag and a backpack."

He reached back in and retrieved the other two items, then searched the space again to be sure he didn't miss anything. "That's it."

Sarah tugged at the backpack zipper.

"Hold on a second," Porter said. He pulled a pair of latex gloves from his pocket and handed them to her. "Put those on first."

She frowned. "Do you honestly think this is evidence? It's probably just kids again. One of the smarter ones hid his own bed so he wouldn't have to make his prom princess lie down on that filthy mattress."

"Best to be safe until we know for sure." Porter put on a pair of his own.

Sarah slipped on the gloves and went back to work on the zipper.

"It's rusty, doesn't want to move." She grimaced and it finally gave, opening with a metallic rip.

Stale, musty air came out of the bag. The scent of something worse came up from the bottom.

"You better let me do that," Porter told her, reaching for the back-pack.

Porter shined his light down inside while trying to breathe through his mouth. Then he began removing items from the center pocket of the bag, placing them in a row on the floor. When the bag was empty, he leaned back, studying the items under the light.

"Why does it smell so bad?"

"Water got in at some point, recently I'd guess. Everything's rotted, stagnant. It's been down there a long time," Porter replied.

He counted six shirts, four pairs of jeans, socks, and undergarments, both men's and women's. The clothes were damp, the material crumbling under his touch. One of the socks was balled up, the end folded in on itself. Doing his best not to damage the material, Porter pulled it open and smoothed it out, revealing a bulge, something inside the sock.

He exchanged a look with Sarah, reached in, grasped the contents, and set it on the floor.

Porter's heart thudded in his chest. "Get a picture."

Sarah nodded and raised the camera.

A locket, small, gold-plated, on a chain along with a rusty key. After Sarah got a picture, Porter pried the locket open. Although it contained a photograph, the image was faded and lost. On the inside were the initials L.M.

Sarah photographed that too.

82

Clair

Day 3 • 9:14 p.m.

They should have gone back to Metro, tried to get some rest in the war room on that ancient couch that probably began life in Chicago law enforcement back when Al Capone and Diamond Joe Esposito were still shoplifting candy behind their mothers' backs. That couch with its faded brown leather, cracked and creased, and padding that had gone as hard as the floor.

Clair needed that couch.

Clair needed to sleep.

"I know I still have one," Nash grumbled beside her, flipping through the keys on his ring. "It's one of these."

He selected a gold one and slipped it into Porter's apartment door. The key didn't turn.

Wrong key.

Nash pulled it back out, metal grinding on metal.

"Why do you have so many?"

The big man shrugged. "I move, the old key stays, new key gets added. You do this enough and you end up with a lot of them."

"Most people toss the old ones or turn them back in when they move. You're not supposed to keep them."

"Are you moonlighting for the key police now? How the hell do you find time for that?"

Nash tried another, silver this time, with an octagonal head. It didn't work either.

"All I'm saying is you should have around three tops. The one for your car, your apartment, and the war room back at HQ, that's it. No reason for more."

Another gold key, round head. This one slipped in smoothly. This key turned the deadbolt.

Nash pushed open the door. "If I didn't keep my old keys, I wouldn't be able to do things like this."

"Sam? Are you home?" Clair wasn't sure why she called out, but she did. They had knocked three times, and nobody answered.

The apartment was dark.

Nash reached inside and turned on the living room light.

They both saw the toppled chair.

"Holy hell," Nash said.

Clair drew her gun and began checking each room, turning on lights as she went.

Nash remained in the living room. He walked slowly around the room, toward the chair. "Clair, he's not here. This isn't a break-in."

Clair returned from the bedroom, the bathroom light blazing behind her. She shouldered her weapon. Her eyes landed on the cell phone on the coffee table. She reached down and picked up the iPhone. Her thumb pressed the home button. Nothing happened. "Sam's phone, it's turned off."

Nash wasn't listening to her, though. He was leaning down beside the La-Z-Boy chair, his fingers running over the loose material at the bottom, the Velcro fasteners.

"What are you doing?" Clair knelt beside him.

Nash leaned back, leaned against the sofa. "There's something I need to tell you, and you're going to be pissed."

"What?"

"The diary."

"What about the diary?"

Nash drew in a deep breath, let it out slowly. "Sam never turned it in to Evidence. He withheld it." Nash raised a hand, silencing her before she could say something. "He planned to. He was going to. But not yet. He wanted to wait until after Bishop was caught, locked up. He felt that if he submitted that book to evidence, the press would get ahold of it, sensationalize the text, turn Bishop into something larger than life. He was convinced that was why Bishop had planted the book in the first place, and he thought that if he didn't turn it in, if he didn't let the diary out at all, it would throw Bishop off his game, maybe make him slip up. Porter said Bishop had a temper. He figured if he got him mad, Bishop might make a mistake, something that might give us a chance to catch him."

"And you knew about this? Went along with him?"

Nash nodded slowly. "At first I told him I'd give it a week. That week turned into a month, then that became four months. Time went by, and it seemed less and less important."

"I mentioned the diary in my reports. There's a record," Clair said.

"I did too. I didn't withhold anything. Sam knew that. He said it wouldn't matter. If someone asked, he'd say he checked the diary in a long time ago, blame it on the evidence room or the system, because they're always losing evidence. You know Sam, he'd come up with something."

Clair nodded at the chair. "That's where he kept it?"

"Yeah."

Clair reached a hand up inside the chair, felt around. "Good spot." She pulled her hand out and leaned back against the couch beside Nash with a resigned sigh. "So where is he?"

Nash's eyes fell on Sam's phone, still in Clair's hand. "Best guess? He found something in that diary, and he's chasing the lead."

"Why leave his phone? Why not tell us?"

"Sam's keeping us out, protecting us."

"He's on suspension. He was told to stay away from this. Even if he marches Bishop into Metro, they'll take his badge. He's done."

"I don't think he cares, not anymore. Not since Heather. Her death changed him. Losing Bishop in that building—it all changed him. I think he sees catching Bishop as unfinished business. I think he'll do whatever it takes to bring him in, then he's out anyway. He wants to exit on his own terms. He feels Bishop is still loose because of him, his mistake, and he wants to be the one to bring him in, to end all of this."

"That's dangerous."

"He doesn't care."

"He shouldn't be alone."

"That's what he wants," Nash said.

Clair drew her legs up to her chest and wrapped her arms around them. "The boy in the truck, Nash, that was horrible. If this is Bishop, he's gotten much worse."

"He's always been trying to tell us something. We need to look for that. Search for his message. That leads us to Larissa, leads us to him." His voice was soft, monotone. "Clair-bear, we need to share what we know with the FBI, the diary too. We can't hold back anymore, not something like this."

"I know." A yawn washed over her, and Clair tried to suppress it, a hand over her mouth. Sitting still, that was bad. If they didn't keep moving, she'd fall asleep right here. "As soon as we get back."

Beside her, Nash yawned too.

"We rest for five minutes, then we head back to Metro."

Nash was already sleeping though, snoring softly.

83

Porter

Day 3 • 9:44 p.m.

Porter felt the weight of Bishop's knife in his pocket.

This was not going well. This was not going well at all. I slipped my hand into the pocket of my jeans searching for the familiar hilt of my Buck knife. If I had it, I could slash this man across the neck. I'd cut right through all his chins and let his blood loose like a faucet. I was fast. I knew I was fast. But was I fast enough? Surely I could kill him before this overweight waste of a man could react, right? Father would want me to kill him. Mother too. They would. I knew they would.

Bishop's words rattled back at him from the diary.

They stood outside the Carter trailer after photographing everything. They bagged the locket and key. The clothes went back into the backpack. They left it on the floor of the bedroom, the floorboards and mattress still up.

Above, the moon crept out, pushing aside dark curtains in an effort to steal a peek at the earth below. The air turned decidedly cold, nothing like the weather in Chicago, but there was a deep, humid chill to it, one that teased Porter's bones.

Sarah wanted to go to town, find a hotel, get rest. She didn't have to say it again. He saw it in her eyes. She was tired. She had had enough for one night.

Porter turned away from her and stared back at the woods lining the property behind both houses, at the small path leading into those woods.

There was a flutter in his stomach. His skin tingled.

The beam of Sarah's flashlight went from the ground at Porter's feet, swept across the yard, then met with his, illuminating the mouth of the path. "Nobody has been living out here for years. Why do you think that path is still there? Shouldn't it have grown over by now?"

"Animals, maybe. Or the same kids who party here in the trailer." *Or something else. Something worse.*

The knife felt warm. He hadn't realized he even put his hand back in his pocket. His fingers slipped over the surface of the handle.

"You can stay here," he offered.

Sarah was already shaking her head. "You're not going out there alone."

With that, they crossed the lawn toward the path, stepping over the trunk of a small fallen tree before disappearing down the path's throat, the beams of their flashlights dueling with the dark.

84

Poole

Day 3 • 9:49 p.m.

"I've been through that same box about a dozen times, the accounting records of the crazy and deranged," a voice said.

Poole looked up from the stack of spreadsheets at the woman standing in the doorway. She wore a pink cap and a purple scarf draped over an unzipped heavy jacket. He had seen her before.

"May I come in?" she asked.

He leaned back in the chair and nodded, then rubbed his temples. The pain at the back of his head had worked around to the front and sides. "What can I do for you?"

She crossed the room and reached out a hand. "We've never been formally introduced. Detective Clair Norton. I was on the 4MK Task Force with Detectives Porter and Nash before you and your team stepped in and stole the case from us."

Poole took her hand. "Special Agent Frank Poole."

"I already know that. Did you miss the part where I said I was a detective?"

He didn't need this right now. "What can I do for you, Detective?"

"I need you to come across the hall."

"To the war room? Porter said I'm not allowed in the war room. He and that other guy made it very clear the last time I was in there."

"Thanks to you and your friends, Sam has been given a little time off. While he's gone, I'm in charge over there," she said.

"What does that have to do with me?"

"Someone dropped your chocolate into our peanut butter."

Poole followed Detective Clair Norton across the hall to the war room. The tension was thick as he entered. Tired eyes were on him. He nodded at Detective Nash as he pulled up a chair at the conference table. Nash was the only person he recognized of the three people already seated.

"Frank," Nash muttered, giving him a weak wave.

Clair introduced him to the two others at the table. "This is Sophie Rodriguez with Missing Children, and the disheveled mess over there in the corner is Edwin Klozowski. He heads our Information Technology Division."

"Call me Kloz," Klozowski stood and offered his hand across the table.

"No sucking up to the feds," Clair said.

Klozowski withdrew his hand and returned to his chair. "Right."

"What happened to your head?" Nash asked. "You're all banged up."

Poole told them about the houses on Forty-First, Diener, and Bishop.

Nash and Clair exchanged a look. Clair was first to speak. "I'm so sorry."

Poole nodded once.

"Are they going to let you continue working the case?" Nash asked.

Poole shrugged. "Nobody has said they're not. Not yet, anyway. The Chicago office is short-staffed as is. Most agents are working a recent terror threat that came in. They might bring someone else in, but for now I'm all they've got with BAU experience. Nobody knows this case better than me." He looked around the room. "Except maybe all of you."

"And Sam," Klozowski said quietly. "He knows the case better than any of us."

Poole said, "I've tried to reach him, several times. I'm just getting voice mail on his phone."

Again, Nash and Clair exchanged a look. "Nash and I just came from his apartment. We found his cell phone sitting on a table in his living room, switched off, and his favorite chair was overturned, lying on its side."

"Do you think Bishop got to him?"

"No. We think he left on his own. His suitcase was gone. We think he went somewhere," Clair said.

"Someplace he didn't want us to know about," Nash added.

"Where would he go?"

Nobody had an answer to that.

"Could he be working with Bishop? Helping him somehow?"

"No way," Nash said.

Clair folded her arms. "Not a chance."

Poole studied their faces. "What do you know about Bishop's diary?"

The room grew quiet again. Looks passed among the group, but they said nothing.

Poole blew out a breath and stood, turned toward the door. "I don't have time for this."

Nash unfolded his arms, set both palms on the table. His eyes swung from Clair to Klozowski. "Wait, Frank. Please sit."

Poole lowered himself back into the chair. "You know where it is, don't you?"

Clair looked to Nash. Nash said, "Sam held it back."

"From Evidence?"

"From the press. Checking the diary into Evidence would be no different from sending it to the newspapers. It would leak. Something like that would most definitely leak."

"So he withheld evidence? All of you let him do that?"

"Sam held the book back. I knew he had it, only Sam and me, nobody else." Nash turned his hands over, looked at his palms.

"Where is the diary now?"

"Sam hid it under the La-Z-Boy in his living room, the overturned chair we found."

"So Sam has it with him? Wherever he is?"

"Yeah."

"Nobody made a copy?"

"We didn't want any copies."

Poole let all of this sink in, then turned to Clair. "Is this why you brought me over here? To come clean?"

Klozowski let out a soft laugh. "Oh boy, icing and cake and all that."

"What does that mean?"

"There's more," Clair said. She pulled an eight-by-ten photo from a manila folder on the table and slid it over to him.

Poole picked up the picture. It was a photograph of a boy, frozen beneath layers of ice, in the cab of a pickup truck.

Clair stood up and retrieved another picture from the whiteboard at the front of the room. She set it down in front of Poole. This one showed a close-up of a windshield, taken from a traffic camera.

"That's Bishop," Poole stated flatly.

"It's the same truck," Clair told him. "That truck was also caught on a security camera at Jackson Park three weeks ago. Our unsub used it to tow a water tank into the park, then used water from the tank to help conceal the body of Ella Reynolds beneath the surface of the lagoon. The tank was stolen from Tanks A Lot, an aquarium store downtown. Libby McInley, the sister of Bishop's fifth victim, applied for a job at Tanks A Lot. She worked there for one day. I think she was only there long enough to scope the place out for Bishop. Somehow, they're working together. They *were* working together."

Poole stared at both photographs. "When did you learn all of this?"

"In the past few hours," Clair told him. "All of it."

"Do you have an ID on the boy?"

"Not yet. The body went downtown. They're working on it."

"Are you aware of what happened to Libby McInley? How we found her?" Poole asked.

"We saw the report."

"You saw the report," Poole muttered. He still couldn't close his eyes without seeing Libby McInley. Now Agent Diener too. Bishop's face when he opened that door.

You're not Sam Porter.

A smile on his face.

Poole looked at the whiteboards at the front of the room, at the girls' images staring back at him. Then he turned back to the people sitting around the conference table, their eyes on him. "Porter said these cases weren't tied to Bishop."

"Sam was wrong."

"Withholding evidence, holding back that diary, in what is now a federal case, could not only cost you your badges but land some of you in jail. That diary could be key, and now we don't have it. We don't know where it is."

"They had nothing to do with it. That's on me and Sam," Nash repeated.

The room dropped into silence again, filling with nervous energy thick enough to crackle.

Clair's eyes met Nash's across the table. Both turned away. Sophie's gaze was locked on the small screen of her phone, although it didn't look like she was actually reading anything, just unwilling to face the others.

After nearly a full minute, Poole stood. "Wait here."

He left them sitting at the table.

Behind him, Klozowski muttered, "We're so fucked."

Poole returned a moment later with one of the whiteboards from the FBI room across the hall. He slid it beside the others at the front of the room, then started back across the hall.

"You're not gonna report us?" Klozowski called after him.

"Right now, we're going to work the case."

Clair let out the breath she had been holding.

85

Kati

Day 3 • 9:52 p.m.

The man in the black knit cap sat across from her at the small kitchen table, his dark eyes bloodshot, lined with red, the left more than the right. He seemed to favor this eye. As he watched her, his head turned slightly as if watching her with the left eye while the right focused on something in the distance, something behind her.

Kati's hands and feet were bound to the metal chair with zip ties.

They were tight.

Far too tight.

Kati kept wiggling her fingers to keep the circulation up.

She tried to focus on him, to keep her eyes on him as one would be expected to do during a civilized conversation. She tried not to look at the wound on the side of his head, caked with dried blood. She tried not to stare too long at the black knit cap rubbing against that nasty red flesh. She tried not to look at the dark cocoa stains on the table and floor, now dry and crusty. Most of all, she refused to look down at the blood on the floor, the thick splatter where Wesley fell, the round pool that trickled out into streams on the floor, then thin branches, finally ending in drops on the linoleum and up the wall.

She couldn't look at that.

She wouldn't look at that.

The man held a bottle of pills in his right hand, gripping tightly enough to turn his fingers white.

Kati tried to glimpse the label, but his hand covered most of it. He was shaking, just a little. He had been worse before he took one of the pills.

"Tell me again," he said, leaning a little closer to her. She smelled his breath. She didn't want to smell his breath. She also knew the only chance she had at escape was to win over his trust. She needed to give him a reason to need her, something that other girl in the basement couldn't or wouldn't provide, something his victims were not willing to provide.

"Can you loosen my hands and feet? I promise I won't try to run. It hurts. I'm still having trouble concentrating, and this pain doesn't help." She rattled her wrists against the chair to emphasize her point, but then decided she shouldn't do that. She shouldn't show any sign of strength, of defiance, only weakness, only submission.

"Pain sharpens the thoughts. If you use it properly, pain will help your focus, not diminish it."

His speech had become clearer since the pill, the lisp almost gone. He was sweating now, though, a slight shimmer on his brow and neck.

"I want Wesley to see," Kati said. "Can you show Wesley too? So we can both tell you? I think it would be helpful to learn if we both saw the same thing, don't you think?"

His eyes left her for a moment, dropping to the floor, looking to the place she refused to look, before focusing on her again, his lips thin. "We're not going to talk about Wesley. I don't want to talk about him anymore. I want you to tell me again."

Kati pulled at her bound hands again, quietly this time. The left one felt looser than the right but not enough to pull free—at least, she didn't think so. She couldn't be sure. "I don't know that I can put it into words. I saw something beautiful, magical. Like standing inside of music or tasting the emotion of an artist as he captures his subject's breath. There are no words, nothing that really compares."

"You said you saw the face of God."

The lisp again, subtle, on the words *said, saw,* and *face.*

"I . . . I think it was all God. I think he was all around me. I felt a warmth, something big all around me. Have you ever drifted off to sleep and first felt like you were falling for a brief second, then that turned into floating, a perfect weightlessness without pain, without any pressure on your body? There was no discernible sound at all, yet I also heard the most beautiful soothing sound, like nothing and everything all at once, almost like being in two different places at the same time."

"Could you see yourself?"

Kati thought about this for a second, then shook her head. The finger of her left hand was nearly able to slip out of the zip tie. "No, nothing like that. I think that only happens in the movies or on TV. But . . . I did feel free, though, free of my body, free of my body's constraints."

Her finger nearly slipped the tie, then snapped back. If he heard the plastic against the frame of the chair, he didn't acknowledge the sound. His finger tapped against the pill bottle.

Win his trust, Kati told herself. Stay calm. If she remained calm, he would stay calm. Tell him what he wants to hear. Her mind drifted to the girl in the basement, the girl who was probably dying in the basement after swallowing glass rather than allowing this monster to hurt her. She'd rather die on her own terms than let this guy touch her. Kati admired her, but she had no desire to die. She would get out of here.

Above the sink there was a window—dark outside, but she could make out the faint outline of the neighbor's house, no more than ten feet away. A light glowed in one of the windows, and she thought she saw movement behind white curtains.

Kati licked her lips. They were dry and chapped. "May I have some water?"

The man stared at her, and at first she wasn't sure he heard her. She was about to ask again when he stood and went to the sink, pulled a cloudy glass from the drying rack on the counter, and filled it with water from the tap. As he returned to the table, she could see particles floating in the water, remnants of whatever had been in the glass before, unwashed, filthy.

The man in the black knit cap stood beside her and tipped the water glass against her lips. Kati drank. She drank and tried not to think about what she saw in the glass. Complacent, willing, unconcerned. These words floated through her mind, all the things she knew she needed to appear to be to survive. The water tasted sour. She smiled as he lifted the glass away. She would not show any discomfort.

His hand trembled as he set the glass on the table and returned to his seat. She wasn't sure if he trembled because of nerves or whatever was wrong with him, but she was certain it wasn't out of fear or weakness. She wouldn't make the mistake of believing that.

"When you put me in that tank," she went on, "I was blindfolded. I woke up in the dark, I didn't know where I was. Then I was in the water, body-temperature water, then falling and silence, then . . ." Her voice trailed off; her eyes met his. "Then I was perfect, everything was perfect. No fear. No wants. No needs. Calm. Serene. Ideal."

The man studied her, his mouth open just enough to allow a trickle of spit down the left side. He made no move to wipe it away. The index finger on the hand that held the pill bottle twitched, tapping at the plastic. With his free hand, he rubbed his pointer finger and thumb together, making a small, circular pattern. "Why should I believe you?" he finally said.

"I have no reason to lie."

"No?"

"I was dead. The other girl told me I was dead. You brought me back, you saved me."

"Your heart stopped. You were dead for a little over three minutes. I brought you back. Maybe it wasn't long enough. Maybe you didn't see anything. You're just telling me what you think I want to hear."

"I wouldn't do that."

"I think we need to do it again. Longer this time. Five minutes, maybe six. The brain dies after five — it should have been longer than five," he told her. The twitching against the bottle intensified as he spoke, the words coming faster, urgent. "Less than five may not be enough."

Kati pulled at her bindings, tugged hard on her left. She couldn't slip out, though. "Who is . . . Maybelle?"

He drew in a deep breath and leaned back in his chair.

"Maybelle Markel?" Kati said. "Yeah, Markel, that's it."

"Where did you hear that name?"

"It came to me when I was there, in that place. I . . . heard it. Like someone whispering to me or maybe shouting from a great distance, I'm not exactly sure. Who is she?"

He took another pill. He fought with the bottle cap, got it open, and swallowed one dry.

"You said you have a daughter. You said these are her clothes I'm wearing. Is that her name? Is your daughter's name Maybelle Markel?"

"I must have told you."

"You didn't."

He looked puzzled as he shuffled through his memories trying to remember if he said her name, the pills lifting the haze from his eyes.

Kati tugged her left hand again, hard this time, almost pulled free, but her hand snapped back. She might have cut herself on the zip tie this time. Not only did the base of her wrist hurt, but she felt warmth there, wetness. She wondered if the slickness of blood might help her slip free. "I think Maybelle wants you to know she's okay. That she's at peace."

"Is that what she said? What she told you?" There was an anxiousness to his voice that wasn't there before. "Are you certain?" The lisp on *certain*.

Kati nodded. "Yes, I think so."

His bloodshot eyes blinked, then locked on her, peering into her, through her. He stood up with such speed and force, the tabletop went with him, tilting up and to the side as the glass flew across the room and shattered. The corner of the table caught Kati in the rib cage like a battering ram, sending her chair tumbling back. The chair snagged for a second on the cabinets behind her before falling to the side, painfully pinning Kati's arm against the floor, caught beneath her own weight.

The word "Liar!" belted from him, a scream of anger and raw emotion.

Kati screamed too. She screamed as she fell. But she was silent now, her eyes fixed on the place Wesley had fallen, only inches from her face. She felt his sticky blood in her hair, and she could see the small, lighter spot at the center of the bloody pool, the place where his head had rested on the floor.

From the corner of her eye, barely visible now from such a harsh angle, she could also see the drawing she noticed when the man had brought her into the kitchen with Wesley. Attached to the refrigerator with a Domino's Pizza magnet, a drawing of a house with a dog, a father, and a daughter standing in front of it, nothing more than stick figures, holding each other's hands. The bottom right corner of the drawing was signed Maybelle Markel, in thick, blocky purple letters.

Someone came into the room then. The front door opened and closed. Frantic footsteps down the hall. "What have you done?"

"She lied. She didn't see. None of them. Not one."

"Everyone will see soon enough."

86

Poole

Day 3 • 9:52 p.m.

Special Agent Frank Poole, Detectives Clair Norton and Brian Nash of Chicago Metro, Sophie Rodriguez from Missing Children, and Edwin Klozowski from Information Technology sat at the conference table in the war room, all eyes on the six whiteboards at the front of the room.

Behind them the coffeemaker beeped. Nobody got up.

"This is overwhelming," Klozowski finally said, the first to speak in nearly five minutes.

It *was* overwhelming, Poole thought. Sixteen years with the Bureau, four with the Behavioral Science Unit out of Quantico before transferring to Chicago. He had never seen anything like this, not in an investigation, not in all the case histories he studied. There was no rhyme or reason to it, no real pattern. Serial killers always kept to a pattern, a signature. That pattern may evolve as the killer tuned his efforts, became more comfortable in his skin, but they were never random. There was always a pattern.

Why couldn't he see the pattern?

"There's too much noise," Poole said quietly.

Nash turned toward him, frowning. "What does that mean?"

"We need to get rid of the noise."

Poole stood up and went to the front of the room, his eyes fixed on the boards.

"I think we've lost him," Klozowski said.

Poole stood there for a moment, taking in the text, every word, every letter, every curved fumble of the dry-erase marker, he memorized it all. Then he turned the first board around backward, all those words lost to the back, replaced by a clean, white surface. He turned the next one and the one after that, until all six faced the wall and they all stared at nothing.

Kloz snickered, leaned back in his chair. "Now I know we've lost him."

Poole walked around to the back of the boards and pulled all the photographs down, picked up a black marker from one of the trays, and returned to the front. "We've learned a lot over the past few days, too much. We need to filter out the noise and focus on what is really important, find the real evidence, piece it together as if it were fresh."

"Puzzle it out," Kloz said.

Nash and Clair both glared at him. He shrugged.

Poole took the photograph of Anson Bishop and taped it to the top center of the board. He then sorted through the remaining photographs in his hand, placing the following beneath Bishop's picture:

Ella Reynolds
Lili Davies
Floyd Reynolds
Randal Davies
Libby McInley
Larissa Biel
Darlene Biel
John Doe/Truck

"These are the people directly impacted by this case," Poole stated. "The victims or intended victims."

Clair asked, "Who does that leave?"

Poole held up the remaining pictures in his hand. "Three of the spouses—Leeann Reynolds, Grace Davies, and Larry Biel, and the remaining children of the families." He set the pictures on the conference table, facedown. "If we find a reason to connect these people to the case, other than relations, we'll put them back on the board. Let's focus on the others for now."

Nash drummed his fingers over the tabletop. "If this is all somehow Bishop, and he's following the same MO as his past victims, that means the children were killed because of something their parents did. The kids aren't the focus."

"But he also killed the parents this time," Sophie interjected.

"And look at how he killed the children," Clair said. "Both girls drowned in salt water. This unknown boy frozen in the truck. They were all tortured."

"He didn't remove the eyes, ear, or tongue on any of the children, which is a major departure," Nash pointed out. "Completely different from what he did in the past."

"He did with Libby McInley," Poole reminded them. "He killed her, just like he would have his past victims."

"Not *exactly* like his past victims," Clair said. "Her toes and fingers were removed. He's never done that before."

"More torture," said Nash. "An escalation, maybe?"

"A different kind of torture, different from everything else," Poole said. He gathered the coffee cups from the table and went to the machine, began to fill them. "Fingers and toes are usually removed to get information. This is a major break from the norm for him. With all his other victims, he removed the eyes, ear, and tongue to send a message to whoever found the bodies, to taunt law enforcement, to sensationalize the murders. He went after the past victims because of information he already possessed, everything he learned from Talbot's business activities. He didn't need to learn anything from those victims. He had it all."

Poole returned to the table and passed out the coffee.

Clair reached for her mug and took a sip. "So Libby McInley is different from all the rest—she knew something, something he needed, something he was willing to torture to learn."

Poole returned to the board at the front. "He was willing to torture Libby more than anyone else in order to get some information."

He removed the picture of Libby McInley from the center of the board and placed it at the top right. "Her murder is nothing like these others. Let's separate her for now too."

"What do we know about Libby McInley? What makes her such a special target?" Nash asked.

Poole rattled off the information from her file. "Charged in March 2007 and convicted in July 2007 of manslaughter for the vehicular death of one Franklin Kirby, sentenced to ten years, of which she served seven and a few months before being released on parole six weeks ago."

"What was the name of her victim?" Nash asked.

"Franklin Kirby." Poole took a step toward the conference table. "That name meant something to Porter too, but he didn't expand on what he knew. Who is he?"

"Holy hell, how did we miss that?" Kloz blurted out.

Clair shook her head. "He's in Bishop's diary. Kirby worked for Talbot. He stole a lot of money from him and ultimately ran off with Bishop's mother when Bishop was a kid. He also shot and killed Bishop's father."

"The diary again." Poole frowned. "I need to see that book."

"Let me try and get this straight," Nash said, "because I *have* read the diary. Kirby kills Bishop's father. Kirby runs off with Bishop's mother. Libby McInley accidentally hits and kills Kirby with her car. Bishop kills Barbara McInley, Libby's sister, in retaliation for her killing Kirby, then he ultimately kills Libby, even though the two of them are somehow working together? That doesn't make any sense. Bishop would have been dancing in the street with Kirby dead."

Kloz cleared his throat. "What if Bishop didn't kill Libby? Maybe somebody else did and just made it look like he killed her. That might explain why her fingers and toes were cut off. Somebody other than Bishop did it. Somebody after something."

"Who?"

Shuffling in his chair, Klozowski went on. "What if Bishop didn't kill Barbara McInley either?"

Clair scratched at the back of her head. "We know he did."

"Do we?"

Silence again.

Kloz wrapped his hands around his mug. He looked down at the coffee swirling inside. "Every one of Bishop's initial victims died because their families were involved in some type of criminal activity, every single one, except his fifth victim, Barbara McInley. Her death was attributed to her sister's hit-and-run. An accident." He turned to Nash. "Like you said, Bishop had no reason to kill her, not for killing Kirby, that's for sure."

"Who, then?" Poole asked.

Kloz answered quietly. "Bishop's mother."

87

Poole

Day 3 • 9:55 p.m.

"Bishop's mother?" Poole frowned.

Klozowski nodded. "She was romantically involved with Kirby. She's never been caught. Who knows? Libby's fingers and toes, that could have been revenge. Cut off an ear, take out the tongue and eyes, and drop them in little white boxes . . . it's not hard to copy Bishop's signature."

"The white boxes, were they the same kind Bishop used in the original killings?" Clair asked.

Poole nodded. "Yeah, perfect match."

"If Bishop's mother is running around out there, we don't know her capabilities. Considering all the information her son put together, I don't think it's too much of a stretch for her to match the box," Nash said. "She had resources, all that money Carter's husband stole from Talbot."

Poole paced between the boards and the table. "Back at Porter's apartment, he pointed out McInley's murder as different from the others. He said Bishop had seemed a little preoccupied with her, the fact that she was the only blonde of all the victims."

"I remember that," Clair said. "Bishop stood there for a second, stared at the picture. Said it was an *anomaly*, his word."

Poole walked slowly back to the board and wrote *Killed by Bish-*

op's Mother? next to Libby McInley's photo, then he stepped behind the boards again before returning to the conference table with an old Polaroid and the lock of blond hair, both in evidence bags. He set them on the table.

"What do these mean to all of you?"

Clair picked up the Polaroid. "Where did you find this?" She showed it to Nash and Klozowski.

"In a drawer at Libby's house, hidden under some clothes, along with the lock of hair."

Clair set the picture back down. "Bishop mentioned some photos in the diary. This could be one of them. If it is, one of these women is Bishop's mother, and the other is their neighbor, Lisa Carter."

"We tried running facial recognition on both women, but we didn't get anything. The age of the image and the angle of the shot don't help. What about the hair? Was that mentioned in the diary too?"

"No. Maybe it's Libby's?" Clair offered.

"It's not a match for Libby or Barbara."

"How about Kirby?" Kloz said. "He had long, blond hair."

Nash pulled the evidence bag closer. "Why would Libby have Kirby's hair? Where would she get it?"

Nobody had an answer to that.

Poole went back to the board and added the information about the photo and hair. He scribbled the name KALYN SELKE too. "So all of you are aware, there's this too—Bishop helped her get IDs under this name. They corresponded while she was in prison."

"Do you know how?" Clair asked.

Poole shook his head. "I haven't had a chance to get down to the prison yet. After talking to her parole officer, we did learn she was having trouble adjusting to being out. He thought she wanted to go back."

"Where was she? Stateville?"

"Yeah. We also found a .45 at her house, which is a clear parole violation," Poole told them. "She knew someone was after her. If what you're telling me about Kirby and the mother is true, that makes sense. We just need to figure out why Bishop would protect her."

Poole returned his attention to the boards. "Okay. This is good. This is really good, we've got something different to go on, with Libby McInley anyway. Let's take a closer look at the rest."

Poole took a few steps to the left, leaving the Libby McInley board behind him, his focus back on the first whiteboard with ANSON BISHOP written at the top and photographs of the seven missing or dead beneath him.

Nash cleared his throat. "Back to what I said earlier. If this is all somehow Bishop, and he's following the same MO as his past victims, that means the children were killed because of something their parents did. The kids aren't the focus."

"Nash is right," Clair said. "Can you rearrange the pictures? Put the adults on top and the children under them?"

Poole nodded and reordered the images:

<u>Floyd Reynolds</u>
Ella Reynolds
<u>Randal Davies</u>
Lili Davies
<u>Darlene Biel</u>
Larissa Biel

He held up the picture of the boy frozen inside the cab of the Toyota Tundra. "That leaves your unknown boy."

"We need to identify him quickly, then hone in on his parents," Clair said. "They might be his next targets."

"What do we know about the other parents?"

Clair found her phone and loaded her Notes app. "Floyd Reynolds, worked for UniMed America Healthcare. He was in insurance sales. We couldn't find any debt or financial problems. No red flags with his home life. His wife said he went out to search for their daughter. The unsub strangled him with piano wire inside the family car, and his body was found in their backyard, hidden inside a snowman. There was a boot print on the back of the driver's seat. We think the unsub placed his foot there for leverage when strangling Reynolds. A size eleven."

"We don't have a record of Bishop's shoe size, do we?"

"Nope."

Poole added this information to the board, then pointed at Randal Davies with the marker. "What about Mr. Davies?"

"He was a doctor. Oncologist. Worked at Stroger Hospital. Like Reynolds, no problems with his home life or his finances. He was killed with a high dose of lisinopril, a medication normally used to treat high blood pressure, something he was not prescribed. We think the unsub broke into the Davies home via the back door. The lisinopril was concentrated and placed in the family coffeemaker. He was the only member of the household known to drink coffee."

Poole frowned. "So either the unsub knew this or didn't really care who died."

"The kitchen had several large uncovered windows. They provide visibility from the road," Nash explained. "The unsub could have learned who drank what with a little surveillance."

"That makes sense. I don't think the adult targets are random, not even within the same household. If this is Bishop, he's got a reason for each victim," Poole said. "That leaves your only adult female victim."

"Yeah, Darlene Biel. We've got an officer stationed at the hospital guarding her room. She's stable but currently in an induced coma. Our unsub injected cyanide into her toothpaste tube. She ingested the poison brushing her teeth at what should have been a safe house." Clair drew in a breath and looked down. "That was on me. She was in my custody, my care."

Nash reached for her shoulder. "You saved her life. Anyone else, and she would be dead right now."

He told Poole how she forced Darlene Biel to drink liquid soap.

"The base in the soap countered the acidic properties of the cyanide? I'm impressed. Where did you learn that?"

Clair said, "Back in high school, my science teacher accidentally poisoned himself with cyanide. When he realized what happened, he ran out of the room into the boys' bathroom and drank the soap. He lived. I guess it stuck with me."

"Don't be too hard on yourself," Poole told her. "Cyanide works fast. Another minute or two, and she would have been dead. Being in that safe house with you probably saved her life. If this had happened at home, she probably wouldn't have survived."

Clair ignored the praise. By the crease in her forehead, Poole knew she was already thinking ahead. When she spoke, she answered the question he was about to put out to the group. "Biel was, I mean, *is* a pharmaceutical sales rep. She travels a lot, had a go-bag ready when we asked her and her husband to leave their home. The poisoned toothpaste was in that bag. CSI tested the shared toothpaste on the bathroom counter in the master bedroom, and it came up clean. Like with Randal Davies, the unsub targeted her specifically. He had advance knowledge, knew about her bag, and went after her."

"Anyone else see a pattern emerging here?"

"They all work in the medical field—we've got a doctor and two sales reps," Nash said.

"What do the spouses do for work?"

Clair glanced down at her notes. "Grace Davies and Leeann Reynolds are both stay-at-home mothers. Larry Biel works construction."

"All nonmedical."

"All nonmedical," Clair agreed. "Definite potential pattern there."

Poole was nodding, studying the text on the board. "Okay, that's good. We can work with that." He pointed at Ella Reynolds's name. "Let's talk about the children."

Clair turned to the other woman across the conference table. "Sophie, do you want to—"

Sophie was already nodding. "Yeah, okay. Ella Reynolds, fifteen years old. Her body was found on February twelfth under the ice at Jackson Park Lagoon. This initially threw us because the lagoon had been frozen since early January, at least twenty days before she went missing. We've since learned Anson Bishop cut a hole in the ice, placed her body in the water, then added water from the stolen tank, creating new ice at the same level as the old. We believe she was taken from Logan Square, about seven minutes from her house. We know she recently purchased a car at Cars R Us, a nearby dealer. She was making payments directly. Her parents had no idea. She only recently got her learner's permit."

"She was found wearing the clothing of our second victim, Lili Davies," Clair said, weighing in. "That just smells like something Bishop would do to try and sensationalize the crime and draw attention."

"I agree," Poole said. "It's part of the noise I mentioned at the start of this. Let's leave that out for now. We can always put it back, if it becomes relevant. What do we know about Lili?"

Sophie went on. "Seventeen years old. She was last seen walking to school at Wilcox Academy on February twelfth. She didn't make it. The school is close, only four blocks from her home. Her body was found at Leigh Gallery, where she worked. She was posed in a storage room at the back, clearly meant to be discovered. Although the unsub used a black electrical cord around the neck to prop her up, it was clear she was already dead. Like Reynolds, she died from repeatedly drowning in salt water. As Clair said, she was found in Ella Reynolds's clothing, so the unsub somehow switched them."

Klozowski poked his head up from his laptop. "Didn't you say something about her trying to buy a car too?"

Clair nodded. "Sophie and I spoke to her best friend, Gabrielle Deegan. She said Lili's father told her he'd buy her a car at graduation, but she wanted something sooner."

"Any connection to the car lot where the first girl bought a car?" Poole asked.

"They didn't know her," Nash said. "We checked out the dealership staff and couldn't find any real connection there. Every teenager wants a car. I think this is just another coincidence. More noise, like you said."

Poole turned back to the board. "Okay, what about Larissa Biel?"

"Larissa is different," Sophie said. "She only went missing as of this morning, and there's no body. There's a good chance she's still alive. At this point, we don't know much more than that. She had planned to go to a dance at school tonight, and she was home when both parents left for work this morning. Her mother had planned a spa day as a surprise. If not for that, we probably still wouldn't know she was missing."

"Judging by what we've seen with Ella Reynolds, and particularly Lili Davies, she doesn't have much time. Davies died within a day of her disappearance," Clair said, turning to Klozowski. "Any luck with her laptop or phone?"

"Her parents installed KidBSafe on the laptop. Teenagers have been sharing the override to that one for nearly two years now. We found the hacks installed on her computer. Larissa could essentially turn the monitoring software on and off whenever she wanted to and limit what her parents could see." Kloz shifted his weight. "We also found PrivaShield running in the background. PrivaShield destroys cache data as it's created, basically erasing digital fingerprints. This girl is smart. She gave her parents just enough data that they could feel like they were monitoring her, then hid the rest. We're still digging, but the laptop may be a bust. We think she had her cell phone on her when she was abducted. We tracked her movements this morning to the corner of West Chicago Avenue and North Damen, and then the signal drops. Most likely, the unsub removed the battery or destroyed the phone. We filed an emergency request for the data, but the phone company hasn't produced it yet. I'll report back as soon as I know something."

Poole returned to the conference table. He studied the photo of the boy frozen inside the cab of the pickup truck, then turned it toward the others. "That leaves us with him."

"I'm sure Eisley is doing everything he can to get us an ID, but the ice will slow things down," Clair said, studying the picture of the boy frozen inside the cab of the truck.

"The truck is registered to Kalyn Selke," Klozowski said.

"Libby McInley's alias," Nash said. "Another dead end."

"Yeah."

Poole turned back to the boards. "Is that everything?"

"We haven't talked about the obituaries," Nash replied.

He turned back to the table. "Obituaries?"

Clair nodded. "A call came in this morning on 911, an older woman claiming that Floyd Reynolds had died twice. His obituary ran in today's paper and last Wednesday. When we dug deeper, we found more. Apparently our unsub has been running obituaries for his victims in the local papers before attempting to kill them."

Poole had stopped listening. "Died twice," he said slowly before turning back to the boards. He found the board with the poems and flipped it back over so the others could read them. "I think Bishop killed Special Agent Diener because he saw these poems. They were written on the wall in the abandoned house. See how certain words are underlined? *Death* is the only word that appears twice." He explained how the poems had been cut out of the drywall and removed.

"Look at some of the other underlined words," Clair said. "*Ice, water, fear* . . . all of this fits the kills."

"Did you run a trace on the 911 call?"

All heads turned toward Klozowski. He held up a finger for a moment, then frowned. "According to the report, the call came in from Lasting Harmony Retirement Center down by the loop. Staff says it was a ninety-three-year-old woman named Ingrid Nesbit—she reads the obituaries daily and got all ruffled when she caught the dupes for Floyd Reynolds. She insisted on making the call."

"Dead end," Nash grumbled.

Clair was still studying the board. "If the poems tie in and he wanted us to find all this, why cut them out? Why kill Diener?"

Poole sighed. "I think he wanted Porter to find all of this, not me. Probably not you either."

Clair turned to Klozowski. "You said all the bogus obituaries were filed from the same computer, right? Anything on the trace?"

Klozowski didn't answer her. Instead, his eyes were glued to his screen.

"Kloz?"

"Ah, no. Nothing on the IP trace, but if that computer pops up anywhere on the city's Wi-Fi, I'll see it right away. I think . . ." His voice trailed off, and he leaned in closer.

"What is it?" Clair asked.

"I see something, it might be nothing. It's probably just my brain looking for something that isn't really there," Klozowski replied.

Clair stood up and walked over to him. "Spit it out, Kloz. Before I'm forced to hit you again."

"I've been plotting out the locations where the children were abducted and bodies have been found on an area map. If I draw lines from one to the other, they more or less center around John H. Stroger, Jr. Hospital."

Nash leaned over to get a look at the map. "That's where Randal Davies worked."

"Insurance and pharmaceutical sales. I imagine our other victims are there a lot too," Clair said. "Darlene Biel is there right now."

Poole leaned in. "If I obtain a list of employees, can you cross-reference that against obituary data? Maybe we'll get lucky and find his next target before something else happens."

Kloz was already typing. "Oh yeah, I'm all over that."

Nash had stood up and was staring at the boards. "We're still missing something."

"What?" Poole asked.

"I'm not so sure Bishop is doing all of this on his own. Even if he somehow had help from Libby McInley, this is just too much for one person. There's still something bigger going on here."

"Maybe."

"You can't play God without being acquainted with the devil," Nash read aloud. "Is that what he's doing here with these kids? Killing them and bringing them back? Playing God?"

". . . with the devil," Clair said.

"All of the poems are about life and death. Maybe that's what he's trying to tell us." Poole brushed back his hair. "I've been getting sleep in patches. I'm having trouble focusing."

That was when Poole's phone rang.

He pulled the phone from his pocket and looked down at the small screen: UNKNOWN CALLER.

He pressed the Talk button.

A voice spoke before he could say anything.

"Frank, this is Sam."

88

Poole

Day 3 • 10:15 p.m.

Poole's heart thudded. He set the phone down on the conference table and pressed a button. "Sam, I'm in the war room with your team. I've got you on speaker."

"You're not allowed in the war room."

"I brought him in, Sam," Clair answered. "The case has gotten complicated. There's a link to Bishop. More than a link. He's all over it."

Poole leaned in close. "Where are you? Where is the diary?"

He heard Porter breathing on the other end, but the man did not reply.

Poole looked up at the others, then back to the phone. "Libby McInley is dead."

Porter said nothing.

"We found her bound to her bed. Ear, eyes, tongue, in white boxes, identical to Bishop's other victims. Her fingers and toes were removed too. She was tortured. Every inch of her body had been cut."

When Porter spoke, his voice was even, measured. "It wasn't Bishop. Bishop wouldn't kill Libby McInley any more than he killed her sister."

Poole looked up at Klozowski. "Your IT guy thinks it was Bishop's mother. I'd like to know what you think."

Again Porter went silent.

Poole heard Porter talking to someone, muffled, the phone covered, and then he returned to the call.

"Sam?"

"I'm going to text you an address. When you arrive at that address, follow the path at the back of the property. It's overgrown, but if you look close you'll find it, like a deer path. It will lead you to a lake. You'll need a team. You'll want to sweep the lake," Porter told him.

"Where are you, Sam?"

"When you get to the lake, look for the cat."

"You're not making sense, Sam. If you—"

The line went dead.

Poole cursed under his breath.

The phone vibrated and an address appeared:

> 12 Jenkins Crawl Road
> Simpsonville, SC

"He must have found it," Nash said, still staring at the phone.

"Found what?"

"Bishop's childhood home."

"I don't like this," Clair said. "Why is he being so secretive? That didn't sound like him. Who was he talking to?"

Klozowski had entered the address into a browser on his computer. He turned the screen around so everyone could see. "That's in the middle of nowhere."

"I'm not sure why I should trust him at all," Poole said. "He stole the diary. He's clearly holding something back. Libby's death didn't seem to surprise him. What else does he know?"

Nash leaned back in his chair. "I think if he knew something he thought would be useful to us, he would have shared it. He's got no reason to hide anything."

"Yet he disappeared with the diary and left his phone behind so we couldn't track him."

"Sam's working the case," Nash said. "You can trust him."

Poole clucked his tongue, then nodded. "I'll call the Charlotte office and get them out there right away. We have a jet at O'Hare. I can be there in a few hours."

Clair rose and went to the boards. "If you can get us that list of employees at Stroger Hospital, we can work that angle. Maybe we can box Bishop in from both sides."

Poole nodded and disappeared out the door, his walk quickening to a run.

Evidence Board

ANSON BISHOP

Floyd Reynolds — UniMed America Healthcare/Insurance Sales
  — Strangled/body hidden in snowman

Ella Reynolds — Found in Jackson Park Lagoon/recently bought
  car — drowned, salt water

Randal Davies — Oncologist. Worked at John H. Stroger, Jr.
  Hospital — overdosed with lisinopril

Lili Davies — Found posed inside stockroom of Leigh Gallery —
  drowned, salt water

Darlene Biel — Pharmaceutical sales rep — poisoned with
  cyanide

Larissa Biel — Missing from corner of West Chicago Avenue and
  North Damen as of 2/14 morning

Unknown Boy

LIBBY McINLEY
Killed by Bishop's mother?
Has photo of Bishop's mother and neighbor/Carter
Lock of blond hair — possibly Kirby? How would she get
  it?
IDs in the name of Kalyn Selke/obtained with Bishop's
  help
Corresponded with Bishop while in prison/means
  unknown
.45 in possession
Felt safe in prison, not on outside

POEMS
Because I could not stop for Death,
He kindly stopped for me;

The carriage held but just ourselves
And Immortality.

A telling analogy for life and death:
Compare the two of them to water and ice.
Water draws together to become ice,
And ice disperses again to become water.
Whatever has died is sure to be born again;
Whatever is born comes around again to dying.
As ice and water do one another no harm,
So life and death, the two of them, are fine.

Let us return Home, let us go back,
Useless is this reckoning of seeking and getting,
Delight permeates all of today.
From the blue ocean of death
Life is flowing like nectar.
In life there is death; in death there is life.
So where is fear, where is fear?
The birds in the sky are singing "No death, no death!"
Day and night the tide of Immortality
Is descending here on earth.

You can't play God without being acquainted with the devil.

UNDERLINED WORDS

ice

water

life

death

Home

fear

death

89

Porter

Day 3 • 10:16 p.m.

Sam removed the battery from the phone and threw both pieces out into the center of the lake. The water swallowed them whole, harsh ripples rolling out from the center until they faded away to nothing, another secret beneath the blanket of black.

"Why toss the phone? You told him where we are," Sarah said beside him.

Porter knelt back down a few feet from the water's edge, his fingers covered in dirt. He had been digging.

The path had led them about a quarter mile into the woods and ended at a small clearing just as the diary described. A small clearing, looking out over the lake.

Bishop said the water froze during the winter.

That had been a lie.

While temperatures in South Carolina could fall below freezing, the winters were much milder than farther north, nothing like those in Chicago. Even if they dropped below freezing, they never seemed to hold there long enough for the ground to freeze, most definitely not a large body of water like a lake. This was by no means a big lake, but it was big enough to escape the worst of the cold, of that he was certain. Bishop had probably only written that to help conceal the location. Porter could think of no other reason. Misdirection.

He knelt in the dirt. Sarah held both flashlights. The beams were focused on the base of the large oak tree looming over the clearing, a laurel oak. At the base of the tree was a small hole. Porter didn't have to dig very deep at all. Part of it had been sticking out of the ground. It caught Sarah's eye right away.

A white metal lunchbox, covered in rust.

Porter didn't expect to find the skeleton of a dead cat.

He didn't expect to find this either.

The lunchbox was open now. Inside was an envelope, the paper yellowed with age, bound to a composition book with black string. The envelope addressed simply—

Mother

"Sam, why'd you toss the phone?" Sarah asked again.

Porter took the bound package from the box and handed it to her. "I'm not worried about Poole knowing where we've been, I'm more concerned about him learning where we're going," he told her.

"What about Bishop? He gave you that phone for a reason."

"We need to shake him up, disrupt him. We're not his puppets. If he can't reach us with that phone, he'll need to find some other way. Maybe this will flush him out," Porter said.

He took Bishop's diary from his pocket and put it in the lunchbox before closing the lid and tossing a little dirt on top, nearly covering the Hello Kitty image stamped into the rusty metal.

Bishop's cat.

"Come on," he said. "Let's get out of here."

90

Poole

Day 3 • 10:23 p.m.

"Sir, I need to see this through," Poole said, tugging the steering wheel of his Jeep Cherokee hard left. He skirted four cars at a standstill in the right lane.

Why is there traffic? It's damn near eleven o'clock at night.

A 727 buzzed over him, the belly exposed as it approached O'Hare Airport.

"You should be on administrative leave. You lost your partner today. The last place you need to be is in the field," SAIC Hurless said through the Jeep's speakerphone.

"Clear the jet, sir. I'm nearly to the airport."

"You need to turn around, come back to the field office, and brief me so we can get someone else on this," Hurless said.

Poole took a deep breath, tried to calm himself. He jerked the wheel and barely missed a brown Mitsubishi Outlander trying to make a left turn. The driver hit his horn and held it down.

"According to Tech, he called you from a burner phone, and the nearest cell tower matches the location data he gave you, so he was standing somewhere close to that lake he mentioned. I pulled up satellite photos, but there's not much to see. The tree cover is so heavy, you can't make out what's happening on the ground. This is odd . . ."

"What?"

"The phone was a burner purchased and activated in New Orleans," Hurless said, his voice flat, sounded like he was reading.

"New Orleans? Could that be a mistake?"

Bishop was in Chicago as of a few hours ago. Porter was outside of Greenville, South Carolina, middle of nowhere.

"The signal died right after he hung up with you. Probably pulled the battery to avoid a trace. Run through it again. What did Porter tell you?"

Poole recounted the conversation again, word for word.

"I don't like this. Porter is too much of a wild card," Hurless said when he finished. "If he's working with Bishop, this may be a smokescreen."

"I think Libby McInley is somehow the key to everything, the key to catching Bishop. Porter knows more than he's telling us, but he hasn't steered us wrong. If he says we need to sweep a lake in South Carolina, I think we've got to believe him. The team is still processing the two houses from earlier, so we've got nothing else to go on right now. I need to do this. Please clear that jet."

Poole took the airport exit from Kennedy and followed the signs toward Fixed-Base Operator hangars, where they housed the charters and private flights. "Bishop somehow communicated with Libby McInley when she was in Stateville Correctional. We need to know how he was able to talk to her and help her obtain the fake identification. We figure that out, we're one step closer. I follow Porter's bread crumbs and we take another step. Hold on a second, sir—"

Poole pulled up to the security gate and passed his identification to the guard. Something clicked when he saw the man in uniform. "I'd check the security guards at the prison, sir, all the correctional officers. That's got to be it. Mail, phones, and electronics are all under constant surveillance. That only leaves the human element."

The security guard handed him a clipboard, pointed to a line, and Poole signed. The man then pointed to a lot on the right, mouthing the words, "Anywhere over there."

Poole nodded and pulled the Jeep into a space next to the small federal building shared by Homeland, FBI, and ATF.

He shifted into Park.

"I'm here, sir. What do you want to do?"

SAIC Hurless sighed. "I ordered them to fuel the plane ten minutes ago. You should be wheels up in twenty. I'll reach out to the local field office while you're in the air. That's Bob Granger in Charlotte. We go way back. I know him from the academy. He can scramble the local sheriff's office and find Porter's lake. Put a team in the water. Touch base with me when you're back on the ground."

"Thank you, sir."

"You better be right on this."

91

Porter
Day 3 • 10:26 p.m.

Porter and Sarah had made their way back to the rental car in relative silence. Porter drove, and Sarah was on the phone booking flight reservations.

She cupped her hand over the microphone. "The next flight doesn't leave until four in the morning. That gives us a little over five hours. Should I book it?"

"What?"

She repeated the question.

"Yeah, sorry. My mind is racing right now."

He stared out the windshield at the road, at the white stripes flying past and disappearing behind them. There were very few cars out at this time of the night. For this he was grateful. It felt like he and Sarah had the road to themselves, the lights of Greenville approaching in the distance. "Maybe we should find a hotel room near the airport, someplace we can get cleaned up and change."

Sarah finalized the reservation and disconnected the call. "May I remind you, you still haven't bought me dinner? As first dates go, this one has been unique, I'll give you that, but I'm not sure I'm ready to rush into a one-hour stop-and-bop motel with you, Mr. Porter."

The bound package they'd found in the lunchbox at the lake sat in the center console, the word *Mother* barely visible in the dim light of the envelope, Bishop's voice, his words, shouting out from the composition book.

Dinner.

They hadn't eaten since New Orleans.

His stomach gurgled.

Thirty minutes later Porter sat on one of the double beds inside a small room at the Greenville Airport Motel 8. Taco Bell wrappers littered the table near the door. Sarah was in the shower.

The package felt heavy, heavier than it probably should, not necessarily with the weight of paper but with something else. He couldn't put his finger on it. Someone's life trapped inside.

Or the rantings of a madman.

He felt that way about the diary when he first read it, but two hours ago he had been standing in the very place where the events inside it had played out.

The Carters.

His mother.

His father.

The two men Porter later learned were Kirby and Briggs.

All of them.

All of it, true.

The envelope and composition book were bound together with a piece of black string. He couldn't help but wonder if it came from the same roll he'd used when he tied all those boxes.

Porter removed the string, opened the envelope addressed to Mother, and unfolded the pages. The paper crinkled under his touch.

How long had they been there?

How long had this letter waited for a mother who never appeared?

Porter recognized the handwriting immediately, a younger version of the writing in the diary.

Momma. I know you have always wanted me to call you Mother, but I really just want to call you Momma. Is that so wrong?

Momma

Momma

Momma

Momma.

Sorry, Mother.

I am so sorry. I am sorry for whatever I did that would make you want to leave me behind. I am so sorry for all that I did that would make you want to run away without me.

Did you leave because you didn't have a choice?

Did you leave because those men came to the house and you had to get away?

That's it, isn't it?

You wouldn't leave me otherwise. Not like this.

I was too slow getting back from the lake. If I had gotten back faster, you would have told me to hop in the car with a skippity jump, loaded up my bags, and all of us would have gotten away together. We would have started a new life together and left this one in the rearview mirror, blurred by the dust behind that green Plymouth.

I didn't want to write this letter, but the doctor told me I had to. He also told me he wouldn't read it, but I know that he will. Father taught me to recognize a lie, and Dr. Joseph Oglesby is not a very good liar. He thinks he is, but he is not, no ma'am, not in the slightest. His dead little eyes shrink whenever he tells a fib, thirty-two of them in our last session alone.

Hello, Dr.

You should cut your hair. The comb-over is not fooling anyone. You look silly.

I'm sorry.

I shouldn't say such things.

Father taught me better than that.

He once told me it is better to shower someone with compliments, let them swim in them until they're drowning. They'll reach for you and hold on tight, your friend forever.

Not Mother, though, not my mother, not you. If you realized I was giving away too many compliments, you'd probably tell me to take them back.

The two of you are different.

Were different.

Father.

Oh, my father.

I can't write about that now. I know Dr. Oglesby wants me to but I can't, it hurts too much. It hurts almost as much as when I dug up the spot at the lake under my cat, when I found my knife.

I knew what that knife meant.

You left me, Mother.

As much as I'd like to believe you didn't leave me intentionally, as much as I'd like to believe you had no choice but to run off without me, I know that is not true.

I knew the moment I saw that knife.

Why do you hate me, Mother?

Why ~~do~~ did you hate Father so?

After the house, after the fire—Do you know about the fire?—After the fire I was brought to the Camden Treatment Center just outside of Charleston.

The people here are very nice, even Dr. Oglesby with all his lies. They gave me my own room. There is a window, but it doesn't open. No summer breezes for me, only the steady hum of the air conditioner.

Dr. Oglesby asked me to keep a diary.

He gave me a black and white composition book and told me it would make the perfect diary.

I told him only girls wrote in diaries, and he told me a journal then, I should keep a journal, that's what boys do.

I told him I would think about it.

I'm a smart boy. I know he only wants me to write things down so he can read them, so he can better understand me.

Would that be so wrong?

To be understood?

Don't worry, Mother. I won't tell him your secrets.

Your secrets are safe with me.

Most of them.

Your ~~loving~~ son,

AB

P.S. Tell Mrs. Carter I said hello, the man with the long blond hair too. I'm sure one day I will see all of you again. I'll keep my knife close until that day, I'll keep it sharp. Thank you for returning it to me.

"Anything good?"

Porter looked up.

Sarah stood at the bathroom door wearing a white towel, another wrapped around her long hair in that way only women seemed to know how to do, steam escaping from behind her.

Porter caught himself staring at her tanned legs and forced himself to find her face.

"Maybe I should get dressed."

"No. Yes. I mean, go ahead. I'm going to get in the shower." Porter swallowed, his face burned.

This isn't high school. Pull it together.

Looking away, Porter dropped the letter on top of the composition book and crossed the room, entered the bathroom, and closed the door at his back.

She smelled like lilacs.

92

Porter

Day 4 • 3:42 a.m.

Sarah took the window seat.

She looked exhausted.

Porter fell into the seat beside her, realized he was sitting on the seat belt, then stood back up long enough to find both ends. He sat down again, buckled the belt, and pulled the excess so it was snug.

Sarah was watching him with a grin. "Do you honestly think that flimsy little belt is going to do a lick of good if this plane decides to take a header into solid ground somewhere over Alabama?"

"I don't want the attendant to yell at me. Sometimes, if you're nice to them and follow all the rules, they'll give you the full can of soda instead of just a cup."

She opened her mouth, about to say something, then changed her mind and leaned back in her seat, closing her eyes. "Wake me when we get there, Detective Sam Porter."

"Thank you."

"For what?"

"For coming with me. I thought I wanted to do this alone, but it's better with you here," he told her.

"Very few things are better in life when you're alone."

"I'm beginning to realize that."

"I'm glad I could be of service," she said groggily. "Maybe pie."

"What?"

"Pie might be better alone. More pie for me."

"I didn't realize there was pie."

"Not on the plane, maybe after we land. There should always be pie."

"Sleep tight, Ms. Werner."

Somehow she did just that, falling asleep even before the cabin doors closed.

The flight was only about two-thirds full. The seat beside him was empty.

Sam waited until they were in the air, then turned on the small overhead light and opened the composition book to the first page, Bishop's words melting away all else.

93

Diary

"Are you comfortable, Anson?"

He smiled at me, but it wasn't a real smile. This was the kind of smile one wears at a dinner party or a fundraiser or an award banquet, the kind that disappears the moment the smilee disappears behind a closed door away from prying eyes. I have never been to a dinner party or a fundraiser or an award banquet, but I've read about them. Mother once brought home a People *magazine, and the pages were filled with these smiles, polite but empty.*

"Would you like something to drink?"

"No, sir."

"So polite," Dr. Oglesby said, glancing down at his notes. "You've been here a week, and I feel we barely know each other."

He wasn't a very large man, maybe an inch or two taller than I. Although everyone called him "Dr.," I had yet to see him wearing a white lab coat. Today he wore a gray and black argyle sweater and khaki pants. He was slightly overweight. The pudge around his belly bloomed out over the top of his pants as he crossed his legs. Not much. He probably exercised a few days each week, just a little bit—the weight wanted to come out, his body wanted to be fat, but he kept his potential for obesity in check. For now, anyway. I couldn't help but wonder how he would look in another ten years. Would he change his mind about the lab coat? If I were a doctor, I would definitely wear a white lab coat.

His office was a large box.

The walls were painted an off-white and decorated with degrees and photographs of Dr. Oglesby fake-smiling beside other people fake-smiling. Unlike the other desks at Camden Treatment Center, his was made of wood, most likely something he brought in himself. Most here were made of the same gray metal.

We sat in the chairs in front of the desk, facing each other. Apparently during one of the degree programs posted on the wall, the good doctor was told it was better to face one's patient on equal ground, so rather than sit in the plush leather chair behind the desk, he came out here with the common folk.

A large Oriental rug covered most of the tile floor, clearly a fake. I had never seen a real Oriental rug before, or a fake Oriental rug for that matter, but there was something about this one that screamed imitation. Maybe it was the mystery stain in the far corner, the one nearly hidden by a potted fern.

"One week," he muttered, tapping at the clipboard in his lap. "Were you taking any medications, Anson? Prior to your stay here? Anything at all?"

He had asked me this question before, four times now. I gave him the same answer I did the other times.

"No."

"Because you seem jittery, like someone going through the final stages of withdrawal. A few of the nurses have made note of this in your file. You've also been experiencing night sweats and tremors. These things are all signs of withdrawal."

I said nothing.

"Was it chlorpromazine or maybe fluphenazine? Possibly haloperidol or loxapine?"

I remained silent.

"Haloperidol? You see, when I said that one, I noticed a slight tic beneath your left eye. That tells me you know that particular drug. What reason would a boy your age have for knowing a drug like that *unless the medication was prescribed and you saw the name on the bottle every day?"*

My face flushed. I drew in a deep, even breath.

"Haloperidol is not the type of medication you want to quit cold turkey. If a physician deems it appropriate to adjust or remove this medication from a patient's treatment, that patient would be weaned off over a length of time. In some cases, another, less impactful medication might be added temporarily to a treatment regimen to lessen the more harmful effects of reduction."

Dr. Joseph Oglesby wore glasses. The lenses weren't especially thick, and I couldn't help but wonder if he actually needed them. He seemed like the kind of man who would wear glasses simply to bolster his role as a doctor, to help play the part. He wore his glasses on a silver chain around his neck and put them on and took them off with a regular frequency, punctuation at the end of a sentence rather than a visual aid. Wearing them around his neck on a chain reminded me of a librarian. He was no librarian, though. I could see the dust on the books lining his shelves from where I sat.

"A sudden stoppage of haloperidol can lead to insomnia, restlessness, anxiety, agitation, depression, vertigo, seizures, even hallucinations. See how your foot is tapping on the floor? That fast patter? That is a definite indicator. Is there a reason you don't want to take your medication, Anson? Is that why you're lying to me?"

I stopped my foot. I didn't realize I had been tapping my foot.

I would not tap my foot.

The doctor raised the tip of his pen to his lip, his eyes on me, then wrote something down in the file. "Because it has been a week, you are through the worst. I see no reason to pick it back up at this point. Should you feel the need to take it, you'll tell me? We can revisit the use of medication together?"

I didn't want to nod, but I did anyway.

The smile again, thin, only at the edge of his lips.

94

Diary

"Are you ready to talk about the fire, Anson?"

He saw my leg tap before I was able to stop it. I placed a hand on my knee.

"Do you know how many bodies were found inside the house?"

I would not let my leg tap.

"Three. I've been in close contact with the local authorities since the start of your visit with us, and they have yet to make a proper identification on even one of them. Because the bodies were burned so badly, they're working with dental records. Without something to compare them to, they're having a tough time. They're waiting for one of two things to happen: either someone will be reported missing and a comparison of dental records will reveal a match, or you provide us with information that leads to identification. The authorities believe you know who those people are. They desperately want to speak to you about it, but since you're a minor and currently under my care, they're not permitted to do so. That could change, of course—all I have to do is sign a couple of forms and they'll be able to sweep right in here and take you away to someplace where they'll try and make you talk. I can't imagine such a place would be pleasant, and I would absolutely hate to see something like that happen to a fine young man such as yourself, but I *can only hold the wolves at bay for so long. Do you know what a district attorney is, Anson?"*

I knew what a district attorney was. They appeared fairly often in my comic books, but I would not tell him so. I had no intention of telling him anything.

"Was one of the men your father, Anson?"

My leg did not tap. His eyes were on me, a hawk on a mouse.

"Of the three bodies found inside your house, all were male. According to the police, your father hasn't reported to work since the fire. That leads them to believe he was killed in the fire. They're concerned about your mother too. She seems to have disappeared as well. They're quite concerned, actually. I think some of them may suspect she started the fire. The house was covered in an accelerant, most likely gasoline. From what I've been told, the place was saturated. Somebody had been thorough in their efforts. Did your parents get along? Did your mother have any reason to hurt your father? Was he hurting her? Did he beat her?"

"Father would never lay a hand on Mother."

I didn't want to talk. I knew I shouldn't talk, but I would not allow someone to say something wicked of Father. Not this man, not anybody.

"But your father was in the house when it happened, wasn't he?"

"I don't know. I was at the lake."

The doctor slipped his glasses on, pushing them up the bridge of his nose. "You told the firemen and later the policemen you had been fishing at the lake for hours and came home when you saw the smoke, yet you carried no tackle box or fishing pole and they found nothing at the lake to indicate you had either. They think you lied."

"I don't lie."

"You lied to me about your medication. You lied about taking haloperidol, a very serious drug."

"That wasn't a lie, that was a fib."

"What is the difference between a lie and a fib, Anson?"

My leg tapped, but only once.

"Do you know where your mother went, Anson? After she started the fire that killed your father?"

Mother hadn't killed Father, and Mother didn't start the fire. I wanted to tell him that. I wanted to shout it out. I wanted to jump from this chair, take the pen from his hand, and embed it deep in his neck and watch the blood spurt out all over his argyle sweater and fake-smile pictures on the wall. I didn't, though. I said nothing.

"A mother's instincts to protect her young are some of the fiercest known to man. Did your father hurt you? Did he touch you in a bad way? Is that why she wanted him dead?"

"Father would never hurt me either."

"You were examined at the hospital prior to coming here, and they found no evidence of abuse, so I suppose that is true. Unfortunately, I don't know how thorough they were in their examination. I have faith. My staff would have covered all bases, but you were taken to a county hospital and I can't vouch for the skill and ability of the people working at a place like that. Some of those places can be downright barbaric, like stepping into a third-world tent city."

"I was skipping rocks."

"What?"

"I never told the firemen or the police I was fishing. I was skipping rocks at the lake. I like to skip rocks."

"That is not what it says in the police report, Anson. Lying or fibbing are both bad, not things you want to do with me."

"The report is wrong."

He removed his glasses, and I watched them fall and dangle around his neck.

The window in his office didn't have bars on it. Rain began to fall.

"Where did you go to school, Anson?"

"Mother homeschooled me."

"Really? That is interesting."

"Why?"

"Remember the tests we gave you on your second day? You scored extremely high on all of them."

"I enjoy tests. They're fun."

"Your mother must be a very intelligent woman. What does she do for a living?"

"I told you, she works in publishing."

He scribbled at his notes but did not glance down. "You did tell me that, but there is no record of her being employed, not recently, not at all. Your parents filed joint tax returns, and no employment has ever appeared for her. The IRS performed a detailed search at the request of the district attorney I mentioned earlier. That man is a bit of a bulldog, and he's itching for the opportunity to talk to your mother."

"I don't know where she is."

"Does it bother you that she left you? Those protective instincts I mentioned, I imagine it would be terribly difficult for a mother to abandon her only child and completely cut contact, just write him off as if he didn't exist at all, throw him away like last night's trash. I'm not sure what would drive a woman to do that. What did you do to make her hate you so?"

This time when my leg began to tap, I did not stop it. Instead, I watched the rain outside.

95

Poole

Day 4 • 4:38 a.m.

Poole had touched down at Greenville-Spartanburg International Airport at a little past one in the morning. A black Subaru Forester with federal plates was waiting for him at the tarmac, driven by SAIC Robert Granger. The man's eyes were red and heavy.

He offered his hand and shouted over the engine noise winding down from the jet. "You must be Frank. Welcome to South Carolina."

Poole put him in his mid-fifties only because SAIC Hurless was fifty-four and he mentioned they knew each other from the academy. Granger looked far older than fifty-four. If Poole had met the man on the street, he would have easily tacked on ten years. Heavyset and bald, he wore thick glasses and a bushy goatee. Poole found this odd because the FBI dress code did not permit facial hair beyond a mustache. The rules in the South must be lax.

Granger gestured toward the passenger door, and both men climbed in the car. They were moving away from the jet before Poole had his seat belt on. Granger waved at the security station before coasting through and heading for the highway. "So, 4MK, huh? Down here?"

"We think he's still in Chicago, but apparently this lake is connected to him somehow," Poole told him.

"It took some doing, but I finally got Sheriff Banister on the phone a little after midnight. That's Sheriff Hana Banister. You'll like her, she's a bit of a firecracker. Been sheriff around Simpsonville for the better part of twenty years, keeps running unopposed, which is fine with the locals. Not many people out there, and they're not too big on change. She said she's got two experienced divers in town. I had three in Charlotte, so we rounded them all up and got them out to your lake straightaway. She's familiar with the property, said it's been deserted since a fire wiped out the main house. There's a trailer out there the owners used to rent out. Teenagers use it nowadays for things teenagers do. From what she told me, not much to look at."

"Can the divers work in the dark?"

Granger leaned up over the steering wheel and maneuvered around a slow-moving semi. "Didn't seem to faze my guys at all. They jump at just about any chance to get in the water."

"How far is this place?"

Granger glanced at the GPS on his phone. "We're about thirty minutes out. Looks like this place is buried good and deep."

Two hours later Poole stood at the edge of the lake, watching the divers as Granger and Sheriff Banister (who was very much the firecracker) barked orders at their teams.

A generator hummed in the distance, with snakes of cords running off in various directions. Large floodlights had been erected at the water's edge, the bright beams illuminating the black pool.

One of the divers broke the surface and raised her hand. "I've got another one! Twenty feet down, directly below me. I've got a cord on it, affixing a balloon now." She pulled a small canister from her belt and flicked a switch. The canister popped and released a self-inflating bright orange balloon. She attached the cord she held in her other hand to the base and set it bobbing in the water.

"Holy Christ, how many is that now?" Banister said from somewhere behind Poole.

Poole glanced to his right, at the black body bags lining the shore. "Four. That makes four."

"Complete body or partial?" Granger shouted out to the diver.

"Complete." The diver replaced her regulator and disappeared back below the surface, the beam of her high-powered flashlight quickly fading away.

They found small garbage bags containing remains as well, six of those so far. Only one had been opened, containing a human leg bone. Each of the others was carefully placed inside clear plastic bags while still below the surface, then brought up and stored in plastic bins in an effort to not contaminate the contents and preserve the findings. They would be opened at the medical examiner's office at the federal building back in Charlotte. Sheriff Banister made no squabble about relinquishing jurisdiction to Poole and Granger. This was clearly beyond her department's available resources.

Poole pressed his hands together. This wasn't Chicago cold by any means, but the air off the lake had a bite to it. Sheriff Banister stood behind him, the beam of her flashlight pointing down toward the base of one of the large trees. "Agent Poole? I think I've got your cat."

When you get to the lake, look for the cat.

He walked over to her and followed the beam of her flashlight.

A rusted metal lunchbox was buried at the base of a laurel tree. He'd walked the entire perimeter of the lake when he first got here, studying the ground for any sign of a cat. He expected to find whatever Porter was talking about near the shore, then the first body was found and he forgot all about the cat. This was about ten feet back, hidden in the trees.

Poole bent down and brushed the dirt from the surface.

Hello Kitty.

"Cute." He looked up at the sheriff. "Do you have any gloves?"

"Yeah, here." She pulled a pair of latex gloves from her jacket pocket and handed them down. Some of her graying blond hair fell loose from her ponytail. She pulled out the rubber band holding it all in place, twisted the hair together into one tight lock, then replaced the band. She did all this with one hand—the other, still holding the flashlight on the lunchbox, didn't falter.

Poole couldn't help but wonder if she handled a gun with the same dexterity, if she ever had cause to use her weapon out here.

"I've got one!" came another shout from the lake.

Five now.

Granger came over, the beam of his flashlight joining Banister's. "That it? What you were trying to find?"

Poole released the rusted metal latch on the front of the lunchbox and opened the lid. The diary stared back at him from inside. "I'll need to see the property records, plat records, whatever you have for this place, the houses we passed on the way in too."

Banister leaned down, her breath white in the chilled air. "They're stored down at town hall. I'll make a call, wake some folks up."

96

Diary

The overhead fluorescents buzzed with the sound of a million bees hidden somewhere in the ceiling, the harsh light dripping down like their wasted honey. I tried to ignore the sound, found that I could not, and laid my head back down on the thin pillow they provided me.

My room was only about six feet wide and eight or so deep. They called it my room, and I accepted this definition even though my subconscious whispered that the room was more of a cell. Rooms were not locked whenever you were directed inside. Rooms had windows that opened. My room had neither of those things.

My first night here, I woke in the middle of the night and crawled from my bed to use the bathroom. The moment my feet touched the cold floor, I suppose I knew something was different, but it wasn't until I reached the place where my bedroom door should have been that I fully awoke and realized I was not at home at all but some strange place.

Not my room.

Not my bed.

Someplace else entirely.

The urge to relieve myself left. I crawled back into the narrow bed. I didn't get up again until the bright lights above turned on at precisely 6:00 a.m., the bees awakening to their preprogrammed day.

They would remain on until exactly ten o'clock. There was no clock in the room, nor could I see one from the small window in the door, but my internal clock was precise. From the earliest age, Father taught me to mark time within my mind. He taught me to recognize the steady tick of a clock somewhere in a little nook of my subconscious, a clock far more accurate than any hanging on a wall once you learned to trust it.

There were no clocks in our house.

I was not permitted to wear a watch.

There was only my internal clock, tested regularly by Father.

He would ask me for the time, sometimes at the most peculiar of moments. If I was off by more than a minute, there would be repercussions. I won't speak of the repercussions, but needless to say, I was rarely wrong.

Father also taught me to suppress time. He compared the skill to meditation but said it was much more. I never had much of a need for this particular skill, but he told me I someday might and I eagerly welcomed anything he was willing to teach me. Suppressing time allowed me to simply close my eyes and shut down. I could do this for five minutes or five hours, the interval determined at the start. Unlike sleep, I could keep my brain active, focused on a particular problem, or I could close that down too and allow instances that would normally be passed swimming in boredom to go by in a flash.

When they locked me in my room like this, I suppressed time.

I understood what they were trying to do. I was only permitted outside my room to use the bathroom and to visit with Dr. Oglesby. The remainder of the time was spent in this room. They wanted me to grow bored. They wanted me to loathe this room. They wanted me to welcome the time away, long for my next session with the doctor. While I'm sure this worked with previous occupants of my room, such tricks would not work with me, not as long as I could suppress time. Not as long as I used this as an opportunity to review my current situation, to find a solution, to puzzle it out.

The fluorescent lights turned on at 6:00 a.m. and off again at 10:00 p.m., and then the cycle would repeat. Eight of those repeats now. The time was currently 4:32 in the afternoon of my eighth day *in this place. There was no escape from my room. The window was sealed tight. Even if I could get it open, I would not fit between the bars on the outside. I could pick the lock at my door if I had something with which to pick the lock, but I did not. My room was the fifth on this side of the hallway; the bathroom was across the hall and to the right. Although I hadn't seen the residents of those other rooms, I heard them, particularly at night. I had identified three male voices and two female. The female voice two rooms down on my side of the hallway sounded to be about fifteen years old.*

She cried at night. She cried every night.

I did not know her name. They didn't use names here; only Dr. Oglesby used names.

The hallway was about fifty feet long in total. When they took me from my room to Dr. Oglesby's office, we went to the left, passing nothing but closed doors. When I returned from Dr. Oglesby's office, I made careful notes of the other end of the hallway—a nurses' station on the left, a guard at the right, and a sealed door between them. I had yet to see this door opened, but I heard it each time, an electronic buzz followed by the release of the lock. I imagined this was controlled from somewhere near the guard's position, but it was possible the nurses had access as well. My mind's eye pictured a small button, grimy from years of random fingers.

There were cameras at either end of the hallway, dark, black eyes staring down from small bubbles in the ceiling. I had not found a camera in Dr. Oglesby's office, but I was fairly sure he had one. The one in my room was hidden in the air vent next to the fluorescent light, watching from above. It did not make a sound, but I felt it blink.

I'm curious, Doctor, are you sitting at your desk watching me right now on some monitor? Insights abound, are you adding to your little notepad? I picture you writing furiously, each word more meaningless than the last. Poor little Anson Bishop, orphan born of fire.

The girl down the hall was crying again. Odd, considering the time.

97

Porter

Day 4 • 7:13 a.m.

Sarah's phone dinged.

At first Porter wasn't sure what the sound was or where it came from, but then he spotted Sarah's phone lying on her lap.

She stirred gently, nestled against his shoulder, and went back to sleep.

The phone dinged again.

The overhead lights came to life, and a voice blared out from the intercom. "Attention, passengers, please place your seat backs and tray tables in the upright position as we begin descent into New Orleans. The local time is seven thirteen a.m., and the temperature is fifty-nine degrees. We truly enjoyed flying with you and hope you enjoy your stay in the Big Easy."

Sarah's eyes fluttered open. She squinted against the harsh light. "Good morning, sunshine," she muttered, smacking her lips.

Her phone dinged again.

"I thought those had to be in airplane mode or this whole bundle of metal would come crashing down."

"Lucky you got that seat belt to protect you." She picked up the phone and glanced down at the display. "When you get close to the ground, they start picking up the towers again." She frowned. "I'm getting text messages. They're not for me, though. They're for you."

"What?"

"Look." She handed him the phone.

> *You shouldn't have destroyed the phone, Sam.*
> *That wasn't nice.*
> *Not at all.*

"How did Bishop get your number?"

Sarah shrugged, "Oh, I don't know. Maybe the sign outside my office, a phone book, the Internet, one of my cards. Maybe his mother gave it to him. I'm a lawyer, Sam. My number is everywhere."

Porter typed: Bishop?

Nothing for a moment, then: Did you enjoy your trip down Memory Lane?

Porter typed: I found your cat.

Bishop responded: Don't you mean, "we" found your cat?

Porter looked over at Sarah. Her eyes were locked on the phone.

BISHOP: It's okay, Sam. I know you're not alone. I'm happy for you. Sarah seems like a lovely woman. Heather would like her. I'm sure they would be fast friends.

PORTER: I have Libby's locket.

No response.

PORTER: It's her locket, right? Under the floorboards in the Carters' trailer? Who was she to you? You know she's dead, right?

No response.

PORTER: Bishop?

BISHOP: I miss my mother, Sam. I desperately need to speak to her about Libby.

PORTER: Turn yourself in. I'll arrange for adjoining cells.

BISHOP: No need. You're going to bring her to me.

"The fuck I am," Porter said.

PORTER: She's not going anywhere.

BISHOP: I'm sending you a picture now, Sam. You're not going to like it. We'll need to talk about it after you look.

The phone dinged, a tiny image loaded on the small screen—two girls, unconscious on a concrete floor.

BISHOP: Are you there, Sam?

Sarah pinched the image, expanding it, bringing in more detail.

One of the girls was wrapped in a green quilt, her face a deathly pale, blood on her lips. The other girl looked like she had been plucked from a river, her clothing and hair wet and matted down.

Porter didn't recognize either of them.

PORTER: Who are they?

BISHOP: Guests of a friend. They're not doing well, though. I'm afraid if I leave them in his care much longer, they may end up suffering the same fate as Ella Reynolds and Lili Davies. You wouldn't want that? More blood on your hands? We're going to trade, you and I. My mother for the girls. A simple tit for tat like old times. You still owe me . . . for the last one.

PORTER: I won't do it.

BISHOP: There are always more girls, Sam.

BISHOP: Alert your friends in blue and they're both dead. I still have plenty of boxes . . .

BISHOP: Leave all your cash in the prison locker at check-in.

PORTER: No.

BISHOP: There's one more thing, Sam. You're not going to like this, not in the slightest, but on the off chance you are willing to let the girls die, I got my hands on something truly spectacular, something that goes boom. I don't want it to go boom, but I'll let it, if you don't bring me Mother. Nobody has enough boxes for that.

BISHOP: BOTH you and Ms. Werner must go. They won't release her to you alone. After all, an inmate is entitled to proper representation. Wouldn't you agree?

BISHOP: You have until 8 p.m. Any later and

"Any later and what?" Porter said.

"No signal. We must have lost the tower."

They both jerked in their seats as the wheels came down on the runway, the plane quickly decelerating, the airport outbuildings rushing past their small window.

Sarah's eyes were fixed on the phone. "Try now, signal is back."

PORTER: Bishop?

MESSAGE NOT DELIVERED!

Porter pressed the small red link that read TRY AGAIN.

MESSAGE NOT DELIVERED!

Again.

MESSAGE NOT DELIVERED!

"What the hell does that mean?" Porter frowned.

"Maybe he pulled the battery," Sarah replied. "Or chucked the phone in a lake." She turned back to Porter. "So much for disrupting him. We didn't slow him down."

Porter scrolled through the texts. When he got back to the picture of the girls, his stomach sank.

98

Porter

Day 4 • 7:57 a.m.

"We've got another hour until visiting opens up," Porter said from the passenger seat of Sarah Werner's BMW.

They'd driven straight from the airport to the prison.

He didn't have a choice.

He knew that.

"She'll be restrained," Sarah offered. "She can't get away. Just keep her close, and when you know the girls are safe, take her back into custody. Technically, she's not leaving custody. Maybe handcuff yourself to her. Isn't that what you cops do? Hell, I don't know."

Sarah had received an e-mail from the prison ten minutes after Bishop broke contact, an automated response that said documentation regarding inmate #2138 had been received and processed, along with about twenty pages of canned information regarding prisoner custodian release and responsibilities.

Porter tried calling the number Bishop used to text and received a recording. "The number you have dialed is no longer in service or has been disconnected. Please check . . ." He had heard the message before. He hung up.

"How much cash do you have left?" Sarah asked.

Porter let out a sigh and patted the inside pocket of his jacket. "Twenty-three hundred and twelve dollars."

She parked in the middle of the lot, the nose of the car pointing at the visitor entrance. "They open at nine to the general public, but lawyers are allowed in any time after eight."

"I should do this alone," Porter said. "I'm already in trouble. There's no reason for you to get wrapped up in all this."

"Oh, I think I'm twisted up good and tight in all of it at this point."

"This is a prison break. You'll be on camera. At the very least, you'll be disbarred."

"You give the worst pep talks."

"You don't need to throw your life away over this."

Sarah sighed. "Bishop was clear. He said we both need to go in, so we're both going in. I just need to stop sweating first."

"You're sweating? It's cold."

"It's probably related to the shaking. I'd like for that to stop too."

She was shaking. Porter watched her hand bouncing nervously on the steering wheel. "I'm going in alone. Fuck Bishop, he's—"

Sarah turned off the ignition and was out the door before he could finish his thought. "Let's go, Detective."

"Shit," Porter muttered. He took out Bishop's knife and Libby's locket, tossed them both into the glove box, then fumbled with his seat belt and chased after her.

At this early hour the visitor center was deserted. As before, the guard asked for Porter's driver's license, then Porter was asked to remove his belt and shoelaces. He placed these inside one of the lockers along with his wallet and jacket, the cash still in the jacket pocket. The guard closed the small door and handed him the key. He was then patted down and swept with a handheld metal detector. When the guard cleared him, he stepped into the adjoining hallway. Sarah joined him a moment later.

"Now what?" Porter asked.

As if in response, the metal door beside them buzzed and opened. Another guard stepped through, the door closing behind him. Weidner. He was on a cell phone. He held up a finger and nodded at them. When he finished the call, he ushered them into a small anteroom. "Wait here, please."

Every time the door in the hallway buzzed, Porter's heart throbbed in his chest.

The door buzzed five times before Weidner returned with two other guards behind him. Between them, Jane Doe shuffled along, her arms and legs in restraints.

Weidner produced a clipboard and handed it to Porter. "Sign here, here, and here, please."

Porter felt Doe's eyes on him, burning into the side of his head as he scribbled his name.

"This is a day pass. Get her back here no later than five tonight. The restraints must stay on at all times. She is wearing a monitoring device on her ankle and cannot leave Orleans Parish. If she does, you will be in violation of the court order."

Court order? How had Bishop—

Weidner went on. "Normally a prison guard would be required to join you, but because you are law enforcement and she's being released into your custody as part of an ongoing investigation, that is solely your call. Would you like one or more guards to accompany you?"

Porter shook his head.

Weidner handed him a business card. A small key was taped to the back. "If for some reason you are unable to return her by five tonight, Detective, call that number and inform the duty chief."

Porter slid the business card into his pocket.

Weidner took the clipboard, flipped to the second page, and handed it to Sarah. "As her attorney, I'll need you to sign here, authorizing the release into Detective Porter's custody."

Sarah signed and returned the paperwork to him.

He studied both pages, then nodded at the guards behind him, then up at the camera in the corner of the hallway. The door buzzed again, and the two men led Jane Doe back inside, the steel door closing at their backs.

Weidner turned back to Sarah and Porter. "Pick up your possessions, then pull your car around to gate 12 at the side of the visitors center."

He left then, disappearing behind the locked door.

Porter and Sarah stared at each other for a moment. The entire exchange had taken less than five minutes.

Back at the lockers, they retrieved their possessions. Porter noted his jacket was considerably lighter without the cash in the pocket.

When they pulled up to gate 12, Jane Doe stood inside the chainlink fence, flanked by the two guards. There was a loud buzz, and the chainlink opened like the metal doors inside the prison. The guards led her to Sarah's waiting BMW and helped her into the backseat, closing the door behind her.

Jane Doe smiled from the backseat. "We need to go to your office, Ms. Werner. Chop, chop."

99

Gabby

Day 4 • 8:03 a.m.

Gabby Deegan was lying in bed trolling Instagram.

Someone had made the hashtag #LiliDaviesMemorial, and it quickly filled up with random pictures of Lili from people at school—people she didn't know, people who didn't know Lili. It made Gabby sick.

What gave them the right to weigh in now?

The hashtag contained numerous posts from Ally Winters and Magen Plants. Neither of them gave two shits when Lili was alive, and now all of a sudden they act like they were besties? The last time Ally saw Lili, she told her her hair looked ratty and she needed to go to a real stylist, no more Bargain Cuts at the mall. Last year Magen took Lili's underwear from her locker during gym class and hid it in the school library. Gabby and Lili spent nearly an hour looking for them and got busted for missing fourth period. Bitch-cunts, the lot of them. That wasn't the worst part, though—random strangers posted images, and some of them were horrible. There were pictures of the Leigh Gallery. Some people even posed for selfies with the sign outside the gallery. @EddieKnowsStuff in West Virginia posted a picture of Buffalo Bill from that old movie *The Silence of the Lambs*, with the caption "She DID NOT put the lotion in the basket!" Not someone who knew her, just some a-hole who should have his social media privileges revoked.

The faculty at Wilcox Academy had organized a candlelight vigil for tonight. Gabby wasn't sure she would go. What was the point? A bunch of people standing around holding candles wasn't going to bring her back, and they all knew she was Lili's best friend. Everyone would be staring at her.

She closed Instagram and opened iMessage. She scrolled through all the car pictures they had shared over the past few months. Lili would never own a car, she would never drive, she would never be married, she would never have babies, she would never . . .

The tears came again, and Gabby tried to fight them back. She hadn't washed off all her makeup before bed, and she could only imagine what her eyeliner looked like.

"You okay in there, baby?" her mom said from the other side of the door.

"Yeah."

The handle jiggled. "Why is this locked?"

Gabby didn't reply. She wiped at her eyes.

"Maybe you should eat breakfast. You'll feel better if you eat something."

Right. Cap'n Crunch fixes everything.

"Maybe later, Mom."

Gabby rolled over, the sheets tangling around her legs. She opened the photo app on her phone and scrolled through Lili's album, hundreds of images, pictures of them at the park, downtown, at school. She saved some of their Snapchats here too. They liked to use Snapchat for their private conversations because messages disappeared the instant they were viewed by all recipients. They were free to say whatever they wanted away from the prying eyes of parents who read *everything*. They were careful to use iMessage too, for the things they wanted their parents to see, but the real conversations took place on Snapchat. If Lili said something she wanted to keep, like her comment about Philip Krendal's butt-crack in science class, Gabby took a screenshot before the message disappeared from Snapchat and saved it in Lili's photo album — password protected and hidden, parent-proof, as it should be. Unlike the Instagram memorial, these pictures made Gabby smile. Lili was the queen of the one-line tag. She liked to send pictures of her Lhasa apso, Scrappy, with little snippets of dialogue. Grumpy Cat had nothing on her. There were pictures of cars too, not the ones she found online but the ones she found at local dealers that she really liked. The next time her dad brought up buying a car, she planned to show him one she wanted locally, a *specific* car, see if she could talk him into going down to the dealer and making an offer, call his bluff. Her favorite was a 2010 Camaro she'd found downtown, cherry red with black upholstery. If she rolled into the school lot driving that, she would have turned all the boys' heads—the girls' too.

Gabby paused at another picture. In this one Lili was holding up her iPad to her camera screen next to her smiling face. The caption read: "#WinnerWinnerChickenDinner." Gabby had completely forgotten about it. Lili had won some kind of contest online for a local driving school. Gabby told her it was probably a scam. She figured they used the contest to draw kids down there, then try to upsell them into a pricey package. Half the driving schools in Chicago did it, ever since the state made thirty hours of lessons mandatory before you could obtain your license. Lili said she was going to check it out anyway, but if she did, she never had the chance to tell Gabby what happened. She'd have gone with her.

Gabby sat up in bed.

She remembered what the police asked her. Would Lili get into the car with a stranger? Her answer had been no, but . . .

She pinched the image and zoomed in until she could read the name of the driving school: Designated Driver. It took her all of ten seconds to find their address.

Twenty minutes later she was dressed and out the door. Her mom didn't even hear her leave.

100

Porter

Day 4 • 8:24 a.m.

"Pull off there, to the side, Sarah. May I call you Sarah?"

Porter knew they shouldn't be following this woman's instructions blindly. He understood this was the wrong thing to do, yet that was exactly what they were doing.

They left the prison with her in the backseat, watching them, watching the outside world as it rushed past.

Sarah did as she was told, pulling the BMW not into one of the parking spaces at the front of the building but into the alley running along the side.

"Put the car in park and beep your horn twice."

The horn echoed off the buildings on either side, a residual slap.

"You look a bit peaked, Detective. You should try breathing every few minutes. It does wonders for the circulatory system."

Porter ignored her.

Someone had come out of the alley across the street. Porter recognized him, the same homeless man he had watched urinate on the sidewalk.

Was that really only twenty-four hours ago?

"May I have the key, Detective?"

Porter nearly asked her what key, then remembered the business card. He dug it out of his pocket and passed the card to her.

"I'd like to do something about these handcuffs and leg restraints as well."

"They stay on."

"We have a long ride ahead of us."

"Life can be very cruel sometimes," Porter muttered.

She smiled again, a slight curl at the base of her lip. "Yes, I suppose it can."

He didn't like that smile.

He didn't like it one bit.

The homeless man knocked at the window, then turned, watching across the street.

Porter watched as she pulled the key from the back of the business card, bent down, and released the ankle monitor. The small box began beeping immediately.

"Won't they know?" Sarah asked, watching in the rearview mirror.

Jane Doe rolled down the window and handed the monitor to the waiting man. He affixed it to his own ankle.

The beeping stopped.

The homeless man gave the roof of the car another tap and returned to the alley across the street, not a word between them.

Porter said, "Those ankle monitors aren't as reliable as the general public might like to believe. They store data when they can't reach a cell tower and upload the data as a batch when they make contact. The older ones, the ones in circulation for a while, regularly report false removal data. Too much jiggling over time of parts not meant to be jiggled. The monitoring center usually programs in a window—if the device reports a problem lasting longer than a minute, an alert goes off, less than a minute, and it's ignored. They would have programmed a geo-fence before they released her. As long as she doesn't leave the geofence, nobody will be the wiser. I saw that guy yesterday, and even my cab driver said he didn't belong. I'm guessing he's been waiting for us."

Sarah took this all in, her eyes glancing nervously at the rearview mirror, then back to Sam.

Without turning in his seat: "Where exactly are we going?"

"Didn't my boy tell you? Chicago, of course. I'll give you the exact address when we're closer to the city."

That smile again.

That wicked little grin.

"I'd like to read Anson's letter now. May I have it, please?"

Porter wanted to say no.

He wanted to tell her to fuck off, sit back, and shut up, but he didn't. Instead he reached into the glove box, retrieved the crinkled yellow pages, and tossed them into the backseat.

He heard her scrambling to retrieve them but did not look.

He would not look.

"Wasn't there a diary too? I do so miss his words."

Porter closed the glove box on the knife and locket before she could glimpse them, then opened the black and white composition book where he had left off. "You can have it when I'm done."

Jane looked to Sarah, their eyes meeting in the rearview mirror. "I believe Anson gave you until eight o'clock tonight. I suggest we get going. Wouldn't want to keep him waiting. He has a temper, that one. I understand he has playthings. Chop, chop."

Porter said, "Not another word out of you unless you're spoken to. Do we understand each other?"

Jane raised her cuffed hand to her lips and turned an invisible key before returning to her letter.

Sarah took one last nervous look in the mirror at the woman behind her, backed out onto the road, and put the BMW in drive, speeding forward. "Chicago it is," she said. "Nothing like a good road trip."

101

Diary

Doctor Oglesby wore a green argyle sweater today, again with khaki pants. I could only imagine argyle growing wild in his closet, slowly taking over the solids and plaids with their evasive patterns. Could you spray for argyle? Maybe there was a way to hold it at bay. Did wearing argyle on the regular cause one to morph into a doctor of the mind? If he wore a Grateful Dead T-shirt, shorts, and flip-flops every day rather than the sweaters, would he be a different man because of his choices? Would the clothing cause his personality to shift? Can the clothes change the man? Or does it work the other way around? A change in personality first, which then leads to a desire to wear more casual clothing. I wasn't—

"Anson? Where are you right now?"

"I'm sorry."

"You don't have to apologize, it's fine. I'm just curious where your mind takes you when leave the room like that."

"I was right here. I didn't go anywhere."

"You were physically right here, but your mind was in a distant place. What were you thinking about?"

The glasses were off again, dangling around his neck.

"Who is the girl down the hall from me?"

"What girl?"

"Two doors down."

The doctor frowned at this. "Have you met?"

On went the glasses, a scribble in his notepad.

I shook my head. "I've heard her crying. She seems very sad."

"Does that make you feel sad?"

"Should it?"

"Do you ever cry, Anson?"

I had to think about this, maybe the first compelling thing the doctor asked of me since I got here. I couldn't remember the last time I had cried. Father taught me to cry, I could cry at will, I could summon tears with the snap of my fingers, but I didn't remember ever needing to do so, even when—no, not then. I wouldn't think about that. The last time I think I cried was after Ridley's puppies. I didn't want to talk about the puppies either, not now, not ever. Father once told me although I knew how to cry, real men do not. Real men never cry. Dirty Harry would be far less threatening if he broke down into tears while waving his gun at the bad guys, or worse—when they pointed their guns at him.

"When you learned you were alone, when you first realized both your parents were gone and you were all alone, did you cry then?"

"Yes."

I said this only because I knew it was what he wanted to hear, the correct answer. I had not shed a tear—there was no point. Crying would not have helped or changed anything. Crying would have been a waste of time. I did not waste time. I did not let emotion control me.

"Yet, you haven't cried at all since arriving here."

Glasses off again.

"There is no shame in crying, Anson. Emotional reactions to situations and our environment aid our body in coping with the current predicament. Bottling up emotion, holding such things inside, that can be dangerous. Have you ever taken a can of soda and shaken it up real good, then popped the top?"

"I don't drink soda."

"Shaking the can causes the gases inside to become agitated. Opening the can allows that agitation to be released. If you don't open the can, all that energy remains inside and it can be damaging, all those molecules running into each other, getting angrier and angrier as they realize they're trapped with no place to go. Shake a can and leave it to fester long enough, and the soda will taste bad when you eventually do open it."

"Soda is bad for you."

"The girl down the hall from you, she cries because something horrible has happened to her. I can't share the details of another patient, but the things that have happened to her were unimaginable, something I wouldn't wish on anyone, not even someone who lies or fibs to me. She cries because crying makes her feel better. She cries because crying helps her heal. Crying is a normal reaction, it is the right reaction. I worry far more about someone who doesn't cry than I do about a girl like her. I don't want to worry about you, Anson, but I do."

"I'm fine."

"Yes, well—" Dr. Oglesby stood and went around to the other side of his desk. He pulled open the top left drawer and took out a plastic ziplock bag. There was writing on the outside, but I couldn't make out what it said. Inside the bag was my Ranger Buck knife.

He set the bag down on the desk between us, then came back around to his chair. With his pen, he poked at the bag, turning it slightly. "That's a nice knife, Anson. Did your father give you that?"

"Yes."

"I bet you'd like to have it back."

"Yes."

"What if I were to keep it? Or maybe throw it away? I suppose I could even give it to someone on the staff. Seems silly to let such a nice knife go to waste."

"It doesn't belong to you."

"No? I think it does. Possession is nine-tenths of the law. Have you ever heard that expression? The police gave the knife to me for safekeeping. A knife is a weapon. I'm not so sure a boy like you should possess a weapon."

My eyes fixed on him.

I wanted to look at the knife, but that was also what he wanted me to do. I wouldn't do what he wanted me to do, no sir.

He gave the bag another poke and eased back into his chair. "If I were to return the knife to you, what do you suppose you'd do with it? Would I be in danger? Would my staff have reason for concern? What does a boy who doesn't cry do with a knife like that?"

Something was absent from that plastic bag, something I desperately wanted to ask him about but knew I couldn't. The picture of Mother and Mrs. Carter had been in my pocket too. Where was the picture?

I imagined Dr. Oglesby holding the picture in the dark, studying it, filthy thoughts running through his little head. Filthy thoughts he'd no doubt wipe away with a discarded argyle sweater.

That would not do.

That would not do at all.

I looked at the knife. "It makes a good screwdriver, and I've used it to open boxes. Sometimes I cut the bark off old trees, or pick rocks out from the tires of Father or Mother's cars. A pocketknife is a useful tool to have on you, but if you prefer to hold on to my knife for now, if that makes you feel more comfortable, that's fine."

Dr. Oglesby smiled. "I'm glad you approve, Anson. And you are one hundred percent correct. I had a Swiss Army knife when I was a boy your age. I carried that knife with me everywhere I went."

Father once told me Swiss Army knives were a joke, bulky and unnecessarily bogged down with useless clutter. A real man could get by with nothing but a knife. Any man who felt the need to carry a corkscrew, scissors, and metal toothpick in his pocket was not resourceful. That was the kind of man who cried. Dirty Harry would never carry a Swiss Army knife. I did not mention this, though, because the doctor seemed pleased with my last response.

The doctor scratched the side of his nose, studied his finger, then nodded back at the desk. "You know, Anson, before the police gave that to me, they ran the blade through a series of tests. I'm not sure exactly what they were looking for, but something compelled them to study your knife very carefully."

I thought about Mr. Carter then, his final visit to the lake. Father had cut him up into tiny pieces neatly wrapped in plastic and tasked me with sending those pieces to the bottom of the lake. I punctured each plastic bag with my knife before chucking them into the water, *weighed down with rocks. Best to give the fish a taste, Father once told me.*

"You know what they found, Anson?" He reached for his glasses, thought better of it, and leaned forward instead. "Your knife had been scrubbed and soaked in bleach, every nook and cranny. Might as well have been brand new. Considering you only used it for things like opening boxes, picking at rocks and bark, and the occasional screwdriver, it seems odd to me that you would use bleach on it. I imagine the police were curious about this too."

"I like to keep a clean blade."

He said nothing then, he said nothing for a long time, then: "Yes, I suppose you would."

Ten minutes later he led me from his office back down the hall to my own room.

Nurse Gilman always smiled up at me when the doctor led me past the nurses' station. Today I smiled back, then bent to adjust my slipper—it was large, and my foot sometimes slipped out.

102

Clair
Day 4 • 8:28 a.m.

Kloz had been right, the little shit knocker.

So far, he'd tied eight more obituaries belonging to employees at John H. Stroger, Jr. Hospital, employees who were very much alive.

Once he matched the employee names, Clair worked with the hospital's HR department to reach out to each one and communicate what was happening, dispatching cars to fetch them.

She spent most of the night gathering them all here, at the hospital. Each person had been told to not to bring anything at all—no food, no toiletries, no books, no cell phones, not one single personal possession other than the clothing on their backs. All would be provided once they arrived. Those with families were told to bring their families. Nobody was permitted to make a phone call, not before leaving or after arriving.

She gathered them here, in the hospital's cafeteria.

They were pissed.

Stir-craziness set in quickly, and most staffers were just longing for their shift to start so they could leave the room. It was worse for the children and spouses, but this made the most sense. The cafeteria was at the center of the hospital, easily guarded. They had plenty of food and shelter. She couldn't accommodate this many people at a safe house, not even in multiple safe houses. The department didn't have the resources.

She saw Nash enter from the far end of the room, spot her, and cross the cafeteria, taking in what was beginning to look like a refugee camp.

"We've got an ID on the boy in the truck," he told her. "His name was Wesley Hartzler. He's a Jehovah's Witness. Went missing sometime yesterday. He attended services first thing in the morning, then they spread out around town to try and recruit."

"Do they know where he went?"

Nash shook his head. "They don't file a flight plan or anything. Sounds like it was completely unorganized. Everyone goes out the door and heads off in different directions."

"Was he alone?"

"He paired off with a girl named Kati Quigley. I just hung up with her mother. She's missing too. We put out an Amber Alert. I told both sets of parents to meet us here so we can get statements. Figured that would be faster. There's more," he said. "Eisley said cause of death on the boy was blunt-force trauma to the head. No water in the lungs."

"So he wasn't tortured?"

"I'm thinking he just got in the way and our unsub kept the girl."

Clair opened the notes app on her phone and ran through the names Kloz gave her. "We don't have obituaries for Quigley or Hartzler."

Nash shrugged. "Maybe they both got in the way. Jehovah's Witnesses show up on our unsub's doorstep, probably out of the blue, they see something they shouldn't . . ." His voice trailed off, but Clair knew where he was going. She glanced around the room. Of the eight potential victims Kloz identified, four had children. All the children were accounted for. They were all here.

Nash followed her eyes. "If he took her, it was because she was convenient, not because we kept him from one of these kids. The fact that we found the boy and not her tells me she's still alive."

"He could be torturing her right now."

"We're getting close."

"Were they on foot? Get uniforms to their starting point, have them branch out on a house-to-house. Make sure they go in pairs— we don't want someone stumbling into Bishop or the unsub alone."

"Already happening. I spoke to Dispatch right after I hung up with Eisley. I'm heading out there now."

Clair nodded, then dialed Agent Poole.

Seven hundred and eight miles away, Special Agent Poole answered on the second ring. Clair told him about Wesley Hartzler, and that they'd located all Bishop's potential victims and gotten them safely to the hospital.

"When we hang up, I want you to call SAIC Hurless. He's my commanding officer. Fill him in on the house-to-house. He can get you more bodies," Poole told her.

Clair felt people watching her in the cafeteria, her every movement telegraphed and documented by the eyes of the people she brought here. She walked past the two officers stationed at the cafeteria entrance out into the hallway. "We interrupted Bishop's endgame. He's going to retaliate."

"You can't think about that. You need to focus on keeping those people safe. We'll find him." Poole sounded like he was shuffling papers. His voice dropped lower. "I've got five more bodies down here in that lake, Detective. Possibly a sixth body. Dismembered. The pieces sunk in plastic bags and weighed down with rocks, just rotting away in the water."

"Jesus."

"I've got the diary too. Porter left it for me." More rustling of papers, and then he went on. "The mailbox on the adjoining house said 'Bishop.' I'm down at the county property appraiser's office, going through records."

Clair said, "We ran searches on that a few months ago but hit a wall. There's no national database, so we threw darts at possible counties. The municipalities with records only go back so far electronically, and there are a lot of Bishops out there. Our search was limited to Illinois and the surrounding states. We never considered South Carolina."

"Yeah, well, sometimes you have to dig the old fash . . ." he trailed off.

"Find something?"

No reply.

"Agent Poole?"

"Does Sam have any kind of connection to South Carolina?"

"He . . . he did his time as a rookie in Charleston I think, before coming to Chicago. Why?"

"What year did he come to Chicago?"

"Why?"

Poole let out a breath, the weight of his words heavy. "The property with the lake and the two surrounding houses, all of it is in his name."

103

Gabby
Day 4 • 8:49 a.m.

Gabby Deegan got off the number 57 bus at West Roosevelt and walked the three blocks to Designated Driver in the falling snow, nearly slipping twice on the icy sidewalk.

The building wasn't very large, a squat, square structure with a flat roof surrounded by half a dozen small white hatchbacks covered in branding for Designated Driver and the words STUDENT DRIVER plastered on every available surface in bright red. The cars were layered in snow, no doubt sidelined by the weather.

Gabby pulled open the front door, fighting the wind, and ducked inside. A woman in her mid-fifties looked up from a copy of the *Tribune* and frowned at her. "We're closed today, sweetie. I just came in to catch up on some paperwork. I can make you an appointment for next week after this weather breaks."

Pulling off her gloves and hat, Gabby approached the counter. It smelled like burnt coffee. "I'm actually not here to make an appointment."

The woman's frown deepened. She returned to her paper. "Well, we're not buying anything either."

"I think a friend of mine was in here a few days ago. I'm trying to find her." She loaded a picture of Lili Davies on her phone and held it toward the woman.

The woman's eyes met Gabby's, and for a second Gabby thought she was going to ask her to leave again. Then she set down the paper and looked at the phone. "Pretty little thing, looks familiar." She reached for the phone and held it close to her face, squinting. "I don't know how you kids can use these little things. Mine is as big as a tablet."

"She would have been in here earlier this week."

Her head tilted to the side. She glanced at her newspaper, then handed the phone back to Gabby, frowning again. "I don't know what game you're playing, but I don't appreciate it."

"I'm not—"

The woman behind the counter picked up her newspaper and folded the front page over, setting it down in front of Gabby. "I should call the police and report you."

Gabby looked down at this morning's *Tribune*. Lili's picture was on the front page, along with that of two other girls, girls she didn't know. There was a boy too. The headline read: KILLER CLAIMS THIRD VICTIM, ANOTHER MISSING. POLICE STUMPED.

"Was she in here?"

"Of course not, I'd remember something like that. You go telling people that she was, and your parents will be hearing from our lawyers."

Gabby wanted to push the issue, to shout at this woman, make her check the records, but she didn't. Her eyes had fixed on the small stack of business cards on the counter beside her. She grabbed one, put on her hat and gloves, and pushed back out into the cold.

Once outside, she loaded the picture Lili had sent her back onto her phone. She pinched the image and zoomed in on the iPad in Lili's hand, on the message that said she won, then she glanced at the business card, then at the front of the building.

The phone number on the card, the building, and even the cars ended with 0000. The one on Lili's iPad, the number she had been told to call to claim her prize, was completely different, and even the area code didn't match.

Gabby dialed the number Lili had been given and pressed the phone tight against her ear, sealing out the howling wind. Her call was answered on the fifth ring. Gabby could see the woman inside the small building, still reading her paper.

"Designated Driver Driving School, how may I help you?" The voice on the other end of the line was gruff, a man's voice. He had trouble pronouncing the *s* in *school*.

104

Poole
Day 4 • 8:50 a.m.

"I didn't mean to eavesdrop on your call earlier, but I did, so I gotta ask, who is Sam?"

Sheriff Hana Banister sat on a stool across the table from Poole, files and boxes laid out between them. She had apologized repeatedly about the lack of computerized records. The county was small, their budget was smaller, and every time the matter came up, a more urgent need for the funds vetoed any plan to enter legacy data into the current system, which only went back a handful of years.

Poole had the property deeds in a neat stack at his side, Porter's name glaring at him. "Detective Sam Porter with Chicago Metro. Until recently, he was the lead investigator on the 4MK task force."

"What happened, recently?"

Poole couldn't tell her, not yet. He wasn't sure what he was dealing with yet. "He let the case get to him, he let it go personal." Poole finished with the current box and slid it aside. "I don't see his name anywhere else, only that particular piece of property."

Banister sat back on her stool, stifling a yawn. "The name Porter doesn't ring any bells, and I grew up around here. I was born in the clinic four doors down from this very building, actually. This is a fairly close-knit community, farmers mostly. A few of the families have sold off over the years to developers, but I like to think I've got a good handle on the people. We get our share of rowdy teenagers and such, but that's mainly because there isn't much else to do. Until this morning, the last murder we had was nearly six years ago, when Edison Lindley's wife took it upon herself to end his cheating ways with the help of a heaping spoonful of arsenic in his soup. She called it in too and was waiting on her porch when I got there, glass of lemonade in her hand. Not exactly the crime of the century."

Pool said. "You mentioned developers. Do you know the name Arthur Talbot or Talbot Enterprises?"

"I do know the name, but only from the news—crazy what happened to him. If he set his eye on property out here, I would have heard about it at town hall. Property sales are usually talked about before I give the crime report." Banister raised a legal-size folder above her head. "Got it."

"Got what?"

"The report on the fire out there that destroyed the main house."

She opened the folder on the table and began flipping through the contents. "August, 1995. Way before my time. Ruled arson on the spot. Tom Langlin wrote it up. He's retired now but still lives in the area. I can drive you out to his place if you think it would be helpful. According to this, the entire area reeked of gasoline. By the time the trucks arrived, the house was a total loss. They found three bodies inside, all male. Cause of death says undetermined due to condition on account of the fire. One survivor, an Anson Bishop, twelve years old. He had been fishing out at the lake and came back when he saw the smoke. They believe his father was one of the men found inside. His mother was suspected of starting the fire—looks like she disappeared. Her information went out on the wire, but she was never located. The trailer behind the house had been rented to a Simon and Lisa Carter. They also went missing after the fire. No hits on their wire report either. The boy went to the Camden Treatment Center not too far from here."

"May I see that?"

She passed him the file.

Poole's phone rang. He answered the call on speaker.

"Frank? This is Granger. I just hung up with Hurless, filled him in on everything. They're still searching the water, but I think we've found them all. Five complete bodies and at least one more in bags. We don't have enough bags for more than one body, but I suppose it's possible the remains came from multiple sources. We won't know for sure until the medical examiner has a look. I'm having everything transported back to Charlotte, our closest lab."

"Thanks. Keep me posted on what you find. If you can't reach me, go to Hurless."

"I'm back at what's left of that house right now. Obvious fire. My office tried to pull records, but they're coming up blank."

"I've got the file in my hand. I'll have Sheriff Banister scan and e-mail it to you."

"What does it say?"

Poole repeated what Banister told him.

"The trailer survived the fire, and it looks like someone has been in there recently. The back bedroom has been ransacked—somebody moved the bed, tore up the floor. We got a backpack full of clothes. Some camping gear. It's strewn all over the room. Somebody was looking for something."

Poole glanced at the diary sitting on the edge of the table. "I think that was Detective Porter."

"Can't tell if he found whatever he wanted. We're shipping all this back to Charlotte too. We'll photograph everything. I'm gonna try and get some heavy equipment out here to go through the remains of that house. It's been a while, but we may find something that ties back to the bodies at the lake."

Poole's phone vibrated on the table. The caller ID popped up. "That's SAIC Hurless on my other line. I've got to go. Keep me posted."

"You got it."

Poole thumbed the display and answered the other call. "Agent Poole."

"Frank. I think we got something. You're gonna need to get back on the plane."

"What is it?"

"You were right about the prison guards at Stateville. I spoke to the warden. We've got a guard who was suspected of passing information for Libby McInley, but nothing was actually proven, so he wasn't charged. He transferred shortly after all of this played out. Guess where he went?"

"Where?"

"New Orleans."

Porter's disposable phone.

"That's our connection to Porter. Any record of the two of them knowing each other or working together?"

"Nothing yet, but I just got this. I'll put people on it right away," Hurless told him. "His name is Vincent Weidner. He's working now, on the clock until four this afternoon. You need to get out there. The Orleans warden said he'd try and stall him, keep him on site after his shift if he has to. They're not going to say anything to him until you arrive—we don't want to tip him off. Granger told me what turned up at the lake. We need to find out what this guard knows and get on Porter's heels. He's deep in this."

Poole told him about the property records.

"Get on him. None of this slips out. I don't want the media running some half-baked story."

"Yes, sir."

"I spoke to Detective Norton too. I've got four teams on their way to help with the house-to-house. I'll put in a call to Porter's captain too. He needs to know what's going on. We're close, Frank."

"Yes, sir."

Hurless disconnected.

Poole looked up at Sheriff Banister. "Can you drive me to the airport in Greenville?"

She nodded.

Poole handed her one of his cards. "You find anything else, call me or SAIC Hurless. His number's on the back. Send that file over to Granger too, as soon as you can."

Scooping up the diary, he started for the door. He'd read it on the plane.

105

Diary

Seven minutes past three in the morning.

I lie awake.

The girl two doors down is crying again, she is crying something fierce.

I'm staring at the ceiling.

My knife no doubt back in Dr. Oglesby's desk drawer.

With the picture?

I wasn't sure about this. I imagined Dr. Oglesby would keep the picture close. I wanted to see it. If I closed my eyes, I saw the photograph in perfect detail. I had no trouble recalling Mrs. Carter's body wrapped in the sheets, lying with Mother. I remembered this as easily as I remembered the day I saw her at the lake, then back in her kitchen—

She was shaking. "I think I wanted you to see. I watched you walk out there with your fishing pole. I knew you'd be there."

"Why would you . . ."

"Sometimes a woman wants to be desired, is all." She took another drink. "Do you think I'm pretty?"

I did think she was pretty.

I wanted the photograph back. The idea of Dr. Oglesby holding my picture, studying it, soaking in that image, this churned my stom-

ach. He wasn't meant to see that picture. That wasn't meant for him at all.

A loud cry. A choked cry.

Nurse Gilman's shoes tapping down the tile floor.

She would comfort the girl. This was becoming the pattern. An extended cry, the sound of Nurse Gilman, the click of the girl's door, then eventually muffled sobs and silence.

I rolled the paper clip between my fingers beneath my sheets, mindful of the camera I was certain watched me from the air vent.

I had picked the paper clip up off the tile floor when I bent down to adjust my slipper earlier. I don't know who dropped it, I didn't care—all that mattered was that I had it now. I knew I could pick my lock with it, and I would do exactly that, when it was time to go. It was not time to go yet.

Another muffled sob from the room two doors down, then nothing.

What did she look like?

How old was she?

What happened to her?

I could almost picture her. Nurse Gilman's arms around this frail thing wrapped in sheets, the two of them—

I couldn't leave without the picture. I couldn't leave without my knife.

I would have to go at night.

The staff was thinnest at night.

I never heard more than two nurses in the halls at night, sometimes only one, and of course there was the guard at the end of the hall to consider. I would need to escape my room, get down the hall, past the nurses' station to the doctor's office, pick his lock (a Kwikset, much easier to pick than the one on my door). Inside, I could retrieve my knife.

I needed my knife.

Without my knife, the guard and nurses would be a problem.

I couldn't get to my knife without passing the guard and the nurses, though, and this was also a problem. This was a serious problem for sure.

There were also the cameras.

Father would know what to do. Father always knew what to do.

The rain had not stopped, a steady patter against my window.

The power was flickering.

If the power went out, would there be a backup generator?

I imagined there was.

Or maybe there wasn't.

Or maybe there was.

Nurse Gilman had a nice smile.

I wondered if the girl two doors down ever smiled. What was her smile like?

I closed my eyes again and thought about the hallway.

Father would puzzle it out.

I would puzzle it out.

106

Clair

Day 4 • 10:12 a.m.

Clair and Kloz hovered over the speakerphone in the small office Klozowski had claimed as his own upon arriving at John H. Stroger, Jr. Hospital. Nothing more than an unused exam room, really. Stacked floor to ceiling with boxes and outdated equipment, the room was down the hall from the cafeteria and blissfully out of sight of the people in there.

Nash was on the other end of the phone line, and Clair told him and Kloz what Poole had told her.

Nash must have covered the phone. He shouted something she couldn't make out, muffled, then came back to the call. "It's bullshit, you know that, right?"

Klozowski's face had grown pale, nearly translucent in the light cast by his large laptop screen. "That's got to be Bishop," he said. "He fudged the county property records somehow."

Clair wanted to believe that. "Electronic, maybe. But paper? Poole said he had to dig through a dozen boxes and old file cabinets with the sheriff in the basement of a municipal building to track this down. Even if Bishop could get in, and I've got no doubt he could, it sounded like they were so disorganized down there, how would Bishop know where to find the original to swap it out?"

Kloz's brain was churning. She could see it in his eyes. "I don't even think it would be that simple. Think about it, a paper document? He would have to break in twice. Once to steal the original, then again to replace the original with the fake. He'd need time with the original to duplicate everything—fonts, format, paper type . . . electronic records are easy—hack in, a couple keystrokes, and you're out clean. Paper is old school, it's tough."

"Not impossible, though," Nash said.

"Okay, we need to focus," Clair said. "We can't get distracted. Anything on the search?"

"Four blocks down. Between the feds and our guys, we've got a lot of people out here. This weather is tough, slow moving," Nash told them.

She turned back to Kloz. "Did you match anyone else to the obits?"

Kloz sighed, then picked up a pen and began twirling it between his fingers, his eyes returning to his laptop. "I need more data."

"I got you data. The hospital gave you access to all their employee records."

Kloz nodded. "And that was very helpful. I was able to match up eight more potential victims against the obituary data we received from all the city papers. They're all in that tent city you've constructed in the cafeteria. Here's the problem, though. If you go back to our original three adult victims, Reynolds, Davies, and Biel, only Davies actually worked at the hospital. Reynolds worked for UniMed America Healthcare in insurance sales, and Darlene Biel is a pharmaceutical sales rep. The hospital doesn't have employee names on their vendors."

"So, let's get them," Clair said.

Kloz snapped his fingers. "Like that, huh? Do you know how many vendors a hospital this size works with?"

"We don't have time to play Trivial Pursuit, Kloz."

"Two hundred and thirty-three," he told them. "I got that list about twenty minutes ago, and I've got my team back at Metro reaching out to all of them, but it's going to take time."

Clair said, "So you found eight potential victims here at the hospital, but since two out of three original victims worked outside of this building, that means his total victim pool is much larger?"

Kloz nodded slowly. "That's what I'm saying. We're protecting eight families, but that's not going to slow Bishop, or our unsub, or both down. He'll shrug it off and just move on to someone else on the list."

Clair was looking at Klozowski's screen. "Is that all of them?"

"That's what we have so far, yeah."

She studied the names. "I think . . . I think we need to focus on the smaller picture, look at what we have, not so much what we don't. Bishop's not targeting these people randomly. There's a pattern."

"That's how we got here," Kloz told her. "They all work in the medical field."

"Yeah, but what do they do in the medical field? What ties them all together? There's a thread. We're just not seeing it."

Kloz used the pen and began ticking off the potential victims by occupation. "Insurance sales, oncologist, pharmaceutical sales, an X-ray tech, an MRI tech, two nurses, a surgeon, a surgical nurse, a scheduling assistant, and the woman who runs Patient Intake downstairs. Do you see a pattern? 'Cause I'm pretty good with patterns, and I'm coming up blank."

Clair took the pen from Kloz's hand and set it down on the make-shift desk. "I still don't see what any of these people have to do with what he did to the kids, drowning them like he did. There's a secondary element at play here."

"It's got to be revenge for something the parents did, something we're still not seeing," Nash replied from the speakerphone. "Punish the children for the parents' mistakes, that's Bishop's MO."

Clair's cell phone rang. She pulled it from her pocket. "Sophie Rodriguez." She hit the Accept button. "Sophie? You're on speaker. I'm here with Kloz, and we've got Nash on the other line."

The woman was breathing heavily, out of breath. "Where are you? It's Gabrielle Deegan. We need to talk."

107

Poole
Day 4 • 12:58 p.m.

The flight from Greenville to New Orleans took a little over three hours. They ran into some turbulence over Alabama, which made it feel as if the G4 might drop out of the sky. The small aircraft made the types of noises you didn't want to hear in a plane—creaks and groans and protests. Although Poole was a seasoned flyer, this would have been more than enough to rattle him had he noticed any of it. He didn't, though. He had been completely engrossed in Bishop's diary for the duration of the flight.

Poole burned through the small composition book, turning each page faster than the last, and when he reached the end, he began to go back through the various pages he'd dog-eared, the ones related to specifics at the property in South Carolina, the lake and shell of a house and trailer. He also folded over the pages concerning Bishop's parents.

Damn near all the pages were now folded.

What the hell should he make of this?

Why had Porter held the diary back?

Why had he *really* held it back?

You can't play God without being acquainted with the devil.

The words rolled back into Poole's consciousness like a freight train.

How deep was Porter willing to go?

Much of the diary rang true, but there was something off about the text. Not only minor details like the Volkswagen rotting away in the driveway rather than the Porsche originally mentioned, or the trailer in the backyard rather than the house Bishop said belonged to their neighbors, the Carters. There was something else, something deeper. The entire text had a fairy-tale feel, a Beaver Cleaver shimmer that crossed the line between documentary fact and carefully crafted fiction. Somewhere within that shimmer the truth lived, he was sure. The words were those of a little boy, the memories of a child who walked that property, who lived there, that was part of it for sure. The world seen through a child's eyes was much different than that of an adult, and the story had been documented as such. If this diary had been written by a child, that would make sense. Poole had seen Bishop's handwriting, though. He had studied his handwriting closely. An individual's handwriting evolves over time, as a person ages. The style surely finds root in our childhood, but as we age, some edges grow sharper while early edges can grow soft. A child's handwriting always has a tenderness to it, a hesitation, as our brain recalls how a letter or word should look before we commit that letter or word to paper. As we get older, that fades and we pull more from our subconscious. A child's writing, although it may appear sloppy, is usually meticulously thought out, done slowly, while as adults we rush through the words, take shortcuts. At Quantico, Poole took a series of handwriting analysis courses, and the one thing that always stood out was the difference between a child and an adult's writing.

The language here, the word choice, the flow—it was very much the work of a child, yet the handwriting itself belonged to an adult. Poole was sure if he compared the diary to current writing samples from Bishop, this fact would solidify. Bishop wrote it recently. Not just the opening page taunting police, but all of it, yet he tried to make the story sound like the words of a child.

That thought, that singular thought, made him suspect of all that he read.

Poole had no doubt much of the diary was true.

He also believed other segments were not.

Bishop didn't write this simply to tell a story. He wrote the diary to control the narrative, plant seeds in the minds of those who read his words, play those who followed him. Of all he just read, he only knew one thing for certain—the dismembered body they found in the lake was most likely that of Simon Carter. How his body got there and who ultimately killed him couldn't be determined by this text, only by the evidence they would eventually uncover.

The diary did not provide any explanation for the other five bodies they found, nor did it provide a true explanation for the bodies found in the house, and nothing about the fire. The only explanations offered were those Bishop wanted them to believe—to buy into that was dangerous. Poole wasn't about to do that.

He felt the diary should be approached from a very different angle. The book should be treated as a laundry list of facts Bishop wanted them to believe, whether they were true or not. Understanding why Bishop wanted to communicate this particular message, and not the diary text itself, would lead to the truth.

Poole wiped at his eyes and looked out the small window. He watched the clouds give way to green below, roads and buildings take shape, the airport come into view followed by the runway. When the plane's wheels touched pavement, they did so with a skilled bump, barely noticeable, a far cry from the roller coaster ride of only a few hours earlier.

As they taxied toward the federal hangar on the north end of the airport, a white SUV drove out from a small parking lot on the side of the building: his ride to the prison.

Poole grabbed the diary and had the small hatch of the plane open even before the G4 stopped moving.

108

Diary

"I received a rather interesting call from the police this morning. Would you like to know what they asked me?"

Red argyle.

Today's sweater.

The doctor had had pancakes or waffles for breakfast. There was a small syrup stain below the collar. I could smell the sugar. This made me hungry. I had been given Cheerios and milk, a favorite of mine to be sure, but most definitely not as good as pancakes or waffles.

I missed Mother's pancakes. She made terrific pancakes.

"Anson, you're wandering again. When someone is speaking to you, you need to attempt to focus on their voice. It helps to look them in their eyes, try to shut down the babble in your head."

I had been looking at the doctor's eyes, although I didn't see him.

I could look right through the doctor if I wanted to, just as easily as I could see inside that head of his and—

"Anson."

I smelled the syrup on the air.

I looked at his eyes.

I smiled.

"Yes, Doctor?"

"Would you like to know what the police asked me?"

"Yes, Doctor. I would like that very much."

He glanced down at his notes. "This was a Detective Welderman with the Greenville PD. He said they have been out to your house a number of times to interview your neighbors, the"—he fumbled through his notes again—"Carters, Simon, and Lisa. Apparently they haven't returned home. That prompted them to check with Simon Carter's place of employ, and he hasn't been to work in some time. His wife, who did not work, appears to be missing as well."

The doctor's eyes remained on his notepad for a second, scanning the text, then he looked up at me and frowned. "So we have four adults, including your parents, either missing or dead. Three bodies found after a horrible fire in your house, a fire that has been confirmed as arson, and we have one boy, a boy who does not appear to cry, left behind and now sitting across from me in my office." The glasses came off again, but this time there wasn't the showmanship behind it. He pulled them from his nose and let them drop to his chest. "I've got to tell you, Anson, this doesn't look good. This doesn't look good at all. The police are most certainly in an uproar. They want to talk to you. They want to talk to you desperately. Of course, I told them that they couldn't. You're a minor under my care, and I wouldn't subject you to that." He leaned forward, lowered his voice. "Not an hour after I hung up the phone with Detective Welderman, I got another call from that attorney general I mentioned to you the other day. Do you remember him? The one who wanted to speak to your mother. He told me it would be in my best interest to allow the police to speak to you, with me in attendance, of course. He was fairly insistent. He asked to see my notes as well. I told him our conversations were strictly confidential, that absolutely everything you've told me is considered private, and there was no way that was going to happen. I pushed back, Anson, I pushed back hard on your behalf. But these people, the police, the attorney general . . . they seem to think you were somehow involved in all this, and I have to be honest, you haven't told me anything that would make me believe oth-

erwise. I can only hold the wolves at bay for so long, Anson. You need to tell me what happened."

My knife was sitting on his desk again. I don't think he'd left it out, because today it was on the corner of the desk, nearest me, not where he had placed it yesterday. I could reach the blade if I wanted to. I could have it out of that plastic bag and embedded in the good doctor's neck before he could scribble potentially dangerous on his little notepad, certainly before he could underline it.

Potentially dangerous

He was watching me again, allowing the ticks of silence to stack one atop the other like Jenga blocks. I knew he would spend the next hour sitting here quietly, waiting for me to speak. He used this tactic repeatedly, his efforts so transparent.

"Father set the fire and left with Mother."

The glasses went back on. "Well, that's an interesting thought, but why would he leave his car? Why leave her car too? Where did they go? Why leave without you?"

"I don't know where they went, and I don't know why they left me behind."

"Who were the dead men in your house?"

"I don't know."

"Where are your neighbors?"

"I don't know."

"Who set the fire?"

"Father."

He wanted to ask me about the picture. I knew he had it, probably on him, probably in the pocket of those khaki pants or hidden somewhere between the pages of his notepad.

"Why would your father set the fire?"

"I don't know."

"Who were those other men, the ones we found in the house, were they there to hurt him? Did they try to hurt your mother?"

I didn't like this.

I didn't like this one bit.

The rapid fire of questions. I was answering too fast.

I was providing answers without taking the opportunity to fully think them through. He was controlling the conversation. Father would not approve. I needed to control the conversation. Paint and corners, paint and corners. I was being—

"Anson, do you know the term kinesics?"

I shook my head.

"Kinesics is the interpretation of body motion, body language. Facial expressions, gestures, nonverbal behavior related to any part of the body. I have had extensive training in kinesics, the interpretation of body language, and this training allows me to know when someone is not being honest with me. We've already discussed how I feel about people who lie or fib. When someone lies or fibs verbally, the rest of their body offers clues that allow me to see through these lies and fibs. The longer I speak to someone, the easier this becomes. Eventually, it becomes impossible for someone to effectively tell me a lie. You and I, Anson, are nearing that point. What does this mean for you? Well, it means that you can continue to lie to me, and I will know you are lying, or you can tell me the truth, in which case I will also know you are telling the truth. It means you have arrived at a crossroad and you need to make a decision. You can begin to answer my questions truthfully, which will fall under the protection of doctor/patient privilege and cannot be used against you. Or you can continue to try and lie to me. Should you decide to take that path, there will be little I can do for you." Oglesby leaned back in his chair. "As your doctor, I will allow the detectives to question you and pursue whatever course of action they deem fit. I will aid that attorney general in his pursuits. You will be transferred from this facility to someplace far less hospitable, the kind of place where a young, good-looking boy such as yourself is considered currency, nothing more than a thing, a possession to be used and discarded. You will be broken and die a little each day, and there will be no coming back. Once a boy finds himself in a place like that, there is never coming back, there is only deeper into the abyss. You'll spend your days with a shovel, digging a deeper hole to hide in only to find the monsters prefer the dark and will gladly follow."

He removed his glasses. "I want to help you, Anson. I hope you see that, but we're running out of time."

He concluded our session then, nearly ten minutes later than usual, and led me back down the hall, past the nurses' station, to my room.

The girl's door was open as we passed, Nurse Gilman delivering her lunch. The girl sat on her bed, her legs pulled tight to her chest. She watched me as I walked past, and I watched her.

I could not look away, even if I wanted to.

109

Clair

Day 4 • 1:12 p.m.

"I told you, we don't run contests. I have no idea what that is."

Clair stared at the woman behind the counter at the Designated Driver driving school. She felt the blood heating her face. The woman stared at her blankly, defiantly. Clair wanted to reach across the counter and pull her over. Kloz had taken the image of Lili Davies holding her iPad, enhanced it, and blown the picture up so they could make out the detail. The version Clair had on her phone clearly showed this building and some of the cars out front. "Look at the pictures again," Clair said, pushing the photo sheet of the missing and dead children across the counter at the woman.

She glanced down, then back at Clair. "I told you, I haven't seen any of them. None of those kids have ever set foot in here. I'd know. Anybody could have taken a picture of this place and mocked it up. That's not our phone number, it's bogus."

The phone number in the picture, the one Gabby Deegan had called earlier that morning, currently rang through to a voice mail box that had not been set up. Kloz tried to trace the number, but it came up as a burner phone, no longer online. He and Nash were working with the phone company to try and trace back Gabby's call from earlier and possibly pin down a location.

Gabby sat in a chair at the corner of the small building, Sophie next to her, holding the girl's hand. "Okay, run through it one more time for me, sweetheart," Sophie said.

Gabby wiped at her eyes. "I should never have let her go by herself. It's my fault. If I had gone with her, she'd still be alive."

"Tell us about the phone call, about the man who answered. What did he say to you? Did you hear any strange noises? Anything that might tell us where he was?"

Gabby shook her head. "I hung up right after he answered. He sounded funny. I . . . I could see inside here, I could see her. She didn't answer the call. I don't think the phone in here even rang."

"I haven't gotten a call all day. It's been dead," the woman said.

"Sounded funny, how?" Clair asked, walking over.

"Like he just woke up, sleepy, I guess. He couldn't say the word *school* right."

"He had a stutter?"

Gabby frowned. "No, not a stutter. I'm not sure what you call it. He couldn't say the letter *s*—well, he could say it, just not right. He pronounced it *thcool*."

"A lisp?" the woman behind the counter asked. "Is that what you mean? He had a lisp?"

Gabby was nodding. "Yeah, that's it. A lisp."

Clair went back over to the counter. "Does that mean something to you?"

The woman picked up the phone and began dialing. "I need to call the owner."

Clair took the phone from her and hung it back up. "You need to tell me whatever it is you know."

Her eyes jumped from Clair to Gabby, then to Sophie, then back again. She drew in a deep breath. "One of our instructors, he has a bad lisp. It came on recently. A side effect, I think."

"Side effect of what?"

She came out from behind the counter and went to the wall on the left side of the office, to a series of employee photographs. She reached up and took one down off the wall. "Paul Upchurch. He's been with us for nearly ten years. About six months ago, he started smelling things that weren't there. He kept telling me I smelled like almonds and vanilla. I thought he was trying to be nice. He was always sweet. The nicest guy. Funny too. Then he started to get the shakes. They'd come on randomly and disappear just as fast. The owner pulled him out of rotation, made him see a doctor. We can't risk something happening to one of our instructors with a kid in the car. He went for a series of tests, over the course of a week or so. Anyway, the doctors said he had a brain tumor. I don't remember the specifics. He explained it, but it was all so technical, went over my head."

Cancer, Clair thought.

Insurance.

Oncologist.

Pharmaceuticals.

X-ray.

MRI.

Surgeon.

Hospital.

"Where is Paul Upchurch now?"

"Home, I imagine. He's had three surgeries that I'm aware of, maybe more. We haven't heard from him for over a week. I was thinking about driving over and checking on him if he didn't call in over the next few days."

"I need an address."

"Sure, okay." Her eyes were still on the picture in her hand. A man in his early thirties, smiling back. "Paul wouldn't hurt anyone, he's really the sweetest guy. Terrible, what he's going through. He's so young, very spiritual, a good soul too."

Clair was already dialing Nash.

110

Poole

Day 4 • 3:47 p.m.

Poole heard the warden step back into his office and close the door behind him.

"Oh hell, we've got a problem," the man said. "This is worse than we thought."

Another man had returned with the warden.

Poole stood up from the rickety chair at the warden's desk, his legs still stiff from the flight.

Warden Vina gestured to the man beside him. "This is Captain Fred Direnzo. He runs security for the prison. Captain, this is Frank Poole with the FBI. Please tell him what you told me."

Poole shook his hand. It was cold and clammy. The man was nervous.

He didn't like where this was going.

He didn't like it one bit.

Direnzo cleared his throat. "After SAIC Hurless called, we put a tight noose around Weidner. We didn't want to spook him, so the plan was to let him go about his normal day and keep an eye on him through the security cameras until you got here. This way, you could talk to him and he wouldn't get a chance to concoct some kind of story to cover his tracks. Always best to approach these scenarios with the element of surprise, right?"

Poole nodded.

Captain Direnzo glanced at the warden, then back at Poole. "He slipped out. I'm not sure how, but somehow he got out."

"When?"

The warden raised both hands, palms out. "Before you get too excited, we got him. I called the local PD, and they cornered him in his apartment, not far from here. Caught him in the middle of packing a bag. They're bringing him back, shouldn't be more than twenty or thirty minutes. Please continue, Captain."

Direnzo nodded. "The cameras are meant to monitor the inmates, not necessarily the guards, so there are blind spots in various places the guards can access. He changed out of uniform in the locker room and left with the three p.m. crew, but like the warden said, we got him. He's not going anywhere, I promise you that. We started backtracking Weidner's steps today, tried to get a better handle on whatever he was up to. Looks like he used a fraudulent court order to arrange for the release of a prisoner at 0800 this morning."

"Who?"

The warden handed a file to Poole. "We don't have a name on her. No ID, and she's not in the system. Just another Jane Doe, picked up for felony grifting. Here's the thing, though. Your detective, Sam Porter, he was here to see her yesterday, spent three and a half hours with her and her attorney in one of the interview rooms. He told me she was somehow connected to the 4MK murders in Chicago."

"Is there tape?"

"Cameras are disabled whenever a prisoner is in consultation with their attorney."

"Who's her attorney?"

"A local, Sarah Werner," the warden said. "We've got a trace on Jane Doe's ankle monitor. She's at her attorney's office. The data is live. She's not going anywhere without our knowledge."

"Can I see her cell?"

"We already tossed it. There's nothing there."

"I'd like to see it for myself."

• • •

Her cell truly had been tossed.

Poole stepped into the small room, feeling the walls on all sides closing in on him.

The mattress stood on its side, up against the wall, revealing the metal cot beneath it. Some clothing was scattered on the floor: a T-shirt and two pairs of sweatpants. The contents of a shampoo bottle and toothpaste tube had been emptied into the sink.

"Sometimes prisoners hide small objects in those. Shivs, mostly."

"Find anything?"

"Nope."

Poole stepped over to the mattress and began running his fingers across the edges, the seams.

"We checked that too," Captain Direnzo said. "Nothing."

Poole looked anyway but didn't find any openings in the material.

"Like I said, there's nothing here."

Poole sighed and dropped the mattress back onto the cot. The metal rattled. His eyes fixed on the wall, on the words scratched into the paint. They weren't alone. The entire cell was covered in text, years' worth of prisoners' thoughts captured in time, left for the next occupant. Poole knew these words, though. They jumped out at him:

Let us return <u>Home</u>, let us go back,
Useless is this reckoning of seeking and getting,
Delight permeates all of today.
From the blue ocean of death
Life is flowing like nectar.
In life there is death; in death there is life.
So where is fear, where is <u>fear</u>?
The birds in the sky are singing "No death, no <u>death</u>!"
Day and night the tide of Immortality
Is descending here on earth.

Home, fear, death, all underlined, as they were in the house back in Chicago. This was followed by one additional line:

Original sin will be the death of you.

"What the hell is that supposed to mean?"

Captain Direnzo stood behind him, reading over his shoulder. Poole hadn't noticed him enter the cell.

Poole ran a finger over the words, bits of paint flaking off beneath his touch. This had been added to the wall of words recently, new graffiti among the layers of old. "It's a play on the Bible, original sin. Shakespeare said it meant 'the sins of the father are to be laid upon the children.' Essentially, we are responsible for the sins of our ancestors, and they are responsible for ours."

"Shakespeare, huh? Our little Jane Doe didn't seem like much of a Shakespeare fan to me."

The radio on Captain Direnzo's shoulder beeped, and he pressed a button. The warden's voice crackled through the small speaker. "Captain? Weidner's back. Please escort our friend to interview room three when you're done."

"Copy that."

III

Diary

Night again.

No rain.

When Nurse Gilman brought my dinner, I asked her about the girl two doors down, but she wouldn't tell me anything about her, not even her name. I hoped for her name. Instead, she only placed my tray on my bed and smiled. "You should eat," she said.

I didn't want to eat. I wanted to know the girl's name. I wanted to speak to her. I wanted to get close enough to her to feel the warmth of her skin, her breath.

I heard her cry. I wanted to know if she could laugh.

I didn't eat.

I didn't notice when Nurse Gilman left my room.

My food went cold sitting on the corner of my bed.

I did not want to talk to the police.

I didn't want to meet the attorney general the doctor mentioned.

I most certainly did not want to be transferred to the place he talked about.

It was time I left.

Father would want me to puzzle it out. I had a plan.

At night there was one guard and two nurses. The doctors were gone, and everyone else was tucked in their rooms.

I would go at night.

I would wait for the girl to cry.

I didn't want her to cry.

I didn't want her to cry ever again, but I knew she would, and when she did, at least one of the nurses would open her door and go into her room to comfort her. When I was certain one of the nurses was in her room, I would pick my lock, go down the hall, and slip into her room too.

I would then make the nurse scream.

I hoped it would not be Nurse Gilman I found in the girl's room but one of the others. I liked Nurse Gilman. But even if it was Nurse Gilman, I would make her scream. Father taught me how. I would make her scream loud enough to draw the other nurse and the guard into the girl's room. I would get them all inside that room two doors down from mine and—

Let me stop here for a moment, give pause.

I want to be clear.

I don't want to hurt anyone.

Nobody needs to get hurt.

The last thing I want to do is hurt someone.

But I will.

They need to stay in that room, and I need to leave.

That is the only acceptable outcome.

I hope I won't have to hurt anyone.

I don't want the girl to see me hurt anyone.

I will lock them all in that room, then I will go to the doctor's office and get my knife. I know this is a risk, but I feel it is an acceptable risk.

Then I will leave.

I'll take the security camera footage with me. The recorder is probably at the guard's desk.

If I have my knife, if I had to hurt someone in that room, in the girl's room, if I had to hurt someone before I could get out and lock them inside, I might have to go back and finish hurting them. That's what Father would want me to do. Mother would tell me I had to hurt the girl too. I had to finish hurting them all, then take the camera footage and leave. Father and Mother would agree on this.

I did not want to hurt the girl, but I would.

A night escape presented one problem, a serious problem, one I wasn't sure I could overcome. I desperately wanted to say goodbye to Dr. Oglesby.

112

Nash

Day 4 • 4:06 p.m.

"Nash, can you hear me?" Espinosa's voice crackled in the small earpiece hidden beneath Nash's thick jacket hood.

Nash resisted the urge to tap at it. "Copy, SWAT leader, coming in clear."

"Ready in three." This was Brogan, out of breath, his voice slightly muffled. He and his team had parked one block over and were trudging through the snow, attempting to approach the back of the house unnoticed.

Clair had gotten an address for this Paul Upchurch from Designated Driver, and Klozowski had confirmed it with DMV and county records. His name appeared on the deed. He had owned the property for the better part of ten years.

Nash sat in Connie, two blocks down Upchurch's street. She had a wad of smoke caught in her throat. The exhaust sputtered as she coughed it out. A large Amazon.com box sat in the passenger seat. Inside the box were an assault rifle and two flat ten-pound weights. He wore body armor beneath his thick fleece coat.

"I can see the back of the house now," Brogan said. "We've got three windows on the second floor, a small one at the attic, and two on the ground level. Shit—"

"What is it?" Espinosa asked.

"The backyard is fenced in, four-foot chainlink. We're in two feet of snow as is, looks like the drifts nearly reach the top of the fence. We'll need to get over. I'm holding the team behind the house one yard over. As soon as we leave this location, we'll be exposed. I'd estimate thirty seconds to cross to the fence, ten to get over, another twenty to reach the back door and attempt a breach. We've got no place to hide in all that space. It's wide open back here."

"Copy," Espinosa said. "Nash, you go on my mark. If you see a doorbell, don't ring it. Knock. A lot of the doorbells in these old houses don't work, and you won't be able to tell from the outside— ringing it and waiting can cost us time. Just knock loudly. The moment you do, I'll give a five count. We'll give Upchurch time to answer. On five, our vans will come in from both ends of the road. Brogan and his guys will breach from the back door." He paused for a second. "You'll be standing on a small front porch. Looks like we've got nine steps with one turn leading up to it with a railing. It's going to be tight, not much room to maneuver. If Upchurch opens the door, rush him, run right over him with the weight of that box as a battering ram. My guys will be right behind you. They'll secure him. Just try to stun him and get out of the way."

"What if he doesn't answer?"

"If he doesn't answer, I'll need you to skirt out of our path. My team will come up behind you and take the door down, then they'll hit the house while Brogan's guys come in and secure from the back. Brogan?"

"Yes, sir?"

"Both teams will secure the main level. Then I want you to go down, get the basement and any subbasements. I'll head high and get the second floor and the attic."

"Copy."

"Nash. Do your best to stay out of our way. You don't have headgear on. I don't want to lose anyone to a lucky shot."

"I'd prefer not to get lost," Nash said.

"Hold—" Espinosa said. Then: "Our ambulances are here. Both will come in behind the SWAT vans on either end of the road, followed by the patrol cars to seal off the block on the off chance this guy gets out of the house. All teams in place?"

"Back of house, in place," Brogan said.

"East street, copy."

"West street, copy."

"Patrol 6, 144, 38, and 1218, all in place."

Silence.

"Nash?" Brogan again.

Nash drew in a deep breath. "I'm ready, copy."

"Okay, pull up on the house whenever you're ready. Number eighty-three on your right. Blue with white trim. We'll follow your lead."

"Copy."

Nash drew a deep breath through his mouth, held it, then let it out slowly from his nose.

This didn't do shit to calm him.

His hands were shaking. His heart was pounding. He had been involved with hundreds of raids over the course of his career, yet this feeling never diminished. Porter had once told him the day it did, the day you entered something like this calm, was the day you got shot.

"Ready or not, here we come," he said.

Connie's gearshift always stuck in Park. He put some muscle behind it and dropped her into Drive. The old car crept forward.

"Slow and steady, Nash, mindful of the ice. They plowed this morning, but the street's a mess again," Espinosa said. "Six more houses up on the right. You'll see it when you hit the top of that hill."

Nash's tires fought for purchase. There was a sweet spot when driving on snow and ice. Too fast or too slow, and cars slid, grappled for hold. Connie wanted to go faster, but he held her back. He saw the blue and white trim of the peaked roof first, and then the address numbers came into view next to the front door. There were a couple cars parked on the street, nothing but giant white mounds under all the snow, color, make, and model indiscernible. The space in front of the house was empty, though, and long enough that he didn't have to parallel park. Nash guided the car in and slipped her back into Park.

Espinosa crackled again in the small earpiece. "Nash at target, all teams stand by for my go."

Nash considered leaving the car running. Would a delivery driver leave the car running? He never paid attention. That made sense, though, in this cold. In and out, in and out, no reason to shut it off.

Upchurch could use your car to run.

He seriously doubted Upchurch would get all the way to the street, but the thought was enough for him to kill the engine and pocket the keys. Connie's motor sputtered again, realized she was no longer running, then went quiet with a groan.

Nash scooped up the Amazon box, opened his door, and stepped out into the storm. The snow had kicked up again, flakes an inch thick. He knew this would compromise visibility. The wind lashed at his bare cheeks as he stepped around the car and made his way to where he imagined the sidewalk probably was, lost beneath a blanket of snow.

"We've got movement," Espinosa said in his ear. "Second-floor curtain on the left."

Nash hadn't seen it.

He was at the steps.

He took them carefully, one hand holding the box, the other gripping the metal railing.

When he reached the small porch at the top, he saw a doorbell, began to reach for it, then remembered what Espinosa had told him only a few minutes earlier.

Focus, asshat. Focus.

He wanted to look behind him. He wanted to look up and down the street to confirm everyone was where they said they were, but he didn't. Instead, he knocked at the door—three heavy knocks, enough to hurt his knuckles.

From the corner of his eye, he caught sight of the SWAT vans approaching quickly from both ends of the street. They skidded to a stop in the middle of the road, the back doors already open, men in black body armor spilling out.

In his ear, Espinosa called out orders. "Go, go, go!"

Nobody answered the door.

Nash could see inside through a thin window beside the door—nobody. When he heard boots crunching through the snow on the steps behind him, he pivoted to the left, away from the door. Thomas or Tibideaux, he couldn't tell who, attacked the old wood-frame door with a large black metal battering ram—two hits and the deadbolt buckled, the door slammed in, and men in black streamed past him into the house.

Another loud bang rang out from the back, rattling the windows. A stun grenade.

Brogan: "We're in! I've got a body on the kitchen table! Female! Otherwise, kitchen clear!"

"Living room, clear!"

"Basement steps—heading down!"

"This is Espinosa, at second-floor landing." His voice low, a whisper. "Bathroom, clear. Bedroom one, clear. Bedroom two—"

His voice dropped off. Nash pushed the earpiece deeper into his ear.

"Freeze! Don't move! Don't—"

Nash pulled the assault rifle from the Amazon box and ran inside. The steps leading to the second floor were at the back of the living room. He took them two at a time. On the small landing at the top, Espinosa had his weapon trained on something or someone in the second bedroom. Another member of his team stood behind him, his gun pointed at the floor.

Nash watched Espinosa step into the room.

Brogan's voice came over his earpiece again, no longer shouting. "Oh hell, what the fuck is this . . . Christ . . . we've got another body down here, another girl. Basement otherwise clear."

113

Poole

Day 4 • 4:06 p.m.

Weidner sat in a metal chair bolted to the floor behind a matching table. His eyes darted around the room, his fingers fidgeted, tripping over one another, one hand on the table, the other on his lap.

Poole watched him through the one-way window. "Did he say anything when they picked him up?"

Warden Vina shook his head. "Didn't put up any kind of fight, just surrendered. He had a bag packed, a little over two thousand in cash, and a bus ticket to Chicago. Ten more minutes, and he might have slipped out."

"Mind if I talk to him?"

The warden shrugged. "He's not talking to me. I gave it a go already. Be my guest."

Captain Direnzo stood to Poole's left. He felt the heat rising off the man.

"He's all yours when I'm done," Poole told him.

Direnzo grunted but said nothing.

Poole opened the metal door separating the two rooms and stepped into the interview space, closing the door behind him.

Weidner looked up, then back to his hand on the table.

Poole took the chair across from him. "Hello, Vincent. I'm Special Agent Frank Poole with the FBI. Sounds like you have had quite an eventful morning. Why don't you start by telling me who Libby McInley is to you?"

Weidner's fingers stopped tapping. "Lawyer. Sarah Werner. Right now."

"You can most certainly go that route. I imagine you've worked in the system long enough to understand how this will play out if you do, though," Poole said. "If you don't help me, if you run interference with a lawyer, I can't help you. That means we go full boat on all the charges—aiding and abetting, orchestrating a prison break, fleeing law enforcement . . . you're looking at a lot of time. You answer a few questions, you help me, then I can help you." Poole leaned in closer, across the table. "I want to be clear on something, Vincent. I'm not here for you. You're a means to an end for me, that's all. I've got no reason to be hard on you. On the other side of that glass, though, you've got the warden and your captain, neither of whom are happy with you. I leave you here with them, and they'll make an example out of you. They'll use you to prove a point. You help me, I'll take you back with me to Chicago and we avoid all that. You were heading there anyway, right? Forget the bus. I've got a jet on the tarmac at Louis Armstrong."

Weidner leaned forward. "Lawyer. Sarah Werner. Now."

"Tell me about Anson Bishop. Why are you helping him?"

Weidner said nothing.

"Who was the woman you helped escape? Is she Bishop's mother?"

Silence.

Poole would spend the next two hours in this room with Weidner.

114

Nash

Day 4 • 4:07 p.m.

Nash stepped to the open doorway.

Espinosa was inside the small room, his weapon trained on a man sitting at a desk in front of the window, the same window where they caught movement from the outside.

The man had seen them approach.

He did not attempt to flee.

The man sat there, his back to them, his head hung low, staring at the desk. Both his hands rested on the desktop, fingers splayed. "I have no weapon."

Espinosa was on him then. He pulled a thick zip tie from the back of his belt, grabbed the man's left arm and yanked it behind his back, then the right, fastening them together behind the chair with the tie. The other SWAT officer, Tibideaux, kept his rifle trained on the man, the muzzle pointed at his head.

Nash's eyes were fixed on a large surgical incision beginning at the man's left ear and running up under a black knit cap. The flesh was red and inflamed, crusted with dried blood. He crossed the room, nearly tripping over a pile of clothing, and pulled off the black cap.

The man was almost bald, his head shaved a few days ago, the hair growing back in thin, irregular patches.

"The chemo does that. I'm sorry, I must look awful. I apologize."

He had a lisp, trouble with the word *sorry*.

"Paul Upchurch?" Espinosa said, lifting the man from the chair. "You have the right to remain silent . . ."

Espinosa's words dropped into the background. Nash found himself studying the room.

A little girl's room. Pink and bright. The small bed covered with a Hello Kitty quilt and stuffed animals. The walls were filled with drawings. Some appeared to be done by a child, and others by the talented hand of an adult, perfectly lined and colored.

In the corner of the room stood a mannequin, child-size, the shape of a little girl. The mannequin was dressed in little girls' clothing. A red sweater, blue shorts. As Espinosa dragged Paul Upchurch away from the desk, Nash saw the drawings where the man's hands had rested, drawings of a young girl in the same clothing as the mannequin. Apparently, he had been attempting to color them, but they had become a scribbled mess. Uncapped colored pens littered the desk.

"Please, don't hurt her," the man said as Espinosa and Tibideaux led him past the mannequin and out the room, his bloodshot eyes on the images.

"Detective Nash?" Brogan said from the earpiece.

"Yeah?"

"We need you in the kitchen."

"On my way."

When Nash reached the bottom of the stairs, he caught sight of Upchurch in the upper hallways, now surrounded by SWAT, moving toward the steps. Nash heard him sobbing over the exposed microphones, but he didn't care.

He crossed the small, sparsely furnished living room.

Two men flanked the kitchen table in the next room.

On the table was the body of a young girl, dressed in the same red sweater and blue shorts as the mannequin and drawings upstairs. Her hands lay crossed on her chest, palms up. Resting in her open palms—a small white box sealed tight with a black string.

"She's alive but unconscious," Brogan said, his fingers tenderly feeling her head. "I've got dry blood here, but I don't see a wound." He turned back to Nash. "We've got another girl in the basement. She's unconscious too. No visible wounds."

Nash's eyes fixed on the white box in her hands. "Could they be drugged?"

"Maybe."

The paramedics burst in then, surrounded her. A woman and two men. Within moments a blood pressure cuff was around her arm. One man held her eyelid open and studied her eye with a penlight, while the female paramedic held her wrist. "Pulse is sixty-three."

"Pressure is 102 over 70."

Fingers ran over her torso, head, and extremities. "No signs of physical trauma. I don't think the blood is hers. I think it's from there—" She nodded toward the puddle on the floor, streaked and crusted into the linoleum.

Nash hadn't noticed it until now.

They wheeled a stretcher through the door, set up next to the table.

"Wait." Nash pulled a pair of latex gloves from his pocket and carefully lifted the white box from her outstretched hands.

The paramedics moved the girl to the stretcher, began fastening her in.

Nash set the small box down on the table and tugged at the black string. It fell away.

Nash didn't notice the silence that fell over the room, nor did he realize everyone had stopped moving, including the paramedics. He lifted the small lid and set it aside.

Clearly one of Bishop's boxes.

Inside, a small silver key with blue plastic on the head, J.H.S.H. carved into the metal, rested on a bed of cotton. Nash lifted it out and set it beside the box. There was nothing else inside.

"I think that's a hospital locker key," the female paramedic said. She turned to the man still holding the blood pressure cuff. "Rick? What do you think? Stroger key, right? J.H.S.H.?"

He nodded, faced Brogan. "You said there was another girl?"

"She's in the basement. Same condition. Drugged, I think. Lacerations around her mouth, but they look superficial."

The paramedic pointed at the girl on the stretcher, at her leg. "She's got a needle mark on her thigh. Definitely a recent injection site. Based on her initial vitals, my guess would be propofol or some other sedative. She's stable, which is consistent with a pharmaceutical-induced state—high-grade, not homegrown. If she were unconscious due to trauma, her vitals would be irregular." He turned back to the others. "Kat, you and Diaz get her in the bus, ride with her to Stroger. Tell Mike to meet me down in the basement with a flatbed stretcher. We'll get the other girl and follow behind you. Draw blood en route, radio ahead for a full tox screen on both."

She nodded and took one end of the stretcher; her partner took the other, and together they wheeled the unconscious girl out of the small kitchen.

Nash followed the remaining paramedic, who disappeared down the stairs at the back of the kitchen into the mouth of darkness below, Brogan behind him.

115

Diary

For the next three days, I thought about kinesics.

I thought about Father.

I thought about Mother.

I thought about what the doctor had told me about the police and the bad place he said I would go.

I listened to the girl cry. In the deepest of night, I listened to her cry.

I pulled within myself and sealed out all the rest.

Her sobs were warm to me, they were her touch, her fingers reaching across the distance of our two rooms as if we were mere inches apart. I imagined her lying in her own bed, able to hear the pitter-patter of my heartbeat, and wanting to listen for it, the only thing to bring her comfort between the hellish thoughts that brought on those cries.

I imagine they came each day to take me to the doctor, but I did not remember these things. The world outside my mind became darkness, a black place, a distant void. As Father taught me, I suppressed time, I swam in it, got lost in the waves.

116

Nash
Day 4 • 5:23 p.m.

After more than an hour inside, he felt the walls of Upchurch's house closing in. Nash dialed Clair at the hospital. "Clair, this is bad, really bad. Bishop and this guy . . ." He pressed the phone to his ear and slowly crossed the basement, retracing his steps from the makeshift cage to the large freezer converted into a water tank next to the stairs, then back again, carefully using the clear step plates placed on the floor to prevent contamination. He found himself standing inside the cage. CSI techs scoured every surface. He watched one carefully collect bloody vomit from the far corner.

Clair sounded like she was walking and talking, out of breath. "We've positively ID'ed the girl you found upstairs as Kati Quigley, the Jehovah's Witness who went missing yesterday afternoon with the boy we found in the truck, Wesley Hartzler. She's stable and in ICU, still unconscious. The tox screen confirmed propofol in her system. They're going to let her sleep it off. As soon as she wakes up, I'll talk to her. She has several electrical burn marks on her body. They appear to be superficial, no permanent damage."

Nash's eyes dropped to a series of car batteries positioned beside the water tank. He had already told Clair about that. He didn't want to think about it. "How about Larissa Biel?"

Clair said something to someone else, then returned to the call.

"She's in critical condition. Drugged too, which looks like a blessing. She went into surgery about thirty minutes ago." Clair's voice dropped lower. "They made her swallow glass. She has lacerations in her mouth, her throat, her stomach. She's all torn up inside. I can't imagine how painful that must have been."

Nash closed his eyes. "What are we looking at here, Clair? This is way beyond anything Bishop has done in the past. What is his connection to Upchurch?"

"I've been trying to reach Poole, but his phone is going to voice mail. Kloz has been looking for something to tie the two of them together since we got his name, but he's coming up blank. We've always profiled Bishop as a loner. None of it makes sense. We think they converted the freezer into some kind of deprivation tank."

"A what?"

"A deprivation tank. They were popular in the fifties. Salt water is heated to exactly 93.5 degrees, basically skin temperature. Once you're inside, all your senses are gone—you can't see or hear anything from the outside. With the water at skin temp, you'd feel like you were floating. They're supposed to be relaxing, a Zen thing."

Nash's eyes fell to the rusty metal of the jumper cables next to the tank. "This was anything but relaxing."

Clair's phone beeped. "Hold on a second. I've got another call."

Nash watched one of the CSI techs bag a green quilt from the corner of the cage, gently folding it before placing it inside the large evidence bag.

He had to get out of there.

He took the stairs back to the kitchen and slowly crossed the room, waiting for Clair to return. When she finally did, he was on the second level, outside the room with the mannequin and all the drawings.

"Nash?"

"Yeah, I'm still here."

"That was the patrol team taking Upchurch to Metro. He passed out in the back of their car. They're rerouting to here."

"Passed out?"

"They said he started screaming, tried to reach his head but couldn't with his hands cuffed behind his back. Banged his head against the door. Next best thing, I guess. They think he had a seizure or something."

"Could it be some kind of trick? An attempt to escape?"

"Doesn't sound like it, but we're not taking any chances. I told them not to open the back until they get here. The patrol car with the key you sent over just arrived. I'm on my way down to grab it, see if I can match it to a locker. I'll ask the officers to stick around and help secure Upchurch. He's not going anywhere."

"Okay, let me know what you find. I'll stay here until CSI wraps up." He had entered the small room. Some of the drawings had been bagged, others laid out on the bed, CSI photographing all.

117

Clair

Day 4 • 6:07 p.m.

Clair followed an orderly off the elevator to the third floor, down the corridor, toward the east end of the building. The woman was talking to her over her shoulder. "This is the only other locker room we have. If that key didn't fit any of the lockers downstairs, it's got to be up here."

Clair had been all over the hospital, stopping only to visit Kati Quigley (still unconscious) and supervise the unloading of Paul Upchurch. He had been cuffed to a gurney upon arrival at the emergency entrance and brought to a private room with two uniforms stationed outside.

He wasn't going anywhere.

She had been told he was conscious but physically unable to speak, the result of whatever attack he suffered on the way in. The attending physician had been instructed to contact her the moment he uttered anything coherent.

The orderly stopped at a door at the end of the hall and unlocked it with a key from her ring. The lights came on automatically. She held the door as Clair stepped inside. "Thanks, Sue."

"I wish you had two, this would go faster," Sue said. "Left side is women, right side is men."

Lockers lined all the outer walls, with two more rows positioned at the center of the room, benches spaced between. A wall separated the two halves.

Clair took out her cell phone to try Poole again.

"That's not going to work in here," Sue said. "This whole floor is a dead space because of the radiology equipment down the hall. You'll either have to go upstairs or down to the first level. They have repeaters down there."

Clair frowned and dropped the phone back into her pocket.

Poole would have to wait.

Turning to the first row of lockers on her right, she slipped the key into the one at the top right, tried to turn it, then pulled it out and moved on to the next locker. One down, about three million more to go.

118

Diary

The doctor was staring at me.

Back in his office.

My knife on the corner of his desk.

A heavy hand on my shoulder belonging to someone I could not see.

The doctor leaned in close.

His breath smelled of onions.

"Anson?"

I should take my knife.

I should forget my plan and take my knife and—

I screamed.

I screamed so loud the sound burned at my throat, a thousand razorblades rushing up and out.

Suppressed time.

Back in my room.

On my bed.

Staring at the ceiling.

I wanted to leave, but the girl did not cry anymore.

My plan did not work if she did not cry.

More days of this.

More nights of this.

Why didn't I take my knife?

119

Poole

Day 4 • 6:38 p.m.

Frank Poole stepped out of the interview room for the umpteenth time and leaned against the wall in the hallway. If he didn't think he'd break his hand, he'd probably punch the cinder block.

"That guy is not gonna talk," Direnzo said. "I'd offer to take a run at him if I thought it would help, but I've seen enough guys like that. You've got a double whammy—as a guard, he knows the routine better than most, and he won't crack. He knows you're only allowed to push so far."

"Did our team find anything at his apartment?"

The captain shook his head. "The man lives in a shoebox, and I use the term *lives* loosely. No pictures on the wall, no television, no furniture other than a folding table and chair in the kitchen and a mattress on the bedroom floor. My guys said they caught him packing, but I get the impression he was already packed. I don't think he ever unpacked. Nola was a temporary stop for him. He got that woman out this morning, his work here is done. He was moving on."

"What about Stateville?"

"Warden Vina has been chasing the Stateville warden all afternoon. No luck yet. The guy is either very busy or ducking his calls." Direnzo clucked his tongue. "I've been at this for going on twenty-five years now. I'm suspicious of everyone, so feel free to completely ignore me, but my gut says that with your boss calling, my boss calling, and who knows who else calling, the Stateville warden is scrambling to clean house internally. Unless someone drops in, I don't think anyone will hear from him until he's got his shit together and a nice, plausible story in place for whatever Weidner did over there."

Libby McInley.

Direnzo turned to the one-way window. Weidner's expression had only tightened in the past few hours, resolved. "Here's problem number two—he asked for a lawyer more than two hours ago. Even by New Orleans standards, you're pushing more than one limit there. Technically, neither of us should be talking to him anymore."

"You said you called her, right?"

"Yeah, no answer, though. Straight to voice mail on her cell and office numbers."

"How about Jane Doe?"

"We let her be, just like you asked. She hasn't left the general vicinity of Werner's office. The tracker in her ankle monitor has her across the street in an alley. There's some abandoned buildings over there, not much to look at. She's waiting for something or someone for sure. New Orleans PD has undercover cars at all the egress points. They're keeping a safe distance, monitoring all traffic in and out. We're thinking she'll cut the monitor off when her ride shows up. She won't get far."

"No sign of Porter?"

"Nothing yet. Looks like he left her there. Must've gone with Werner somewhere and hasn't come back. Or Werner is inside and taking a page from the Stateville warden and ignoring her phone. No way to know for sure. She lives in an apartment upstairs. She could hole up for days without a reason to come out."

When Poole had updated SAIC Hurless, his supervisor had felt Porter busted the woman out and Bishop was coming for her. Most likely they were set to meet in that alley. The lawyer wouldn't risk an exchange in her office. Outside her office, she could claim some kind of deniability. Poole didn't understand why she involved herself at all. Why risk her license? Her livelihood? Possibly, even her freedom.

Of course, all Hurless's suspicions were based on his theory that

Sam Porter was working with Bishop, but that still didn't feel right to Poole. He tried to believe it, tried to make the theory work, but something didn't fit.

Hurless had left strict instructions—watch for Porter, use Bishop's mother as bait. Monitor the area, close in when Bishop was spotted. Until then, hang back.

Poole was spinning wheels. He had nothing else. "Can you give me a ride out there?"

120

Clair

Day 4 • 7:13 p.m.

When Clair slipped the silver key engraved with j.h.s.h. into locker 1812 and turned it, she didn't expect anything to happen. She expected the key to freeze in place like it had on every other locker she'd tried in the past few hours. She didn't expect it to turn, and she surely didn't expect it to unlock.

"Sue?"

Her orderly/locker tour guide glanced up from a paperback copy of the latest Nora Roberts novel and pulled the earbuds from her ears. "Yes, ma'am?"

"Who does locker eighteen-twelve belong to?"

Sue brushed a strand of blond hair from her eyes and began flipping through the folder at her side. She stopped on the third or fourth page and ran a finger down the list. "That is . . . shit."

"Whose is it?"

"Dr. Randal Davies, Oncology. He . . . he died, day before last. The whole hospital is talking about it. Severe stroke, but he was healthy as a horse. His daughter . . ."

Clair had stopped listening.

She tugged at the locker door, opened it slowly.

Inside she found a thick folder, nearly two inches thick. Sitting atop the folder was a bright red apple. A hypodermic needle stuck out from the side.

Clair pulled a pair of latex gloves from her pocket and slipped them on. "Sue? Can you get my bag? I think it's still in the admin office." She would need evidence bags.

With two fingers, she gingerly removed the apple from the locker and turned it in her hand. The flesh around the needle was slightly discolored, but otherwise the apple showed no sign of age. She carefully set it down on the bench behind her and reached back in for the folder, both hands this time. She removed the bulky folder from the locker and placed it on the bench beside the apple.

The label read: PAUL EDWARD UPCHURCH.

Inside the folder she found at least two hundred pages, some fastened to the sides, others loose. Reports, notes, test results, imaging—all dating back nearly a year. At the very top, written in familiar blocky letters, was a note:

Hello, Detective Norton, or maybe Detective Nash? I imagine one of you. I hope you have been well. Better than others.

B

121

Diary

I haven't been writing.

I've lost track of the days.

Father would be mad.

Father would be mad indeed.

It was 3:24 in the afternoon, I knew that much, my internal clock, but I had no idea of the day or how long I had been here now. So much of the same, each sameness blurring into the next.

When the door to my room clicked with the turn of the lock, I looked up to find Dr. Oglesby standing in the opening.

"How are you today, Anson?"

"Fine."

The word came out soft and low and seemed to take him by surprise, the first time I had spoken or responded to him in days.

I sat on the edge of my bed, then stood up, stretching my legs.

Normally, the doctor smiled when he came for me for our sessions. Today he did not. His eyes darted around my room—my empty lunch tray on the dresser, yesterday's clothing rumpled in a pile on the chair—the paper clip was tucked under the corner of my mattress and I thought I saw his eyes linger even there for a second, although I was sure to be careful when I placed it, mindful of the camera.

"Let's go, Anson."

He opened the door wider and gestured for me to go first.

At the nurses' station, Nurse Gilman did not smile as we passed; instead, she looked down at some papers on her desk and shuffled them.

The girl's door was open.

I looked inside, hoping to see her propped up on her bed. She was not in the room. There were no sheets on the bed, and the room was completely empty—more so, soulless.

"Where is she?"

The doctor put a hand on my shoulder, pressed me forward. "Come along now, Anson."

There were two men sitting outside the doctor's office, both in rumpled suits. They looked up as we approached.

One of the men stood up. "Is this him?"

The doctor's grip on my shoulder tightened, and then he let go. "Detective, this is Anson Bishop. Anson, this is the detective I told you about, Detective Welderman, and his partner, Detective . . . I'm sorry, I forgot your name."

The other man stood up, smoothing out his slacks. "Stocks, Ezra Stocks."

"Go ahead and turn around, Anson. Put your hands behind your back," Detective Welderman said.

I did as I was told.

Cold steel slipped over my wrists and clicked tight.

Handcuffs.

The detective clicked both sides one more time, until they bit into my wrists. "They're tight."

"Yep."

I thought about the paper clip under my mattress. I could open the handcuffs with the paper clip.

"Let's go." Welderman again, pushing at my back.

Detective Stocks led the way past the guard desk, through the metal door that opened with an electronic buzz, then down a series of hallways, an elevator, and finally out the front door. I could hear Dr. Oglesby behind me, talking in a hushed tone with Detective Welderman, but I could not make out the words.

A white Chevy Malibu waited at the curb, the paint covered in a layer of dirt and grime. Stocks opened the back door.

I planted my feet firmly on the ground. Welderman pulled up on the handcuffs, causing my arms to rotate painfully at my shoulders. "Keep moving, kid."

He pushed me toward the car.

"Can I speak to the boy for one second? Privately?" Dr. Oglesby said from behind me.

"Keep it fast." The grip on my handcuffs dropped away, and both detectives went around to the front of the car. Stocks pulled a pack of cigarettes from his pocket. Welderman raised a hand. "No time," I heard him say.

The doctor turned me toward him and kneeled on the sidewalk. "I gave you every opportunity to talk to me, Anson, every opportunity. There is nothing else I can do for you."

"Where is the girl?" I asked. "Where did she go?"

"You need to cooperate with these men. You're young, you can get through this."

"I want my knife back."

The doctor leaned in close. I thought he was going to hug me. Then came a whisper in my ear: "What knife?"

The doctor stood up, took a step back from me. "Good luck, Anson. I wish you nothing but the best."

He gave the detectives a wave, and both men returned.

Stocks forced me into the backseat, closing the door with a thud.

122

Porter

Day 4 • 8:01 p.m.

They made surprisingly good time.

Porter glanced over on more than one occasion and caught the speedometer deep in the red, though Sarah insisted that her BMW was police-proof.

As the lights of Chicago came into view, Sarah finally slowed, not because she was worried but because they hit traffic.

"Take exit 26A," Jane said. She hadn't said a word for the entire drive.

Porter had tried to get her talk early on, prompting her with leading questions from Bishop's diary—questions about the Carters, Franklin Kirby and Riggs, her husband, even Bishop—but she said nothing, only looked at him with steely eyes or back out the window at the rolling countryside.

"Chatty Cathy finally speaks," Sarah said, merging to the right. "Where exactly are we going?"

"Take exit 26A," she repeated.

"26A, check. Then what?"

She said nothing.

Sarah rolled her eyes. "Fine, but give me enough warning to get in the right lane so we don't get caught in traffic."

The city grew near and soon wrapped around them, the tall buildings looming above.

The air *looked* cold.

Snow had fallen recently, every surface covered in a bright white sheen. Porter knew by morning the snow along the highway would take on a dull gray look, black in some spots, but for now it was crisp and white. His jacket was still in the trunk—there had been no need for it in New Orleans. Sarah was still in short sleeves.

The BMW slowed, and Sarah followed the edge of the off-ramp as it twisted down and below the highway. The plows had been through, but he cautioned her anyway, unsure of how much experience she had driving in these conditions.

"At the bottom of the ramp, take Independence and follow it south to Hamilton."

Porter knew the area. They were heading toward West Garfield and K-town. "This is not a good neighborhood."

"We're not here to sightsee. We're also late."

"It's two minutes past eight," Porter told her.

"Anson was very clear."

"I don't like this," Sarah said, her eyes on the various men standing at street corners, eyeing them as they drove past.

South Independence Boulevard made a slight jog to the right, then became North Hamilton Avenue.

"Make a left on Washington."

Sarah did as she was told.

"There. Pull in there. Pull around back."

Porter pressed his head against the window and looked up. "This is the Guyon Hotel, isn't it? I thought they demoed this place years ago."

Jane stared out the window like she'd caught sight of an old friend. "Many people have tried, but she's a fickle bitch. Just swats the developers away like mosquitoes. The federal government declared it a historic landmark in '85. She's not going anywhere."

Sarah pulled into the lot at the back and shifted the car into Park. "Now what?"

"Now, we go inside."

"How? It's boarded up."

Porter studied the building. Sarah was right. Plywood covered every opening from the ground level to the fifth floor. The fifth was out of reach, the fire escapes long ago removed. A chainlink fence also surrounded the structure. Places like this were a haven for gangs and the homeless.

"As I've already pointed out, we're late. Let me out of this car."

123

Poole

Day 4 • 8:07 p.m.

"Are you sure she's in there?" Poole had been on his share of stake-outs, more than he could count at this point, but his patience had come to an end. He caught himself drumming his fingers on the passenger door while Direnzo flipped through a paperback.

"I can call in again," Direnzo said. "But as of fifteen minutes ago, she was in that alley. There's no other way out. We've got movement and vitals. She's there."

Poole had called SAIC Hurless twice since they arrived, and he insisted they only observe, wait for Bishop. Porter wouldn't bust her out of prison only to leave her in an alley. They were coming back.

Poole not only believed Hurless was wrong, but he was also beginning to believe Bishop was nowhere near here. Everything about this situation felt wrong. "What does it take to remove one of your monitors?"

"We went over this back at the prison—can't be done."

"Anything can be done. Tell me again."

"Each monitor has a unique key that can't be copied. If someone cuts it off, we see a continued drop in vitals. There's an alarm. The key for Jane Doe number 2138 is right where it's supposed to be. We checked that too."

"Does Weidner have access to the keys?"

"We have her key," Direnzo said. "There's only one."

Poole cursed himself for not realizing it sooner. "Weidner knows you'd check the key—he'd switch them. He'd swap the key with one you wouldn't be looking for so nothing would be out of place. That's what I would do."

"You go in that alley and we're blown. There's no going back."

Poole was already out the door.

124

Clair
Day 4 • 8:08 p.m.

Clair hung up with Nash.

He was still at the house.

She and Kloz had Upchurch's patient file spread out on a table, searching the text. They found references to everyone currently in the cafeteria, but it didn't stop there. They found a dozen other names scattered throughout the various documents. She had patrol cars running all over the city picking up anyone mentioned and bringing them back here.

"Here's one more," Kloz said. "Angelique Waltimyer. She's a nurse in the ER downstairs. Looks like Upchurch came in about a month ago and was held overnight."

Clair nodded to Sue behind her. They had recruited the orderly in their roundup efforts. Sue was already on the phone, dialing downstairs.

"I don't care if she's plugging a gunshot wound with her index finger. I want her up here," Clair said, returning to the folder.

"This guy has had three surgeries so far, all performed here," Kloz said. "They might as well install a zipper on his head. They scrape away the tumor and it comes right back. The first one was the size of a golf ball . . . and get this—it grew that big in only a few weeks."

"They're prepping him for another surgery right now," Clair muttered. "I hope the fucker dies on the table."

"I'm not sure how he's even still alive. They took out so much of his brain, he could be a politician."

"Detective?"

Clair looked up. Dr. Hirsch stood in the open doorway. A balding man of about fifty, with small round glasses and a bright purple tie. "Yes?"

"Kati Quigley just woke up. Her parents are with her."

Clair glanced at Klozowski.

"Go, I've got this," he said.

Clair rushed out the door, the doctor behind her. In the elevator, she asked, "Any word on Larissa Biel?"

Dr. Hirsch scratched at his chin. "Still in surgery. I think she'll pull through, but repairing this kind of damage can be time-consuming. She's with Dr. Crandal. He's a phenomenal surgeon. I know he called for a specialist to look at her throat, specifically her vocal cords. If there's going to be any permanent damage, it will be speech related. Too early to tell, but we should know soon. I'd expect them to be in there at least another hour."

The elevator doors opened. They turned left and followed the hall.

Kati Quigley was in a private room on the second floor, a uniformed officer stationed outside her door. Clair could see her through the door's thin observation window. She was sitting up, her hands animated. Her mother and father stood on the left side of her bed. The doctor pulled open the door and ushered Clair inside. Kati and her parents all looked up.

Kati's father stepped between Clair and the bed. "Oh no, she needs to rest. She can give a statement once she's gotten her strength back." He had been wearing a suit, but his jacket and tie were on one of the chairs in the corner. Kloz said he was a lawyer.

"It's fine, Dad. I'm okay. I want to help."

Kati's mother reached down and squeezed her daughter's hand. "Of course you do, but your father's right."

Clair felt the roadblock going up and wanted to knock these people over and push past them, but instead she counted to five in her head, drew a breath, and forced a smile. "I completely understand, Mr. and Mrs. Quigley, I do. I promise, I won't take a lot of her time. It's always best to do this when events are fresh. Dr. Hirsch here will monitor her. If at any time she's under duress, we'll stop."

"Dammit, Dad. This is important!"

"Kati!" Her mother glared.

"I'm sorry, Mom," Kati said. "Please let me talk to her."

Her father didn't move. "You have the monster who did this in custody, right?"

"We think there were two."

"Please, Dad?"

He closed his eyes, shaking his head. "Okay, but only for a minute."

"Thank you." Clair stepped past him and sat on the right side of the bed, opposite Kati's mother. She took out her cell phone and set it on top of the sheets. She reached out and took Kati's free hand, the one with the IV in it. "I'm so glad you're safe. Do you mind if I record this?"

"No. It's okay."

"Please tell me everything you remember. Start from the beginning and take your time. Sometimes the smallest of details can be the most important."

Kati nodded. Her face crinkled and she sneezed.

"Bless you," Mrs. Quigley said.

Clair handed Kati a tissue from the bedside table.

The girl dabbed at her watering eyes.

125

Poole
Day 4 • 8:08 p.m.

Poole rounded the corner, and a dozen eyes were upon him from within the alley, frozen stares. A woman of about fifty with colored beads in her tangled gray hair stepped aside and pressed against the wall of the building at her back. With her foot, she tugged a cardboard box to her side.

Poole raised his badge. She turned and nodded toward the back of the alley.

The alley was about eight feet wide and thirty deep, lined with large cardboard boxes and makeshift tents constructed of anything from sheets to garbage bags held together with duct tape. The air stank of piss and rotten food.

She nodded again.

Poole followed her gaze.

A refrigerator box along the wall at the left about twenty feet in.

The people in the alley began to move away from it, spreading out in all directions. Three ran past him and out the front. Poole heard officers grab them at the sidewalk.

He approached the refrigerator box with his hand on the butt of his gun. When only a few feet away, he kicked at the side. "I'm Special Agent Frank Poole with the FBI. I need you to come out of there."

A hand poked out the opening at the opposite end, then another.

Poole watched as a man in a filthy blue shirt and jeans shuffled out. "Don't shoot."

Direnzo came up behind Poole, his weapon drawn. "Shit."

The homeless man had an ankle monitor on his leg.

Poole spun past Direnzo. "Werner's office! Now!"

126

Porter

Day 4 • 8:09 p.m.

"Pop the trunk," Porter said.

They had parked just outside the fence at the rear corner of the hotel.

Porter was first out of the car. He rounded the back and grabbed his coat as well as Sarah's. After the warmth of New Orleans, it felt like he was stepping out into a bucket of ice. He handed Sarah's coat to her as she exited the car, then opened the back door and helped their passenger to her feet. He draped his coat over her shoulders.

"Aren't you the gentleman," she said.

Porter didn't care whether or not she was cold. He wanted to further restrict the use of her hands. Although still handcuffed, he didn't trust her in the slightest. "How are we getting in?"

"Oh, I think you already know." She ducked through a break in the chainlink fence and started across the parking lot toward the back of the building with Sarah chasing after her.

Porter understood then. He ran back around to the passenger side and opened the glove box. He tore open the plastic bag with the chain containing the locket and key.

His eyes fell on the second bag with the knife.

He tore that bag open too, dropping both into his pocket before closing the door, and ran after the two women.

Without plows to attend to the grounds, the snow surrounding the Guyon Hotel had climbed to staggering heights. The wind drove it against the building and swept drifts up to nearly the second floor along the back and sides. The white powder swirled loosely at the surface, a fine mist over a lake of white.

Porter quickly realized there were three sets of tracks in the snow ahead of him. From Sarah, Bishop's mother, and another. Bishop was already here, most likely alone. His tracks had already begun to fill back in. A few hours, and they would be gone altogether.

He caught up with the women at a heavy metal door in a small brick alcove beside a loading dock.

Sarah stood off to the side, glaring at the other woman.

Bishop's mother was humming "Baby, It's Cold Outside" behind a Cheshire cat grin.

She nodded at the deadbolt. "Chop chop, Detective."

Porter frowned at her, then shoved a hand into his pocket and retrieved the chain with Libby's locket and key.

His hand was shaking when he fumbled it into the lock. He wanted to blame that on the cold.

The key turned smoothly. Someone had recently oiled the lock. The deadbolt slid back with a clunk. Porter tugged the door open and gestured the women inside, pulling it shut behind him, the icy wind arguing with a howl.

Sarah pulled out her cell phone and activated the flashlight.

They were standing in a kitchen. Or, more appropriately, what used to be a kitchen.

Most of the appliances had been stripped away long ago along with many of the industrial stainless steel tables. All that remained was the unwanted clutter. The ceiling had given way in various places, adding chunks of plaster and rotten boards to the mix.

"What a hellhole," Sarah said, sweeping the light across the room.

Porter stepped deeper into the room, avoiding the mess on the floor. "Where's Bishop?"

"This way." Jane Doe shuffled forward, her ankles still in restraints.

Porter and Sarah followed her past a series of rusted-out stoves and some old wooden crates stacked floor to ceiling on the left.

A set of swinging double doors with round windows at eye level had once separated the kitchen from the lobby, but now one door was lying flat on the floor and the other held to the wall at a precarious angle from the remaining hinge. Candles flickered from the other side of the opening.

They stepped through into the lobby, coming out behind a counter overlooking the once grand space. A popcorn machine, now old and filled with spiderwebs, stood in the far corner.

"A medium-size buttered popcorn contains more fat than a breakfast of bacon and eggs, a Big Mac and fries, and a steak dinner combined," Bishop said from somewhere in the room. "Maybe that's why we never ate popcorn at the Bishop house, right, Mother?"

Porter peered out into the dark, at the shadows dancing against the walls and ceiling to some unheard song.

"Over here, Sam. You'll need to give your eyes a little time to adjust."

A bell dinged, and Porter swung around toward the front door, which was all boarded up. Bishop stood beside the large door, next to the bellhops' station. There was a gun in his hand, but the barrel pointed toward the floor. It looked like a .38. His hair was longer than the last time Porter had seen him, the scruff of a beard covering his face. Porter had expected a disguise of some sort, possibly dyed hair, but no—this was the Bishop he knew, the man who haunted him.

Porter took a few steps forward, putting himself between Bishop and Sarah. "You never struck me as the gun type."

"This?" Bishop raised it and smiled, waved the gun about. "Desperate times."

Bishop peered past Porter. "Hello, Mother. How have you been?"

Before she could answer, Porter took another step forward. "Where's the bomb, Bishop? You said if I got her here, if I brought her to you, you'd tell me where you planted it. You said you'd release the girls too."

"I did say that, didn't I?" He scratched at the side of his head with the stubby barrel of the .38. "I do believe I gave you a timetable too, didn't I? You're late, Sam, woefully late. It's never polite to keep someone waiting, but under the current circumstances, tardiness can be downright deadly. I always pegged you as Mr. Punctual."

Porter felt the weight of the knife in his pocket pressing against his leg.

"We got here as fast as we could," Sarah said from behind him.

Bishop dropped the gun and paced in a circle around the bellhop station. "I suppose you did. That *was* quite a drive, wasn't it? A bit presumptuous of me to make this so difficult for you, for *all* of you." He leaned back, the old wood frame groaning under his weight. "You can relax, nobody has died, not yet. There's always time for that. Unfortunately, your lateness does cut into the time we get to spend together. I had hoped we would have a chance to talk, to discuss everything you've seen in the past few days, but now, now I'm afraid we simply can't. Not to the extent such a conversation deserves, anyway. That bomb is still tick, tick, ticking away. Our Boy Scout here would like to see to that. I think we all have pressing matters to attend to."

Bishop took a few steps forward, the .38 at his side. "You could have removed her shackles, Sam. They're a little barbaric, don't you think?"

His mother shuffled forward, closer to him. "It's good to see you, Anson. So good."

Bishop smiled. "You remember this place, don't you? So many fond memories for you, I'm sure." He turned and looked up at the ornate ceiling, his eyes drifting over the crumbling millwork and intricate patterns above. "There are ghosts in these walls, Sam. Can you hear them screaming? I can, like it was yesterday — Libby loudest of all."

Porter reached over and grabbed the woman at his side by her hair. He pulled her close, the sound of her chains jangling beneath his coat. With his free hand, he snatched the knife from his pocket, flicked open the blade, and pressed the sharp steel against her pale, exposed throat. "This is the last time I am going to ask, you crazy shit. Where is the bomb? Where are the girls?"

Bishop smiled and raised the gun. "Thanks for bringing my knife,

Sam. Maybe we can swap for the gun when we're done here? I like that knife."

He started across the room, the barrel growing larger with each step.

The woman pushed back against Sam. "We're even now, Anson. I can't run anymore. I did everything you asked of me. Everything."

"Yeah? Almost," Bishop said.

The .38 went off with an explosion loud enough to rattle what remained of the windows.

Sarah screamed.

Jane Doe's head jerked into Sam's chest.

"Now, maybe," Bishop said. "Yeah, now I think we're even."

127

Poole

Day 4 • 8:09 p.m.

"It's that one!" Direnzo shouted. "The shotgun with the green and white trim!"

Poole darted across the street, the alley at his back. A taxi screeched to a stop, fishtailing. The driver shouted something, but Poole couldn't make out what he said, wasn't sure he wanted to.

Werner's office was dark.

He peered through one of the windows and saw the dim outline of a deserted desk and some chairs at the back of the room.

No movement.

At the door, he pounded with his fist. "Sarah Werner. I'm Special Agent Frank Poole with the FBI. I need you to open this door!"

No response from inside.

He shuffled back onto the small porch and tried to see through one of the second-floor windows. Too dark.

Poole returned to the door, tried the knob.

Locked.

"Sarah Werner!"

He pounded again.

Nothing.

Poole pulled the Glock from his shoulder holster and used the butt to break one of the door's windowpanes. He reached through, mindful of the glass, and twisted the deadbolt.

He opened the door and stepped inside, his free hand groping the wall until he found the light switch and flicked it on.

"Sarah? Sam? I'm coming in! If you're in here, I need you to come downstairs with your hands above your head."

From above, the floor groaned. The barrel of his gun instinctively pointed toward the sound. Poole couldn't be sure if it was the result of someone moving upstairs or one of the many sounds made by old buildings as they sagged and settled slowly into the dirt.

He crossed the room, his eyes darting over each shadow, every alcove. The office offered little in the way of hiding places, even with all the clutter.

At the back of the small office, a hallway led off further into the dark, the office lights held back by the opening and the ornate millwork. Poole drew in a breath and started toward it. His gun rounded the corner first, and as he followed, he prepared to pull the trigger on whatever waited on the other side. He found nothing but a staircase leading to the second floor. He considered turning on these lights too, then thought better of it. If someone was up there, they didn't need to know he was on his way just yet. Let them think he was still downstairs.

He tentatively placed a foot on the first step, then followed it with his weight, unsure of whether or not it would betray him with some kind of sound. Nothing but silence.

Poole ascended the stairs, his eyes adjusting to the dark above, the shape of an opening coming into focus as he drew nearer, some kind of alcove, a closed door beyond that.

His hand wrapped around the cold metal of the doorknob. He turned it slowly, careful not to make a sound. The lock wasn't engaged. There was a slight pop as the cylinder pulled free of the strike box.

The door swung into the room.

The smell hit him all at once.

Decay, rot.

The lights were off, the room crowded with the dark.

Poole stepped inside and switched on the light, then wished he hadn't.

A woman stared at him from the couch, her vacant eyes clouded over, milky. She slumped there, leaning awkwardly to the side. Her face was pale, the blood having drained away to lower ground some time ago. This accentuated the dark, black hole in her forehead, a puckered gunshot wound. She had been eating when it happened, a plate of something unrecognizable spilled on her lap and the vacant cushion beside her.

Her killer probably stood right where Poole did now, surprising her from this very doorway.

He approached the body, knelt at her side.

This wasn't the woman from the prison, couldn't be. This body had been here for at least a week, maybe as long as two, decomposition hungrily eating away at what was once a living thing. She wore a silver ring on her right hand, the finger plump and swollen like a hot dog around the metal.

"Shit," Captain Direnzo said from behind him. "That's Sarah Werner."

Poole hadn't heard him come in.

128

Porter

Day 4 • 8:14 p.m.

"Mother, give Sam your phone, please," Bishop said, smoke from the gun distorting the air at his face.

Sarah's hand reached out, held the phone out to him. "Anson, baby, why would you tell this nice man your father was dead? We raised you better than that. That whole little book of yours is scribbled full of lies."

The body fell from Porter's hands, crumpled at his feet.

He dropped the knife.

His heart thudded.

Bishop knelt, retrieved the knife, and set the .38 down on the counter next to the popcorn machine.

"Not all of the book, Mother. Only some. Little white lies here and there. You were always so good at those."

Porter's eyes flew from Sarah's outstretched hand, to the phone, to the body on the ground.

"You look pale, Sam. You should sit. I worry about you sometimes." Bishop reached to his side and grabbed an old wooden chair from a pile of ruined furniture and shook the dust off. The floral print on the back and seat was riddled with holes, worn through to the stuffing. Something had chewed on one of the legs. Bishop slid the chair behind him and Porter dropped into it, his own legs becoming Jell-O.

"What the fuck is this?" he breathed. "I don't . . ."

"Language, Sam."

Sarah rolled her eyes. "Christ, Anson. You're no better than your father."

Porter looked down at the body at his feet. The bullet had left a small, round hole in her forehead and very little blood. There was no exit wound, probably a hollow-point, lodged inside. Her eyes stared forward, her last words trapped forever on her lips.

We're even now, Anson. I can't run anymore. I did everything you asked of me.

Everything.

"Who . . . ?" The word sputtered out, caught on the edge of his tongue.

Bishop knelt beside the body on the floor, looked into her vacant eyes. "Her name was Rose Finicky, and she deserved to die, she deserved to die a hundred times over—hardly pure at all."

"Finicky?"

"Yes."

"Who . . . Did she kill Libby? Is that why . . . ?"

"I wish we had time to go into all that, but like I said earlier, you're late. The world waits for no one, and we have a lot of balls in the air today."

Porter felt Sarah's eyes on him. Bishop's mother. He couldn't look at her, though. He couldn't see her face. Not now, maybe not ever. He somehow knew she was smiling, and that made this all the worse. "Are you going to kill her too?"

Sarah shuffled, "He won't hurt me. Will you, Anson?"

"No? We'll see. We'll see about that."

"I brought Finicky here, just like you asked," Sarah shot back.

Bishop tilted his head and smiled. "And she brought you . . . just like I asked. Funny, how things have a way of working themselves out."

Bishop brushed the blade of the knife against his pants leg, closed it, then dropped it into his pocket.

"Finicky did some horrible things. Many of them here, right in this building." Bishop said. "And I had been searching for her for a very long time, nearly as long as I searched for Mother. Both had reasons to hide, of course, some more than others, but nobody hides forever."

Porter's eyes returned to the gun on the counter. He was only about four feet away. He could get to it. "If your father is still alive, where is he? Why make up some story about his death?"

Bishop let out a soft chuckle. "He hasn't figured it out yet, Mother."

"Not yet, but he will. I've got faith," Sarah said. She came up behind him and ran her hand through Porter's hair.

Porter dove for the gun.

He was off the chair and pushing past her before she could react. His hand fell over the gun, and he scooped it off the counter, shuffled to the side, and leveled the weapon on both of them. "Neither of you move."

Bishop smiled. "Sam, that's not going to—"

Sam fired a round past Bishop's head. The report echoed through the room, the bullet landing in the far wall with a thud.

Bishop's mother let out a soft gasp. "I told you he'd shoot you, Anson."

"He didn't shoot me, Mother."

"Give me your phone."

"Give Detective Porter your phone, Mother."

"I tried to give him my phone earlier, and he got twisted all out of sorts." She stepped forward and handed the phone to him.

Porter snatched it from her hand and swiped at the screen with his finger. "Get back beside him."

No signal.

"You'll want to go upstairs to place a call. These old buildings are not cell-phone friendly at all. I left something for you in room 405. It will work just fine in there. You can call when you go up."

Porter glanced around the room and located the stairs winding up from the far corner. "We'll all go up. You're going to tell me where the bomb is, where those girls are, then you're both going to jail. If you don't, I'll shoot again, maybe her this time. Maybe this time I won't intentionally miss."

Bishop shoved his hands into his pockets. "I want to thank you for bringing Mother to me, Sam. Finicky as well. Two birds. My ability to travel lately has been a bit . . . restricted. You've been so helpful. The last few months have been challenging, but it's coming together now. I feel good about the future, I really do."

"Toward the stairs, now."

Bishop smiled. "You're going to let us leave, Sam. Then you're going to head upstairs to room 405 and make a phone call. Not the phone call bouncing around your head right now, something altogether different."

"Last warning—toward the stairs."

Bishop reached over, took his mother's hand, and smiled. "You're going to do exactly as I say, Sam. Here's why."

129

Kloz

Day 4 • 9:11 p.m.

Klozowski stepped back into his makeshift office at John H. Stroger, Jr. Hospital and carefully crossed back to his computer with two cups of coffee, one in each hand, the contents of Paul Upchurch's file strategically placed across every flat surface in the room.

He'd spent the past two hours going through every page, identifying every name, then working with the team they had in place to round everyone up and bring them here. Thirty-two others in total, not counting spouses and children. They brought in so many people, Clair had been forced to spread out from the cafeteria and take over two adjoining employee lounges. She was in there now, trying to keep the large group calm, organize the uniforms, and get statements.

Most of these people had no idea why they had been dragged down here by the police. From what she said, only a handful recognized Upchurch by name. His condition, as horrible as it may be, wasn't uncommon. Anyone dealing with death on a daily basis learned to tune it out, compartmentalize.

Kati Quigley was awake and talking up a storm. Clair told him what the girl went through, both girls. Kloz blocked it out. He could compartmentalize with the best of them.

Larissa Biel had come out of surgery twenty minutes earlier. She was in recovery with her father. Once she woke, she'd be moved into a double room with her mother, who also regained consciousness—both expected to make full recoveries.

Kloz set the two cups of coffee down and cracked his knuckles.

Now he'd search the obits and put a nice bow on this project.

His bed was calling out to him, and he'd be wrapped up in those glorious sheets soon.

A small red box blinked at the corner of his laptop screen.

Kloz clicked on it, expanding the alert message.

"Shit."

He scrambled through the papers surrounding his computer, nearly knocked over one of the coffees, and picked up his phone, hitting Clair's speed-dial button. The call went straight to voice mail.

"Shit. Shit. Shit."

He dialed Nash.

One ring.

Two rings.

Three—

"Yeah?"

"Hey, where are you?"

"Still at the Upchurch house. I probably have another hour here. Why?"

"Remember the trace I set up on Bishop's laptop?"

"Yeah."

"We got a hit, and it's close."

"Text me the address. Espinosa too—his team just left."

130

Clair

Day 4 • 9:15 p.m.

Clair was about ready to scream.

She had the absolute worst headache, and the three Advil she'd swallowed did nothing for it.

She stood in the middle of the cafeteria, surrounded by at least forty or fifty people—adults, children, medical staff—everyone Kloz had identified from all the documents they'd put together, everyone they'd tied to the dozens of obituaries planted by Bishop, all these people shouting either at her or at one another.

Nobody wanted to be here.

The faster she could get them out, the better.

She'd spent an hour with Kati Quigley and couldn't shake the images of what the girl told her. She had just been told Larissa Biel was awake too. Larissa's father tracked her down, said he searched all over the hospital for her. Larissa couldn't speak. The doctors wanted her to rest her throat, but she was able to write. She began writing the moment she woke, and based on her father's hysterical state, her story might be worse than Kati's.

"I need everyone to shut up!"

A few heads turned. The noise softened for a moment, then roared back to life.

Clair climbed up a chair and onto one of the tables. "The sooner you all listen to me, the faster I can get you out of here!" She waved a stack of questionnaires above her head. "If you haven't turned in the forms I passed out earlier, I need you to complete them and hand them in to one of the officers!"

A little girl screamed about five feet away from her, screamed for no reason other than to add to the chaos. The girl's mother scooped her up and rocked her, but that did little good.

From the corner of her eye, she spotted Dr. Morton ducking back into the cafeteria. He saw her too and quickly turned away.

She left strict instructions that nobody was to leave this room, but the various medical professionals they rounded up into this makeshift protective custody seemed to treat her orders as more of a suggestion. Nearly everyone had come and gone at least once. Most had done so many times as their pagers and phones summoned them to various parts of the hospital. There was little she could do about this. In many cases, lives were ultimately at stake, not just their own, and none of these people were really obligated to stay. She was certain a few had snuck out and not come back at all.

Clair's phone vibrated in her pocket.

She fished it out.

Sarah Werner.

She didn't know a Sarah Werner. She would have to wait.

Clair pressed Decline. She noticed that she had missed two calls from Kloz.

She'd head back there next.

He was analyzing Upchurch's file and may have found something. The lab was also working on a substance found in that needle sticking out of the apple. If they couldn't reach her, they would pass the results on to him.

Her phone rang again.

Sarah Werner.

She hit the answer button and pressed the phone to her ear, covering the other ear with her hand. "This is Detective Norton!"

The voice on the other end was male, but she couldn't make out what he said. It was too loud in here. "Hold on—give me a second!"

She climbed down off the table, pushed through the crowd and out into the hallway. When she reached the elevators, she tried again. "Sorry, this is Detective Norton. What can I do for you?"

"Do you have Paul Upchurch?"

"Who is this?"

"It's me, Clair."

"Sam?"

"Yeah."

She turned. One of the patrolmen guarding the cafeteria was watching her. She took a few more steps down the hallway and turned her back on him. "Where are you?"

"I . . . I thought he had a bomb. He made me think he had a bomb, but it's not a bomb. Not a bomb at all . . ."

"Sam, you're not making sense. Who are you talking about? Upchurch? We got him. He doesn't have a bomb."

"Do you . . . do you have the girls? The two girls? Larissa Biel and the other one?"

"Yes, Sam. They're safe. Both of them. They'll be okay."

Wait. Something was wrong.

This wasn't right.

"Sam, how do you know about Larissa Biel? She disappeared after you left. We haven't told anyone about Quigley. Have you been talking to Nash or that FBI agent, Frank Poole?"

"Oh, Clair. I fucked up. I fucked up bad."

"What's going on, Sam? Talk to me."

Porter drew in a deep breath. "Is Paul Upchurch alive?"

"Yes. Espinosa's team took him into custody without incident. Nash said it was like he was waiting for them. He went peacefully. On the ride to Metro, he had a seizure and passed out. They brought him here to Stroger, and he's in surgery. Stage four brain cancer. It doesn't look good."

"Glioblastoma. He has a glioblastoma," Sam said softly.

"How do you know that? How do you even know his name? Who have you been talking to?"

Silence.

"Sam?"

"Where are the girls?"

"They're here too."

"Christ."

"Sam? What is it?"

Porter drew in another breath. "You need to isolate them. Isolate them and anyone who came into contact with them immediately. Don't let anyone leave."

"Why?"

Silence again.

"Sam, you're scaring me."

"Bishop said he injected both girls with a concentrated version of the SARS virus. He told me where he got the virus, and I believe him. He also said he left a sample for you in the hospital to confirm. He told me to tell you, 'Snow White didn't know better, either.' Does that mean anything to you?"

"We found an apple with a syringe stuck into it," Clair told him, the words catching in her throat. "The apple was sitting on top of Paul Upchurch's file."

"Clair, listen to me carefully. I'm going to give you a name. Are you ready?"

No.

"Go ahead."

"Dr. Ryan Beyer. He's a neurosurgeon at Johns Hopkins. He specializes in something called *focused ultrasound therapy.* Apparently this is some kind of treatment that can help Upchurch, but his insurance wouldn't cover it. Even though it's extremely effective, the treatment is still considered experimental. Bishop believes everything they've done so far has been a waste of time. He felt all the people involved in Upchurch's treatment failed him—the doctors, nurses, insurance, medication providers. He targeted everyone involved because he felt the system murdered Upchurch. He thinks insurance took the cheap way out, he believes everyone else just went along with business as usual, and he is not willing to let this guy die."

"How do you know all this?"

"As soon as we hang up, you need to locate this Dr. Beyer and get him there. Bishop said . . ."

Porter's voice trailed off, then he came back. "Bishop said he has more of the virus, and if Upchurch dies, he's going to inject random people around the city. Find this guy. Isolate anyone who came in contact with the girls. You need to contain this."

"Are you with Bishop now?"

"I have to go, Clair. I'm so sorry. I'm sorry for everything."

Porter disconnected, and the line went dead.

All the voices in the cafeteria came to her then, a growing mass of angry voices seeping into the hallway past the two patrolmen trying to hold them back.

Clair looked down at the remaining questionnaires in her hand. She had made sure everyone had one right after she spent over an hour with Kati Quigley.

The forms slipped from her fingers and fell to the floor.

An ache roiled through her, deep in her bones.

Clair sneezed.

131

Nash

Day 4 • 9:43 p.m.

Espinosa counted silently with his fingers, holding up five—

Four.

Three.

Two.

One.

Brogan rammed the door and burst through, the heavy wood splintering and cracking down the center.

"Go!"

"Go!"

Nash watched the SWAT team disappear into room 405 of the Guyon Hotel one at a time until he was alone in the dilapidated hallway. They found a body down in the lobby. A woman in a prison jumpsuit and restraints, an execution wound in her head.

Klozowski had traced the signal to here. Something about triangulating Wi-Fi transmitters in the neighborhood. Espinosa then used a handheld gizmo of some sort to seek out the only electrical signal in the building, somewhere behind the door to room 405.

"Hands in the air!"

"Don't move!"

"He's got a gun!"

Nash wasn't sure which voice belonged to whom, the shouts overlapping between his earpiece and the open doorway.

Another crash. *Second door?*

"Nash! Get in here. Now!"

Nash crossed the hallway to the door, the Kevlar vest cutting into his waist, making it difficult to breathe.

He stepped through the doorway, into room 405, lit by a dozen or so candles and the concentrated beams of the flashlights mounted on the half dozen assault rifles all pointing to the same spot.

A man.

His back to the door. His hands raised above his head. A laptop glowed on an antique desk before him. A dozen or so black and white composition notebooks sat stacked beside the computer, a .38 sitting off to the side.

"Sam?"

Porter began to turn in the chair.

"Don't—" Tibideaux said.

"Stand down!" Nash shouted. "Sam? What are you doing here?"

Porter looked down at the edge of the desk, closed his eyes.

Espinosa and Thomas both had their rifles pointed at the walls, the beams of their flashlights crawling over the faded floral wallpaper and the dozens of pictures hung about the room, all framed.

Nash followed the light and stepped closer, studied one of the frames.

It was a photograph of Sam, a much younger Sam, forties maybe. He was smiling at the camera. A boy stood at his side, also smiling. A boy of about fourteen or fifteen.

Espinosa frowned. "Is that?"

"I think it's Anson Bishop," Nash said, his voice low. He glanced at two others. "All of them."

Nash crossed the room, went to Porter. "Sam? What is this?"

Porter opened his mouth to speak, but nothing came out.

On the screen of the laptop, glowing bright enough to light Porter's face—

Hello Sam,

    I imagine you're confused.

    I imagine you have questions.

132

Diary

I did not know where the police station was.

For that matter, I wasn't sure where the Camden Treatment Center was located either. I had no idea where I'd spent the past few weeks.

We drove for a long time.

I watched the city of Charleston roll past outside my window. None of the buildings were very tall. Father once told me city ordinances prevented builders from reaching too close to the sky.

I wanted to hurt the doctor.

The anger that swelled within me was greater than any I'd ever experienced, but I did my best to suppress it. Like time, anger could be held in check, it could be bottled and stored, it could be opened when it was most needed.

I would open that bottle when the time was right, I would pop that cork.

Neither detective said a word.

I expected a flurry of questions, but nothing came. They did not speak to me, they did not speak to each other.

I said nothing in return, letting the silence speak for itself.

Outside, I recognized nothing of where we were, the city behind us now.

Detective Welderman glanced at me in the rearview mirror more than once. I met his gaze.

We turned off the two-lane road that took us about thirty minutes outside of the city. We turned off the blacktop onto a gravel lane with tall weeds growing on either side.

We did not stop at the police station, and this should have worried me, but I didn't let it.

We stopped at a large farmhouse at the end of the gravel road. A woman of about Mother's age saw us, waved, and came to the car. She had brown hair, cropped short, and wore a yellow dress with white dots.

Detective Welderman gave me another look in the mirror, then both men got out of the car.

The doors in the back did not have handles. Even if I weren't handcuffed, I could not get out on my own.

The detectives went to the woman, and the three of them spoke. I could not hear what was said, but it was accompanied by the occasional glance back at the car, back at me.

Welderman stood with the woman when Detective Stocks finally opened my door and helped me out.

The woman let out a soft gasp. "My, are those really necessary?"

Detective Stocks's face went red. "Turn around, kid."

He removed the handcuffs.

I rubbed at my wrists.

Welderman opened the trunk of the car and took out a green duffel bag. He handed the bag to the woman. "The hospital put together some clothes. Not much, they didn't have much in his size. He lost everything in the fire."

The woman came around to me then, stood in front of me and smiled. "Anson, my name is Ms. Finicky. You're going to be staying with me for a while."

Looking back over her shoulder, she called out, "Paul? Come here. Meet your new roommate."

I hadn't seen him standing there, this boy on the porch, tall and lanky. He emerged from the only shadow able to evade the climbing sun. He pattered across the gravel and took the bag from the woman, extending his free hand. "Hi, Anson, I'm Paul Upchurch. You're going to like it here."

Detective Stocks snickered at this.

The woman's eyes narrowed, then her smile returned. "Take him upstairs, Paul. Show him to his new room."

"Yes, ma'am."

"Anson?" Detective Welderman said.

I looked up at him, at the scowl on his face.

"We know what you did, Anson. We all do. It won't take us long to prove, we just need to put a few pieces together. Feel free to unpack. Those clothes are only on loan. You'll get new clothes soon enough— a new room, a new roommate too."

I smiled up at him, at Detective Stocks. "Thank you for the ride, Detectives. It was a pleasure meeting you both."

I followed Paul Upchurch.

I followed Paul into the gaping mouth of that farmhouse.

The house was much bigger than it appeared from the outside. Maybe it was the many dividing walls breaking up the many rooms, or it could have been because the house was much deeper than wide, maybe a combination of both, but I felt I was lost the moment I stepped inside.

I paused in the small living room, past the foyer, and looked back out through the front door. Paul had told me to leave it open.

The two detectives were still out there, wrapped up in conversation with Ms. Finicky. The world seemed brighter outside, just past that doorway. There was a stillness to the air inside this house, not stale or musty, just still. I couldn't help but think of the air trapped inside a coffin shortly after the lid was nailed tight.

"What is Ms. Finicky's first name?" I asked.

Paul stopped at the base of a staircase and looked back at me. "Who cares?"

"I care."

The other boy shrugged. "Dunno. She's just Ms. Finicky, always has been. Finicky, Finicky, Finicky. Not Fin or Mrs. Finicky, maybe ma'am *but never* you. *I imagine the other kids have come up with a few good names for her over the years, but you can bet nobody is going to say any of them to her face."*

"Other kids?"

He paused again, five steps up, two before the landing. "You do know where you are, right? They told you? Sometimes they do, sometimes they don't. We all trudge through that door from our own path. Some are old hacks and others are fresh to the game. You don't have that scared, deer-about-to-meet-bumper look on your face, so I assumed your rodeo has been running for a while now."

He came back down the stairs, took my hand, and pumped vigorously. "You, my friend, have just entered the System. Congratulations! I'm afraid there's no cake or welcome wagon, just little ol' me, but there are worse things to run into when you step into a stranger's house. You'd think there'd be an instructional video or a pamphlet or something, but funds are tight. If there were a video in the works, I'd like to see Rod Serling narrate. That guy is awesome. Old school, but awesome."

Paul jumped back up the stairs to the landing and spun in a circle with his arms up high, his voice dropping an octave. "There is a fifth dimension beyond that which is known to man. It is a dimension as vast as space and as timeless as infinity. It is the middle ground between light and shadow, between science and superstition, and it lies between the pit of man's fears and the summit of his knowledge. This is the dimension of imagination. It is an area which we call"—he *stopped spinning and steadied himself on the railing*—"*the Finicky House for Wayward Children."*

I couldn't help but laugh. I had never heard so many words come out of one mouth so fast.

He nodded toward the top of the large staircase. "Onward."

Pictures of children lined the walls with such abundance, the flowered wallpaper beneath was barely visible. At least a hundred, maybe more. Boys and girls of all ages, some smiling, others not, all standing in the driveway with the large house looming at their backs.

Paul pointed at a brown frame near the top. "I'm right here.

Don't worry, you'll get your turn in front of the camera soon enough, we all do."

There was something about the way he said this, something in the tone of his voice, the way he trailed off, his thoughts lingering a little longer than his words.

"How many kids are here?"

He reached the top of the stairs and turned back around. "You are number eight, my friend. Three girls and five boys, ranging in age from seven to sixteen. I myself am fifteen. Three more years and they'll be forced to unleash me upon the unsuspecting world. May God have mercy on them all."

I reached the top of the stairs, which opened on a long, narrow hallway—more photographs up here, nearly every inch of wall space, closed doors sandwiched between them on either side.

Paul pointed to a closed door on the left. "That there is Vincent Weidner. We don't talk to Vincent Weidner. Avoid Vincent Weidner and he will avoid you. That seems to be best for all."

He crossed the hall and opened the second door on the right. "This here is us, only a couple solos in this place. Most of us double up. That's still better than some of the places I've been. I once shared a room with six other kids, and it was smaller than this one. You couldn't sleep without someone else's foot in your face." He ducked inside, then poked his head back out. "Bathroom is the door at the end of the hall on this side. Right side is boys, left side is girls. Leave the door open when you exit so everyone else knows it's vacant. We keep matches in the medicine cabinet to take care of the aroma after a most glorious evacuation, and the latest girly magazine can be found in a plastic bag in the bowl—be sure to seal that ziplock back up. Nobody likes soggy porn. Return everything to where you found it upon exit, or there will be repercussions. We take turns cleaning. A schedule is on the refrigerator downstairs."

Paul ducked back into the room. "You coming?"

I stood there for a moment, outside the room, and looked up and down the narrow hallway at all the pictures on the wall. Ms. Finicky *wasn't very old; I wondered how long she had been doing this, how many children had passed through here.*

I stepped into the room.

Bunkbeds.

I'd always wanted a bunkbed.

The duffel bag containing my loaner clothes sat in the middle of the bottom bunk.

"I've got seniority, so I officially lay claim to the top," Paul said. "If you outlast me, maybe someday it will be yours. Dare to dream, my friend. Dare to dream."

Like the hallways, the walls of the room were also lined with pictures. Unlike the ones in the hallway, these were not photographs but drawings, cartoons, and sketches. "Are these yours?"

Paul nodded proudly. "Every last one is a Paul Upchurch original." He crossed the room to a small desk, picked up a sketchpad, and carried it over. "I've been working on my own comic. It's about this little girl who is constantly stepping in all kinds of trouble. Just because it's about a girl doesn't make me a queer or anything. She's a major tomboy and she's a little sexy, right? I've done some serious market research, and I determined that by using a girl as the main character, the comic book will appeal to all kids." He tapped at the side of his head. "Always thinking . . . you've got to consider these things, because I'm sure the publishers do."

I studied the image of the girl. She was cute. About our age, with a mischievous little smile curling up at the corner of her mouth and a glisten in her eyes. The detail was amazing. I had read my share of comics and was a bit of a connoisseur. Paul's drawing was as good, if not better, than most I had seen.

"Do you have a name for the comic book?"

Paul's eyes brightened. "Do I have a name, of course I have a name. I call it The Misadventures of Maybelle Markel.*"*

"You're very good."

Paul lifted the sketchpad to his lips and kissed the drawing. "She's like the daughter I never had. Baby girl here is going to make her daddy a rich man one of these days."

I heard a sob then, a soft, muted cry from behind the closed door across the hall.

I knew that sound, that cry.

Paul set the sketchpad back down on the desk, then followed my gaze to the door. "She came in yesterday, hasn't really been out of her room yet. She kept most of us up last night with the waterworks, but we all try to cut some slack when someone first gets here. The other girls have been taking shifts with her so she's not alone." He paused, his thoughts elsewhere. "Some fosters can be rough. She'll like it here. You will too. I think Ms. Finicky said her name was Libby."

I took a step closer to the door.

I felt Paul's hand on my arm. His fingers tightened.

The boy's voice dropped low, barely a breath. "I think they listen to us. Be careful what you say."

To be concluded . . .

Acknowledgments

Special thanks to my agent, Kristin Nelson, for finding a home for Sam Porter and his story. Tim Mudie, who edited this book with a sharp eye. And my first readers — Summer Schrader, Jenny Milchman, Erin Kwiatkowski, Darlene Begovich, and Jennifer Henkes — all of whom helped me shape what I found after cracking the pages of Bishop's diary and poking around in his mind.

Thanks to my wonderful wife, Dayna, for believing . . . for being you.

Finally, to Anson Bishop — are you ready to finish this little dance?

JD

Don't miss the third and final 4MK thriller:

The Sixth Wicked Child

by J. D. Barker

Turn the page for a sneak preview . . .

"Hey shithead, this look like a fucking bed-and-breakfast to you?"

The voice was gruff, gravelly. At this hour, it had to be a cop, security guard, or maybe just an angry homeowner. Whoever it was, Tray Stouffer didn't move within the folds of the musty quilt. Sometimes, when you're still enough, they go away. Sometimes, they get bored.

The boot came again—fast, hard. Direct hit to the stomach.

Tray wanted to shout out, to grab the leg and fight back. Didn't, though. Remained perfectly still.

"Goddamn it, I'm talking to you!"

Another kick, harder than the last, right in the ribs.

Tray grunted, couldn't help it. Pulled the quilt tighter.

"Do you have any idea what you and your friends do to resale value when you camp out here? You scare the kids half to death. The older folk won't leave the building. They shouldn't have to step over a piece of garbage like you just to run to the store."

Homeowner, then.

Tray had heard it all before.

"Do you know what *I'm* doing out here at five in the morning while you're taking a nap? While you're all snug on our front stoop? I just got off a ten-hour shift at Delphine's Bakery. Did twelve hours the night before in that devil's asshole of a kitchen. Gotta go back in another ten. I do that to pay for this place. I do that to contribute. You'll never catch me living on streets like you lazy shits. Get a damn job! Make something of yourself!"

At fourteen, there was no work. Not the legal kind. Not without some kind of parental consent, and *that* was never going to happen.

Tray braced for another kick.

Instead, the man grabbed ahold of the quilt and yanked it away, tossed it to the side. The quilt landed in a slushy puddle of half-melted snow at the base of the steps.

Tray shivered, coiled up, ready for another kick.

"Hey, you're a chick. You're just a kid," the man said, the anger dropping from his voice. "I shouldn't have done that. What's your name?"

"Tracy," she said. "Most people call me Tray." She regretted the words the moment they left her lips. She knew what happened whenever she talked to one of them. When she opened up. Best to just keep her mouth shut, stay invisible.

The man knelt down, a paper sack dangled from his left hand. He wasn't very old, maybe mid-twenties. Heavy coat. Brown hair tucked under a black watch cap. Hazel eyes. Whatever was in the sack smelled delicious.

He caught her looking at it. "Tray, my name is Emmitt. Are you hungry?"

She nodded. Knowing this too was a mistake. But she *was* hungry. So hungry.

He reached into the paper sack and took out a small loaf of bread. Steam floated from the crusty surface through the icy Chicago air and for a moment, Tray forgot about the bitter wind coming off the lake, howling through the street each time it kicked up.

Her stomach gurgled, loud enough for both of them to hear.

Emmitt tore off a piece of bread and handed it to her. She devoured it in two bites, barely bothering to chew. Possibly the best bread she's ever eaten.

"Do you want more?"

Tray nodded, although she knew she shouldn't.

Emmitt let out a breath. He reached out and stroked her cheek with the side of his pointer finger. Drifting from her face to her neck, slipping beneath the collar of her sweater. "Why don't you come inside with me? You can have all the bread you want. I've got more food, too. A warm shower. A comfortable bed. I'll—"

With both arms, Tray slammed the man in his shoulders. He had been precariously balanced, kneeling down on one knee like that, and he wasn't prepared for the blow. He rolled backward, the sack tumbled from his hands, and his head slammed into the metal railing from the building's staircase. "You little bitch!"

Before he could get up, Tray was on her feet. She grabbed the paper sack, scooped up her backpack, and raced down the five steps, snagged her quilt, and took off down Mercer. He wouldn't chase her; they rarely did, but sometimes—

"Stay the hell away from here! I catch you again, I'm calling the cops!"

When Tray did risk a glance back, Emmitt had stood, gathered up his things, and was pushing through the door into the building. Even from this distance, she imagined she could feel the warmth of that hallway.

She didn't slow until she reached the gates of Rose Hill Cemetery. At this hour, they were locked, but she was thin, and a moment later she had wiggled through the wrought iron bars to the other side, pulling her backpack and quilt behind her.

Chicago had its share of shelters, but she'd gone that route too. At this hour, they'd be locked tight. All locked their doors somewhere between 7 p.m. and midnight, and none would admit you after hours. Even if they did, it wouldn't matter, they'd be full. Sometimes the lines started as early as noon, and there was never enough room. Besides, Tray felt safer on the streets. There were "Emmitts" everywhere, especially in the shelters, and the only thing worse than running into an Emmitt on the stoop of some building or in an alley shielded from the wind, was being locked overnight in a shelter with one. Sometimes, more than one. Emmitts tend to stick together and hunt in packs.

Tray wasn't afraid of the cemetery. After two years on the streets, she'd slept in each one at least once. Rose Hill was one of her favorites on account of the mausoleums. Unlike Oakwood or Graceland,

Rose Hill didn't lock the mausoleums at night. And while there were several security guards, on a cold night like tonight, they'd be in the office playing cards, watching television, or even sleeping. She'd seen them enough through the windows.

She stomped up Tranquility Lane through the fresh snow. She wasn't too worried about the tracks behind her; she knew the wind would take care of those. They'd be gone in an hour or so. There was no reason to take chances, though, so when she reached the top of the hill, rather than making the left at Bliss Road, she cut across Tranquility and ducked down into the small patch of woods running along the side of Bliss.

Although there were no lights, the moon was nearly full, and when the reflection pond came into view, Tray couldn't help but stop and look at it. The icy surface glistened under the thin layer of fresh snow. Marble statues stood silently along the edge of the water, stone benches between. This was such a peaceful place. So quiet.

Tray didn't see her at first, not at first, this woman kneeling at the water's edge, facing away. Long, blond hair trailing down her back. She looked like one of the statues, unmoving, facing the pond like that. Her skin was so pale, nearly white, almost as colorless as her white dress. She wore no shoes on her bare feet, no coat, only the white dress of a material so thin, it was nearly translucent.

Tray didn't speak, instead, she drew closer. Close enough to realize the thin layer of snow that covered everything else, covered this girl, too. And when she circled around to her side, she realized it wasn't a girl at all, but a woman, this kneeling woman with her hands clasped together near her breasts as if lost in prayer, her head tilted to the side. The stark whiteness of her, every inch of her, was broken by the thin line of red, down the side of her face, from under her hair. There was another from the side of her left eye, a stream of red tears, and yet a third from the corner of her mouth—this one painting her lips the brightest rose.

At her knees, sitting in the snow, was a silver serving tray. The kind you might find at a fancy dinner party, a high-priced restaurant, the sort of place Tray already knew, even at fourteen, she'd never see in her lifetime beyond television or the movies.

On that tray were three small white boxes. Each sealed tight with black string.

Behind the boxes, propped up against this woman's chest, was a cardboard sign not unlike the ones Tray had used numerous times to raise money for food. Only she had never used these three particular words before. The sign simply read:

FATHER, FORGIVE ME

Tray did the only thing she could do. She ran.

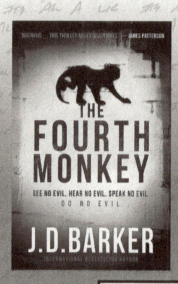 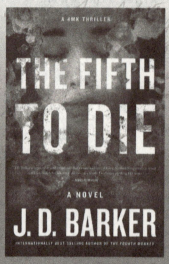